I0769881

The Butcher and the Ballerina

THE
BUTCHER
AND THE
BALLERINA
KRIS K. HAINES

Copyright © 2024 by Kris K. Haines

Cover Design and Chapter Header illustration by Rena Violet (coversbyviolet.com)

Developmental Editing by Susan Barnes Editing (susanbarnesediting.com)

Copy Editing by Noah Sky Editing (noah-sky-editing.com)

All rights reserved.

No part of this book may be reproduced in any form or by any electronic or mechanical means, including information storage and retrieval systems, without written permission from the author, except for the use of brief quotations in a book review.

This is a work of fiction. Names, characters, places and incidents are the products of the author's imagination. Any resemblance to actual persons, living or dead, or locales is entirely coincidental.

ISBN-13: 979-8-9879402-7-3

For anyone who has ever felt caged.
Break those bars and glow.

CONTENT WARNING

This book contains subject matter that might be difficult for some readers, including strong language, graphic sexual content, violence and gore, colonial oppression, sexual assault (not the main couple), parental death, and substance abuse. Reader discretion is advised. The mental health of my readers is of the utmost importance to me. If you feel that there is a trigger that is not mentioned above, please do not hesitate to contact me via the form on my website: kriskhainesbooks.com.

PRONUNCIATION GUIDE

Characters
Ronin Matakos - ROH-nihn mah-TAH-kohs
Mireille Valette - mih-RAY vah-LET

Belen Erabis - BAY-lehn AIR-ah-biss
Cecelia Beruglia - seh-SEE-lee-ah beh-RUH-lee-ah
Dimi - DIH-mee
Eamon Erabis - AY-mahn AIR-ah-biss
Hugo Skanisse - HYOO-goh skah-NEESE
Irina Amiel - ee-REE-nah AH-mee-ell
Juliet - JOO-lee-et
Julius Kosera - JOO-lee-uhs koh-SEHR-ah
Jurgev Otto - YER-gehv aw-toh
Layla Fetar - LAY-lah feh-TAHR
Leonin Erabis - LEE-oh-nihn AIR-ah-biss
Larissa Bisere - lah-RIH-sah bee-SEHR
Mattias Bisere - mah-TEE-ahs bee-SEHR
Mila Erabis - MEE-lah AIR-ah-biss
Mistress Klovia - [mistress] KLOH-vee-ah

Nostrata Otto - nohs-TRAH-tah aw-toh
Nero Beruglia - NEE-roh beh-RUH-lee-ah
Odelle Carmina - oh-DELL cahr-MEE-nah
Piretti - pih-REH-tee
Selene Matakos - seh-LEEN mah-TAH-kohs
Sharae - shah-RAY
Sorenno - suh-REHN-oh
Tristan Erabis - TRIS-tehn AIR-ah-biss
Vivienne Valois - vih-vee-EHN vahl-WAH

Places
Aethalia - eh-THAL-ee-ah
Akti - AHK-tee
Brachos - BROCK-ohs
Cernodas - SEHR-noh-dass
Delos - DEH-lohs
Denevrae - DEH-neh-vray
Diachre - dee-AHK-rah
Ethyrios - ih-THEE-ree-ohs
Icthian Mountains - ICK-thee-ahn [mountains]
Kheimos - KAI-mohs
Listhima - LISS-tee-mah
Nephes - NEH-fehs
Oread Woods - ORE-ee-add [woods]
Sea of Thetis - [sea of] THAY-tiss
Syvalle - see-VAHL-ay

Terms
Adelphinae - ah-DELL-fee-nay
Aguaver - AAH-gwah-ver
Amatu - uh-MAH-too
Anaemos - ah-NAY-mohs
Aramaelish - ah-rah-MAY-lish

Delirium - duh-LEER-ee-uhm

Dienses - dee-EHN-sees

The Delphine - [the] dell-FEEN

drachas - DRAH-kahs

Faurana - fowh-RAHN-ah

Iae Tombilae, Iae Nost Thanatem Sompros - yai TOHM-bee-lay, yai nohst THAH-nah-tehm SOHM-prohs

Ignesh Tremani - ihg-NESH treh-MAH-nee

Inom Than - ee-NOHM thahn

Nyctima - NICK-tee-mah

Psychis - SIGH-kiss

Raetyndra meos, amaternum mei - ray-TIHN-drah MAY-ohs, ah-mah-TEHR-nuhm MAY-ee

Stygios - STIH-gee-ohs

Teles Chrysos - TEH-less KREE-sohs

Thakavi - thah-KAH-vee

Typhon steel - TIE-fuhn [steel]

Vestan - VEST-an

Citizens of Ethyrios

<u>**FAE**</u>

Nearly immortal, magical, humanoid beings.
Descendants of the High Gods. Divided into three sub-
species.

Windriders: Winged sub-species, both of feather and of
flesh. Ability to fly. Ability to manipulate air and control
wind. Descendants of Anaemos.

Beastrunners: Sub-species of mammalian bi-forms.
Ability to switch between beast and humanoid forms at
will. Descendants of Faurana.

Deathstalkers: Venomous sub-species. Ability to
paralyze another Fae with a bite from their three-inch
fangs. A full Deathstalker bite is instantly fatal for
humans. Descendants of Stygios.

<u>**HUMANS**</u>
Mortal and non-magical. No sub-species.

Gods of Ethyrios

<u>HIGH GODS</u>

Anaemos: The Father, High God of Spirit and Sky
Faurana: The Mother, High Goddess of Land and Life
Stygios: The Reaper, High God of Death and Destruction

<u>GODS</u>

Letha: The Stranger, Goddess of Oblivion
Nemosyna: The Chronicler, Goddess of Memory
Dienses: The Jester, God of Merriment
Amatu: The Lover, Goddess of Love
Vestan: The Warrior, God of War
Thakavi: The Scholar, God of Wisdom
Ker: The Killer, Goddess of Violence

Adelphinae: The Creator, The Fallen Goddess*

*Adelphinae's story has been stripped from Ethyrios's histories.

Territories of Ethyrios

<u>CONTINENTAL</u>

Akti: Southern coastal region. Capital: Rhamnos.
Brachos: Northwest region. Capital: Diachre.
Cernodas: Eastern region. Capital: Aethalia.
Nephes: Central region and home to the Imperial Capital, Delos.
Northern Territories: Northeast region. Capital: Kheimos.
Syvalle: North central region. Capital: Thalestria.

<u>COLONIAL</u>

Northern Colonies. Capital: Thalenn.
Northern Middle Colonies. Capital: Primarvia.
Southern Middle Colonies. Capital: Vaengya.
Southern Colonies. Capital: Meridon.

CHAPTER ONE

*I*n the cage fighting rings of Kheimos, there was only one rule: no magic.

In a city full of Fae where magic was a hard thing to avoid, the restriction leveled the playing field and added tension to the fights.

Deathstalkers wore mouth guards to disarm their venomous bite. Windriders sported nessite-lined cuffs to prevent them from summoning the wind.

And Beastrunners, like Ronin Matakos, were forbidden to shift into their animal forms.

But Ronin wasn't a stickler for rules. Not anymore.

So when his opponent—a scrawny, but scrappy hyena bi-form named Ned—swiped at his chest with claws extended, Ronin revealed his own much larger, sharper ones.

The referee slammed a fist on the cage. "Against the fucking rules."

"He doesn't want to take a chance on these, anyways." Ronin's savage smile revealed thick fangs. Ned trembled.

"So are those," the referee grunted. "Put 'em away before I end the fight."

A chorus of boos swelled in the stands. The crowd was out for blood. What did they care how it was spilled?

Retracting his claws and rushing across the ring, Ned's bare feet splashed in a leftover puddle of viscera as he reared back and smashed his skull into Ronin's forehead.

Ronin staggered and Ned swung, wearing himself out as fists, feet, elbows, and knees collided in a symphony of grunts and fleshy smacks.

Ned even managed to sneak a bite to Ronin's neck.

"You trying to fucking mark me, baby?" Ronin ripped his opponent away and threw him against the cage with an echoing clang.

Loosing a mad cackle, Ned scrambled back toward Ronin, who swept his leg out and dropped the other male to the floor.

Ronin pounced.

Locking his knees around Ned's hips, Ronin lost himself to the euphoric frenzy of knuckles cracking teeth, crushing cartilage, and breaking bone. Blood flew from his fists, soaking the cage as the crowd roared its approval.

Wrath of Vestan, he fucking *loved* this part. Violence was his favorite high.

Well, top three at least.

Groans burst from the handful of risk-takers daring enough to bet against him, the current champion of the Northern Territories and the perennial odds-on favorite.

The referee called the fight, then strode into the cage to raise Ronin's wrist and declare him the winner.

The crowd surged to its feet.

"Butcher! Butcher! Butcher!"

A contented growl rumbled through Ronin's mind.

They call for me, his wolf purred. *Let me come out and bask in their glory.*

No fucking chance, Ronin grumbled back.

He hadn't let his beast out in nearly three centuries.

He couldn't, even if he wanted to.

Ronin took in the rapturous crowd, allowing himself a moment to savor their admiration, then ripped his wrist away from the referee and exited the ring.

His was always the last fight of the night—the marquee bout that kept the crowd in the stands, betting more *drachas* than they could afford and ordering more greasy food and over-priced drinks. Ronin got a cut of the night's earnings, so he didn't complain about being kept in the reeking, blood-soaked arena well past midnight.

Ronin stalked into the locker room, then shucked off his sparring pants and unwrapped his fists.

Blood came away on his fingertips—his or the hyena's, he couldn't tell. Likely a mixture of both, based on the scents. Ned had been dragged to the healing wing. Ronin's opponents usually were. Beating the shit out of them ensured he'd have the shower to himself after-wards, at least for as long as it took the staff to coun-teract the healing suppressant the Fae fighters consumed.

He stepped into the stall, and scalding water erupted from the faucet, streaming over his muscled shoulders as he dipped his head, palms resting against the tiles.

Casting a glow upon the steam, ice-blue tattoos swirled across his arms and torso—a cage of the Empire's making.

Three centuries ago, during the Empire's war with

the humans, Ronin's white wolf had slaughtered over two thousand mortal soldiers on the battlefields of Aethalia, delivering the Fae a decisive victory. The feat earned him a new nickname—the Butcher—and he was celebrated across the territories. Cheered at parties. Showered with gifts. Revered as a continental war hero. Emperor Leonin Erabis himself had even commissioned a grand portrait of Ronin's wolf for the palace in Delos.

Ronin Matakos had been on top of the world.

For a time.

Everything had changed during the Accord negotiations, when the Emperor yielded to some very assertive human voices who weren't too keen on letting the most notorious killer of their kind go unchecked. A political concession and nothing more; the humans were headed for the colonies and Ronin was staying on the continent, so how much of a threat could he really pose? Not to mention, the war was over.

Though Ronin could manage small displays—thickening his fangs, elongating his fingernails into claws, even popping out his white tail—the tattoos prevented him from making a full transformation.

At the time, Ronin had been furious about the sanction. Why should he be punished by the very Empire whose orders he'd been following? For becoming the weapon *they'd* trained him to become? Besides, it wasn't as if he'd killed innocents on those fields. Those human soldiers had been just as capable of savagery, demonstrated by the Fae casualties piling up in the months prior.

But three hundred years later, he only nurtured a quiet rage over his caging. Had begrudgingly resigned himself to his fate.

His wolf, however, had not. The caging of a Beastrunner's animal was a very specific type of torture. With no outlet or means of release, it was a daily occurrence that the beast howled and snarled and ripped against Ronin's chest, begging to be unleashed.

Over the years, there were only three things that Ronin had ever found to calm the creature: fighting, fucking, and Delirium, Trophonios's glorious invention. The elixir, brewed from human memories, held Ronin and many of his fellow Fae within its addictive thrall.

Ronin could feel his wolf within him now, curled against his heart, bathing in the afterglow of the night's violence.

Footsteps clacked against the tiled floor and Ronin whipped his head around, droplets splattering the wall.

Dimi, a Deathstalker female who worked for the fight promoter Sorreno, plunked a hefty sack of *drachas* on top of the stall's ledge.

"Your cut for the night." Dimi's forked tongue slithered across her lips as she dragged her serpent's eyes up Ronin's glistening, naked body. "And the boss has a message for you."

Ronin shook the water from his hair, then wrapped a towel around his waist.

"Tell Sorreno I'm fucking done for the night." He ran a hand through his wet, white strands. A calculated move to pop his biceps.

"But not done fucking, we hope." Dimi's pupils dilated.

They'd enjoyed each other before. In this very locker room, in fact. She'd been a spry and enthusiastic partner, but he had a taste for fresh meat tonight—the gorgeous new Windrider waitress at the Frosted Crystal who'd been flirting with him for the past week. And was about to earn a very generous tip.

"Anyway, we didn't mean *that* boss," Dimi said. "We meant the big boss. Skanisse."

Ronin reigned in his shock. The High Councilor of the Northern Territories had been at the fight tonight?

Dimi handed Ronin a slip of paper. "Told us to give this to your hot ass."

Ronin snickered. "He didn't say *hot*."

"Added that bit ourselves." She winked. "You seem tense, Butcher. You want to burn off some energy before you go?" Her head tilted back as Ronin towered over her.

"You wanna play with me again, Dimi?"

Her eyes slid shut and a quivering breath parted her lips. "*Please.*"

High *Gods*, Ronin could never resist it when they begged. Wielding his savage beauty was one of the few weapons left in his arsenal.

He cuffed her throat, her pulse pounding against his fingertips, then traced the tip of his tongue down one of her fangs, careful to avoid the pointed end. She shuddered, the bitter scent of her venom prickling his nose.

"I'm not in the mood for seconds tonight," he whispered against her lips before nudging her out of the way and heading for his locker.

Dimi's hissing laughter followed her out of the humid room. "Someday, Matakos. You'll cave again."

Not fucking likely, he thought as he changed into his typical all-black uniform: a long-sleeved t-shirt, utility pants, and loosely-laced boots.

Shrugging on his leather jacket, he plopped onto the bench and opened the note. Messages from High Councilor Skanisse were rare, and since his caging, Ronin had done his best to stay out of the Imperial orbit. But given his history and reputation, the Empire—and its representatives—did occasionally come calling.

Written in the High Councilor's familiar chicken-scratch was a short message: *Imperial Affairs HQ. Tomorrow morning at eight.*

Ronin groaned. *Way* too fucking early. Especially given his plans for the remainder of his night.

He ripped up the note, then tossed the pieces in his locker and slung his equipment bag over his shoulder.

As he rushed through the empty underground halls of the arena, he wondered what Skanisse wanted this time. When Ronin had previously been summoned, he'd been nothing more than a glorified babysitter. Dragged around to some secretive event or another, the cornerstone of Skanisse's wall of muscle.

Ronin slipped out a side door and into the hazy night, welcomed by the halos of magically-powered street lights. Snowflakes needled his face and hands, melting upon contact with his Beastunner heat.

As he trudged through the slushy streets, his thoughts turned to the Crystal's new waitress and the plans he had for her taut little body.

Whatever Skanisse wanted tomorrow morning, he wasn't about to let it mess with his post-fight ritual.

CHAPTER TWO

Mireille Valette disentangled herself from the scratchy sheets and glanced toward the clock on the nightstand.

Shit. She was due at the theater in less than an hour.

Get on with it, a low, sly voice sighed into her mind. *We've spent far too much time with this disgusting specimen already.*

Mireille snickered, ignoring her wolf. Though she didn't disagree with the assessment.

Her current mark, the Deathstalker male she'd spent the afternoon with, was still sleeping soundly next to her, face down on the pillow with his pale arms circled above his head.

She rose from the bed as quietly as possible, trying not to wake him, then padded into the tiny bathroom to ensure the veiling potion she'd dosed herself with earlier hadn't yet worn off. Though her facial features were still unrecognizable in the mirror, strands of copper now wove through the black hair she'd donned for this assignment.

She and her wolf would have to work quickly.

The Deathstalker's back steadily rose and fell as she crept back into the bedroom, plucked up her discarded clothes, and dressed.

Slinking into the cramped living area, she asked her wolf, *Where is it?*

The creature sniffed at the shack's stale air, retching. *This place smells like a dumpster. But I'm getting a hint of something behind the couch.*

Mireille padded over and eased the lopsided lump of torn cushions away from the wall. A bundle of dust-streaked cloth lay nestled against the trim. She reached down to grab it, then slid the couch back into place.

Crossing to the kitchenette, she unwrapped the bundle atop a crusty table and let out a satisfied grunt.

The scepter—a relic of the Fallen Goddess and one of many that Mireille had acquired in her work for the Empire over the years—was topped with a fire opal that glistened in the early evening sunlight.

How this male had gotten his hands on the scepter was completely beyond Mireille. She knew he wasn't keeping it for himself. He was one of many links in a chain that would lead to the scepter's delivery into the hands of someone far more powerful. And wealthy.

There were a number of buyers throughout the continent willing to pay hefty sums for these relics, and one buyer in particular here in the Northern Territories who Mireille was almost certain was the intended recipient. Most of these pieces were useless, their power having faded just as much as the Goddess who'd inspired their creation.

But every so often, about one in fifty jobs, she'd come across a functioning relic, one imbued with a power that could threaten the Empire's dominance.

Which is exactly why they employed Fae like Mireille to hunt them down and ensure they didn't fall into the hands of their enemies. Enemies who hadn't counted on their errand boy being so easily undone by a pretty face.

All Mireille, or Merina as she had dubbed herself today, had to do when she'd met him at the bar was bat her eyelashes and ask what he did for work. A few probing questions—to which she already knew the answers since she'd been tracking him for weeks—and he'd all but admitted he had the scepter. Couldn't help bragging about how much he was going to earn as soon as he delivered it.

She'd gifted him a little gasp, running her fingers through his cornsilk hair and saying how much it turned her on that he was defying the Empire by trafficking illegal relics.

The idiot had dragged her out of the bar and brought her to this crumpled shack in the Southlake district on the outskirts of Kheimos. Three hours of drunken, unsatisfying fucking later—an attempt to allay his suspicions and wear him out so she could perform her search and sneak away without the mess of killing him—and her assignment was nearly complete.

Thank the High Gods for stupid, easily manipulated males. They made these jobs so much easier.

She shrugged on her jacket, patting the pocket over her left breast where she kept her standard-issue Typhon steel dagger, then unzipped her bag.

A sleep-worn voice rasped from the bedroom doorway. "Merina? Why are you dressed?"

Fuck, Mireille thought, her shoulders dipping.

Her wolf licked her chops, delighted. *Looks like we're going to have to make a mess after all.*

The Deathstalker wore a confused smile and a sheet around his waist. "Come back to bed."

Mireille angled herself in front of her bag and the unwrapped scepter. "I can't. I've got plans tonight that I can't cancel." She grabbed his face, forcing him to look at her and not the bounty behind her. "I'd love to see you again, though. Maybe tomorrow?"

Her wolf chuckled. *He'll be dead by then.*

"Mmmm." He leaned down, his mouth inches from hers. "So eager to see us again? We must not have worn you out enough this afternoon."

Mireille had to stop herself from rolling her eyes. He *had* worn her out, and not in a good way. He'd been a sloppy, greedy lover, only interested in his own needs. She'd faked every single climax, and the cretin about to kiss her hadn't even noticed. Not that she cared; she never sought pleasure with her marks.

He crashed his mouth down onto hers with too much force, too much tongue and teeth, and she fought the urge to retch.

She pushed him back into the bedroom, releasing soft whimpers that only served to make him kiss her harder. She unlatched her lips, and he crawled up the bed. Straddling his waist, she shivered with disgust as he dragged his hands up her thighs, pushing his cold fingers up under her shirt.

"You wanna go again?" he asked. "We'll be fast."

Sweetheart, you've been fast every single time, her wolf crooned and Mireille nearly snorted.

He cocked his head, reaching for her hair. "Hey, what happened to your—"

She whipped out her dagger and pointed the tip at his heart.

His eyebrows crashed together as his fangs popped down. "What is this?"

He tensed, poised to strike, and she pushed the dagger down further. "Don't even think about it."

He snarled, then turned his head, nearly slicing her wrist with a venom-filled fang.

She called upon the strength of her wolf, putting her full weight upon the dagger and plunging it into his heart. A bubble of green blood burst from his mouth as his limp limbs fell to the bed.

Typhon steel to the heart was one of the quickest, most effective ways to deliver True Death to a Fae.

Mireille crawled off the Deathstalker's body then covered it with a sheet and wiped the blood off her hands and dagger. She slipped the weapon into her jacket as she returned to the kitchenette, then rewrapped the scepter and placed it in her bag. She wouldn't have time to deliver it to Imperial Affairs tonight; she'd barely have time to make it to the theater.

She glanced back into the bedroom. Patches of bright green blood seeped through the sheet and tiny rivulets snaked across the stripped mattress, dripping onto the floor.

Let me out, her wolf whined. *I can clean up your tracks. And I haven't had a proper snack in days.*

We don't have time for that, Mireille snarled back.

You're no fun.

Mireille rushed through the shack, massaging her

cheeks—Sweet Amatu, all those fucking smiles she'd given the male over the past few hours made them ache.

A blast of icy wind greeted her as she opened the door, setting her bag upon the snow-dusted sidewalk.

There's only one way we're going to make it, she coaxed her wolf. *Fancy a run instead of a snack?*

You know how much I hate *shifting when you've taken a veiling potion. This color looks terrible on us,* the creature huffed, but obeyed.

Mireille's limbs lengthened, muscles stretching and bones popping, her clothes transforming into sable fur streaked through with hints of copper. She reached down, cradling the bag gently in her thick fangs, then sprinted around a corner onto the main avenue and headed for the Grand Ethyrian Theater.

Toward her second performance of the day.

THE AUDIENCE EXPLODED into thunderous applause following Mireille's final solo.

She could barely see beyond the edge of the stage, blinded by the lights beaming down from the rafters.

Her false lashes fluttered in her peripheral vision and her pancake make-up cracked as she held yet another broad, aching smile.

She knew she'd been perfect. Flawless. As always. She practiced longer and more often than any other dancer in the company, even with her other job taking up so much of her time.

But one didn't become the prima ballerina of the Kheimos Company, the most revered in Ethyrios outside of the Imperial Ballet in Delos, without a rigorous and unwavering dedication to the craft.

She flicked her gaze up to the front box at the right of the stage. It was dark and empty. As it had been for every single one of her thousands of performances.

She sighed, shaking off her disappointment and waving to her adoring fans. The burgundy curtain lowered, the clapping and shouting muffled beyond the heavy velvet.

"Brilliant, as always." Juliet, a sly-faced Windrider with butter-yellow wings, sauntered up to grip Mireille's hand. "You bitch."

Mireille snorted a laugh.

"No show again?" The young chorus member's voice softened.

She didn't bother answering Juliet, who read the truth in Mireille's silence.

"He'll show up one of these days, Mireille. Don't lose hope."

The kindness and sympathy lacing Juliet's normally sarcastic tone had Mireille on the verge of tears. So she did what any normal, well-adjusted individual would do in that situation.

She turned and fled.

Juliet followed. "What are you going to do after next week when the run is over?"

Other company members and stagehands offered salutes and claps. Mireille acknowledged them with curt nods, but her smile never reappeared. That rare sight was reserved for the audience—and her marks.

"I have plans." Mireille added enough bite to offer Juliet a hint, but as she turned the corner to her dressing room, the young dancer followed.

"Liar," Juliet smirked. "I thought maybe you'd finally deign to practice with me. Maybe even take me out to lunch on your superstar salary."

Mireille paused before her door, and Juliet took the opening.

"There's this new restaurant that just opened a few blocks away. Rishi's? Yogi's? Rogie's?" Juliet snickered. "I can never remember what it's called. The chef came to Kheimos from some coastal village in Brachos. She serves these bold uncooked fish dishes I've been dying to try. Figured if anyone in this company would enjoy eating raw flesh, it would be you."

Mireille laughed despite herself. And a small, shriveled part of her wanted nothing more than to take Juliet up on her offer. Out of all the dancers, she felt a kinship with Juliet. The Windrider's snark rivaled even that of Mireille's wolf. And Juliet took less shit from anyone other than Mireille herself.

But Mireille didn't do *friends*.

She attempted to will Juliet away with a glare. She was sweaty, her make-up itched, and her hair was too tight against her scalp; she'd been hurried when she'd pinned it up earlier. All she wanted to do was strip off her costume, return to her apartment, and take a long, hot bath.

"I'll think about it."

Juliet shook her head. "You've been giving me that answer for nearly as long as that box has been empty." Mireille stiffened. "Not everyone you let in is going to abandon you."

"Goodnight, Juliet," Mireille snapped as she whipped open the door, then slammed it on Juliet's frustrated sigh.

In her dressing room, the largest in the theater, Mireille plopped into the tufted chair before her vanity table and sank her head into her hands.

She didn't know why she bothered to keep that box for her father. He'd never once shown up to claim it. But to open it up to another patron... She wasn't ready to give up that hope yet.

The hope that she'd one day meet the male who'd sired her.

The hope that she might one day learn his name.

She tucked the pain of his centuries-long absence away, her eyes darting to a small ballerina figurine leaning between the mirror's spherical bulbs, and began her post-show routine—a series of steps as carefully choreographed as those she'd just performed.

She removed her shoes, then her costume. Peeled off her tights. Wiped away her make-up. Brushed out her hair—fifty strokes on the right, then the left. And finally, changed into charcoal leggings and an oversized sweatshirt.

Atop the vanity, her commstone began to glow.

She tucked the violet stone underneath her ear and High Councilor Skanisse's squeaky voice flowed into her mind. "You've retrieved the scepter."

It wasn't even a question. The Deathstalker's body must have been discovered in that shack in Southlake.

"Was there ever any doubt?" Mireille purred, burying her grief behind a professional mask—her go-to tactic.

"Did anyone see you?" Skanisse asked in a tight voice.

"You mean other than the dead Deathstalker?"

Skanisse huffed. "You find any evidence that tied him to Otto?"

Mireille bit back a frustrated grunt. Jurgev Otto, the biggest of the big fish in the trade for the Fallen Goddess's relics, had proven to be Mireille's most elusive mark yet. Though she had little doubt that the eccentric Fae billionaire was the intended recipient of that scepter, she'd found nothing that proved it. The only smart move that dead Deathstalker had made earlier today was not revealing the name of his buyer.

Mireille had been trying to get an in with Otto for months. He was a constant presence throughout Kheimos's many clubs and restaurants, often surrounded by a rotating entourage of the snowy city's glitterati. Ancient religious relics weren't the only things he collected.

Mireille had put herself in his path, using veiling potions to alter her appearance with different body types, hair colors, faces, and even genders, each more alluring than the last. Nothing had worked to capture his attention; she'd never even gotten close enough to be rebuffed.

Skanisse was growing impatient with her lack of progress.

"No," Mireille grumbled. "But I—"

"Be here tomorrow morning at eight. I have another matter to discuss with you."

"What other matter?"

"Eight o'clock," Skanisse spat. "And don't forget the scepter."

The connection went dead and Mireille ripped the commstone away from her ear, tossing it onto the vanity.

Fury burned through her veins. She *hated* having to answer to Skanisse. Preening bastard who sat behind a desk all day, had no idea of the dangers and drudgery of the field work Mireille performed for him and his precious Empire. She'd never once failed to deliver in the nearly three centuries she'd worked for the High Councilor, had done everything he'd ever asked of her with her trademark ruthless efficiency, completing every single assignment on time and without getting caught.

And still, she couldn't get a word of praise from the male. She didn't know why she craved it so badly. Still, she supposed she should be grateful that he allowed her to pursue her true passion, to continue to dance as long as it didn't interfere with her other…*duties.*

She pushed up from her chair, trying not to dwell on the lack of information. She preferred to know exactly what she was getting into before a trip to Imperial Affairs headquarters downtown.

Preparation was a singular obsession for Mireille.

And she did *not* appreciate surprises.

Shouldering her bag, she left her dressing room. The theater was empty as she strode to the back entrance. Even Juliet, who sometimes hovered around waiting for her, had given up.

Good.

Mireille preferred being alone. She had neither the time nor the inclination to worry about anyone but herself.

Snow fell as she exited the theater, the flakes catching in her hair, restored to copper now that the veiling potion had fully worn off.

She wondered if any of the other dancers or audience members had noticed that her facial features looked slightly off this evening—her long nose not quite as sharp and her lips thinner than usual, her silver eyes ringed in dark blue.

She doubted it. No one, aside from her wolf, knew the real Mireille Valette.

And she was determined to keep it that way.

CHAPTER THREE

$\mathscr{R}$onin plodded down the snow-packed sidewalks of downtown Kheimos, weaving around very different groups of Fae than what he was used to due to the early hour.

A Windrider couple swung a rosy-cheeked toddler between them, laughing as the child fluttered his downy gray wings in an attempt at fledgling flight.

A pinched-face Beastrunner male in a sharply-tailored suit barked commands into his commstone, head bowed against the wind.

A line of tourists awaited entry into the city's famous art museum, a mix of all three sub-species donning knit hats, puffy coats, and excited smiles.

They all shared something Ronin had been lacking for centuries—a compelling reason to get up in the morning and face the harsh daylight.

Ronin was a creature of the night, preferred the city's seedy underbelly that only exposed itself under cover of darkness. Which there was plenty of this time of year this far north. One of the main reasons Ronin had chosen to come here after his caging rather than returning home.

As he trudged past the tourists, several heads swiveled in his direction. He pulled his hood down lower; the last thing he needed this morning was to be recognized. He was in no mood to entertain anyone's morbid curiosity about his past deeds or his resulting punishment.

Before his caging, fame had been a delightful burden to bear. Infamy was much heavier. And far more barbed.

Head pounding—he'd *definitely* had too much Delirium after the fight last night—he barreled across the street, nearly side-swiping a deliverymale with an armful of packages, and strode up the steps of Imperial Affairs headquarters.

The sprawling complex reminded him of a honeycomb, with its hexagonal windows and all the drones buzzing around doing Skanisse's bidding. All types of Fae in drab navy and charcoal milled about, sipping cups of steaming coffee or rushing into glass-walled conference rooms.

The clinical lobby contained no decorations other than a portrait of Emperor Leonin Erabis, his iridescent black wings and obsidian gaze on proud display, and two flags. The black one bore the Imperial sigil: a Typhon steel broadsword bracketed by feathered wings and radiating lines. The aqua flag beside it showcased the Northern Territories' sigil: a double-headed axe, the favored weapon of Vestan, God of War, on top of a crescent moon.

Night and violence.

Fitting that this is the territory where Ronin ended up.

Adjusting his hood, Ronin offered a sarcastic salute to the stone-faced Beastrunner at the front desk, who boomed in a bass-deep voice, "You're late. Meeting's downstairs." He nodded back toward the bank of elevators. "An escort is waiting for you on sub-level five."

"Cloak-and-dagger shit this time, huh?" Ronin grimaced, earning a grunt as the male buzzed him through a waist-high gate.

The elevators were a recent addition. Though they'd been invented decades ago, Kheimos had been slow to adopt many of the technological advancements sweeping through the continent from Delos. Not as slow as the human colonies, granted, which enjoyed precisely none of the Fae's innovations. Those nearly magic-less islands were practically primordial.

Ronin pressed a button on the wall and waited for the telltale ding. He hated riding in the small, windowless box, a claustrophobic cage that was all too familiar.

He stepped through the opening doors, then leaned on the back bar and massaged his temples, thanking the High Gods that no one had joined him. Glowing numbers ticked off the floors as he descended, clenching his fists against the inevitable stomach drop.

The elevator slowed, and Ronin burst out as soon as the doors parted, not wanting to spend an additional second within the six-by-six-foot death trap.

A Windrider male with tucked wings and a tight face was waiting for him. "You're late."

Ronin huffed a laugh, pushing his hood back. "So they keep telling me."

"Follow me."

The Windrider led Ronin on a circuitous route through narrow, tubular hallways. Jittery due to the elevator ride, his wolf paced and panted within him, sniffing at the dry, recycled air.

Easy buddy, Ronin soothed. *Just a business meeting.*

Fool, his wolf snarled back. *Are you so certain they are not marching you toward True Death?*

They haven't killed us yet. They won't today. Probably.

Ronin wished the creature would calm the fuck down. It would likely be hours until Ronin could get his hands on another Delirium.

The Windrider stopped before a large vault door, then pressed a palm against a black pad in the center. A series of clicks followed by a reverberating clank echoed, and the male twisted the circular handle before hauling the door open to reveal a cavernous space.

White lights flowed overhead and flecks of green glimmered along the curved concrete walls—a nessite treatment to suppress elemental wind magic. And the High Gods knew what other types of wards and spells were in place to deactivate opticorders or listening devices.

Cloak-and-dagger shit, indeed.

Metal scraped across the floor, and Ronin grunted as the Windrider shoved him into a chair across from Hugo Skanisse. The High Councilor's sky-blue feathered wings drooped over his own chair, positioned in front of a tower of shipping containers. Skanisse had a round face, pink cheeks and slick blond hair with too much product in it. He looked like an overgrown baby angel wearing a plastic helmet.

"You're late," the High Councilor squeaked, completing the cherubic effect.

Ronin fought the urge to roll his eyes at his third scolding in less than ten minutes, then dragged his hands up the shaved sides of his head. "Apologies. I got caught up."

Caught up in the moans of that Windrider waitress—fuck, he didn't even remember her name—as she'd come apart beneath him mere hours ago.

Her name was Sharae, his wolf chuffed, and Ronin silently shushed the beast.

"I do hope you'll be more punctual during this assignment." Skanisse puffed his feathers.

"Where am I escorting you this time, boss?"

Lips pinched like a petulant toddler, Skanisse shook his head. "I'm not the one you'll be watching over." He hooked a thumb over his shoulder. "She is."

The female who stepped out from behind the shipping containers had the straightest posture Ronin had ever seen, her shoulders pushed back and her head floating above her long neck as if dangling from a taut string. Not a single strand escaped her coppery red bun, and underneath her jacket and duffel bag, white leg warmers peeked out over her boots.

Another wolf bi-form based on her scent, that unmistakable musk of fur and pheromones. But hers had something soft and cloyingly sweet underneath. Like a flower at peak maturity before decay kissed its petals.

Her silver eyes landed on him as she skidded to a halt, clenching her fists at her sides.

When she spoke, her voice was lovely and melodic, despite her cutting words. "Absolutely not." She clutched the collar of her jacket, her gaze darting to the bunker door in search of a swift exit.

"Sit down, Agent Valette," Skanisse barked. "We've

already discussed this. You don't have a choice in the matter."

Ronin's brows rose as recognition barreled through him. He'd seen that stunning face before, peering out at him from posters and bus stands and store windows throughout the city.

Mireille Valette. The prima ballerina of the Kheimos Company. *She* was an Imperial Affairs agent?

What the fuck kind of meeting was this?

She stiffened at Skanisse's reprimand, then blew out an annoyed breath, dropped her bag, and peeled off her jacket. From across the room, Ronin's Windrider escort ogled the miles-long, black-clad legs beneath her gauzy pink skirt. Not that Ronin could blame him.

The advertisements paled in comparison.

In person, she was all sharp lines and angles—a cold, aristocratic beauty that sliced like a knife. And he imagined many, *many* males would line up and beg to bleed.

She took a seat next to Skanisse, who said, "Mireille, this is—"

"Ronin Matakos. The *Butcher*."

Most of the Fae who referred to him by that nickname did so in some combination of fear or awe.

Neither were present in her greeting. In fact, he thought he noticed a twinge of disgust. She raked her ice-pale gaze across his disheveled attire. "I don't need a fucking partner, Hugo. I've already—"

Skanisse held up a hand, cutting her off, and turned to Ronin. "Mistress Valette is one of the IA's most, if not our absolute most, skilled field agents."

Ronin couldn't help mirroring her obvious distaste. "What does she do, twirl her marks to death?"

Skanisse and Mireille shared a loaded look before the latter muttered, "Un-fucking-believeable."

The High Councilor cleared his throat. "She has been attempting to lure a new mark, but has so far been unsuccessful."

Mireille huffed, crossing her arms. "You haven't even given me—"

Again, Skanisse silenced her with a sharp look, then slid his gaze back to Ronin. "I assume you've heard of Jurgev Otto?"

Ronin nodded, smoothing over his shock.

Jurgev Otto was one of the oldest—and richest—Fae in Ethyrios. A Deathstalker with a taste for the extraordinary, over the centuries Otto had used his vast wealth to acquire a collection of fine art and religious relics that he kept hidden away in his macabre mansion up in the Blackspur Mountains.

"I've heard of him. Why's the Empire siccing a deadly ballerina on him?"

Mireille shot Ronin a sharp glare, but he just grinned at her.

"The IA has been keeping tabs on him." Skanisse leaned forward in his chair, clasping his pudgy hands in his lap. "We've gotten a number of reports over the years of Fae who have allegedly gone missing after visiting his estate. We informed the Empire, but they didn't feel the need to actively probe into his affairs."

"What's the cause for intervention now?"

"You heard about what happened with the Imperial Prince?" Skanisse cocked an eyebrow.

"Who *hasn't* heard about it?"

"Yes, well, the Empire is trying to minimize the fallout. Tamping down on any lingering sentiment for mortals that the Prince's crime may have stirred up."

"What's that got to do with Otto?"

"The majority of Otto's acquisitions these past decades have been illegal relics associated with the Fallen Goddess. You know the tenets of her faith, I assume? Those ridiculous notions that Fae and humans are somehow equal? The Empire fears Otto may have plans to use these relics to undermine the Erabis family's authority. They've ordered us to sniff out his intentions. Infiltrate his estate, retrieve any powerful objects. And end him, if necessary."

Ronin rubbed at his jaw. Of course the Empire didn't care about a few missing Fae. But now that the threat may be aimed squarely in their own direction... Ronin knew exactly what happened to anyone whose interests no longer aligned with the Erabis family, was infinitely familiar with those consequences. He bit back his rising discomfort at the thought of working for them again.

"Why can't you just go up there officially and question him yourself? Why all the subterfuge?"

"It's a delicate political matter," Skanisse sniffed, "as I'm sure you can appreciate. Otto has been very generous with his resources toward the Empire. It wouldn't do for us to make an enemy of him if our suspicions prove to be unfounded."

Fucking typical. Self-interested bastards. Ronin leaned an elbow on the back of his chair. "How are we supposed to infiltrate Otto's estate? Heard he keeps it pretty well locked down."

"He's hosting a gathering at the end of the month and has invited a select number of guests from among the influential circles here in Kheimos. We were hoping

Mireille could score an invite, but she has not been able to entice him with any of her disguises." Ronin flicked his gaze toward Mireille, who was picking at her nails, pretending to ignore the conversation. Ronin guessed Skanisse had told her all this before he'd arrived. "Time to try a more forward approach."

Mireille glowered at Skanisse. "It's too much of a risk. My cover could be blown. And to pair me with a fucking *amateur—*"

"Do you know what Otto enjoys more than anything?" Skanisse dodged Mireille's outburst, aimed his question at Ronin. "The pursuit of the forbidden. We need to play his game. And what better illicit thrill could we offer than to steal the prima ballerina of the Kheimos company away from the infamous Butcher of Aethalia?"

The hairs on the back of Ronin's neck prickled. He had a bad feeling about where Skanisse was headed with this. "I'm not sure I understand."

"Mireille's disguises have not worked because she's only been offering him beauty. But why would a male like that be interested in beauty with no substance? Her *true* persona is where her value lies. A persona which will become infinitely more enticing once Otto believes she has captured the interest of a powerful male with your level of notoriety." Skanisse rustled his wings, enjoying a meaningful pause before he dropped his bomb. "We need you to pose as her lover."

Mireille emitted a disgusted scoff as Ronin asked, "For how long?"

"For as long as it takes. Otto will be attending the final performance of *The Curse of Faurana*. We'll seed a few well-placed rumors around town that you two have been together for months, a fact which you will confirm with a public outing this week. Hopefully, it will be enough for you *both* to score an invite to that event when you see Otto at the Grand Ethyrian on Friday."

Ronin scrubbed a hand down his face. This was certainly not the meeting he'd expected. "Why both of us? If you're just using me as bait, why do I need to attend Otto's event?"

"*If* you two attend, you'll be able to offer Mireille some measure of protection while you're up there."

"Sounds like she'd be able to protect herself."

Mireille's eyes widened at the compliment. "Exactly what I've been telling him."

"Plus, it will double our chances of success should something unfortunate befall one of you." Skanisse offered Ronin a caustic smile.

"This is never going to work," Mireille cut in. "There's no way anyone's going to believe that I would willingly attach myself to *him*."

Ronin sat back and crossed his arms. "What's that supposed to mean?"

"We don't exactly run in the same circles."

He reviewed what he'd heard of her. Current gossip around Kheimos was that Mireille Valette wasn't dating anyone, and rarely showed her face outside of the theater. Had never attended any of the company's parties or charity galas. She'd never even been seen out at dinner.

"From what I've heard, you don't run in any circles at all," Ronin shot at her.

"And from what *I've* heard, you run in too many," Mireille sneered. "Bedroom's practically got a revolving door."

"You keeping tabs on my bedroom?" Ronin winked. "No wonder Skanisse chose me."

Mireille blasted him with such a bloodthirsty look that his wolf's ears perked up.

Ronin didn't understand why she was so furious at the thought of working with a partner.

Or was it the thought of working with him specifically?

HOLY HIGH GODS.

The Butcher of Aethalia was Mireille's new partner? It was worse than if she'd been shackled to some dimwitted neophyte.

The minute she'd rounded those shipping containers and seen him sitting there—that messy white hair, those sleek muscles, that cocky grin that any female would happily ruin her life for—all the blood had rushed from her body.

Of course she knew who he was. One would be hard-pressed to find a Fae on the continent who didn't. He was exactly the type of arrogant, dominant male she'd always steered clear of. And despite his punishment, he was far too convinced of his own charm.

Many of her fellow dancers had fallen prey to that charm, only to be carelessly tossed aside once Ronin had gotten what he wanted.

On a purely physical level, she could understand why they continued to fawn over him despite the warnings being bandied about the theater.

Handsome didn't even cover it.

Ronin Matakos was a special brand of devastating.

He continued to stare at her with those unnerving, uniquely beautiful golden-blue eyes. "Did I do something to piss you off?"

She pinned him in place with her own silver gaze. "I'm just wondering why the IA thinks a caged wolf will be of any use to me."

He snarled, elongating his fingernails into sharp black points. A pathetic imitation of claws. "Oh, I can still slice. Don't you worry about that."

"Hmm. There's quite a bit of shrinkage, if you ask me."

His eyes blazed and he bared his teeth, his tattoos glowing in the dim light as if working to stop a transformation.

Mireille turned to Skanisse. "He's not right for this. Surely, we can find someone else."

Ronin turned to the High Councilor as well. "And she's too uptight. Good luck finding anyone who wants to work with her."

Skanisse pinched the bridge of his nose, sighing heavily. "It's you two or no one. None of the other operatives have as grand a reputation as Mireille. Nor one as infamous as yours, Ronin. Otto won't be swayed by anything less. Emperor Erabis is, let's just say, extremely *keen* to learn precisely what's going on up at that estate. His Imperial Majesty is prepared to make it very worth your while." He produced two small envelopes from his suit jacket and handed one to each of them.

Mireille turned away to open hers. The message written upon the card stole her breath.

We have learned the identity of your father. Upon the successful completion of your assignment, we will reveal it to you.

The backs of Mireille's eyes prickled. As if she wasn't already ruffled by the thought of working with Ronin fucking Matakos, the IA had to throw this at her as well?

She tucked a hand into her pocket, curling her fingers around the ballerina figurine as the memory of another note, one containing an unfulfilled promise, rose in her mind.

For my little pup. I'll see you soon.

Mireille bit back her tears, refused to show them to these two frustrating males. There'd be plenty of time to indulge her feelings later. Alone.

"I'm in," she pronounced to Skanisse, then tucked the card back into the envelope and placed it in her bag, darting a look at Ronin.

Unguarded devastation twisted his irritatingly perfect features as he clutched his own card. She wondered what they'd offered him, but didn't bother asking. He'd probably lie about it anyway.

He swallowed, then composed himself before crushing the card in his fist. "I need some time to think about it."

A burst of panic tore through her chest. Now that she knew how high her own personal stakes were, she *needed* this assignment. And she'd be damned if she let the smarmy asshole sitting across from her jeopardize that.

Skanisse pushed up from his chair, then snapped his fingers. "Piretti." The black-winged Windrider bustled over to hand a file folder to Mireille. "Profiles of Otto and his associates, plus any information the IA has gathered about the inner workings of his estate. The Cathedral of Bones, they call it. Whatever you can't learn from that file, you can research in the archives. Study up."

The High Councilor strode for the vault door, Piretti

hustling behind him, then called out over his shoulder. "Oh, and Matakos? You've got three days before that offer expires. Choose wisely. If you refuse, this mission will not launch. And if it goes poorly, there *will* be consequences. For all of us. Piretti will wait to escort you out of the building when you're ready."

Skanisse ushered Piretti through the door, then hauled it shut with an ominous thud.

Mireille and Ronin surveyed each other. A silent stand-off between two immovable, opposing forces, each a weapon in their own right. And both savvy enough to know that whoever spoke first would lose the upperhand.

A vein jumped in his jaw, and his marbled eyes swirled with emotions she couldn't decipher.

She held up the file folder. "You wanna look through this before you make your decision?"

He shook his head, cracking his knuckles with his thumbs. The popping sound set her teeth on edge, but she tried not to show it as she noted the phrase tattooed there in Aramaelish, the ancient language of the Fae.

Inom Than. Become Death.

The caging of a Beastrunner's animal *was* a kind of death, she supposed, and a twinge of sympathy gripped her. Though it swiftly curdled at his refusal to accept the assignment.

"Don't fuck this up for me, Matakos." She stood from her chair. "I've tangled with enough entitled assholes to last a lifetime. I don't particularly want one for a partner, but if that's the hand I've been dealt, so be it. Be a good boy and play along."

He drew himself out of his own chair and prowled toward her. Instinct had her stepping away until her back crashed against a shipping container. She squared her jaw as she stared up at him, her wolf whining quietly within her.

He slammed a hand against the metal, and the clang reverberated throughout her body. Elongating his canines, he bent down to sniff her neck where her pulse had grown frightened, fluttery wings. Even caged, those teeth could do major damage.

"Do you know what *I've* tangled with enough of to last a lifetime?" he growled as the edge of a fang coasted over her skin, inspiring an uncontrollable shiver. "Little she-wolves who think they can order me around. Though I do love how delicious they taste when they're scared." He lowered his voice. "My favorite fucking prey."

He pushed away from the container and stalked toward the exit.

What a delightful barbarian, her wolf purred. *I think I want to be his prey.*

"Where are you going?" Mireille choked out, struggling to calm herself and ignore her wolf.

He didn't answer, merely pounded on the bunker door then stalked out as soon as Piretti opened it.

She sagged against the shipping container, gulping stale air into her heaving lungs.

Fuck this. If having a partner meant dealing with the terrible, relentless uncertainty of depending on someone other than herself, then Mireille could do without one.

She gathered up the folder, left the bunker, and headed for the archives hall to begin her research.

CHAPTER FOUR

"Got himself banished to the colonies, is what I heard."

Ronin didn't mean to eavesdrop on the conversation at the other end of the bar, but given that he and the two ancient, chatty Windriders were the only patrons in here, there was no avoiding it. Nor could he avoid the surreptitious gazes the two males kept sliding his way. Not like he wasn't used to it.

"'Sa damn shame, if you ask me," the other male murmured into his beer. "Never liked the look of that younger one. High Gods help us all when he takes the throne."

The continent was still reeling from the scandal involving the Imperial heir, though very few details had been leaked about precisely why Prince Tristan Erabis had been stripped of his title and exiled a year ago. The most persistent rumor was that he'd fallen in love with a human woman.

Ronin didn't know which part of that rumor was

more unbelievable—that the young prince had fallen in love with a *human* in the first place, or that he'd been willing to forsake his birthright for her. No love, especially not of a mortal, could have ever persuaded Ronin to give up that kind of power and prestige.

Ronin thought the young prince must be a fucking idiot.

Though to be fair, Ronin was feeling like an idiot himself at the moment.

Scrawled upon that card Skanisse had handed him was an offer he'd craved for centuries.

The Emperor was willing to uncage his wolf.

And he'd fled the IA building like a coward, his heart in his throat and his wolf howling in protest. Had barreled into the first open bar he could find to drown himself in Delirium.

He'd already downed one bottle, and as he brought the second to his lips, his eyes darted out the filmy window to the little storefront across the street.

The truth was, as soon as Ronin had read that note, terror had sunk icy claws into him. He couldn't help but wonder if the Emperor's offer was too good to be true.

He'd had a third of a lifetime to resign himself to surviving without his wolf, had worked hard to kill that most dangerous of emotions: hope.

Could he really trust Leonin Erabis? The male had branded him a monster, ruined Ronin's life and reputation in one fell swoop.

Plus, the offer had come with some rather unsavory stipulations: an assignment where he'd not only have to outwit a dangerous Deathstalker billionaire, but would also have to pose as someone's fucking boyfriend. A role he'd successfully avoided all his life.

Nor did he have any particular desire to do it with the bitchy, uptight redhead who'd already cut him to shreds this morning.

But none of those were the real reason why Ronin had asked for time to think before he accepted.

That reason was staring at him from across the street: the tiny purple door nestled between a tea shop and an apothecary.

He'd never visited a chronomancer before, didn't even really know if he believed in the purported abilities of the Fae females who claimed to have a gift for seeing both into the past and future. Most of them had been priestesses of the Fallen Goddess before the Empire had sacked her temples and forbidden her faith.

His twin sister Selene swore by their readings. Barely made a single decision more complicated than what she was having for breakfast without consulting the mystical females. And according to Selene, they'd yet to steer her wrong.

So, before Ronin made a choice that could drastically alter the course of his life, for good or bad, he thought it couldn't hurt to get some spiritual advice beforehand.

"You want another, handsome?" The Beastrunner bartender propped her hands against the bar, leaning forward and pushing some very impressive cleavage into his face. Ronin's eyes dipped to the sight as he knocked back the rest of his drink, and she licked her lips, shimmying her hips.

We could stay a bit longer, his wolf offered, calmed by the Delirium.

Not today, Ronin snapped back.

Prude.

Ronin paid for his drinks, leaving the pouting

bartender a larger tip than necessary, then pushed out of the dim bar and squinted against the blinding noonday sun.

He crossed the street, the euphoric effects of the elixir tingling through his limbs, and approached the purple door. Before he could even raise his fist to knock, the door opened.

A calm, lovely female voice beckoned him across the threshold. "Welcome, Butcher. She's been expecting you."

She *who*? The Fallen Goddess? More likely, this was the greeting the chronomancer used on all her victims. Er, clients.

Though he couldn't yet explain how she'd known it was him. He glanced around the doorframe, searching for an opticorder, but didn't see one. Didn't mean there wasn't one there, just that it wasn't visible.

He pushed through a gauzy curtain and entered a circular room. Seated at the table was a Windrider female with mint-green wings, wearing a shimmery white robe and veil. Her palms bracketed a white obelisk carved with a symbol that Ronin recognized.

Teles, the symbol associated with the Fallen Goddess —a circle bisected by a vertical line.

A bold display this day and age. Though, the fact that the Empire didn't even care enough to shut these establishments down told Ronin all he needed to know about the accuracy of whatever he was about to hear.

Still, he felt compelled to do this. Maybe it was the cumulative effect of Selene's ramblings. Either way, he knew he couldn't make a decision about the assignment without hearing what the chronomancer had to say.

"Please, have a seat," she said. "And tell me what troubles you today?"

"If *she's* been waiting for me, shouldn't you know that already?" Ronin cocked a skeptical brow.

"She sees you have many troubles. Neither you nor I have the time for her to examine them all for you this day."

His wolf chuckled. *Savage.*

Ronin sat back in his chair, crossed an arm over his chest and scratched at his biceps. "Don't we need to discuss payment before we begin?"

The female angled her head and blinked her violet eyes. "She does not charge for her readings. Time belongs to us all. However, if you are pleased at the end of the session, you may feel inclined to offer a donation to her disciples." She gestured toward a small cabinet laden with an overflowing bowl of *drachas* and other trinkets: jeweled necklaces, a golden platter, a silver pocketwatch, and several chunks of god-touched stones in red, purple, and deep blue. "So again I will ask, Ronin Matakos, what troubles you today?"

"I..." He didn't even know where to start. How to phrase the question to ensure he'd receive a helpful answer. "I was offered a chance this morning to get something back that I lost a long time ago. Something I didn't believe I would ever get back. I want to know if I should take the chance, if the situation will work out, in the end."

Crinkles formed at the corner of her eyes, as if she were smiling beneath her veil. "A very worthy question. Different from the trivialities that most of your fellow citizens arrive here with. She will be pleased to have such a challenge."

The female gripped the obelisk, one hand stacked

above the other, and began to rub her hands up and down.

His wolf snickered.

Child, Ronin shushed him.

"Place your palms on the table and close your eyes," the female commanded softly. "Repeat your question within your mind."

Ronin did as he was told, the purple tablecloth catching on his calluses.

Will I really get my wolf back? he asked into his mind.

At first, he could hear nothing but the gentle sounds of the female breathing deeply through her nose, her hands swishing over the obelisk.

So he asked again. *Will I get my wolf back?*

The female's hands stilled and her feathers rattled as a warm breeze churned through the small room, caressing over Ronin's skin and stirring his hair.

The scent it bore was nothing that Ronin recognized. Something ancient and mossy and brimming with both life and rot. He shivered as a multi-faceted voice penetrated his mind.

You ask the wrong question, the voice said, sounding like thousands of voices strung together into a timeless melody. *Ask again.*

Will my wolf and I be reunited?

That is the same question. And you already know the answer. Your wolf never left you.

Ronin clenched his hands into fists. He was beginning to think that this was the second stupid decision he'd made today. Though he didn't see how the voice could be a trick. He cracked an eye and glanced toward the female across the table, then nearly jumped out of his chair.

Her eyes had gone an opaque shade of white and even

without the pupils, he could tell she was staring straight at him. It was fucking unnerving.

He closed his own eyes, trying to come up with a way to phrase the question that would get him the information he needed.

If I take the assignment that was offered to me this morning, will I be happy with the result?

Closer, the voice answered. *Push* deeper. *Is happiness truly all you seek?*

Ronin sought his wolf for back-up, but the creature was utterly silent for once. Bowed in reverence with his head resting on his paws, ears back, tail down. Supplicating to the presence before him.

What *was* Ronin seeking through this assignment? Happiness, yes, but there was something even more important than that.

To be whole again. To prove he wasn't the monster everyone suspected he was. To do some good in this world, for a change.

If I take the assignment, will I find purpose in my life again?

The voice emitted a low hum that vibrated not only through Ronin, but through the room, rattling the Windrider's feathers and jostling the table.

There is a worthy question. Yes, Ronin Matakos. You will. Though it will come at a cost you may not be willing to pay.

He bristled. *What cost?*

This I cannot tell you.

Ronin almost snarled. This was such bullshit. He didn't know why he'd bothered.

Can you at least tell me if the Emperor's offer is legitimate and made in good faith?

The room grew icy, the warm breeze replaced with a glacial blow that pelted Ronin's cheeks.

The current Emperor has no faith, the voice spat. *But the offer was legitimate.*

So I should take the assignment then?

This I cannot tell you.

Ronin felt like he'd set himself up for that one. He wracked his brain, trying to come up with another question to ask, a question that would wash away his indecision and help him choose what to do.

You said if I take the assignment that I will find my purpose again. What is my purpose?

The voice took a long time to answer, what felt like an eternity but was probably only a few minutes. Ronin had almost given up on hearing one when the voice spoke up softly.

You will be afforded the opportunity for many. Restoration. Destruction. Salvation. Abomination. Resurrection. In this moment, all paths remain open. But several are rapidly closing. You must make your choice.

Which paths are closing?

This I cannot tell you.

Ronin slammed a fist upon the table and the voice laughed. Fucking *laughed.*

What can *you tell me?*

You have a role yet to play in this world's history. If you are brave enough to bear it.

And if I'm not?

It was as if all the air was sucked from the room. The breeze snuffed out abruptly and the temperature plummeted. Ronin cracked his eyes to see hoarfrost crawling up the female's wings.

Then this world will be yet another failure in a long string of disappointing experiments. And we will be forced to start over again.

What in Ethyrios did *that* mean?

No fucking pressure, he answered.

You asked for a purpose. What greater purpose could there be than saving your world?

Does this world even deserve to be saved?

Silence blanketed his mind again, and when he looked across the table toward the chronomancer, her eyes were now closed and dancing behind her lids. Calculating.

That remains to be seen. Is there anything else you would like to ask us?

Ah, no. I think I've learned enough, thanks.

Be well, Ronin Matakos. We will see you again. In this world or the next.

The lights in the room flickered back to life and the temperature normalized.

Ronin blew out a long breath.

The Windrider opened her eyes, which had returned to normal, and regarded him with an inscrutable expression. "Are you satisfied with your reading?"

"Sure." Ronin pushed up from the table, feeling even more foolish than when he'd walked in here.

The female bowed her head, her gaze darting to the small donation table. "We thank you for visiting us today."

Ronin fished a few *drachas* from his pocket and tossed them into the bowl, then exited the shop and returned to the snow-covered, sun-drenched streets. He needed another Delirium after that weird fucking session.

She spoke the truth, his wolf piped up.

How do you know that? Ronin aimed for the bar.

You can drown us in Delirium, poison us both all you want, but she would not lie to me, his wolf whined.

I've had enough of the psycho-babble bullshit today, Ronin spat back. *Spare me.*

You only have three days or you will lose this chance.

Why do you fucking care?

Because, his wolf spoke in a low, reverent voice, *she showed me a vision of our future.*

Ronin's heart nearly stopped as his wolf whispered to him again.

And I was free.

CHAPTER FIVE

*M*ireille gently stirred the pot above the burner, trying not to agitate the veiling potion she'd spent the past hour brewing.

She'd used the last of her supply during her assignment with the Deathstalker this past weekend, and she wanted at least one vial on hand before she headed to Otto's estate.

If she went to the estate. It was seeming less and less likely with each passing day.

Ronin hadn't shown up here at IA HQ for the past three days, and, to no one's shock, least of all Mireille's, she'd been forced to begin doing the research into Otto on her own.

Ronin was rapidly running out of time to make his decision. And if he didn't agree to play along, mission incomplete.

Even if, by some miracle, Ronin showed up today and agreed to participate, there was still the pesky task of getting an invite to the event in the first place.

She snorted a bitter laugh at the thought that *all* the males she was currently required to depend on were letting her down.

Well, they could fucking get in line. Males had been letting her down her entire life.

From the side of the lab table, that thick, creamy card beckoned with enticing promise.

We have learned the identity of your father.

She'd been trying to do the same ever since she'd come to Kheimos. But with so little information to go on, even the IA's vast data archives had revealed nothing. Each fruitless effort had dampened that hope in her heart, until it was no more than a faintly smoldering ember.

The Emperor's offer had brought it blazing back to life.

She tried to ignore it, breathed in the bitter-scented steam of the bubbling potion, the result of crushed leaves of dienswort.

The plant was named after Dienses the Jester, God of Merriment. Also a God of trickery, whose mythology was full of stories of altered appearances causing mischief among humans and Fae.

Dienses was one of the many, *many* Gods in Ethyrios's long history of deities. The Jester dated back tens of thousands of years, a Lesser God of the ancient humans and one who ruled before the two species had discovered each other and the reign of the Fallen Goddess, Adelphinae, had supplanted them.

Dienses had, as always, gotten the last laugh when the Empire had suppressed the Fallen Goddess's influence and re-instated the Fae High Gods and human Lesser Gods to worship.

High Gods, Lesser Gods, Fallen Goddesses. While Mireille grasped the concept of divinity, she wasn't sure she believed any of them actually existed.

There'd certainly been no talk of Gods in anything more than an intellectual capacity during her ascetic childhood in the Oread Woods, a vast sprawl of evergreens and birches that lined the border between Cernodas and the Northern Territories.

The only *Gods* who'd been worshiped in the tiny cabin that Mireille shared with her mother Vivienne were practicality, industriousness, and ruthless efficiency.

She could almost hear her mother's voice as she stirred the potion.

Gently, Mireille. You mustn't get excited and ruin it. And do not *overmix it. Be deliberate in your motions.*

Her mother had taught her how to make many potions, poultices, tinctures, and extracts from the veritable bounty of nature that had grown around their cabin.

Mireille had learned at a very young age that the best way to win her mother's affections—so infrequently given—was to complete her chores and tasks on time and without error. Any mistakes were met with swift reprisals and often meant being sent to bed without dinner.

And though her childhood had been calm, it was entirely devoid of emotion. No laughter. Certainly no crying. Mireille had a vivid memory of falling in their small kitchen as a toddler and banging her knee against a chair. She'd burst into tears and something else had awakened within her, her wolf attempting to come out. Her mother had smacked her so hard that her tears instantly dried and her wolf retreated with a frightened whine.

Vivienne had an irrational fear about Mireille shifting. As if she wasn't sure what such an act would reveal. She hadn't even taught her daughter how to do it; Mireille had learned on her own. Though Vivienne herself did go out in wolf-form to hunt every few weeks.

Mireille had spent the majority of her childhood learning to master her feelings, lest she suffer her mother's harsh punishments.

There were only two instances when her mother had ever strayed from her own principles. When reason and practicality had abandoned Vivienne Valois and the choices she'd made were entirely based on emotions.

The first was anger.

One night, when Mireille was five, a visitor had arrived at the cabin. Vivienne had taken one look out the window and her face had drained of color. She'd hustled Mireille into her bedroom and locked the door.

Ear pressed against the wood, Mireille had heard her mother shouting at the stranger.

Mireille had never met another Fae, so the sound of the male's voice, raised to meet her mother's, shocked and excited her. She wanted to meet him too, didn't understand why her mother wouldn't let her.

Mireille had barely been able to make out what they were saying, though a few choice snippets stuck with her, even after all these years.

…needs to understand who she is…

…no idea how hard this had been for us…

…I'm sorry, Vivi. Truly I am…

After the voices had faded, Vivienne, eyes red and swollen, came to let Mireille out of her bedroom.

Mireille had never seen her mother look like that before, and she was frightened.

"Who was that?"

"No one important." Vivienne's cool countenance returned. "Just an old friend. Someone I knew from Before."

Before. To Mireille's five-year-old mind, the word held the weight of a physical place. The name of a town, perhaps? The one where Vivienne had lived with her pack before she'd fled, pregnant and alone?

"You are never to ask me about him again. It's for your own protection, Mireille," Vivienne had pronounced before fleeing to her own bedroom.

The next day, Mireille had gone out to forage behind their cabin and noticed something gleaming through the needles at the base of a pine tree.

A small wooden box.

She'd snuck it back into her room and when she'd opened the lid, a tinkling melody began to play. A small figurine wearing a pretty pink skirt sprang up, spinning along with the music.

There was a note in the box as well.

For my little pup. I'll see you soon.

And even though she was young and certainly not privy to the ways of the world, Mireille knew that the male who'd visited the cabin the previous night was her father. And he'd left her a gift.

She'd hidden the note beneath her mattress, the box beneath her bed, and for weeks, months, years, expected him to return like he'd promised.

At night, alone in her bedroom, Mireille would open the box and mimic the small ballerina. Irina, she'd named her, after Irina Amiel, the legendary prima ballerina of the Imperial Ballet in Delos. A fact Mireille had learned from the books her mother insisted she study as her sole means of education.

Mireille would twirl around her room, pretending to be Irina, imagining that if she could maintain the spin for as long as the music played, somehow her father would know. He'd realize she was perfect and he would come back to rescue her from her mother's suffocating clutches.

But he never did.

So Mireille bore it. Did everything Vivienne ever asked of her. Suppressed her feelings and dreams and lived a life of colorless drudgery, with her untrained dancing as her only outlet. Imagined the life she might have one day if her mother ever let her go.

Her wish came sooner, and with far more violence, than Mireille could've anticipated.

The day after Mireille turned twenty-one, two males had arrived at the cabin.

The instant Vivienne scented them prowling through the pines, she'd snarled at Mireille to stay inside, then burst through the door and shifted into her wolf.

Watching through the window, Mireille saw her mother—that proud, copper she-wolf so similar to her own—stare down the two enormous males, one gray and one black.

"Did you think you could hide from the pack forever?" the black wolf growled. "Give the child over, and we'll leave."

"*Never*," Vivianne barked, launching for the gray wolf.

Despite her confused feelings about the woman who controlled her entire existence, Mireille couldn't stand by and watch her mother get eaten alive. So she rushed from the cabin and called upon her own wolf.

The fight was *vicious.*

It was the most alive Mireille had felt in years. Maybe ever.

Blood and fur flew as yips and snarls and howls rent the night, Vivienne fighting with a ferocity that Mireille had never witnessed. Mother and daughter pushed the two wolves further into the woods and finally chased them off.

"Psycho bitches," the black wolf had growled over a torn shoulder as he and his companion fled. "You're not worth the effort."

Mireille and Vivienne limped back to the cabin, but before they even made it to the steps, Vivienne collapsed in the grass, shifting back into her humanoid form.

And revealing a sight Mireille would never forget for as long as she lived.

Her mother's terrified silver eyes swirling madly, her mouth opening and closing. And where her neck should have been, nothing but a gaping, meaty wound. Mireille was amazed her mother had made it through the fight, let alone back to the cabin. Streams of blood pulsated from the torn skin and muscle as Vivienne emitted watery gasps, trying to catch breaths that would never again fill her lungs.

Mireille shifted as well, wincing at the deep gash on her right forearm. She dimly recalled the gray wolf's jaws sinking into her own wolf's leg and tearing out a chunk of flesh.

She crashed to her knees, grasping her mother's hand. It was all she could do. The wound was far too aggressive for even a Fae's healing abilities to fix.

Vivienne gripped Mireille's hand, pulling her closer with the last bit of strength in her failing body, and wheezed, "Your…father…"

She never finished her confession. Life drained from her eyes, her limbs slackening, and Mireille knew she was gone.

Vivienne would have been proud of the stoic calm that overtook Mireille as she sat there, bathed in moonlight, not shedding a single tear despite the complicated grief that froze her in place for hours. Her mother had died protecting her, a final act of love and sacrifice. But she'd also died protecting her own secrets. Mireille was simultaneously furious and heartbroken. Vivienne may not have been kind, but she was the only companionship Mireille had ever known.

She buried her mother at sunrise in the field behind their cabin.

And by the time the sun rose to its peak in the noonday sky, Mireille had buried her sorrow as well.

She fled to Kheimos, made a new life for herself there. Took a job with Imperial Affairs that allowed her to use the skills her mother had taught her—the intellect she'd gleaned from the books, her ability to remain unflappably emotionless no matter the circumstances, her talent with potions brewing. She was so good at her job that Skanisse hadn't objected when she'd requested to pursue her dancing as well. And she'd climbed to the very top of that field with the same single-minded focus and ruthless efficiency she'd gleaned from Vivienne.

She'd changed her last name from Valois to Valette, keeping a hint of her mother's original surname. Though it was a risk, especially with her mother's pack members still at large, she couldn't bear to change it completely.

What if her father ever came looking for her?

She pulled the ballerina figurine from her pocket, holding it in her right hand as she caressed the long, silver scar on her forearm with her left. Two reminders of everything she'd lost.

"Whatcha working on?" a low voice drawled, breaking her from her reverie. She turned toward the open door of the laboratory.

High Gods, Ronin looked like shit.

His clothes were especially disheveled today. And was he wearing his shirt inside out? Purple crescents lurked beneath his eyes, and his white hair was limp and greasy—unwashed for days.

Mireille glanced at the clock on the wall. "Only three days and twenty-seven minutes late. You must've been anxious to see me."

He shrugged, leaning against the door frame. "Needed some time to think."

"And?" Mireille asked, her heart in her throat, her eyes glued to her potion. Though the fact that he'd come at all was promising, she couldn't bear to look at him. Maybe he'd only come to let her down.

She distracted herself by decanting the clear liquid into a small vial, then screwed on a silver lid and placed it in her bag.

"I'm fucking here, aren't I?" he mumbled.

Relief poured through Mireille's veins as she stood from her seat, then gathered her bag and flicked off the lights.

"Follow me," she said. "You've got a lot to catch up on."

CHAPTER SIX

Ronin followed Mireille down the sparse hallways, the harsh lights buzzing overhead.

He'd never seen someone move so gracefully. She glided along the concrete, her steps silent and her back rod-straight.

She turned through a windowed door, *ARCHIVES* printed on the glass.

"Good morning, Sonya." She offered a kind smile to the female Windrider behind the desk. So she *was* capable of being cordial. Just not to him.

The cream-winged Fae smiled back. "At it again, I see? I left the room set-up for you." Sonya passed a plastic card to Mireille. "Thank the High Gods the IA is finally taking those complaints seriously and looking into Otto."

Ronin stepped up to the desk. "What complaints?"

The Windrider gave Ronin a questioning look and Mireille piped up, "He's my partner on this one. You can answer him."

"Partner?" Sonya barked a laugh. "Where's he been the past three days, then? And since when do *you* need a partner?"

Mireille side-eyed Ronin. "I've been asking myself the same question. He certainly wouldn't have been my first choice."

That makes two of us, Ronin thought. "What *complaints?*" he asked again.

"Not very polite, is he?" Sonya cocked an eyebrow at Mireille, who returned a conspiratorial grin.

"And rather impatient, given he was nearly a half-hour late this morning as well."

Sonya patted Mireille's hand. "Well, if anyone can turn him around, I'm sure it's you, dear."

Ronin stared at the two females, slack-jawed. Unused to being so thoroughly ignored.

"What complaints have you heard?" Mireille asked.

Sonya answered *her,* and Ronin bit his tongue to keep from throwing his hands up in consternation. Like he needed this bullshit on top of the massive hangover he was nursing. He'd gone on a bit of a bender after that visit to the chronomancer.

"I gave you the reports about those Fae who disappeared, right? Their loved ones were sure they'd been at the estate, but Otto and his associates somehow managed to persuade the IA they were lying." Sonya frowned. "I never bought it. Grease the right palms, and rich bastards like Otto can make any story disappear."

"Right." Mireille nodded. "Thought maybe you were talking about something else. I haven't gotten to those files yet."

"Maybe your new *partner* can help." Sonya aimed a shit-eating grin at Ronin, who merely grunted back.

Mireille swept away from the desk, and Ronin hustled to keep up.

"Be nice to her, Butcher!" Sonya called out. So she *had* known who he was.

Mireille wended her way around empty tables and stacks of books, then stopped at the last door in the back corner of the hall. She swiped the card across a black panel, a beep sounded, and the door swung open. The lights flickered on, revealing a windowless room containing a table piled with documents and open filing boxes.

"Have you searched through all this already?" Ronin asked, incredulous, as Mireille settled into a chair and motioned for him to take the one beside it.

From her bag she pulled the original folder, the one Skanisse had given them days ago, and plopped it onto the table. "What did you think I've been doing for the past three days while you were out"—she sniffed, her upper lip curling—"fucking females and getting plastered on Delirium?"

"Had some sinning to work out of my system before shackling myself to your prim ass." Ronin stretched his legs out under the table and cupped his hands behind his head.

"I hope you enjoyed yourself." She pushed the folder toward him, her silver eyes dragging over his muscled arms as if she couldn't help herself. "But now it's time to work. You need to read this."

He didn't budge. Maybe even flexed a little. "If you've already read it, why don't you just tell me what you've learned and spare me the homework."

"Lazy ass," she muttered under her breath. "You planning to just coast along and let me do all the work for you?"

"Again," Ronin said, chewing on a fingernail, "if you've already read through all this, what's the point of me wasting my time? You're the super-spy genius, right? What could I possibly find that you haven't?"

Mireille's fists clenched, her teeth grinding. He'd caught her. No way would she admit she might've missed something.

She glared at him, but opened the folder, then brought a hand to her neck to smooth a few red curls that had escaped her bun. The movement washed her scent over him, that odd mix of musk and ripe flowers, and his wolf perked up.

Tell her to let her hair down, the creature purred. *We want to see her wild and untamed.*

Ronin ignored him as Mireille removed several photographs from the folder and pushed one across the table.

"Otto."

Ronin rolled his eyes. "I know what Otto looks like."

Her face was tight, like an exasperated school teacher, her fingertips lingering on the photo's edge.

He snatched it up for a closer look. He was still amazed by the clarity opticorders could achieve, a Fae invention about a century after the war. Before that, all visual representations were drawn or painted. Whether the device had been invented by science or magic, Ronin didn't know. Though he supposed, in Ethyrios, they were one in the same.

Thanks to his severe, triangular face, Otto looked even more serpentine than most Deathstalkers. Dark, vertical pupils stood in stark contrast to his pale yellow irises, and his nose was so flat it nearly disappeared into his ghostly skin. His black hair was short and slicked back from his forehead. In this particular photo, his sharp fangs were popped, extending past lavender lips to his pointed chin.

A notorious dandy, he wore an impeccably tailored three-piece suit in a loud purple-and-green plaid, and the stunning female clinging to his arm wore a long fur coat in matching purple.

Otto was staring at the female with such predatory possessiveness that Ronin shivered. The Deathstalker's intensity was legendary, though Ronin suspected one didn't earn the kind of wealth Otto had acquired without it.

He handed the photo back to Mireille. "Your future boyfriend looks dangerous. Like he might just eat you alive." Mireille sniffed, not taking the bait, and he wondered why he had such an urge to rile her. "Assuming you know who that female is?" Mireille shook her head. "I can't remember her name. Veronica? Vanessa? Something with a V. Former mistress of one of the Emperor's cousins. She left the male for Otto. Skanisse wasn't wrong about him being a famefucker."

"How do *you* know that?" Though her tone was incredulous, he swore she looked impressed.

"He brought her to a few of my fights a while back. Haven't seen them together since, though. Rumor around town is she left him. Went back to the Emperor's cousin. Good news for you. Nothing heals a broken-hearted male like a good rebound fuck."

She vented a disgusted scoff, then slapped another photo onto the table. It had been taken on the same day, though the view was wider. Otto was helping Veronica-Vanessa into a black sedan on some street in

Kheimos. Two Fae stood behind him, one male and one female.

Mireille pointed at the male. "Julius Kosera, but everyone refers to him as the Greyhorn. Rhinoceros bi-form and Otto's personal muscle."

"I know him, too. Defeated him in the arena decades ago."

Kosera had been furious about the loss at the time, though he'd never returned to challenge Ronin again. Guess he'd found himself a new job.

The towering Beastrunner was nearly seven feet tall, his bulging muscles threatening to split the seams of his black suit jacket. His skin was a dull shade of gray, reminiscent of sun-dried mud, and his bald head showcased a squished face, two beady, black eyes and a long hooked nose.

"She's the one you have to look out for though." Mireille tapped on the female. She was short, barely crested Kosera's ribs, with straight hair that fell to her waist in contrasting sheets of white and black. Dressed head to toe in black leather, her small, shapely frame was accentuated by a corset-like belt filled with gleaming blades. "Layla Fetar. Honey badger bi-form. Otto's fixer."

Ronin let out a low whistle. The female was beautiful and deadly, her deep brown eyes lit with sharp cunning and violent menace. He thought it convenient for Otto that he had a honey badger bi-form in his employ. There weren't many left on the continent, and their blood could be used as an antidote to Deathstalker venom, which was fatal for humans and could lead to True Death for other Fae, if the antivenom wasn't administered quickly enough.

"She looks like a *real* fun time," Ronin smirked.

"This isn't a joke," Mireille spat, swiping up the photo. "She used to be a Shadow Maiden."

Ronin's brows rose. The Shadow Maidens were a group of lethal females tasked with personal security for Empress Mila and Princess Belen. Trained from birth to kill in a thousand different ways. It was considered a great honor to be chosen for the position, one typically held for life.

"Why'd she defect? I can't believe the Empire would have allowed such a thing."

"That information isn't in any of these files."

Ronin dragged a thumb across his lower lip. "A hundred *drachas* says I can persuade her to tell me."

Mireille's eyes flashed with heat before she huffed a grunt. She tossed another folder onto the table, and he chuckled at her irritation. "Shipping intake forms."

"Sounds fascinating."

"They were actually." She opened the folder and pulled out several marked documents. "Most of them were full of innocuous things—produce, meats, linens, crates of wine from Nephes. But look at these." She ran a finger down several sheets, pointing to areas where the amount of the shipment was far larger.

He glanced at the entries. "Anastasium. Isn't that—"

"The god-touched stone of Stygios, yes."

"Why would Otto be ordering such a large amount of the god-touched stone of the High God of Death and Destruction? And why wasn't this order flagged?"

"Well, technically it was, if it made it into these archives." Mireille frowned. "But the IA only gets involved if it's over a certain amount. All these were just below the legal limit. He was trying to stay under the IA's radar by spreading the shipments out and burying them among other ordinary items."

"What's anastasium used for?"

Excited curiosity transformed Mireille's cold features into something warm and unnervingly attractive. Ronin tried not to stare. "That's the strange thing—its uses are purely decorative. It's not like mentrite, the god-touched stone of Thakavi, which is mined from a single source in Cernodas to produce commstones. Or polemite, the red stone of Vestan that powers Tartarus." Ronin shivered involuntarily at the name of the infamous prison. "Or even nessite, Anaemos's stone that has the power to suppress wind magic. Anastasium has no uses, because the source of Stygios's power on Ethyrios remains a mystery. If one even exists."

"So what's Otto using it for? Lining his bathtub? Making candlesticks? Paperweights?"

"Has anyone ever told you that you're not as funny as you think you are?"

"Never," he scoffed. "I'm fucking hilarious. Maybe you could find a sense of humor if you spent less time working and more time interacting with people."

Mireille ignored his taunt, placing the shipping intakes back into the folder and rising from her chair, then bent over to pick up another filing box.

Delectable, his wolf crooned.

Ronin stifled a laugh, though he sure as shit didn't disagree. *Pretty sure she hates us, buddy. Don't get your hopes up.*

Mireille hauled the box onto the table in front of Ronin. There were hundreds of folders inside.

"Wrath of Vestan," Ronin choked out, "how are there so many?"

"These are the reports that Sonya was talking about. Review them and see if any patterns jump out at you."

Ronin pulled a folder from the box, then extracted a document written in swooping letters. "What does this say?"

Mireille gaped at him. "You don't speak Aramaelish? I assumed you did, based on that phrase you have tattooed on your knuckles."

Ronin shrugged. "I only know a few words here and there."

Aramaelish was only used as a daily language on the continent sporadically, for official purposes and mostly among the higher class Fae. Which Ronin certainly was not. His parents and sister had only spoken to each other in the common tongue, the language used most often throughout Ethyrios and among the humans as well. Most signs on the continent were written in Aramaelish, so he'd gleaned some. But he certainly couldn't speak or read it.

"Let me guess," he said, "you're fluent."

"Of course I am. It's a necessity that operatives speak it in addition to the common tongue."

"If we're supposed to be dating, *that's* something I should know about you. I don't even know where you're from, what your parents' names are."

She dipped a hand into her pocket, a flicker of the deepest sadness darkening her silver eyes. Shit. Had something happened to her parents? He felt a small stab of guilt for teasing her.

Until she opened her mouth and proved, yet again, what a cold bitch she was.

"I don't want to know anything about you, Butcher. Only what's absolutely necessary. You're a tool to get me through this assignment and nothing more. I don't need your sympathy or your intimacy, and I'm *certainly* not going to offer anything of the kind to you. So, let's just cut the bullshit. Play your role and I'll play mine, and when this is all over, we can go our separate ways."

Ronin whistled and spread his arms across the back of his chair. "She-wolf *does* have claws, after all. What nerve did I just hit, huh?"

Mireille didn't answer, merely scowled, her foot tapping against the floor. "Off fucking limits." She leaned down to pick up her bag.

"Where are you going?"

"Theater. Practice. Files are all yours." She gestured to the bookshelf. "There's an Aramaelish dictionary over there if you need help translating."

"Wouldn't it make more sense for *you* to do this? It'll take me five times as long."

"Guess you'd better get started then." She hauled her bag over her shoulder and headed for the door. "See you tonight."

"What's tonight?" he barked out, halting her.

"Skanisse didn't tell you?" She pinched the bridge of her nose, mumbling, "It's the debut of our fake relationship."

"Oooo, you've finally admitted it's a relationship. Say it again, baby. Tightens my balls."

Her silver eyes blazed and if looks could kill, he'd be bleeding out in his chair right now.

She whipped open the door. "If we're not able to score an invite to that event, or if anyone suspects we're not really a couple, this isn't going to work. And we can *both* say goodbye to our rewards from the Emperor. Dinner. Riashi's. Eight o'clock. Then tomorrow night, he's gotten you a ticket to the ballet. Better hope Otto shows up."

"Can't fucking wait," he grumbled, slouching down in his chair.

"They wanted you on this assignment for a reason, Ronin. And it's not just to be my gorgeous arm candy. Maybe a miracle will occur and you'll find something in those files that I didn't. Do your fucking homework."

The corkboard on the wall rattled as she slammed the door behind her, leaving him alone with his wolf and the files.

Groaning, he strode to the bookshelf to grab the dictionary, then slumped into his seat and plucked out a folder.

He'd prove to that smug little minx that he could find answers, too. That he was just as smart as she clearly thought she was.

It was only hours later, the juicy tidbits of information he'd found piled before him, his eyes scratchy and his back aching in the tiny chair, that he realized Mireille's clever manipulation of his pride.

Maybe she was smarter than him after all.

CHAPTER SEVEN

"Selene, you have to—"

"Can you hear me?"

Ronin's sister's voice was faint and muffled, and he could barely hear her through the commstone. He'd shipped the device to her, thought it would be an easier way for them to communicate versus writing letters, but he didn't anticipate how much trouble his tech-averse twin would have operating it.

"I don't think he can hear me," Selene mumbled to herself. "Stupid stone. How does this work?"

"You've got to—"

"Hello? Ronin?"

"Put the damn stone under your ear, Leenie!"

Selene released an exasperated huff. "Sheesh, Ro, you don't have to shout at me." There was muffled jostling, followed by a few taps and scrapes.

"Hello?" His wolf whimpered at the crystal-clear voice of his twin. Something within Ronin settled, all his restless energy given temporary pause. Selene was the only individual in the world who could soothe him so effectively. Make him feel like he didn't need the fighting or the fucking or the Delirium.

"It's really not that hard to operate," Ronin said. "You're usually so good with new things. I can't believe you're struggling with this."

Selene laughed. She was *not* good with new things. Never had been. It was one of the reasons she'd never left Denevrae, the small village they'd grown up in on the outskirts of Aethalia. She'd stayed behind to keep the cottage after their parents had succumbed to True Death and the Empire had come sniffing around, lured by rumors of the largest white wolf bi-form Ethyrios had ever seen. And to persuade him to become a weapon in their war.

Though they were twins, they were polar opposites—Selene shy and reserved, content to live her cozy, provincial life filled with her painting and her gardening and her healing. Whereas Ronin had been ready to escape the moment he'd learned to shift. He'd wanted a life of grand adventure and daring exploits. Had wanted to become *someone*.

And he *had*.

Just not the kind of someone he'd imagined.

"How are you? Really?" Concern tinged Selene's voice. She'd begged him to come home after his caging, but he'd refused. That would've been even more pathetic than his current existence. "You staying off the Delirium?"

Selene had a moral opposition to the substance. Had never quite given up her worship of Adelphinae and the Creator Goddess's tenets of faith espousing equality between Fae and humans. Selene abhorred that Delirium bastardized the true purpose of emotion feedings, an act of worship and communion between the two species. Plus, Selene was of the opinion that banishing the humans to the colonies and forcing them to sell memories was barbaric. Though, she was careful about who she shared those beliefs with these days.

Ronin could still remember the fights they'd had after he'd agreed to join the war. Selene had been horrified to learn that her twin was going to be used to slaughter as many humans as possible. Had begged him not to go. But he was young and hungry and stupid. And craving the acclaim the Empire had promised him. Besides, he didn't believe in Adelphinae. Didn't believe in the Fae's High Gods either.

Ronin didn't believe in *anything* other than his wolf and his immortality. Everything else was a myth.

Funny that he, too, turned out to be a myth.

Selene and Ronin didn't communicate at all during his years as the Empire's greatest weapon. It was only afterward, when he'd been discarded like a rusted tool, that she'd begun answering his letters again.

Selene's tender heart couldn't abandon Ronin in his time of need, no matter how much he'd defied her principles.

"Well?" she said. "Are you?"

"You know better than to ask me that."

Selene's heavy sigh weighed on his useless conscience. She'd never stopped trying to get him to be better. Whatever the fuck that meant anymore.

"Just be careful, okay? You know how addictive it is."

"I can quit any time I want to."

"I can hear you smirking through this ridiculous

stone, and I know you're lying. You're drinking one now, aren't you?"

"Of course not." He placed his half-consumed bottle of Delirium onto the table as quietly as possible. Right next to the chessboard that sat in stasis, awaiting his sister's move.

Another reason he'd purchased the commstones— playing chess via letters resulted in the slowest games ever.

"I heard that," Selene said at the light chink. "Bishop to d7. Check."

Ronin groaned, moving Selene's bishop across the board and removing his rook. He pinched the bridge of his nose, not in the mood for another of his sister's lectures. But he tolerated them. The High Gods knew no one else cared enough to check up on him.

"I'm fine," Ronin sighed. "For the love of Anaemos, will you stop pestering me about it? Knight to d7."

Ronin tossed Selene's bishop off the board, chuckling as he heard Selene do the same through the commstone.

"Clever move, brother." She clucked her tongue. "What else is going on up there in Kheimos? I'm a bit jealous, actually. It's been unseasonably warm down here. We haven't even had our first snow of the season yet. It doesn't feel like winter without it. Queen to d8. Check."

Fuck, she was good at this game, her aggressive moves a contrast to her shy, sweet demeanor.

And he knew she was angling for an invite. She'd done so in her letters as well. But he'd never allow her to come here. To see what a complete and utter mess his life had become.

Though his apartment was luxurious, purchased with his fight winnings, it certainly didn't look it at the moment. Empty bottles of Delirium and greasy take-out containers lined the counters, discarded boots and dirty clothes piled on chairs.

"Maybe I could come visit this year?" Hesitation quieted her voice.

There it was.

"Not this year, Leenie." He studied the board, searching for his next move.

"You say that every year."

"It's not a good time," he sighed. "Knight to b8. Gotcha."

"You say *that* every year, too." Selene exhaled long and loud, pieces clacking as she removed her queen. "I'm worried about you. You're up there all alone, thousands of miles away from me, participating in those dangerous, no-magic cage fights. Who's going to help you if something happens? Who's going to take care of you?"

"I can take care of myself," he snarled. "Those fights aren't dangerous for me."

"They're not dangerous for the *old* you. The one who had back-up."

Ronin's wolf huffed. *Back-up. Please. If anything, you were* my *back-up. Silly female.*

"I said I can handle myself. Will you fucking stop? High Gods, you sound just like—"

Ronin stopped himself. He knew bringing up their mother would just upset her. Family was more important than anything to Selene, and despite the fact that their parents had passed peacefully, their deaths had hit her hard. Even centuries later, the grief hadn't fully let her go. He didn't need Selene to burst into a crying fit on top of the guilt trip she was laying down.

"My life is about to change in a way that means you won't have to worry about me so much anymore."

"How's that?"

"I have a new assignment. Straight from Imperial Affairs and the High Councilor himself. And if I succeed, they're going to remove my cage."

Selene squealed and Ronin nearly ripped the comm-stone from his ear. "Ro, that's wonderful! Will you come back home then?"

Ronin didn't yet know *what* he would do if he succeeded in getting his wolf back. There were certainly more welcoming places to roam in the fields surrounding Denevrae versus the frozen, lifeless tundra up here.

"Haven't thought that far ahead. I need to complete the assignment first."

He told Selene what he'd been tasked with, protecting another operative and posing as her lover while they worked to gather intel on a suspected enemy of the Empire. He didn't tell Selene who it was. Firstly, the IA probably wouldn't want him spreading the word about it and secondly, he didn't want to give Selene any information that could put her in danger if things went…poorly.

"Posing as a lover, eh?"

Ronin shook his head. Out of all the outrageous things he'd just shared with his twin, somehow he knew that detail was what she'd get hung up on.

"Just a job. Don't get all excited."

"Is she pretty?"

Ronin scrubbed a hand down his face. Yeah, she was fucking gorgeous. Soft and curvy in all the right places with a strong pair of legs that wouldn't quit and an ass he wanted to sink his teeth into. Not to mention that lustrous copper hair and a face that males would start wars over.

"I guess. If uptight killer ice queen with a massive stick up her ass sounds pretty to you."

"Bless the Creator," Selene cackled. "You like her. Either that, or you've finally met a female who's not so eager to throw herself at you."

"Both of those statements are false," Ronin growled.

"Mmhmm. Now I *really* want to come up there so I can meet her."

"Trust me, she's not nearly as fun as I'm making her sound."

"Rook to d8. Checkmate."

"*Fuck*," Ronin exhaled, moving Selene's white rook down the board. His sister had bested him. Again. In all the years they'd been playing together, he'd never been able to beat her.

A knock followed by muffled voices sounded through the stone. "I've gotta go, Ro. I'm having company over tonight."

Ronin bit back a shocked grunt. Selene kept pretty much to herself, but he was pleased to hear she was making friends back home. "Good for you. Now, when you're hosting an orgy, you're going to want to—"

Selene's warm laugh settled over him like a comforting blanket. "You're incorrigible. Trust me, it's not that kind of get-together."

Something about the way she said it made Ronin curious to ask exactly *what* kind of get-together it was, but the voices on the other end grew louder and he didn't want to keep his sister from her guests. Especially since she entertained so rarely.

"Night, Leenie. Have fun at your orgy. Make safe choices."

Selene snickered again. "Have fun with your ice queen. Love you, big bro."

"Love you, too."

Ronin removed the stone and tossed it onto the table next to his half-drunk Delirium and his lost game. He plucked up the bottle and took another long pull before glancing at the clock on his bookshelf. Just before seven.

He groaned, stretching his arms across the back of the cushions, and gazed out the window. Below the sharp, icy fangs of the Blackspurs, a turret of the Otto estate punched through a gap in the trees, bone-shard white through the black skin of evergreens. Ronin shivered. What awaited him and Mireille in that old mansion in the mountains?

He pushed up off his couch and strode into the kitchen to grab another Delirium.

Is that a good idea? his wolf asked in a bored voice.

"Fuck off, furball," Ronin said out loud. "You're the reason I need it."

His wolf snarled, and Ronin headed to the bathroom to get ready for his *date.*

Amatu fucking spare him.

Mireille lingered across from Riashi's, trying to will her feet into motion.

She rubbed her sweaty palms on her wool jacket, and up the street movement caught her eye. Her palms dampened further at the sight of the lone figure stalking through the snow.

Ronin moved like a knife through water, the blistering wind doing nothing to slow his pace. He prowled as if on the hunt.

He's hunting for us, her wolf whispered with a quiver of excitement.

Since when have you ever been excited about a job? Mireille asked.

The most she ever got from her wolf during assignments was a sort of begrudging obedience, only coming to the surface when Mireille needed to call upon her strength or sense of smell. Or to bring her out to shred through a throat. Her wolf rarely paid attention when

Mireille's assignments had necessitated a more intimate type of spycraft.

Run, her wolf begged. *Maybe he'll chase us.*

Mireille snorted. *You'd let him catch us.*

Damn straight, I would.

Mireille ignored her wolf's panting as Ronin jogged up the steps and opened the door, the burbling voices spilling over to where she stood, transfixed.

Once inside the foyer, he shucked off his jacket, patting away the snow, and swiveled his head. Searching for her.

How incredibly absurd this all was. Ronin Matakos didn't date females like Mireille. In fact, from what she knew of his exploits, he didn't date at all.

It was that thought which spurred her into motion. This wasn't a date. It was a job. Might as well get it over with.

Glancing left and right for passing vehicles, she crossed the street and strode into the bustling restaurant.

Ronin pivoted toward her as she opened the door, and he stepped over to take her coat.

"Valette," he crooned.

"Matakos. I'm surprised you showed up."

He cocked an eyebrow, a wry smile twisting his plush lips. "Why wouldn't I?"

"I thought you didn't do *homework.*"

His laughter was low and uncharacteristically warm, sinking into his role. "A night out with a beautiful female can hardly be considered homework." He leaned in to whisper into her ear and a shiver ran down her spine. "Even if this is all for show."

She fought an urge to press in closer as her wolf took a deep whiff of his scent.

Bountiful Faurana, the creature groaned. *He smells incredible.*

Mireille breathed in his fresh, wild scent—wind-tousled pine trees and frosted citrus—then dragged her gaze across his slim gray trousers topped with a fitted navy sweater that showed off his broad chest and muscular arms.

"You look…nice," she said.

His lupine grin had her instantly regretting the platitude. "Holy shit, was that a compliment?"

"Don't get used to it," she grumbled. "Just playing my part."

He performed a similar perusal over her forest green, high-necked dress. It was one of the few she owned that she'd purchased solely for herself and not as a trapping for one of her many disguises. She'd been overtaken by a rare moment of vanity when the salesfemale had gushed over how incredible it made her legs look.

His eyes darkened as they traveled their length. "You look…*nice*, too." The word was loaded as it dripped from his lips.

She tugged at the short, flowing skirt, questioning her decision to wear it.

Please, her wolf piped up. *You know* exactly *why—and for whom—you wore it.*

Okay, fine. Yes, she'd wanted to look good tonight. She'd caught him staring at her a few times in the archives hall this morning. And heated looks like that coming from an attractive, powerful male like him… He'd been on her mind all day.

It was fucking annoying.

Are you going to offer up unhelpful commentary all night long? Mireille snapped at her wolf.

The beast sat back on her haunches, cocked her head and perked up her ears. *Oh my darling, I'm just getting started.*

Ronin cradled the small of Mireille's back, the warmth of his fingers seeping through the thin silk. "Come, our table's ready."

Her wolf let out a euphoric sigh at both the touch and the command, and Mireille bit her tongue to keep from echoing it.

Just a job, she reminded herself.

This was going to be a long, exhausting night.

Twisting heads and muttered whispers followed them through the restaurant, shock at seeing the prima ballerina of the Kheimos Company with the infamous Butcher of Aethalia. Though, there was an equal amount of envy. For both of them, Mireille supposed.

They did make a rather striking couple, each with their own unique grace—Ronin's charming and predatory, Mireille's lithe and elegant.

He ushered her to an intimate table in the corner, then pulled out her chair and placed her napkin in her lap as she sat.

"Sweet Amatu, Matakos. Laying it on a bit thick, don't you think?"

"Just making sure you get the full experience," he answered, settling into his own seat across the table. "I'm guessing this is the first date you've been on in decades. Centuries maybe."

She scoffed. "What makes you think *that?*"

He perused the floppy leather wine menu. "You don't seem like the type of female who regularly goes on dates."

"Really?" She huffed, sitting back and crossing her arms. "And what kind of *female* do I seem like to you?"

He ignored her question. "Tell me I'm wrong. When was the last time someone took you out?"

"You're wrong." She gifted him a victorious smile. "I went on one just a few days ago."

"One that didn't end in you killing someone," he clarified in a low whisper out of the corner of his mouth.

She snapped her menu open. "Keep up this line of questioning and *this* date will end with me killing someone."

He tilted his head back in a hearty laugh. "Vicious." He cocked his head as if listening to some internal voice. "My wolf approves."

Her own wolf opened her mouth, but before the creature could utter a single, vulgar word, Mireille breathed in for a count of six, held it for a count of six, then breathed out for a count of eight, banishing the beast to the depths of her mind. Navigating her unnerving physical attraction to the tattooed male across from her was difficult enough without her wolf piping up with sultry comments every few minutes.

The waiter approached to take their drink order, and, again surprising her with his chivalry, Ronin asked, "Do you prefer red or white?"

"Red."

Ronin ordered a bottle from Nephes, along with Delirium for himself. The waiter rattled off the specials, then bustled away to fetch their drinks.

Ronin placed his elbows on the table, resting his chin upon his inked knuckles as he gazed at her.

"What?" she asked. "Why are you looking at me like that?"

"No reason. Just figured that you've probably prepared a list of questions for us to run through."

She scoffed, then reached into her bag to pull out the…list of questions she had prepared for them to run through.

He laughed. "I knew it."

"Happy to *amuse* you with my predictability."

"I look forward to the day when you surprise me, Valette," he uttered in a low voice that tingled across her limbs. High Gods, Ronin at full charm, even fake charm, was fucking deadly.

She unfolded the sheet of paper, fingers shaking slightly. "Right. Let's get started. Where were you born?"

"Really? You don't know this about me already? It's practically branded on me due to my nickname."

Mireille shrugged. "Just because you gained your infamy there doesn't necessarily mean you were born there."

"You're partly right." Ronin dragged a hand through his tousled white hair. "I was born in a small village just outside of Aethalia called Denevrae. My parents were both wolf bi-forms, though they've since passed. My twin sister—"

"You have a twin sister?"

Ronin grinned. "Is that hard to believe?"

Mireille studied his inherently masculine, and frustratingly perfect, face. "I'm trying to picture you in female form."

"We have the same color hair and eyes, but that's where the similarities end. If not for those two features, you might not even know we were siblings at all."

"What's her name?"

"Selene." Genuine affection crinkled the corners of Ronin's eyes. It made him look younger, less burdened. It also made Mireille's heart gallop in her chest. "She still lives in the cottage where we grew up."

Mireille fiddled with the edges of her napkin, needing to occupy her hands. "Why didn't you go back there? After the war, and after…"

"You can say it." All the warmth drained from his expression. "After I was disgraced? There was nothing there for me anymore. There never had been. Didn't have many other options outside of coming up here to the fighting rings and capitalizing on my fame, so…" He raised his palms. "Here I am. What about you? Where were you from originally?"

The waiter returned with their drinks, uncorking the wine and pouring Mireille a glass. Ronin's pupils dilated as he took a long swig of his Delirium, and the hardness that had overtaken his features softened.

Mireille sipped her wine, letting the dry, oaky taste settle her own nerves. She'd never been comfortable talking about herself. And certainly not about her abnormal upbringing.

"I spent my childhood alone with my mother in the Oread Woods." A thoughtful frown tugged at Ronin's mouth. "What?"

He shook his head. "Not the answer I was expecting."

Mireille returned her glass to the table, tightening a fist around the thin stem. "What *were* you expecting?"

Ronin's marbled gaze bore into her and she pulled her shoulders back, despite her instinct to cower at his intensity.

"I assumed you came from one of those high-class Beastrunner families. Raised by a series of nannies in Delos or something while your rich parents flitted about the continent with their monied friends."

Mireille bristled. "Just the one parent."

Ronin's face twisted in sympathy. "What happened to your father?"

Mireille could hardly bear it. Cold sweat coated her skin, and her head began to pound. Too much sharing. She took a gulping sip of her wine and nearly choked. "Next question."

Ronin regarded her carefully, as if she were a skittish animal. "Alright, I won't pry. But you're the one with the list of questions."

She smoothed the paper, perusing it for a less volatile subject. "What was your most fervent childhood dream?"

Ronin snickered. "Most *fervent*? Did you really use that word? Let me see." He leaned across the table to snatch up the paper.

She pulled it against her chest. "It means—"

"I know what fervent means," he muttered, easing back into his chair. "I'm not *that* dumb. Despite your initial assumptions."

"Says the male who thought I was some rich snob." She pursed her lips. "You gonna answer the question or do you want to review the rest of my vocabulary choices?"

He sighed, smearing the beads of condensation gathering on his Delirium bottle. "I wanted… When I shifted for the first time, my mother fainted."

"*Actually* fainted?"

"Yes."

"What does this have to do with your childhood dream?"

"You got places to be?" he grunted. "I'm getting there."

He took a swig of the elixir, darting his tongue out to

catch a drop on his bottom lip and High Gods help her, Mireille's toes actually curled.

He didn't seem to notice her gawking. "It happened in the back yard of our cottage when I was four. I can still feel the heated, prickly sensation that rushed through my veins when he popped out for the first time."

Mireille remembered her own first shift just as well. As violent and satisfying as an aggressive sneeze. Or a really good orgasm.

She shook *that* unhelpful thought from her mind as he continued, "My mother screamed, then toppled onto the grass. When my father came out to see what all the commotion was about, the look of pride on his face… I'll never forget it. He paraded me around the village after, showing me off, encouraging me to shift. Which I was more than happy to do. Everyone wanted a look at the 'biggest wolf the world had ever known.' That's how my father always referred to me. I got off on it—the shock on their faces that inevitably transformed into awe. I was certain I was destined for greatness. That I was meant to make a mark on this world."

Mireille didn't like where this story was going, but she just sat quietly and listened.

"It's why I leapt at the chance to join the war, when those whispers about my size and power traveled all the way from Denevrae to Delos. Straight into the ears of the Emperor himself. And well, you and everyone else on the continent know how *that* story ends."

"So, you got exactly what you wanted."

"Did I?" Pain and regret dimmed his blue-yellow gaze as his tattoos flickered. He shook it off, smoothed it over with his typical smarmy arrogance. "What about you?

What did the great *Mireille Valette* dream of when she was a little pup?"

"You're looking at it." She leaned back in her chair. "I've achieved precisely what I set out to achieve."

"So you *wanted* to be a prima ballerina who spends half her time dispatching the Empire's enemies but still has no friends or joy in her life?"

Rage poured through her. How *dare* he judge her choices?

"You think your life is so much better? The infamous Butcher of Aethalia, fallen from glory and turned tail to Kheimos. Or can you even show your tail, now that you've been caged?"

Something dangerous flitted through his eyes, his fangs thickening as black claws extended from his fingertips.

"Careful," he whispered, his guttural voice filled with menace. "If you try to bait me, I can't be responsible for what happens to you."

She laughed, even as fear sluiced through her veins. "Put your fangs and claws away, Butcher. You don't scare me."

"I should," he answered, retracting his weapons. "I should *terrify* you. I'm exactly the monster that everyone claims me to be. You'd be wise to recognize it before our temporary partnership ends in bloodshed."

"Well, this date is going *extremely* well, I think." She took another sip of her wine. "Let's just agree that we're both perfectly well-adjusted individuals who've made all the right choices in life and leave it at that."

"Fine," he growled, draining the last of his Delirium and shaking the bottle at the waiter for another. "What other questions are on your list?"

Mireille surveyed the sheet. This was pointless. They had absolutely nothing in common, other than this shared mission, so why bother getting to know one another? But since sitting in silence while they ate their meals sounded even less enticing, she asked another.

"What's your greatest fear?"

He huffed a laugh. "Suffocating under the weight of my reputation."

Her eyes rolled upward. "You're the one still brandishing it."

"As if I have a fucking *choice*," he muttered. "What's yours?"

She took several minutes contemplating her own answer. Did she have any fears? Sometimes she felt a twinge of nervous energy before a performance or an assignment. Not really a fear.

She didn't like getting close to people, but was that due to fear? Or was it a strategic choice, since most people were self-interested assholes?

No, the only thing Mireille truly feared was never learning the truth about her past. Not getting those answers she'd been seeking for centuries. Forever feeling like only half of her outline was filled in.

But *that* was definitely too profound an answer to share with the male seated across from her. He'd likely find some way to taunt her with it. Not to mention, this conversation had taken an uncomfortably heavy turn.

She decided to lighten the mood with one of her smaller fears instead.

"Spiders."

MIREILLE'S ANSWER coaxed a rumbling belly laugh out of Ronin.

"Spiders? I just bared my soul to you and your answer is spiders?"

Mireille shrugged, drawing Ronin's attention to her delicate shoulders and long neck. She really was incredibly beautiful, even if she was infuriatingly difficult to crack. "They're unpredictable."

He laughed louder.

"They appear out of nowhere on their creepy, fuzzy little legs. Some of them jump, and you can never tell which ones can and can't. I'm always worried one is going to crawl into my mouth while I'm sleeping and lay eggs underneath my tongue."

"Fucking *gross*. Who worries about such a thing?"

She plucked up her wine glass, swirling the burgundy liquid. "You asked. I answered."

"Well, when we're up at the Otto estate, I promise to protect you from pregnant nighttime spiders."

She rewarded him with a breathy little laugh and his wolf shivered. *Make her do that again.*

Ronin mentally swatted the creature away. Though he wouldn't mind hearing it again as well.

"One more," he said. "At least *your* answers are entertaining."

She smiled at that—a dazzling, unguarded one—and he made a note of her reaction.

Little she-wolf liked to be praised.

Her enchanting silver eyes scanned the paper before she folded it, creasing the edges precisely, and placed it back in her bag.

When she returned her gaze, it was full of mischief. Something stirred low in his gut.

"What is your biggest fault?" she asked.

He ran his thumb over his bottom lip, delighted to see her glance at the movement. "Other than this face of mine?"

Confusion pinched her brows. "What's wrong with your face?"

"Can't go anywhere without a female or seven collapsing at my feet. So inconvenient. Why do you think I'm always late?"

Mireille's eyes rolled so hard he was worried she might fall right out of her chair. Though, he did notice the corner of her mouth quiver.

It was that tiny tell that encouraged him to share a real answer. He'd already laid himself bare once tonight —the first time in years, decades even, that he'd done so with anyone other than Selene. There was something about Mireille's unapologetic frankness that he appreciated. So different from his sister's endless coddling. It was…refreshing.

"I wish I could stop drinking this." He rolled the empty Delirium bottle between his hands. He hated that he'd already noticed exactly how long it was taking the waiter to bring his second one.

Mireille softened at his confession. "Why'd you start in the first place?"

"It happened after my caging." He couldn't look her in the eye as he ripped the label. "Without the outlet of shifting, it's hard to control my wolf's violent cravings. I get…urges."

Mireille sucked in a sharp breath, and a tangy whiff of fear wafted across the table.

He lifted his eyes and wasn't surprised to find her looking at him quite differently than she had at the start of this dinner.

"It's fine, Mireille. Although you do smell incredibly tasty, I said *difficult* to control. Not impossible. Just don't piss me off and I promise not to eat you."

Another scent joined her fear. A deepening of her musk. Unmistakable.

His wolf perked up again. *Mmmmm. She* wants *us to eat her. We should forget about this boring conversation and ask her if she'd like to come back to our place so we can spread apart her thi—*

Enough, Ronin snarled. *No one's eating anyone tonight.*

His wolf huffed a frustrated breath and settled.

"Anyway, the Delirium helps keep things in check."

Mireille's throat bobbed. "Have you ever tried quitting?"

"Many times." He fought to suppress those memories, the pain roiling through his body, how ill he'd become. It wasn't worth it. The Delirium always beckoned him back. This conversation was getting too fucking depressing. "Your turn. What would you change about yourself?"

She cocked her head, then shot him a coy grin. "Not a fucking thing."

"Why do I feel like I'm the only one taking these questions seriously?" he grumbled. "And why are they so probing? Why didn't we start with some light shit?"

"Like what? Favorite color? What types of music we like? What we do for fun?"

"Exactly."

"Really deep insights into our personalities, those."

"Fine, how about something more practical? How do you take your coffee?"

"Splash of cream, two sugars."

"Predictable," he huffed.

She sneered. "Let me guess. You drink yours black."

"I prefer tea in the morning, thank you very much. How old are you?"

Mireille feigned a shocked gasp. "How dare you ask a lady such a question? How old do you think I am?"

Ronin rubbed his jaw, trailing his gaze down her torso. "You don't look a day over six-hundred."

"Fuck you," she chuckled. "I'm three-hundred-and-eleven. You?"

"Three-hundred-and-twenty-eight. Kinks?"

"Ex-excuse me?" Mireille sputtered.

He folded his arms on the table. "If we're supposed to have been seeing each other for months, I'd certainly know a few of yours by now, don't you think?"

"I'm not sharing that," she answered primly, unable to meet his penetrating stare.

"Ropes." He traced small circles on the tablecloth with his fingertips, relishing the blush creeping up her neck that told him he'd guessed correctly. "Or silks. Or handcuffs. Any kind of restraint, really. You're completely in control everywhere else, so I'm guessing you like to give that up in the bedroom, let someone else take the lead for a change." His eyes darted to her small, trembling fists. "I'm right, aren't I?"

"No one is going to probe us about each other's *kinks*, Ronin."

"Well, just in case they do, mine are—"

"No fucking *way*." A low, female voice broke through the din, and a Windrider with yellow wings sauntered over to their table. "I never thought I'd see the day."

Mireille shifted in her seat, uncomfortable not only with the attention of the female, but the attention her outburst had attracted to their table.

"Hello, Juliet," she murmured, toying with her wine glass.

Juliet's eyes slid toward Ronin, then back to Mireille, a sly smile parting her lips. "Who's your friend?"

Ronin leaned back, drumming his fingers and watching with amusement as Mireille squirmed.

"This…this is my boyfriend." She wrenched the word through gritted teeth. "Ro—"

"Ronin Matakos," Juliet interrupted, offering Ronin a slim hand, her eyes glittering with joy. "I know who you are." She turned back to Mireille. "My, you *do* keep your secrets, Mireille. How long have you two been dating?"

"A few weeks," Mireille answered at the same time as Ronin said, "Several months."

Juliet's gaze bobbed between them, a confused look passing over her face. They probably should have discussed this before they'd come out together tonight.

Ronin laughed softly, then plucked up Mireille's hand from the table, which had gone cold and clammy. He brushed a thumb over her knuckles. "What I meant is, I'd been pursuing her for months before she finally deigned to give me a chance a few weeks ago. In case you hadn't noticed, this one plays rather hard to get."

Mireille flinched at Juliet's knowing laughter, and Ronin squeezed her hand.

"Oh, you don't have to tell *me* that," Juliet said. "I've been trying to convince her to come out with me for years. Good on you."

"How do you two know each other?"

"Juliet dances with me at the Kheimos Company," Mireille answered.

Juliet snorted. "With her? She's being incredibly

modest. We all dance *behind* her. She's the bright, shining star, and we are but mere shadows cast by her presence."

Ronin tried to detect any hint of jealousy or sarcasm in the yellow-winged Fae's words, but found none. Just genuine respect and admiration.

"Have you seen her dance?" Juliet asked him.

"I haven't yet had the pleasure, but I'm very much looking forward to tomorrow night's performance." Ronin aimed an amused smile at Mireille, whose own expression remained guarded.

"Maybe if you're lucky, she'll give you a private dance after." Juliet winked and Ronin laughed heartily.

"Nice to see you, Juliet," Mireille said in a clipped voice. "Enjoy the rest of your evening."

Juliet caught the dismissal in Mireille's tone and shook her head in an exasperated manner. One that informed Ronin the two females had shared many similar exchanges. "Lovely to meet you, Ronin. I'm glad Mireille has found someone to pull her from her lonely existence. Maybe you can convince her to come to dinner with me some time."

"As long as I don't want to keep her all to myself," Ronin said with a waggle of his eyebrows that tugged a sultry chuckle from the young Fae.

"Have fun, you two." Juliet winked over her shoulder as she sashayed away from their table.

Ronin watched her join a group of Fae in the foyer, whispering and gesturing back towards Mireille and Ronin before exiting the restaurant.

Mireille loosed a breath.

"She seems nice," Ronin said.

"She seems *nosy*. The entire city of Kheimos will be talking about us by morning."

"Isn't that the whole point? She clearly admires you and wants to be your friend. Why have you never taken her up on her offer?"

"I don't do friends," Mireille bit out. "For many reasons. Not the least of which is my work for the Empire. I don't want to put her in danger. And I don't have time for friends anyway. My jobs keep me busy enough." Ronin aimed a pointed look at Mireille that she missed completely as she snapped out her menu. "Where in the name of Stygios is our waiter? I'm starving."

Ronin signaled to the waiter that they were ready to order.

The rest of their fake date passed by in rigid, awkward silence. Whatever progress he'd made in trying to get Mireille to open up had been shuttered by Juliet's appearance.

She tensed when he slipped on her jacket and ushered her out to the street, then nearly elbowed him in the stomach as he pressed a goodnight kiss to her cheek. A calculated move for the remaining patrons watching through the windows.

"I'll see you at the archives tomorrow," he said, flagging down a cab and opening the door for her.

She glanced up at him, snowflakes catching in her coppery waves. "I won't be there tomorrow."

"Why?"

"None of your fucking business." She slid across the seat, hauling the door shut behind her.

He huffed out a cloudy sigh as the taillights melted into the night.

Then his wolf released a mournful howl, and Ronin began the long trudge through the slush back to his quiet, lonely apartment.

CHAPTER NINE

Ronin ambled down the red-carpeted aisle of the Grand Ethyrian Theater as the lights flashed to signal the beginning of Friday night's final performance of *The Curse of Faurana.*

He'd never once attended the ballet, and was nearly as bitter about being forced here tonight as he was about the fawning boyfriend role he'd have to play afterward.

He certainly hadn't tried to fit in with the sophisticated crowd, arriving in his utility pants and leather jacket, boots unlaced and hair unkempt.

They'd seated him down in front, dead center, Anaemos spare him. Displeased grunts sounded as he shuffled down the row, knocking knees and crushing toes, then pushed down the velvet cushion and plopped into his narrow chair. His massive body barely fit.

A scoff tickled the back of his neck—a patron annoyed by this mountain of a male blocking their view.

Ronin swiveled, flashing his fangs, and the thin male cowered, mouthing *sorry* before careful averting his eyes.

Ronin scanned the rows around him for any sign of Otto or his hulking bodyguard but they either hadn't arrived yet or they were seated elsewhere. Wrath of Vestan, Skanisse better not have been wrong about Otto's attendance or this would all have been an enormous waste of Ronin's time.

The orchestra began playing the first notes of the overture, a song he was surprised to recognize—one of Selene's favorites. He hummed along, the melody seared into his brain.

The music faded and the curtain parted, revealing a painted backdrop of a farmhouse nestled atop rolling fields of gold and green.

A male dancer bounded onto the scene, dressed in what looked like peasant's garb: a fitted brown tunic and black tights.

Ronin fought the urge to fall asleep as the male leapt and twirled across the stage. He was joined moments later by four female dancers in flowing purple skirts and green tights.

Were they supposed to be flowers? Ronin chuckled out loud, earning a few sidelong glances from his seatmates.

Ronin had no idea what the fuck was going on. He thought the male was supposed to be a farmer, maybe? But he kept having poor luck with his animals and his crops. Despite his efforts, everything he touched was failing. Ronin had to bite his lip to keep from snickering at the dramatic *deaths* of first the flowers, then wheat, then, to Ronin's near uproarious laughter, cows.

As the act drew to a close, the male lead was at his wit's end. He performed an aggressive solo full of pretend shirt-rending and fist-raising, then fell to the floor in supplication, his knees cracking the boards.

The entire stage went dark, save for a single spotlight up by the rafters.

Gasps rippled through the audience as a pair of crimson pointe shoes dipped below the top curtain.

As much as he hated to admit it, Ronin would recognize those legs anywhere.

A stiff red tutu came into view, followed by a bejeweled bodice, a delicate, exposed collarbone, a long neck, and then…

There she was.

Mireille floated down to the stage, the combination of her poised legs, fluttering arms, and beatific face mesmerizing.

Alighting upon the boards, she raised an arm, and Ronin noted a long, silver scar trailing down her right forearm. He hadn't noticed it before, wondered where she'd gotten it. Scars on Fae were quite rare.

She approached the kneeling male, her feet moving so quickly she appeared to be floating, then bent gracefully at the waist and touched his shoulder. He reared back, his mouth wide with rapture.

The stage went entirely dark, the curtain fell, and the auditorium lights flared to life.

"What's happening right now?" Ronin growled to the male seated next to him, a small rodent Beastrunner with buck teeth.

The male shrank from Ronin's glare and stuttered, "In-intermission. A fifteen-minute break before the second act begins."

Ronin crossed his arms, annoyed. He didn't want to

wait even fifteen minutes to watch more of Mireille. So far, she was the only interesting part of this show.

The audience filed out of their seats and Ronin rose with a huff, figured he might as well grab a Delirium during the break.

He purchased a glowing bottle at the refreshment stand, then leaned against the wall to drink it as he awaited the end of intermission.

Many sidelong glances were cast his way, along with murmured speculations about what the Butcher of Aethalia was doing at the ballet. A few brave souls tossed a snarky remark or two about his attire. An even braver Windrider male with tucked black wings came over to congratulate him on his win the other night. And to chat about tomorrow's championship bout. Ronin nearly snarled at the pity he found on the male's face as he not-so-subtly studied Ronin's tattoos.

The flickering lobby lights mercifully ended both the conversation and Ronin's discomfort, and the crowd streamed back into the auditorium.

As he retook his seat, his head loose and woolly from the Delirium, he noted a pair of pale yellow eyes staring down at him from a box close to the stage.

Jurgev Otto dipped his chin in greeting, Julius Kosera a bulging shadow behind him. The Greyhorn looked even more bored than Ronin. Otto refocused his piercing gaze on the stage as if he could force the curtain to rise through sheer will.

Perhaps this evening wouldn't be a waste of time after all.

Ronin settled into his seat and the second act began. Even with the mind-softening effects of the elixir, he couldn't take his eyes off Mireille.

In the role of the High Goddess Faurana, she'd offered blessings of abundance to the farm in exchange for the man's devotion.

A fair exchange until a lovely young female arrived to purchase a bushel of wheat. Ronin recognized the yellow-winged dancer, Juliet, from Riashi's last night.

Juliet and the farmer performed a dance together—a *pas de deux*, Ronin heard one of his seatmates call it—and even as a ballet virgin, Ronin could tell Juliet wasn't nearly as skilled as Mireille.

His leg bobbed impatiently as he awaited her return.

When Mireille re-took the stage, the music shifted. Lively strings and bubbling flutes gave way to droning cellos and booming timpanis as the Goddess ripped the lovers apart.

Ronin held his breath, enraptured, as Mireille executed spins, lunges, and the highest leaps he'd yet seen. Even higher than the Windriders who had wings to assist.

Mireille defied gravity, and his chest swelled at her mastery.

High Gods, she was fucking *incredible*.

Ronin was so caught up that he barely felt his rodent-toothed seatmate tugging on his sleeve.

He bared his teeth at the male, annoyed that his attention had been taken from Mireille's solo, and the male pointed toward the aisle.

A female stagehand was waving at him.

Ronin ignored her. He wanted to see how the ballet ended. Wanted to know what would become of the farmer and the Goddess he'd forsaken. Surely this was some sort of allegory for the perils of denying the High Gods.

The stagehand snapped her fingers, and his seatmates muttered in frustration.

Ronin rolled his eyes and exited the row, knocking knees and crushing toes again. Petty, but he was pissed that they'd get to see the grand finale and he would not.

He followed the stagehand out into the lobby.

"Ronin Matakos, right?"

"You didn't think to confirm that before you interrupted the show to fetch me?" he grumbled.

"Follow me." She turned on her heel and led Ronin through a door marked *Theater Staff and Performers Only*. They traveled down into what Ronin assumed was the backstage area, a maze of low-ceilinged hallways lined with props, painted flats, and racks of costumes.

"She said you should wait in here until the performance has finished." The stagehand opened another door with a star on it, then closed him inside.

Mireille's dressing room was clean and well-organized, not a stray pin or shoe out of place.

On her vanity, a neat row of cosmetics stood in order from smallest to largest, labels facing out. A silver-handled brush sat exactly perpendicular to the edge, and he nudged it slightly off center. Couldn't help himself.

He sank down onto the tufted white couch, crossing an ankle over his leg, and waited for his *girlfriend*.

Applause thundered through the ceiling. The finale. That he didn't get to fucking see.

The stagehand bustled back in, setting an overflowing vase of pale blue roses onto a low table. She beamed at him, making false assumptions about the flowers' origins, and he didn't correct her as she flitted away.

A few moments later, Mireille herself swept in, her silver eyes glancing off him and landing on the bouquet.

"Butcher," she cooed, slightly out of breath from her performance. "You shouldn't have."

"I didn't." He shrugged as Mireille plucked out the card nestled between the blooms.

"Perfect," was all she murmured before handing it to him and twirling a finger. "Turn around. I need to get out of this costume."

"Want some help?" he grinned, earning a deadpan stare.

Worth a try, his wolf piped up.

Ronin dutifully stood, giving Mireille his back. The sounds of rustling tulle and popping buttons sent goose-bumps shivering over his skin as he read the message on the tiny card.

Beautiful blooms for a blossoming beauty. Spare a moment for us after the show? - O

Ronin snickered, even as an unexpected twinge of jealousy squeezed his chest. "Your new boyfriend's quite the poet. Think he uses these lines on all the females?"

Mireille grunted as she struggled to remove some part of her costume. "Thanks to our little date last night and Juliet's gossip-mongering, it looks like I might actually find out."

"You did okay up there," he said, changing a subject that he suddenly had no interest in discussing. The thought of Otto putting his slithery hands on any part of Mireille...

She scoffed. "I missed a step during my solo. Stupid, *stupid* mistake."

"I doubt anyone noticed."

"*I* noticed. I should've practiced more this week instead of spending so much time reviewing those damn files."

Ronin's brows furrowed. "Are you always this hard on yourself?"

"It's the only way to ensure perfection," she said flatly. "You can turn around."

He spun, struck dumb by the outfit she'd changed into for Otto's benefit. For a fleeting, foolish second, he wished she'd worn it for him.

Loose pink pants flowed past her feet, hanging low on her hips and exposing her toned stomach. The wide neckline of her silky crop top bared a creamy shoulder.

Waves of burnished copper tumbled to her waist, and he crossed his arms to keep from stepping toward her and running his hands through it.

Fuck, why were the beautiful ones always the most infuriating?

He swallowed. "I was teasing you, Mireille. You were a marvel."

A gorgeous blush crept across her cheeks before she turned to her vanity and straightened the hairbrush. He bit back a chuckle.

A knock sounded at the door. "Mistress Valette?" The stagehand's voice wobbled. "Y-you have another visitor."

Otto, Ronin mouthed and Mireille nodded, gesturing for him to sit back down.

Which he promptly did, then stifled a groan as Mireille settled into his lap.

The heady combination of her scent, her soft skin, and her perfect ass atop his groin inspired his wolf to howl so loudly he was worried Mireille herself might hear it.

She looped an arm around his shoulder, then swept her hair away from her neck. "Nuzzle me."

"Wh-what?" The haziness he felt could no longer be blamed solely on the Delirium.

"Nuzzle my neck," she commanded through gritted teeth. Ronin's wolf bounded across his heart in playful anticipation. "For Otto."

"Right." Ronin swallowed, his eyes darting to the pulse pounding beneath Mireille's jaw. At least he wasn't the only one affected by their proximity.

He ran his nose along her throat, then placed a hand on the curve of her hip. She exhaled a breathy little whimper, likely unintentional, that shivered down his spine.

"Come in!" Mireille crooned as Ronin replaced his nose with his lips, dragging them along her shoulder as his fingers caressed the edge of her waistband. He could've sworn he felt her press in closer.

Fuck, yes.

Jurgev Otto entered the room, wearing a finely-tailored baby-pink suit peppered with pastel polka dots. His serpent's eyes blew wide at the sight of Mireille tangled up with Ronin. Before the door snicked shut, Ronin caught a sliver of Kosera's broad back.

Mireille ignored Otto as she dragged her fingernails across Ronin's scalp, inspiring a frisson of pleasure. His cock thickened, and he shifted away, didn't want her to know how much her touch affected him. She'd likely use it against him, somehow.

Otto cleared his throat and Mireille finally deigned to address him. "Can I help you?"

Otto's affronted frown had Ronin biting his cheek to keep from cackling. He didn't know which was more entertaining: watching Mireille dance or watching her cut the self-important billionaire down to size.

"We see you received our flowers," Otto said, his gaze lingering on the hand Mireille pressed against Ronin's chest. Maintaining her bored, blasé perusal of the Deathstalker, she moved her hand lower, stroking over Ronin's abs with an appreciative murmur. His wolf yipped with pride.

Playing along, Ronin lengthened his canines, nipping at Mireille's earlobe as her fingertips reached the top of his zipper.

Otto observed the spectacle with barely concealed envy, his pupils dilating and his forked tongue darting past his lips.

Ronin struggled to maintain control, wondering how low, exactly, Mireille was going to dip her hand.

Sweet fucking Amatu, she was good at these games.

Taking pity on Otto—or determined to give Ronin a nasty case of blue balls for messing with her hairbrush—she pushed out of his lap.

She bent down to sniff a rose as Ronin adjusted himself in his pants. "Oh, these were from you? They're beautiful. Thank you, Master...?"

Otto quickly smoothed over his outraged expression, and Ronin covered his mouth to hide a smile. "Otto. Jurgev Otto. You are quite an extraordinary dancer, Mistress Valette." Mireille dipped her head, fluttering her long lashes. The picture of coquettish humility. "Though we did notice a little misstep tonight? During your final solo?"

Mireille cocked an eyebrow at Ronin before returning her attention to Otto. "You're very perceptive, Master Otto. Only a male with an extraordinary attention to detail would have noticed such a thing."

Otto pinched a strand of Mireille's hair, running it

over the sharp black points of his fingernails. To Mireille's credit, she didn't flinch. Though Ronin's hands involuntarily fisted on the back of the couch and his wolf released a burbling growl.

"Too many distractions?" Otto's pale yellow eyes slid to Ronin.

And even though Ronin knew it was fake, the incandescent smile Mireille aimed at him radiated through his chest. "Oh, he's the best kind of distraction. Do you two know each other? This is—"

"Ronin Matakos." Otto spat his name, sneering at Ronin's salt-crusted boots. "We doubt you'd find a single Fae on the continent who hasn't heard of the Butcher of Aethalia. Though we would have said the same thing about ourselves."

Ronin rose from the couch, unable to stomach Otto's oily covetousness. He slung an arm around Mireille's shoulder and she pressed a hand against his stomach again, Otto's eyes flying to the contact.

"You'll have to excuse her." Ronin trailed his fingers through Mireille's hair. It was just as soft as it looked, liquid silk flowing through his fingertips. "She's a woman possessed these days. Only has time for her dancing and, well…me." He gnashed his teeth on the final word.

"A pity." Otto turned to Mireille. "Surely you don't intend to keep up such a rigorous schedule now that your season has ended? We're hosting a gathering up at our estate next week. You should join us."

"Oh, that's unnecessary." Mireille pressed herself closer to Ronin. "We couldn't possibly impose."

"You'd be doing us a favor, honestly. The other guests will be thoroughly impressed that we were able to lure the glittering jewel of the Kheimos Company to our event."

Mireille feigned indecision. "Are you sure?"

"We insist. Bring your Butcher as well, if you must. We're sure at least a few of our guests might be curious to know how he managed to fall down so many rungs of life's ladder from war hero to cage fighter."

Asshole.

"I must." Mireille cupped Ronin's cheek, as if to soothe the sting of Otto's jab. "What do you think, my love? Fancy a holiday at a snowy mountain estate?"

Ronin grabbed her hand and kissed her fingertips. "As long as we're together, I don't care what we do." The corners of her lips jumped at his sickeningly sweet smile.

Otto broke in. "Wonderful. It's settled then. We will send a car to pick you up on Monday morning."

Mireille broke out of Ronin's hold and shook Otto's pasty hand. "Thank you, Master Otto. We look forward to your hospitality."

"Until then, Mistress Valette." Otto pressed his lavender lips to Mireille's knuckles before exiting the dressing room.

Ronin opened his mouth, but Mireille held up a hand, shushing him. She cocked her head, listening for Otto and Kosera's footsteps to fade.

After several minutes, she breathed a sigh of relief and began gathering up her things.

Ronin eyed her with a new respect. "You're good at this."

"What, did you think Skanisse was lying when he said I was a skilled field agent?" Mireille fluffed out her costume and hung it on a rack in the corner.

"No, I…" Ronin leaned a hip against her vanity. "You're just so…"

She whipped around, hands on her hips. "I'm just so *what?*"

He scratched his cheek. "Different than I expected."

Mireille snorted, bending down to pluck up her discarded tights. "Wish I could say the same. If slovenly beast was the look you were going for tonight, bravo, you've succeeded."

Ronin tipped his head back, releasing a hooting laugh. "That's more like it. Never change, Valette."

He could've sworn he saw her lip twitch as she shrugged on her jacket and looped her bag over her shoulder. "See you at the archives hall tomorrow?"

Ronin nodded, then pushed up off the vanity and strode to the door.

As he stepped into the darkened hallway, he tossed a farewell over his shoulder. "Goodnight, *my love.*"

And tried not to snicker at the little growl of frustration Mireille released in his wake.

CHAPTER TEN

Mireille arrived at the archives hall the next morning at eight o'clock sharp, bright and early as usual. She'd already been awake for several hours anyway, had spent the morning in the practice room at the Grand Ethyrian, blissfully alone now that the company's season had officially ended.

She'd gone back to her apartment to shower and change, then come here to IA HQ to continue her research. She figured she'd have at least several hours to herself before Ronin showed up.

She pushed through the windowed door. "Morning, Sonya." She folded her arms—pleasantly sore from her rigorous practice routine—upon the desk. "Can I get the key card, please?"

Sonya gave her a sly look. "Your partner's already back there."

Mireille nearly choked on her tongue. "*My* partner? Ronin Matakos?"

Sonya nodded. "Arrived about an hour ago. Seemed

pretty excited, too, about whatever he has to share with you."

Mireille let out a small shocked sound, then leaned across the desk and lowered her voice. "Any news on that other matter?"

Mireille had been asking Sonya over the years if there were any records of a male that might have been associated with her mother, or any filings about Mireille's birth. Sonya was discreet, one of the few—really the only—colleague that Mireille trusted at the IA, so she didn't worry about revealing her true last name to the kind, motherly Windrider.

And now that the Empire had claimed to have learned her father's identity, she'd hoped that maybe Sonya would find something new in the system.

Sonya dipped her eyes, shaking her head. "I'm sorry, my dear. There's still nothing other than what I've already given you."

Which was nothing more than Mireille herself had already known. A report detailing Vivienne Valois's abandonment of her pack and the birth of her daughter, with no name of the father listed on the certificate. Mireille had often thought about trying to find her mother's pack, visiting them under the guise of a veiling potion to see if she could tease out any information about her father. But it was a risk she was unwilling to take, given what had transpired at the cabin.

Mireille sighed, pushing back from the counter. "Thanks for checking again," she called over her shoulder as she strode to the room at the back of the hall.

Shock stilled her feet when she opened the door. Folders, books, and documents were scattered across every surface, and an array of papers rustled from where they'd been pinned to the corkboard.

Ronin sat at the table, buzzing with excitement. "Valette." He gifted her a genuinely delighted smile, and her stomach flip-flopped.

"Matakos," she answered carefully. "Are you messing with me? What are you doing here so early?"

He stood and pulled out a chair, angling it toward the board and encouraging her to take a seat. "Just eager to show you how wrong you were about my ability to find anything useful."

She huffed a short laugh. "Or how right I was to challenge your studying skills."

He vibrated with impatience as he hustled her into the chair, taking her bag and placing it on the floor.

"Yes, yes, you're a master manipulator, played me perfectly, got me wrapped around your little finger. Need me to keep stroking your ego or can I show you what I found?"

He crossed his burly arms, his onyx brows peeking through his tousled white strands.

Frenzied Dienses, it should be illegal for a male to be that good looking. She wondered why he'd come up here to Kheimos after his caging. He could've easily gone down to Delos, charmed the panties off some rich, widowed female and lived the rest of his days as a well-kept boy toy.

"You don't need my permission," she said. "I'm not your master."

He cocked his head and smirked. "Would you like to be?"

Her stomach gave another stupid little flutter. "High Gods, Ronin, just tell me what you found."

He seemed far too amused by her annoyance, and she scolded herself for letting him rile her. But she couldn't help it. Of all the males she'd dealt with, Ronin had a unique ability for getting under her skin. In more ways than she cared to admit.

"Okay." He clapped his hands and turned to the board. She tried, and failed, not to notice how well his broad shoulders filled out his tight black shirt.

Not relevant. *Focus.*

"These are the reports of the disappearances, the ones the relatives gave to the IA." He tapped on several of the sheets. "Note the dates."

Mireille made a cursory scan.

"*Note* them, Mireille," he scolded. "They'll become important as I continue."

She bit her lip to suppress a laugh. His enthusiasm was unexpected. And kind of adorable. She attached her gaze to each one in turn, cataloging the dates. "Noted."

He side-stepped to the other side of the board, waving his hand across a series of images showing the night sky above the Blackspurs.

Mireille instantly recognized what she was looking at, and High Gods help her, she was actually impressed. "Those are the Scales of Nyctima."

The iridescent, multicolored lights—a rare, natural phenomenon named after Nyctima, the giant pet serpent of Stygios—appeared in the Northern Territories' sky every one-hundred-and-five days. They were said to represent the serpent as she prowled the skies of Ethyrios in search of recently departed souls.

Ronin flashed a smug, closed-lip smile. "These images were taken by the Figroth observatory in the eastern Blackspurs. And guess when they occurred?"

"The same dates those Fae disappeared," Mireille murmured.

"Gold star." Ronin tapped Mireille's nose and she swatted him away. "And guess when the Scales of Nyctima will next grace our illustrious city's sky?"

"Next week." Mireille exhaled a long breath.

Ronin nodded. "When Otto is finally opening up his estate for this event."

Mireille shook her head, surveying Ronin's work. "Nicely done."

"Not just a dumb beast after all." Ronin cracked his knuckles. "Though other than the timing, I'm not sure what else this signifies."

Mireille turned her chair back to the table and Ronin took the one beside her, wafting his enticing, evergreen scent. She rifled through the piles, then found the shipping intake forms she'd been reviewing yesterday.

"So, we know Otto's been ordering large supplies of anastasium, the god-touched stone of Stygios. And now we find out that Fae have disappeared from his estate on nights when a light show named after the High God's snake appears in the sky? Obviously it's not a coincidence. Do you think the lights activate the stones somehow?"

Ronin rubbed at his jaw. "Even if they do, what is Otto using them for?"

"I don't know." Mireille twirled a strand of hair around her finger. She'd left it down today, and she saw Ronin mark the movement. "Unless..."

"Unless what?"

"Well, after we learned that Otto had been taking in shipments of the stone, I went to the Imperial library downtown and checked out a few books about anastasium's uses over the years, just to make sure I wasn't wrong about it being merely decorative. I read through all ten books yesterday—"

"As one does," Ronin cut in.

"Anyway" —Mireille rolled her eyes— "there was an entry in one that said anastasium was originally discovered millennia ago in a small village deep within the Northern Territories called Listhima. The Deathstalkers who lived there used the stone in some kind of religious ritual, but the book was vague on the details. Whatever it was, that knowledge has long since faded from history, along with any mention of a potential source of Stygios's power."

Ronin rubbed a hand up the shaved side of his head, lost in thought, and Mireille had to consciously stop herself from staring.

She'd always thought he was handsome, even before they'd officially met. It was his personality that had been a turn off. Or what she'd assumed was his personality. He *was* cocky, of course...or maybe that wasn't the right word. Because cocky implied an act, a lack of substance hidden behind false bravado.

But now, especially after everything she'd learned on their date, his arrogance held the unmistakable air of legitimacy. He was a male who had been *through it* and come out the other side to tell the tale. A bit more mature —and humble—than she'd expected.

And curse Amatu, Mireille was finding it all so *disgustingly* attractive.

She'd been trying to smother her interest these past few days by being as nasty and standoffish as possible. But despite her efforts, the seeds of a crush were blooming tiny sprigs of life.

He raised his gaze to find her staring. "What?"

"Nothing." She darted her eyes away. "Did you find anything else in the disappearance reports?"

"Fucking *taskmaster*, Valette." His sly grin exposed a sharp canine that had her involuntarily tonguing her own. "But there was one more thing."

He angled his head back toward the board, his tattoos shifting across his taut neck muscles. He tapped his knuckles against one of the disappearance reports. "This Beastrunner female, Larissa Bisere. I know her brother Mattias. Used to fight him in the arena, though he hasn't been back in months. I see him occasionally at the Crystal. I'll reach out, see if he's willing to meet with us after my fight tonight."

"Good," Mireille said, feeling like she should compliment Ronin on all the work he'd done, but not quite ready to give him that satisfaction. "What time?"

"Fight's usually over by midnight. I'll meet you at the Frosted Crystal after. One o'clock? Or is that past your bedtime?"

"It's fine," she snapped. "I'll see you at one. I'm gonna head back over to the Imperial library, see if I can find anything else about anastasium or the Scales of Nyctima. Are you staying?"

"Nothing else to do." He picked up a folder.

Mireille was once again impressed by his dedication, but didn't say anything as she exited the room and shut the door.

Working with someone else wasn't nearly as terrible as she'd anticipated.

CHAPTER ELEVEN

The arena smelled even worse than Mireille could've imagined. A nauseating stew of sweat, blood, cigarette smoke, and cheap cologne that had her wishing she'd gone with her first instinct this evening and just met Ronin at the Frosted Crystal after his fight like they'd agreed.

But she couldn't help it. She was…*curious.*

Honestly, she blamed this stupid crush on her pathetic excuse for a love life. She hadn't had sex with anyone other than her marks for decades, not since that disastrous attempt at a relationship twenty years back.

She and Josef had begun dating while starring together in *Torvolde and Birgitta,* a ballet that chronicled the star-crossed love between Syvalle's first female warrior and the enemy general of an opposing army in the years before the Empire had unified the territories.

It annoyed Mireille that despite being the obvious hero of the story—and the only half of the duo to survive the final curtain—Torvolde's name had been placed before Birgitta's in the title.

The injustice didn't bother Josef, a laid-back Windrider with an easy laugh and the most stunning abs she'd ever seen. Though based on the feel of Ronin's beneath his shirt last night, Josef was about to be unseated.

The two dancers had enjoyed a passionate, months-long affair. Josef had softened Mireille's rougher edges, had allowed her to be a version of herself she'd never tried on before. He didn't balk at her dedication to her jobs, so she'd moved in with him.

She'd thought she'd found the love of her life.

A notion she was abruptly disabused of when she'd caught Josef fucking one of the chorus members back-stage on opening night of the following season. Suddenly, his easy-going nature had made a lot more sense.

Luckily, she'd had the forethought to keep her own apartment. Also luckily, she was the High-Gods-damned prima ballerina, so she'd had Josef's cheating ass booted from the company.

Despite her bruised pride and broken heart, the whole debacle *had* offered one benefit: the reinforcement of Mireille's life-long belief that getting close to anyone, allowing anyone behind her walls, would only cause her pain. And even though she'd learned that lesson the hard way, she felt a renewed justification in her solitary existence.

She'd sworn off relationships since. And had vowed never to mix work and even temporary pleasure again.

Was she breaking that vow tonight by attending Ronin's fight? Surely not. They were supposed to be lovers. How could it be anything other than prudent to learn more about him before they'd face the ultimate test up at the Cathedral of Bones?

She was already learning plenty from the crowd, who were in absolute hysteria over their Butcher. Last week, he'd handily won his bout against a hyena bi-form, but tonight promised much higher stakes. Ronin's opponent, a Windrider from Brachos, was similarly undefeated in his home ring. The night's winner would gain both a hefty purse of *drachas* and the title of cross-continental champion.

Mireille ascended the sticky concrete steps, boots squelching as she elbowed through the rowdy spectators. She'd hidden her signature tresses underneath a navy beanie, and, bundled within her gray wool jacket, she hoped no one would recognize her.

Not really the ballet crowd.

She picked her way to her seat, glancing down toward the current match. A female Deathstalker with two black braids had a female Windrider in a headlock. The bottoms of the latter's white wings dragged across the cage floor, soaking up the spattered blood.

As Mireille sat, the male next to her shot to his feet, cheering at the Windrider bucking out of the Deathstalker's hold, and his drink tipped off the armrest into Mireille's lap.

"Sorry, *sorry.*" He grabbed his empty cup, then patted at her crotch. With his bare hands.

She smacked his hands away with a soft snarl, and he turned back to the fight, muttering something that sounded a lot like *cunt.*

Definitely not the ballet crowd.

She pressed her jacket against her damp thighs, then

swiveled her head toward the concession stand. The tangled mass of bodies flowing through the aisle discouraged her from fetching a pile of napkins.

The fight between the two females ended—the Windrider had pulled off the win—and the announcer, a walrus Beastrunner with hefty tusks on display, stepped to the center of the ring, silencing the spectators.

"Ladies and gentlemales," he said into a floating violet disk that amplified his rumbling voice, "it's time to crown a new continental champion. Are you ready?" The crowd surged upward, shouting and stomping their feet. Mireille joined in, politely clapping her hands.

"All the way from the windy wilds of Diachre, please welcome the brown-winged brute, the fists of fury, the beauty with the braids...*Callum Maloney!*"

A bulky Windrider with fleshy wings jogged into the ring, pounding his fists against his bare chest and roaring at the stands. His ginger hair was braided back from a face that revealed the sarcasm in the announcer's nickname.

Callum Maloney was perhaps the ugliest Fae male Mireille had ever seen.

His black eyes bulged above a bulbous nose, his chin jutting forward in a severe underbite. He looked like one of those toothy, gelatinous fish that stalked the depths of the Sea of Thetis.

Jeers pelted Callum as he taunted the crowd from his side of the ring, bouncing back and forth on his feet.

"And now," the announcer boomed, "the male who needs no introduction—but I'll do it anyway because we all know how much he loves it—put your hands together for our hometown hero, the tattooed terror himself, everyone's favorite white wolf...*RONIN MATAKOS!*"

Thunderous applause wracked the arena as Ronin sauntered into the cage.

"Bu-TCHER! Bu-TCHER! Bu-TCHER!"

The eardrum-bursting cheers faded to a faint hum as Mireille beheld Ronin.

She was no stranger to chiseled males, fellow dancers who spent hours each day honing their forms. But their lithe bodies were marble-smooth—works of art.

Ronin's body was a work of war.

A broad chest covered with swirling tattoos and tiny white hairs. Thick, sculpted arms capable of crushing a skull. Or cradling a female. Divine abdominal muscles, seemingly crafted by Vestan the Warrior God himself.

Mireille couldn't decide what to ogle first. So she just ogled it all.

Josef had most certainly been unseated.

Ronin didn't need to resort to his opponent's theatrics. Dragging his gilded blue gaze across the rapturous crowd, he offered a subtle nod, then took his corner, the portrait of aloof confidence. He rested his hands on his hips, his fingers grazing those insane cuts of muscle that flowed into his loose black sparring pants.

Mireille unbuttoned her jacket, suddenly needing to cool her heated blood.

The announcer addressed the two fighters. "You both know the rules." He paused with a serious look before he threw his head back and cackled. "There are no rules! Except for the one: no magic. Yes, gents?"

Both males affirmed, Maloney fingering the nessite-lined cuffs around his wrists. Not enough nessite to fully paralyze him, but enough to deactivate his wind magic.

"Then let the championship bout begin!" The

announcer hustled out of the cage and slammed the door with a clang.

Mireille's heart leapt into her throat as Maloney scrambled toward Ronin, head lowered as he tried to take him out at the waist.

Ronin crouched, bracing his feet, and his chest met Maloney's with a fleshy smack.

The first few minutes of the fight were more like a dance, the two males meeting and parting, arms, legs, fists and chests colliding. Evenly matched, neither was able to land a blow.

And though Mirielle had never seen Ronin fight, she knew he was holding back. Saving his energy by letting Maloney come to him. A living example of *ruthless efficiency*. Vivienne would have been proud.

The crowd grew restless, screaming at the two fighters to quit stalling and start shedding blood.

Maloney rushed forward, arcing a hook that Ronin caught single-handedly before shoving the male away. Striking out with a wing, Maloney sliced Ronin's shoulder with one of the sharp talons at its apex.

Mireille's hand flew to her mouth and she emitted a little yelp, but Ronin didn't even flinch. Merely shook off the blood before it trailed to his hand and affected his grip.

The next time the two males crashed together was far more vicious. Ronin landed a killer punch to Maloney's temple, red spraying as his eyebrow split.

Mireille could barely watch, fingers wrenched in her lap, as the two males pummeled and ripped each other.

Maloney managed to get Ronin facedown on the floor, tearing apart Ronin's back with his talons.

Ronin roared, and the heart-twisting sound tugged a whimper from Mireille's wolf.

He bucked his hips and threw the Windrider off, and as he stood, blood gushed into his waistband. He bared his teeth in a feral smile, then lifted his palm to beckon Maloney.

More.

Maloney bolted for him, and Ronin captured the Windrider in his massive arms, then slammed him to the concrete. Maloney palmed Ronin's jaw as Ronin squeezed his neck, attempting to choke the life out of him.

Ronin's own face reddened, and beneath him, Maloney's cuffs had lost their faint green glow.

He's wearing fake cuffs, Mireille's wolf growled. *Cheating* ass!

Mireille shot to her feet, watching in horror as Maloney summoned the wind to steal Ronin's breath.

Ronin reared off the Windrider, then staggered to the cage wall and looped his fingers through the grate, steadying himself and clawing at his throat.

The crowd erupted into ferocious shouts, and the referee rushed in. Ronin held up a hand to stop him, and Maloney's wind snuffed out.

Cries of *cheater* and *disqualify him* echoed as Ronin panted, never taking his eyes off his smirking opponent.

"You wanna finish this clean, or are you too chicken-shit?" Ronin ground out through serrated breaths.

There was no answer as the two males sprang for each other. The referee emitted a panicked bark before hustling out of the cage.

Fists collided with faces, feet cracked shins, and blood drenched the cage floor and walls.

A deafening crack sounded, and Mireille saw Ronin holding Maloney's wing in a very unnatural position before smashing the Windrider to the floor.

Any doubt Mireille had about Ronin's capacity for terrible violence washed away as he beat Maloney's face into a bloody pulp.

She should've been terrified. Or at least disgusted.

Instead, her wolf howled with ferocious glee at Ronin's psychotic, red-stained smile. Tingling warmth flooded Mireille's veins before settling into a pulsing ache between her thighs.

Fucking kill him, she thought savagely, and her wolf yipped in agreement.

The referee burst into the ring, breaking Ronin's trance. Maloney was motionless beneath him, save for a slight rise and fall of his chest.

Ronin pushed up, then stumbled backward, nearly toppling over before the referee grabbed his bloodied fist and thrust it upwards.

The crowd lost their fucking minds.

Mireille joined them, hollering and clapping so aggressively that her palms began to burn.

"Our champion!" the referee boomed, beaming at the stands as Ronin swayed unsteadily beside him.

As soon as the referee released his wrist, Ronin collapsed to the concrete.

And the arena erupted into chaos.

CHAPTER TWELVE

By the time Mireille managed to fight her way down the arena steps, nearly half an hour had passed since the end of the fight.

After Ronin had collapsed, nearly taking Mireille's heart with him, he'd been whisked away as the crowd flooded the ring, concerned about their champion.

The concern had swiftly morphed into celebration, as bottles of champagne were popped and boisterous dancing began. It took her another fifteen minutes just to wend through the mayhem.

As she approached the hallway to the locker rooms, she saw Maloney being carried away by two males, a short female trailing behind. The female glanced furtively over her shoulder, and Mireille stopped in her tracks at the white and black hair poking out of her hood.

Layla Fetar.

Had Otto tried to fix the fight, given Maloney those

fake cuffs? An attempt to get Ronin out of the way, have Mireille all to himself up at the estate?

Mireille pressed herself against the wall, bowing her head as she watched Layla trail the two males down the shadowed corridor.

She took a few steps toward their retreating forms before a wave of indecision stilled her.

Where the fuck was *that* coming from? She'd never let anything stop her from chasing down a mark. The smart choice would be to follow them, learn anything she could about what Layla had been doing here tonight before she encountered the female up at the estate. The successful completion of the assignment might very well depend on such knowledge.

But she couldn't shake a nagging sense of guilt.

Ronin had almost been killed tonight. And likely because of her.

She tried to rationalize it away. Ronin had agreed to this job just as willingly as she had, knowing the potentially dangerous consequences.

Still, she didn't want to admit how much the thought of his suffering displeased her.

This. This right here is why she didn't do partners. They made everything so much more fucking complicated.

She lost sight of Layla and the two males, then made her way to the locker entrance.

The spacious room was eerily quiet, the fighters from earlier bouts having long since left the arena. And the High Gods only knew where Layla was taking Maloney. Probably somewhere private to tie up Otto's loose end.

Rushing water sounded as Mireille followed snaking steam past benches and lockers to a door at the other side of the room. As she swung it open, mist clouded her vision and a soft, whimpering sigh filled her ears.

A decidedly *female* sigh.

The fog parted, revealing a scene in the shower stall that had Mireille squeaking to a halt.

She didn't know where to look first.

At the Deathstalker female's face, red lips parted, eyes closed, brows pinched in an expression on the verge of total ecstasy.

At the angry pink welts criss-crossing Ronin's muscled back, the water streaming over his bulging shoulders as he gripped the female's wrists above her head in a single hand.

At the two perfect globes of his ass, clenching as he thrust into her slowly, his other hand clamped onto the pale thigh around his waist.

"I'm close," the Deathstalker breathed.

"Yeah?" Ronin whispered against her neck, hips rolling. "You think you deserve to come after sneaking up on me in the shower again?"

"Y-yes," she whimpered.

He released her leg and slapped her face. "What was that?"

"No."

Ronin squished the female's cheeks, then spit into her open mouth. "Fucking beg me for it."

He shoved his tongue past her lips at the same time as he snapped his hips forward, and she released such a low, primal moan that Mireille's nipples stiffened.

She was pinned in place, couldn't take her eyes off them. Afraid to move lest they hear her and stop.

If they stop, I'm going to be extremely upset with you, her wolf whispered.

If they stop, I'm going to be extremely upset with myself. Mireille steadied herself against a small table, settling in for the grand finale.

Ronin broke the kiss and the female shuddered. "*Please*, Ronin." Her fingers splayed above his grip, and he returned his hand to her quivering thigh.

Ronin increased his pace, and the smacking sounds of their flesh combined with the stalls' humidity made Mireille's head swim. Her knees buckled as she gripped the edge of the table.

"That's my good—"

The table tipped forward, and both it and Mireille clattered to the floor.

Her wolf snarled. *Clumsy* fool.

The Deathstalker's eyes flew open and she shrieked, her foot meeting the tiles with a wet slap. She snatched a towel, and fled the stall.

Ronin's head dipped between his shaking shoulders as Mireille picked herself up, awaiting his reprimands and trying to ignore the string of frustrated curses her wolf was letting loose in her mind.

To her utter shock, Ronin's head flew back as he released peals of uproarious laughter. Mireille was, once again, frozen in place. Didn't know what to do with her hands other than clench and unclench them at her sides.

His laughter subsided, and he shook the water from his white hair, holding a towel in front of his groin as he turned.

Well, that's just great, her wolf growled. *We don't even get to see his co—*

Shut. Up, Mireille spat back.

"Dimi's gonna be furious with you." Ronin snickered. "I'd been edging her for half an hour."

"I… I'm not… What?" Mireille was so rarely at a loss for words. She didn't enjoy the sensation.

"You're wet." Ronin's low murmur snapped Mireille from her trance.

"*What?* You think this is the first time I've seen a couple screwing? I'm not fucking *wet,* Matakos."

"Liar." He winked, pointing to her leggings, still damp from the mess with her seatmate.

"This isn't… Someone spilled a drink on me."

"Sure they did." He gestured to his towel. "You wanna help me with this, *lover,* or…?"

"Holy fucking High Gods," Mireille screamed, aiming for the door. "I'll wait for you out here!"

Ronin's dark chuckle shivered down her spine as she fled the showers.

RONIN SPLAYED a wet hand against the tiles as he tugged his cock with the other, slow and steady. Just how he liked it.

But it wasn't Dimi's face in his mind when he came with a guttural tremble.

It was Mireille's.

His wolf laughed. *We're going to tell her.*

No one but me can hear you, dumbass, Ronin snarled back.

Not for long.

For forever, if you keep this shit up. I'll fail this assignment on purpose.

She wanted us, too. His wolf licked his chops. *Even you could see that.*

The beast wasn't wrong. High Gods, she'd looked so

fucking adorable standing there, gawking at him, her cheeks flaming pink and her silver eyes ablaze with embarrassment and…curiosity.

She didn't want to be turned on by what she saw, but she was. Oh, she fucking was. She had no idea how much ammunition she'd just given him.

He preferred her that way anyway—real emotions, real reactions. Not the wily seductress persona she'd worn last night in front of Otto.

But he sure as Stygios wasn't going to tell her that any time soon.

He cleaned himself off, then towel-dried his hair before poking his head out and asking Mireille to hand him his clothes. He'd change in here—didn't want to torment her any further.

He wondered what she was doing here, anyway. Their meeting with Bisere wasn't until one.

Had she come to watch his fight? How oddly touching.

Fully dressed, he swaggered into the locker room to find Mireille sitting on a bench, back ramrod straight as always, with her legs crossed at the ankles and her hands clasped in her lap.

"Sorry about that," he muttered. Though, why was he apologizing? It's not like there was anything going on between him and Mireille. Nothing real, at least.

"I should have… I should have knocked," she said, with none of the characteristic bite in her voice.

"What are you doing here?" He sprawled out across from her. "We weren't supposed to meet at the Crystal until one."

"I… I wanted to see your fight," she said to her lap.

"Why?"

"You came to the ballet. Figured it was only fair I return the favor. And if anyone asks about it at the estate, my answer will be more authentic."

"Fair enough. But why'd you come down to the locker rooms? You could've just told me at the Crystal that you'd been here."

She snapped her head up, her eyes narrowed. "Professional obligation."

"Little she-wolf was worried about her big, scary boyfriend, wasn't she?" The edge of his lip curled up, and her eyes went molten.

"No." Her teeth were clenched so tightly that a vein pulsed in her jaw.

He shook his head, leaning forward and resting his forearms on his spread knees. He pointed a finger at her forehead. "Did you know that when you lie, you get the cutest little dimple between your eyebrows?"

"I'm not..." Mireille rubbed at the spot. "Otto fixed the fight."

"What?" Ronin jerked upright.

"I saw Layla Fetar and two males hauling Maloney away. Guessing they gave him those fake cuffs."

"Our show at the theater last night worked. Wow, Otto must be completely smitten if he's already trying to kill me after one meeting with you. Bravo."

"You need to be careful when we get up there," Mireille said, her voice edged with panic. "There's no way this will be the only attempt."

"I can handle myself. Plus my hot, deadly girlfriend will protect me, right?" He smirked, then dipped his head, dragging a hand across the back of his neck. He was still sore from the fight. The healing suppressant hadn't fully worn off, and the raw cuts across his back and shoulders rubbed uncomfortably against his shirt. "You find anything else at the Imperial library today?"

She shook her head. "Waste of time."

"Dimi probably feels the same."

Mireille snickered. "Is she your real…"

"Nah. Just a friend who occasionally helps me blow off steam after a fight."

"Does she know about us? About our assignment?"

Ronin sighed. "No, but I guess I'll have to tell her now. I won't give her all the details. Just enough for her to know not to blab about fucking me when I'm supposed to be dating you. She'll be discreet."

Mireille shrugged. "It's not a big deal. I spent an entire afternoon fucking a mark last weekend. Though *he* won't be telling anyone."

She was chuckling when he met her eyes, but the vision that speared for his mind nearly knocked him flat.

Mireille splayed out on a bed, her copper hair fanned across a pillow and her wrists bound in black silks, straining against the headboard as Ronin cupped her breast and licked between her legs.

Frenzied fucking Dienses, he was too hard up. Hence why he'd entertained Dimi's request when she'd ambushed him in the showers earlier. Thought maybe the release would help banish the highly inappropriate things he'd been thinking about his new partner.

Obviously it hadn't worked.

He broke Mireille's stare, then strode to his locker to gather his belongings. "You ready? Mattias should be waiting for us at the club by now. I'll give you some privacy to change."

She glanced down at her attire—dark gray leggings

with a large wet spot and a long-sleeved black top. "Change?"

"*That's* what you thought you were going to wear to a nightclub? Man, you really don't get out much, do you?"

Mireille pursed her lips. "The Frosted Crystal is *not* my scene."

He cocked his head, pushing his tongue into his cheek. "I think we might be able to salvage this." He stepped over the bench as he extended a claw, then sliced through her shirt just underneath the generous swells of her breasts.

"What the fuck, Ronin?" She grabbed for the falling fabric. "This is my favorite shirt! *Asshole*."

"You're the one that didn't dress appropriately." He shrugged. "You would've stuck out like a sore thumb. Now at least everyone will be staring at you for the *right* reason."

"And what reason is that?" She whipped her hands to her hips, the movement lifting her newly-shorn hem and exposing her black lace bra. His wolf began panting.

Ronin whispered against the shell of her ear and if he wasn't mistaken, she might've leaned in a bit closer. "You have an incredibly sexy stomach, *my love*."

The tiny hairs along her nape prickled, and he caught the shift in her scent, though she still looked furious when he backed away.

"Almost as sexy as mine." He winked, lifting his shirt and patting his own well-earned abs, delighted to see her eyes dart there and glaze over. He swept past her and held open the door as she grumbled and tugged on her jacket and beanie.

"Let's go, Valette. The Crystal awaits!"

CHAPTER THIRTEEN

The Frosted Crystal was a glowing, thumping beacon beneath the damp blanket of Kheimos's ever-present snowfall.

A long line of huddled Fae, mostly Beastrunners and Deathstalkers, awaited entry into the exclusive club.

Mireille didn't know why they bothered. Unless you knew someone, or were well-known yourself, there was no chance of getting inside. Windriders were given special preference, but even a few of them were out here, stamping their feet and blowing into clasped fists.

Mireille aimed for the back of the line, but Ronin tugged her toward the front door. "I'm insulted you think *I* have to wait in that line."

He stalked up to the blue rope, nodding to the woolly mammoth Beastrunner bouncer. "Charlie."

"Mezzanine. VIP section," Charlie boomed in a bass-deep voice, his auburn curls dotted with snowflakes. "He's been waiting for you."

Charlie unlatched the rope, and as his russet eyes slid

to Mireille, he let loose such a high-pitched squeal that several Fae in the line covered their ears. "Mireille Valette! What are you doing here? Especially with this cretin."

Ronin scoffed. "*You're* a fan of the ballet?"

Charlie ignored him, towering above Mireille and clutching her hand, his eyes shining with adulation. "It is such an honor to have you here. I attended *The Curse of Faurana* last month and you were magnificent. That final solo? I was in tears."

Charlie ushered her and Ronin past the barrier, earning a few half-hearted murmurs of frustration from the hopeful club-goers. Ronin flashed a wicked grin, elongating his fangs. Many of them cowered.

"If that uncultured beast gives you any trouble tonight, you let me know." Charlie called after her. "And your drinks are on the house."

"Thanks, Charlie!" Ronin tossed back.

"Not yours," the mammoth grumbled. "Just hers."

"Thanks, Charlie!" Mireille mimicked, and Ronin shook his head, amused, before pushing open the red leather door and crossing the threshold into throbbing bedlam.

The Frosted Crystal resembled a wintry circus, the ceiling's red-and-white-striped fabric billowing around a glittering sphere of ice, kept magically frozen.

Throughout the room hung metal cages and rings hosting beautiful male and female performers, their sparkling outfits barely covering their intimate bits.

Ronin shoved through the dance floor, a sweaty, gleaming mass of half-naked bodies writhing to the droning beats. A translucent crystal bar spanned the entire left half of the club, and an array of sinfully attractive bartenders in a state of perpetual motion attempted to serve the patrons waving *drachas* at them.

Above the bar and dance floor, a glass-walled mezzanine ringed the room. Ronin scanned the shadowy alcoves, his gaze catching in the furthest corner, then dragged Mireille through the mob and up a metal staircase.

Once they reached the alcove, Ronin plopped onto the red velvet banquette across from a skinny male Beastrunner—coyote by the scent—with a spiky green mohawk.

A cigarette dangled from the male's lip, wafting an unmistakable smoky, licorice smell.

Lethaphyll.

So named for the Goddess of Oblivion, because consuming too much was just as bad as visiting one of those Shrouded Sisters at her Temples throughout the colonies.

Say goodbye to those memories.

The male's bloodshoot squint informed Mireille that he was well on his way to a visit from the Stranger.

"Mataaaaaaahkos." His shoulders shook with silent laughter.

"Beezie," Ronin chuckled. "You start the party without us?"

"Man, you were s'posed to be here an hour ago." The male tried to blow out a breath between his lips but ended up making an extended raspberry sound.

"Are we really gonna learn anything from this guy?" Mireille whispered, leaning down to Ronin and definitely *not* breathing in his iced citrus and pine scent.

"He's always like this." Ronin tugged Mireille into his lap.

Right. They were in public. Had to put on their show.

Mireille wondered how much Ronin had told... *Beezie?*

She tried not to melt as Ronin curled his hand around her waist, resting his thumb on her bare hip. "Beezie? What kind of name is *that?*"

Ronin's warm huff rumbled through her, and that coupled with the scene she'd witnessed earlier had her mind—and her wolf—conjuring some spectacularly filthy images.

Ronin turned to whisper back, his plush lips grazing across her jaw. "His real name is Mattias Bisere, but no one ever pronounces his last name right. So, Beezie it is. I would say we shouldn't be talking about him right in front of his face, but I'm not sure he's even noticed."

Mattias—Mireille refused to use that ludicrous nick-name—slouched against the banquette, his thin, but well-muscled arms spread across the cushions.

Ronin jostled Mattias's shoulder and his head popped up, the precariously positioned cigarette landing in his lap in a flash of sparks.

"Oh, shit!" Mattias smacked his tight black pants, then tossed the smoldering cigarette into a glass of water where it snuffed out with a hiss. "Matakos. Hey man, I've been waiting for you."

"Yes, we've already established that," Ronin chuckled.

Mattias aimed a hooded gaze at Mireille, then licked his lips. "Who's your yummy friend?"

Ronin brushed Mireille's hair back and planted his chin on her shoulder, gazing at her lovingly. Her trai-torous body flooded with heat. "This is my girlfriend, Mireille. Mireille, this is Mattias."

Mireille extended a hand and Mattias clasped it over

the table. His fingers were rough and dry, but his hand-shake was firmer than she would've expected given his current state.

"High Gods, am I hallucinating? You're fucking stunning. What in Ethyrios are you doing with this asshole?"

Mireille snickered. "A question I ask myself on a daily basis."

Ronin nipped her neck, and a languorous tingle, warm as melted honey, oozed down her spine. "I love it when she's nasty to me."

Mattias shook his head, rolling himself another cigarette, his eyes glued to Mireille's exposed stomach. "I don't blame you."

He placed the cigarette in his mouth, and Mireille nearly fell out of Ronin's lap as he snapped his fingers.

And a kernel of flame burst from Mattias's thumb.

CHAPTER FOURTEEN

*M*ireille's mouth fell open, and Ronin must've felt her tense in his lap because he whispered in her ear, "See? I told you he'd be worthwhile to meet with."

"How…how did you do that?" Mireille asked Mattias, who snuffed out the flame, dragged deeply, and puffed out a cloud of smoke.

Mireille had never met a Fae with elemental fire magic. Nor the other two elemental magics, lightning and water, that had faded away centuries ago. Only the Windriders' ability to control air and summon the wind had remained in Ethyrios after the suppression of the Fallen Goddess.

She was shocked Mattias felt safe enough to put on even that little display. Though truthfully, Mattias didn't seem to be feeling much of anything at the moment.

"Fancy party trick, huh?" Mattias smirked at Ronin. Had he already known about Mattias's gift?

"I knew she'd be impressed." Ronin winked as Mireille continued to gape.

"Where did you get it from?" she asked.

"Showed up after my sister disappeared," Mattias murmured around his cigarette. "No idea why or where it came from."

"Your sister have it too?" Ronin asked.

Mattias shrugged. "Not that I know of."

"What happened to her?"

A shudder ran through Mattias, and he seemed to sober up, sitting up straighter and glancing around the mezzanine. The alcoves were well hidden from each other, and the booming music was so loud that no one would hear them.

"I *know* something bad happened to her up at that estate…" Mattias trailed off, a fearful look in his eyes. "No matter what the IA claims."

"Why did she go in the first place?" Mireille asked.

"She got some kind of cryptic invitation from Otto himself." Mattias brought the cigarette back to his lips with pinched fingers, sucking in a comforting drag. He leaned his head back against the banquette, his mohawk crunching. "Claimed he could help her *unlock her inner power*, or some shit."

"What, like fire?" Ronin shifted forward, his hair tickling Mireille's temple.

Mattias expelled a long exhale. "I don't fucking know, man. Larissa was always… she was super spiritual. Obsessed with the Fallen Goddess. Didn't believe in the High Gods or the Empire. She and our parents used to have screaming matches about it."

Mattias's eyes glazed over, lost in the tempestuous sea of his memories.

Mireille coaxed him back. "So, what makes you think something happened to her up there?"

His face hardened. "Because I followed her."

Ronin stiffened beneath her. "*How*? How did you even get in? And how the fuck did you get back *out*?"

Mattias smirked. "Bought a vial of veiling potion from one of those back-alley apothecaries downtown and snuck in with a shipment of crates. Disguised myself as one of the deliverymales."

"What did you see while you were there?" Mireille was on the edge of her seat. Well, the edge of Ronin's knee, really. Very few people had ever seen the inside of Otto's estate.

"The place is fucking huge and just...so odd looking. You've seen pictures, right? Those tall turrets with all those melting windows. The Cathedral of Bones— weirdest fucking architecture I've ever seen. And the collection he's got in there? Shit from all over the continent, some of it thousands, maybe even tens of thousands of years old. Like walking through a fucking museum. And some of those pieces, man... I couldn't shake the feeling that they were watching back."

Ronin cocked an eyebrow and Mattias let out a bitter little laugh.

"I wasn't on this stuff as much back then." He flicked some ash into an ashtray. "And I wasn't there long, but I saw Larissa having dinner alone with Otto. He was asking her all these questions about our family. Where we were from, where our grandparents were from, shit like that."

"Did the staff not question you?" Ronin was rubbing idle circles against Mireille's hip, goosebumps raising with every pass. She didn't even think he realized he was doing it. It was extremely distracting. Though not entirely unwelcome.

"Nah, they were all so out of it. Think Otto's got them all under some kind of spell."

"What happened after dinner?" Mireille asked, not sure she wanted to know.

Mattias crushed his cigarette into the ashtray, then dipped his head into his hands. "I followed Larissa up to her guest room. She was the only guest there, as far as I could tell. I convinced her that I was, well, me, by telling her things from our childhood that only I would know. We had a huge fight. I tried to convince her to leave with me, but she refused. Whatever promises Otto made to her, she was so eager for them that she wouldn't see reason. I was lucky she didn't drag me out of that room and expose me as an intruder."

"What did you do?" Ronin asked.

"What else *could* I do?" Mattias's amber eyes filled with shame. "I left. Snuck back out on the delivery truck. I was... I hoped that maybe Larissa would come to her senses and return in a few days."

"Did she?" Mireille strained forward.

"In a way, yes." Mattias plucked up a bottle of Aquaver from the table and took a long, deep pull. "She came to me in a dream. Well, her voice at least. Said, *I am one with my power. And I am enough.*"

"What do you think that means?" Ronin asked.

"Fuck if I know." Mattias shook his head. "I thought it meant she was still alive, still up at that estate. But the IA wouldn't take me seriously. And I had no concrete proof, other than my own testimony, that she'd even been there."

"Did you ever go back? To find her or try to confront Otto?" Mireille asked.

"*Fuck*, no. I never want to go near that male or his creepy place again." Mattias shivered. "Jurgev Otto is the fucking manifestation of Stygios himself.

"Death and destruction, that's all he's got to offer."

MATTIAS HAD ALWAYS BEEN a little out there, but even he had never spouted anything as strange as this. And Ronin knew he wasn't lying.

"When did all of this happen?" Mireille piped up.

Ronin was trying to ignore how good, how natural it felt to have her sitting in his lap with his hand at her waist. And High Gods, her fucking *scent*. He could no longer blame the effect it was having on him solely on his wolf.

"'Bout a year ago," Mattias answered.

"And you haven't seen Larissa since?"

Mattias's gaze trailed out into the club, the lights bathing him in a pulsing rainbow. "No." A simple answer, yet weighed down with a year's worth of guilt and regret.

No wonder he needed the lethaphyll. Ronin could relate.

The thought made him instantly, and uncomfortably, aware of how long it had been since he'd had his own fix. He pressed a button on the table to call over a waitress, and Mireille shot him an annoyed look.

She scooted out of his lap, her ass brushing over his cock far too briefly, and settled herself next to Mattias.

"I'm so sorry." She grasped the male's hand, her voice laced with an empathy Ronin had never heard her use.

Like she recognized Mattias's loss, had felt a similar one herself. That missing father she refused to talk to him about, perhaps?

Mattias sighed. "Sorry, I haven't been much help."

Again surprising Ronin with her gentleness, Mireille placed a hand on Mattias's thigh. Ronin's wolf emitted a low growl. "Every little piece of information we can gather before we go up there will help. And if we find any trace of Larissa, if we figure out what happened to her, we'll let you know."

"Thank you." The pained, grateful expression on Mattias's face had Ronin's chest clenching. "Fuck, stunning *and* thoughtful? Again, I'll ask… how did *this* guy score you?"

Mireille aimed a cheeky little smile at Ronin over her shoulder, and winked. "He's not so bad."

And even though he knew it was all for show, goosebumps shivered down his neck.

Mattias pushed up from the banquette and handed the pack of lethaphyll cigarettes to Ronin. "You might need this up there to chill yourself out. That estate is a fucking viper's nest. Watch out you don't get bitten."

Ronin stuffed the pack into his pocket, then stood and shook his friend's hand. "We will. Thanks, Mattias. Take care of yourself."

Mattias shuffled out of the alcove, swallowed by the droning music and throbbing lights.

Ronin crashed back against the banquette. "Well, that was…*interesting.*"

"You're telling me. Did you know about Mattias's fire power?"

Ronin nodded. "He mentioned it to me when I contacted him to arrange this meeting and told him about our assignment. I promised him we wouldn't tell Skanisse."

"What are the chances his sister is still alive?" Mireille shot him a pleading look.

He was about to answer when the waitress he'd summoned finally bustled up to the table, her golden wings flowing behind her. Her mouth formed an excited O before she noticed Mireille and her lips pressed together.

"Can I get you two something?" Her gaze bobbed between them.

Ronin grimaced. "Oh, hey, uh…"

Sharae, his wolf supplied with a laugh.

"…Sharae. Nice to see you again."

"Sure it is," Sharae answered flatly. "Last call. What do you want?"

"I'll take a Delirium. You want anything, Mireille?"

"Aquaver," she said to Sharae, no trace of the previous empathy she'd shown to Mattias. "Straight up with a twist of lime. A *twist*, not a peel. Make sure the bartender doesn't fuck that up."

"Of course." Sharae aimed a saccharine smile at Mireille, then huffed down the mezzanine, wings bouncing.

Ronin loosed a chuckle. "She's gonna spit in your drink."

"What was that all about? She looked like she wanted to use her wind to choke the life out of me."

"Nothing. Had a little fun with her last weekend and haven't seen her since."

"Ronin Matakos, Butcher of hearts," Mireille teased. "Sounds like she'd be better off spitting in *your* drink.

Though based on what I saw earlier, you might be into that."

Ronin leaned back against the banquette, crossing an ankle over his knee, and spread an arm along the back, tracing circles on the plush velvet. Mireille's eyes darted right to his fingers. "Curious, little she-wolf? You never let me tell you what my kinks are."

"I've got a pretty good guess," she muttered. "What were we talking about before your ex-girlfriend showed up?"

"She's not my—"

"Right, Mattias. And the question of what actually happened to his sister."

"Is it worth checking through the archive files again tomorrow before we leave for Otto's on Monday?"

"I don't think so. We're heading to the source itself. Better to see what we can learn up there." Mireille got a far-off, dreamy look and they settled into a comfortable silence, each of them lost in thought as they gazed down upon the sea of Fae still dancing away to the pulsing drumbeats.

And Ronin wondered if Mireille's thoughts matched his own.

What the fuck was going on up at that estate?

And what had the IA gotten them into?

CHAPTER FIFTEEN

As the sleek, black sedan crept up a gravel driveway on Monday afternoon, Ronin couldn't help thinking that the estate's moniker had been spot on.

Cathedral of Bones, indeed.

Three tapered white turrets pierced the surrounding pines like skeletal fingers, intercut with long, thin windows.

The sedan crunched to a halt beside a stone fountain with a statue of a coiled, striking serpent in the center. To the right was an arched entranceway of towering double doors, above which shone a stained-glass window depicting the High God of Death and Destruction himself.

Stygios glowered down from a throne of writhing serpents, his forked tongue poked out over long, sharp fangs. Nyctima twined through his feet, and the yellow glass of his eyes gleamed, cutting through the overcast haze.

Ronin stepped out of the sedan, a chill wind rustling through his hair. He glanced up toward the far left turret, spying a humanoid-shaped shadow watching their arrival from the window. Ronin shivered as he rounded the trunk to retrieve their bags.

"No need, sir." A dark-haired human servant bustled down to the car. "The bags will be brought to your room." He gestured up the stairs, where a regal-looking woman with a tight gray chignon waited. "Mistress Klovia will give you a brief tour of the main house. We hope your stay with us is empowering."

An odd thing to say, Ronin thought. He inspected the man, searching for any sign of the spells Mattias had assumed the human staff were under. The man looked well-cared for, not sickly or tired. Though there *did* seem to be a lack of vitality in his eyes.

Mireille took Ronin's proffered arm, her face carefully neutral as her gaze climbed the ossified towers and stained-glass window.

Mistress Klovia stepped forward to greet them and the white stone doors behind her groaned open, seemingly of their own accord. "Welcome to the Otto estate." Her voice was low and deep, no hint of a smile as she swept an arm across the threshold. "After you."

As Mireille and Ronin were swallowed into the gaping maw, his wolf shuddered. *This place reeks.*

Ronin sniffed the air, smelling nothing but the heady, floral notes of the massive bouquet of pale blue roses sitting atop a round table in the entryway.

Of what? Ronin asked. *Roses?*

No, his wolf whined.

Death.

Mistress Klovia swept ahead of Mireille and Ronin, her low-heeled shoes clacking on the checkered marble floors. "The first floor contains rooms for social gatherings. You may feel free to use the parlors during your stay. However, there is a strict midnight curfew."

Ronin glanced into the rooms they passed, each with soaring ceilings and purposefully arranged couches, chairs, and tables around which groups of Fae were gathered. Bubbling laughter and excited conversations echoed, the walls a veritable gallery of paintings and artistic photographs, plus several maps of the continent and its various territories.

In the third room, a line of beautiful humans stood against one wall, the women in gauzy dresses and the men shirtless above linen pants. Beside them, a stack of Delirium bottles glistened atop a black credenza. Ronin's mouth watered.

The drive to the estate had taken several hours, and he hadn't had a drop of the substance since before he'd left his apartment this morning.

He paused at the parlor entrance as a Deathstalker female wearing a low-cut turquoise bodysuit approached the humans, stopping before a chiseled blond who didn't look a day over twenty-five. The man inclined his head, following the Deathstalker to a red settee where she arranged herself in his lap. She sniffed his neck, coasting her sharp purple fingernails down his chest, and he released a groan of such euphoric ecstasy that Ronin's wolf yipped.

The warm cinnamon scent of the young man's lust

wafted into the hallway as the Deathstalker female began sucking down lungfuls.

Mistress Klovia spoke up. "Refreshments are available here in the northeast parlor, should you require a snack before the opening reception this evening."

The young man's groans increased in volume and frequency, and just as he was about to achieve a very obvious climax, the Deathstalker sank her fangs into his throat, and he crumpled into a pile beneath her.

The female stood, wiping a drop of blood from her lip, then winked a serpentine eye at Ronin. Beside him, Mireille went rigid. He'd never seen her take a drop of Delirium; didn't know what her stance was on fresh emotion feedings either. But given the tension in her body, he guessed she didn't indulge.

"Please don't be shy," Mistress Klovia said. "Master Otto ordered a fresh shipment from the colonies specifically for his honored guests. There's plenty to go around." She turned and snapped at another servant, a bulky man standing sentry in the hallway, who hustled into the parlor to clean up the discarded meal. He grasped the blond's feet and hauled him through a hidden door in the wall before the blood leaking from the bite marks could stain the carpet.

Ronin swallowed. He hadn't had much contact with humans, not since that bloody battle on the fields of Aethalia. And maybe his sister's constant defense of the species had started to sink its claws into him after all, because he felt a pang of horror at such a wasteful, pitiful death.

Still, it didn't take away the unrelenting pull of those bottles of Delirium. His wolf paced and howled within him, just as desperate for a taste as Ronin.

Mireille placed a hand on his chest, and the beast calmed. "Shall we continue on?" She gazed up at him, a question in her silver eyes.

"Y-yes, of course," he coughed, tearing his gaze away from the room as a Beastrunner male entered and began inspecting the feast against the wall.

"This way." Mistress Klovia led them up a marble staircase, then paused at the top. "The guest rooms are here in the east wing."

"What's in the west wing?" Ronin couldn't help asking.

"Those are Master Otto's personal suites. And off-limits to guests."

Mireille squeezed Ronin's arm.

Mistress Klovia led them down a hallway lined with black laquered doors, then stopped at the final one. "Your suite for the duration of your stay. Place your palm against the pad and the room will recognize you. It will open for you and only you while you're here with us."

Mireille flattened a palm against the pad, and Ronin did the same. The door swung inward and before they crossed into the room, Mistress Klovia spoke up again. "The opening reception will be held in the greenhouse at seven o'clock. Take the front staircase, then double back. The entrance to the gardens is through the windowed doors and the greenhouse is just to the right. You can't miss it. The first performance will be held tomorrow morning at sunrise in the gardens."

"Performance?" Mireille asked.

"You're in for quite a treat," Mistress Klovia said, no emotion gracing her slack features. "Master Otto has arranged for a very special guest to sing for you all. Subsequent events will be announced as the week progresses. Breakfast will be delivered to your room promptly at six o'clock. Other than the mandatory performances and dinners, you're free to roam the estate grounds. The galleries are located just west of the gardens. They are quite legendary and very few have had the privilege of touring them. We hope you will have a chance while you're here. Have an empowering stay, Mistress Valette, Master Matakos."

Mistress Klovia offered a subtle nod, then slid down the hall as Ronin and Mireille slipped into their room.

Ronin took a moment to survey the spacious and well-appointed suite, whistling in awe as he approached a wall of windows overlooking the gardens.

Gardens was a generous word this time of year in Kheimos, as there was little greenery poking through the white. But Ronin did spy a rather elaborate hedge maze, topped with fluffy clumps of snow, plus several ice sculptures ringing a flagstone patio. Beyond the gardens, a dense forest of evergreens spanned the entirety of the back yard.

Ronin turned back into the room. A large bed with a white oak frame dominated one half, a fur throw artfully tossed on the end. Opposite the bed, flames danced in the woodless fireplace. Two black leather armchairs with matching ottomans were arranged in front of the mantel and a low marble table between them held—what else—a vase of pale blue roses.

Mireille crossed into the bathroom, an elegant space with a glass-walled shower and a large soaking tub.

A knock sounded at the door, and Ronin opened it. A human servant dropped their bags inside with a bow, then left again.

"Well," Mireille said, walking to the bed and running a

hand along the fur throw, "this is all a bit more luxurious than I expected."

Ronin snorted. "From a billionaire? What did you think we were gonna walk into? Otto sacrificing virgins in the foyer?"

Mireille huffed a laugh. "Something like that. Mistress Klovia seemed a bit...odd. She didn't even flinch when that human was killed right in front of her."

"She seemed just as addled as Mattias warned us they'd be. Brazen of Otto to showcase non-consensual feedings like that."

"I don't think he's particularly concerned about abiding by the Empire's laws. Besides, trafficking humans is rampant throughout the continent. If Emperor Erabis were actually serious about upholding that stipulation of the Accords, he'd do something about it." She chewed her lower lip, as if hesitant to ask her next question. "Have you ever...fed from a human?"

"Not like that. Though it was unavoidable during the war. Those battlefields were awash in human fear and anger. Once you get a taste, it's hard not to crave more. The Delirium helps." Saying the name of the drink out loud made Ronin desperate to get his hands on one. "Have you?"

Mireille shook her head. "I barely had any contact with other *Fae* while I was growing up, let alone humans. I tried Delirium once, but hated the way it made me feel. So out of control of my mind and body." She shuddered. "I don't know how you stomach the stuff."

As if I have a fucking choice.

He didn't throw that at her.

He glanced at the clock on the mantel. "We've got about an hour until the party starts. I'm going to go back downstairs and scope out those parlors while you get ready."

Mireille surveyed him, silver eyes narrowed. As if she could tell the real reason he wanted—*needed*—to go down there.

But she didn't say a word as Ronin left the room to feed his addiction.

CHAPTER SIXTEEN

Mireille applied her lipstick, a deep burgundy shade she never would have chosen for herself, purchased as a replacement for her missing armor—the veiling potions that typically masked her identity during her assignments. And though it would do her no good tonight, she'd brought along the vial she'd concocted last week just in case.

She leaned further over the vanity, her dress hanging open and exposing her back. She couldn't zip it up herself, but she hadn't yet asked Ronin for help. Knowing how she'd reacted to his touch down in Kheimos made her hesitant to indulge the temptation.

Ronin had only spent about thirty minutes *scoping out the parlors*. She knew the real reason he'd gone down there, had felt his vibrating need for a Delirium as soon as they'd come upon the supply downstairs. But she didn't want to call him out on it. If he needed the substance to steady himself, to get him through these next few days, who was she to judge?

"We need to discuss some rules," she said.

"Discuss away."

Through the mirror, she watched as Ronin undressed.

His ice-blue tattoos shimmered across his chest and arms, carving down his thick thighs. Though he wasn't looking at her, she knew that *he* knew she was watching him. And he was taking an abnormally long time shoving his legs into his black suit pants.

Wrenching her gaze back to her face, she smoothed on a second coat of lipstick. "When we're downstairs together, you may touch me, but there's no need to go overboard. Back only, and stay above the ass and below the shoulders."

Ronin snickered, flicking white hair out of his eyes as he buckled his belt. "How long has it been since you've been in a real relationship?"

"Asks the male who doesn't seem to know the meaning of the word." She blotted her lips with a tissue. "Why?"

Ronin shrugged on his dress shirt, his long fingers making quick work of the buttons. "Because a new couple, especially one as attractive as us, wouldn't be able to keep their hands off each other. In any type of crowd."

"So what are you suggesting?" She tilted her head back to sweep mascara up her lashes. "That you're going to bend me over a table and take me in front of the entire room?"

Ronin shot her a heated look. "Exhibitionism one of those secret kinks of yours, Valette?"

"No." She dusted her cheeks with blush to hide the real one threatening to overtake her.

Ronin laughed, a deep rumble that was far sexier than it had any right to be. "Don't worry. I don't have any more desire to touch you down there than you do me. I'll abide by your rules."

She'd pretended so many times before, through all the unwanted but necessary pawing she'd been subjected to from her marks. Her body was a tool she wielded with exacting precision, whether onstage or on assignment. Attraction had never been part of the equation. At least not for her.

This assignment, however, was precariously different. If she ceded an ounce of power to Ronin, let him see just how much he affected her, the consequences could be disastrous.

She'd be damned if she let yet another male stomp through the broken shards inside her chest.

Time to nip this stupid crush in the bud and put up some boundaries.

"Also, since I am the senior agent on the assignment—"

"I'm not an agent at all."

"Don't remind me," she mumbled, then raised her voice, lacing it with all the authority she could muster. "And *don't* interrupt me. Since I am the senior agent on this assignment, you'll do what I tell you. Do not question me, nor offer up suggestions. I don't need your input. And if you think I do, I *really* don't. If I tell you to jump, you ask how high then leap for the sky with a fucking smile on your face."

"Yes, ma'am." Ronin's grin had been growing throughout her speech and by the end, it was practically feral. She felt like she was missing something.

Makeup complete, she gathered her long fall of hair and began twisting it into a bun.

"Leave it down." Ronin's husky command prickled across her exposed flesh.

Her hands stilled as she met his hooded gaze in the mirror. "Why?"

"Because I prefer it that way." He crossed his arms, tugging a thumb across his lower lip, and her stupid wolf rolled over in submission.

"Did you not hear what I just said?" She grabbed a handful of pins from the vanity. "I don't give a shit about your preferences."

He prowled over, towering behind her, the radiant heat of his powerful body warming her back.

"Here's why you should." He reached an arm around her, snatching up the pins, and his breath caressed her nape. "If I can picture my hands fisted in these gorgeous strands, it will help perpetuate our little lie. People will take one whiff of my scent and believe that all I want to do, all night long, is get you back up to this room and bury my face between your legs."

She rolled her eyes, trying to ignore the scintillating heat unfurling in her core. "Fine. If something as simple as my *hairstyle* will make us a more believable couple, I'll leave it down."

She released her hair, and the coppery waves cascaded down her shoulders. Behind her, genuine hunger flashed through Ronin's blue-yellow eyes.

He inched closer, his soft dress shirt tickling her exposed back. "You can drop the hard-ass act this week, too. I can see right through it. You pretend you don't need or want anyone, but the truth is, you're terrified that someone might find out there's absolutely nothing beneath your ice queen exterior." He pressed his mouth against the shell of her ear. "But I can feel it. You want to unleash. You've just been waiting for the right male."

A blaze of molten rage tore through her. The fucking *arrogance* of this beast. "And you think *you're* the right male?"

"I don't want the job."

His words were a well-timed blow, shredding through hidden, vulnerable parts of her heart.

Why did she even *care*?

"Good." She launched her own volley. "We'll get through this assignment—because we have to—and then I can go back to pretending you don't exist. Just like everyone else on the continent after your wolf was caged and you became the nobody you were always meant to be."

"Bitch." He tipped his head back in a barking laugh. "Claw at me all you want. But by the end of this week, you'll be *begging* me to touch you. And not just above your ass and below your shoulders."

"Un-fucking-likely." She bared her teeth even as her useless wolf continued to pant and preen.

Dangerous. He was too dangerous. In more ways than she cared to admit.

She managed to get herself—and her wolf—under control, and side-stepped away, struggling to reach the zipper on the back of her dress.

He vented an exasperated sigh, then tugged her back to him and pulled her hair aside. He zipped her dress, his knuckles trailing up her spine far more tenderly than she deserved, given the vitriol she'd just spewed at him.

He turned her around, then bent down to examine her cheeks, which she knew were flushed from their argument.

Only the argument. Had nothing to do with his gentle touch.

"Perfect. You've got some color now and your breathing is heavy. The other guests might even believe we spent the afternoon enjoying each other before attending this party."

She gawked at him, certain he'd baited her into this fight on purpose, and she almost laughed in admiration.

He opened the door and held out an elbow, which she grudgingly accepted.

Then he ushered her out of the room and into their first test.

CHAPTER SEVENTEEN

The greenhouse on the Otto estate was a sprawling glass and metal structure topped with a central dome, and, rumor had it, outfitted with rare botanical specimens from across the Ethyrian continent.

Mireille was bursting at the seams with excited curiosity. There were plants in here that she'd never even seen in real life, had only read about in books.

"You ready?" Ronin paused outside the entrance. A symphony of tinkling glasses, shrieking laughter, and hearty conversation played beyond the doors.

Mireille's assignments had always felt similar to her ballet performances. They were a chance to be someone else for a night. A chance to shed her baggage. A chance to get out of her own head.

And though this assignment was a bit different—she was playing herself, or at least some heightened version of herself—that familiar thrill fluttered through her stomach.

Tonight, she was *Mireille Valette*. Prima ballerina and badass bitch.

"Ready." She squared her shoulders, and Ronin pushed open the doors.

The humidity sighed over her, tightening her scalp as they stepped across the threshold. The greenhouse was kept warm by magical means to protect the plants from Kheimos's inhospitable conditions.

She'd planned for the heat. Her silky, aquamarine cocktail dress—the color chosen specifically to match Ronin's tattoos—was sleeveless and dipped into a vee at her sternum. The mid-length skirt fluttered around her shins as they walked into the party. Sweat bloomed on the back of her neck, and she cursed herself for letting Ronin talk her into leaving her hair down.

A small balcony overlooked a ring of stone pavers surrounding several rows of rose bushes, each one dripping with fluffy, baby blue blooms.

She leaned closer to Ronin. "Did you know that blue roses don't actually exist in nature? They appear in so many other colors: red, white, yellow, pink, peach, even purple. But not blue. I wonder how Otto's achieved such a beautiful color. Do you think he's treating the soil?"

Ronin shook his head, staring down at her. "Nerd."

"What?"

"Nothing. Just curious if this is the kind of information you're going to regale me with all night. We're not supposed to be studying the plants. We're supposed to be studying Otto and the guests."

Mireille glared at him. "I know that. But there are plants in this building that haven't thrived on the continent in centuries. Aren't you the least bit curious?"

He shrugged. "Not really. Plants aren't the type of

thing that turns me on. Now *that,* however…" He gestured toward a Fae female standing near the low iron fence ringing the rose bushes. She was in quiet conversation with a male, her black and white hair twisted into two buns atop her head. Her dress wasn't much more than a series of carefully-arranged strips around her chest and hips.

Mireille snorted. "You *would* be the type of male that gets turned on by a mark. Be careful with that one, though. Layla Fetar would sooner slit your throat than let you get close enough to fuck her for information. Not to mention, she's already tried to have you killed."

"I do *love* the violent ones." He gripped Mireille's hand and led her down the wrought-iron staircase into the heart of the party. He swiped a Delirium from the tray of a passing waiter, then cracked the cap off with his teeth. She watched the muscles of his throat work as he drained the bottle and tossed it onto a side table.

"Is that a good idea?"

"Back off, narc," he grumbled.

She was about to protest, to order him to slow down, but there was an edge of desperation to his tone that she didn't want to exacerbate.

As they stepped further into the crowd, several heads turned their way, followed by low whispers.

"The Butcher of Aethalia is here."

"…heard they caged his wolf…"

"…odd sort of couple. I wonder how long they've been together…"

"…far more beautiful up close…"

Mireille smiled to herself before realizing that last comment could have been aimed at either of them.

Ronin plucked up another Delirium and Mireille

tensed, though she didn't scold him. Nor did she protest when he grabbed a glass of sparkling pink wine and pressed it into her hand.

Popping bubbles tickled her nose. The drink smelled sweeter than she'd anticipated, like berries and burnt sugar. She took a tentative sip. Delicious. And far too tempting.

She supposed she could say the same about the male standing next to her, sipping his Delirium with a hand resting above the swell of her ass. And just inside the line of her rules.

The conversation around them dampened, and Mireille tilted her gaze toward the balcony.

Otto had arrived.

The Deathstalker was dressed in a tight white suit embroidered with prancing horses. He surveyed his silent guests as he curled long black fingernails over the railing. His popped fangs ruined the intended effect of his warm smile.

"Friends, welcome to the Otto estate!"

The crowd clapped, throwing nervous glances at each other.

"Or the Cathedral of Bones, as some of you so cheekily refer to it." Otto dipped his head, emitting a laugh that sounded more like a hiss. Several of the braver guests chuckled along with him. "We are sure you are all wondering why you've been invited here."

Ronin circled his thumb against Mireille's back, a casually intimate gesture. It was making it hard for her to focus on their host. She darted her eyes to Ronin, but his were glued to Otto.

"We assure you that all will be revealed in due time.

And if you make it to the end of the week, your minds will be opened, your hearts will be changed, and your souls will be invigorated. It will be an empowering journey, to be sure!"

Ronin tensed beside her, hid it with a sip of his Delirium.

"Here, here!" A Beastrunner male with a shaggy black mane saluted with a glass of the same sparkling pink wine Mireille was drinking. Otto bowed in recognition of the toast.

The crowd murmured excitedly, but a pit of dread formed in Mireille's stomach. Clearly, they'd all missed the line *make it to the end of the week.*

Otto clasped his hands in front of his stomach. "The theme of this week is stories. The stories we've been told, the stories we tell each other. Even the stories we tell ourselves."

His eyes flicked to Mireille, and she fought the urge to flinch.

"Throughout the course of our week together, we will endeavor to turn those stories upside down and inside out, an attempt to decipher that which is real and that which is illusion. Delusion, even. The first story begins at sunrise. Until then, please enjoy yourselves." Otto lifted his hands and his gaze toward the ceiling. "Praise the High Gods!"

Mireille thought she caught a hint of sarcasm in Otto's final proclamation, but the crowd echoed him, raising their glasses, then turned back to each other to continue their revelry.

"Odd welcome," Ronin whispered as Otto descended the stairs.

"Yes," Mireille responded, twirling the stem of her wineglass. "We'll focus on mingling and listening tonight. Converse with a few of the guests. We can't approach Otto himself yet and too obviously press our intentions. Let's start with—"

She nearly dropped her glass as Ronin dragged her toward their host.

"Otto!"

So much for subterfuge and subtlety. And was Ronin seriously disobeying her already?

Otto swiveled toward Ronin, his black hair gleaming beneath ribbons of bioluminescent moss strung between the trees. His lavender lips turned down ever so slightly before spreading into an amused smile as he slithered toward them, Julius Kosera a hulking shadow at his back.

"The Butcher of Aethalia," Otto said, his voice fizzy and sibilant. "So pleased that you were able to join us."

Ronin towered over the Deathstalker—he towered over pretty much everyone at the party save Kosera—and extended a tattooed hand towards him. Otto shook it with a limp wrist.

"Where my female goes, I go." Ronin nudged Mireille's elbow, encouraging her to shake Otto's hand as well. Something bloomed in her chest—something she refused to acknowledge—when Ronin called her his *female*.

Otto's hands were cold, his knuckles bulbous and flaky. As if he were molting.

"We are, of course, even more pleased that *you* were able to join us, dear." Otto's forked tongue poked out, catching Mireille's scent. He dragged his eyes down her dress and she shocked herself by instinctually pressing further into Ronin.

The foursome remained silent for an awkwardly long time, Kosera grimacing at Ronin while Otto regarded Mireille with heated curiosity.

She nearly jumped out of her skin when Ronin ran a hand down her hair, tangling his fingers through the strands. "She is lovely, isn't she? I don't know what she sees in a brute like me."

"Indeed," Otto mused. Kosera grunted in agreement as his boss turned to Mireille. "Well, if you find yourself needing a break from your *brute*, come find us. We'd be happy to show you around the galleries."

"Bet you've got some very interesting pieces in there," Ronin piped up, and Mireille had to stop herself from elbowing him in the ribs. High Gods, he was the worst spy *ever*. She silently cursed Skanisse for shackling her to him.

"Our collection rivals even that of Emperor Leonin Erabis himself. You let us know when you're ready for a tour, Mistress Valette." Otto inclined his head, then sauntered over to another group of guests.

Kosera didn't immediately follow. Instead, he sidled up to Ronin, crushing a fist in his hand and cracking his knuckles. "Well, if it isn't the *grand champion*."

Ronin huffed a laugh, smirking as he took a sip of his Delirium. "Don't tell me you're still bitter about our last fight, Greyhorn. That was what, three decades ago? I thought elephants were the ones who never forget, not rhinoceroses."

Kosera's beetle-black eyes glinted with barely restrained fury. "If I'd been able to shift—"

"But you weren't." Ronin squared off against Kosera, shoulders taut. Nearby partygoers cast curious glances in their direction, and Mireille placed a hand on Ronin's arm. A warning. "You lost fair and square. Go whine about it to someone who gives a shit."

Kosera smiled, chapped lips pulling back from crooked, yellow teeth. "You think you're so tough, hiding behind the rules in the arena. That's the only place a broken bastard like you could ever hope to win. Why don't you try me now? Fight me outside that ring and see how long you last."

"Julius!" Otto hissed from across the room.

Kosera glanced over his shoulder, snapping the thread of tension tightening between him and Ronin.

"Looks like your creepy boss needs you." Ronin smirked, gesturing toward Otto with the tip of his bottle. "Better not keep him waiting."

Kosera snarled. "Give me a reason. Just one. Fucking. Reason. I dare you. I'm watching you, Butcher."

"Enjoy the view," Ronin tossed off as Kosera stalked over to his master.

Mireille grabbed Ronin's wrist and pulled him down a narrow, leafy pathway into a shaded alcove. "Are you fucking insane? Did you not listen to a word I said earlier? Why are you trying to bait them *both*?"

"Relax, Valette." Ronin guzzled his Delirium, an infuriating portrait of nonchalance. "Those little conversations were all part of my plan."

"Yeah?" She crossed her arms over her chest. "And what plan would that be, oh wise and terrible spymaster?"

Ronin gazed down at her, still smiling to invoke her fury, his bottle dangling from his tattooed fingers. "Julius is a petty, ineffectual bully. Keeping him focused on his hatred of me will distract him from looking too closely at *you*."

Mireille's hands tightened around her upper arms and she pursed her lips. Not willing to concede that he was making…some kind of sense.

"As for Otto, he needed to see us together. I wanted to make sure he knew I wasn't scared off by his ill-advised plan to get rid of me at the fight last weekend. Plus, we need to keep stoking his jealousy. He's salivating over you already. You'll have him wrapped around your finger in no time."

"Marking your territory, is that it? Swinging your big dick around?"

"You noticed?" He grinned.

She didn't know how it was possible, but she flushed redder, even as she lobbed her retort, "Well, try not to trip over it while we go mingle."

"How are you enjoying the estate so far?"

The shaggy-haired Beastrunner who'd piped up during Otto's welcome—Nero Beruglia, an ocelot bi-form—eyed Mireille's cleavage with blatant hunger.

"We haven't seen much of it yet," Ronin said, tugging her against his side. "You?"

The trio were standing just inside the entrance to one of the pathways, Mireille's blue silk dress and silver scar glistening under the glowing moss.

Behind Nero, a jungle of monstrous leaves shined beneath three unique blooms cased in bell jars. Ropey green vines swirled around heart-shaped petals in varying shades of pink. Ronin wondered why they were underneath glass. He probably didn't want to know.

"It's fascinating, isn't it?" Nero burbled with excitement. "Such a treat to be able to see it all in person."

"Have you come alone?" Mireille's eyes darted to the heart-shaped flowers. *She* probably knew why they were under glass.

"No, my mate is around here somewhere." Nero waved his hand, his honey-colored eyes never leaving Mireille. "Probably talking the ear off some poor hostage."

Mireille emitted a polite, close-lipped laugh. "Are you two friends of Otto's?"

"Never met the male before in my life. Cecelia and I have been speculating for weeks about why we'd been invited."

"Do tell," Ronin chimed in, scanning the party. So far, Otto had been a charming host. He mingled with different groups of guests, regaled them with stories of how he'd acquired his art collection, ensured that glasses were full and food was plentiful.

It was all so fucking...*normal*. Which had Ronin completely on edge, waiting for the other shoe to drop.

"One of our theories has already been confirmed this evening. I wonder if you can tell what it is, Mistress Valette?" Nero offered a sly smile.

Mireille returned it. "Everyone that's been invited is either a Beastrunner or a Deathstalker."

"Not a haughty winged bastard in sight." Nero chuckled. "Curious, that, don't you think?"

"You've got something against Windriders?" Ronin asked.

"I think the better question is, why do *they* have something against the rest of us? Just because their elemental magic never faded, does that give them the right to preside over every single territory?" Nero leaned in closer, lowering his voice. "My family are originally from a town on the coast of Akti, west of the Icthians. If my grandparents are to be believed, our ancestors wielded water magic for millennia before the Erabis family consolidated their Imperial power and changed the fabric of Ethyrios. Not saying they were the cause of it fading, but the timing seems rather convenient, don't you think? How have all the other elemental magics disappeared except for wind?" He glanced out at the party. "I wonder how many other guests here would share a similar story."

Ronin thought back to what he'd seen at the Crystal, the small seed of fire magic that Mattias had possessed.

Nero sipped his wine. "I, for one, cannot wait to see what Otto has in store for us."

"What was it the staff said to us when we arrived?" Mireille placed her hand at Ronin's hip and his wolf shivered. "They hoped we would have an *empowering* stay." She turned back to Nero. "You think he's discovered something about the lost elemental magics?"

"If anyone could, I have a feeling it would be Otto. I suppose we will see, won't we?" Nero raised his glass, dragging his tongue along the rim in a way that felt ominous. "How did you two meet?"

She looked up at Ronin and he said, "It's actually a funny story. Would you like to tell it, love?"

He felt her pulse flutter when he called her love, relishing the effect he had on her. Even if she was too High-Gods-damned stubborn to admit it.

"But you tell it so much better than I do."

Ronin pinched her ass, a chastisement, and she buried her yelp in her wine glass.

"Mireille was my dance teacher."

Nero's gaze bounced between them. "Really? You don't look like the type."

"Dance is a useful skill for a fighter," Ronin said. "It's important to be in tune with your body, to know how to control it precisely. Helps you stay light on your feet, too."

Mireille looked genuinely impressed by his quick lie. And it wasn't a complete lie. He *had* taken dance lessons about a century ago for that very reason.

"Yes," Ronin continued, tucking Mireille under his arm, "she was so impressed by my skills on the dance floor that she practically begged me to take her out dancing for real."

"Come now," Mireille piped up with that mischievous grin that did funny things to his insides. "*You* begged *me* to go out with you." She winked at Nero. "He liked the way I looked in the leotards."

"I have no doubt." Nero's eyes traveled down Mireille's body. "Perhaps you could give me lessons some time as well."

Who is this fool making eyes at our female? Ronin's wolf growled.

She's not our—

Eat him.

Wrath of Vestan, eating people is not the only way to solve a conflict.

But it's the most enjoyable way. Come now, fillet this imbecile. Save me his heart.

Trying not to laugh at his wolf, Ronin smiled, really more a baring of teeth than anything else. "I'm afraid her teaching days are over. I'm her only student at the moment."

Nero sniffed. "Pity. Perhaps a demonstration is in order?" He gestured to the dance floor, where a group of Fae were gyrating to music far more primal than the lyrical melodies that had opened the party.

Ronin imagined taking Mireille's hand and leading her into the heaving mass of bodies. How she might grind that tortuously perfect ass against his cock in time with the beat. How she might reach up and grab the back of his neck. How he might sink his teeth into her bare shoulder and run his hands all over—

"Maybe another night," Mireille answered. "If you'll excuse us, Nero. Pleasure to meet you."

She pulled Ronin further down the pathway as he fought to control his pounding heartbeat.

"The other guests are plenty distracted now," she whispered into his ear, completely oblivious to where his thoughts had strayed. "Let's go poke around Otto's wing while we have the chance."

He downed the rest of his Delirium, an attempt to dull the desire throbbing through his body, and nodded.

"Mmmm." He ran a thumb across her exposed collarbone. "You wanna sneak around with me?"

"You're ridiculous." She shook her head, but that gorgeous color rose on her skin again.

"Are you okay?" He took her wine glass from her. "Did you have too much of this tonight? You looked flushed."

"I'm fine," she snapped. "Just worried that now I'll have to teach you to dance so that when that pompous ass spreads the story of how we met, people will believe it."

"Oh, you don't think I can dance, do you?" Ronin snorted. "I *will* prove you wrong."

"Waiting with bated breath, Matakos."

The sarcastic look she gave him was nearly as tempting as her flush. He was starting to look forward to those looks.

"Come on." He grinned at her. "Let's go make mischief, *love*."

CHAPTER EIGHTEEN

*R*onin led Mireille out of the greenhouse, wrapping an arm around her to keep her warm as they crossed the patio into the main house.

It was dark and quiet inside, splinters of moonlight slicing across the checkered floor.

They hurried past the empty parlors, then took the staircase to the second floor landing before turning down the hallway toward the west wing.

A sense of foreboding washed over Mireille, and her wolf stirred—hackles raised, teeth bared. As if there was an enemy hidden around every corner and the beast was preparing for a fight.

Mireille rubbed at her chest, trying to calm her wolf as she followed Ronin down the corridor.

Otto's wing was even more ornate than the rest of the house. Colorful carpets with intricately-woven patterns lined the floors, likely purchased from artisans in southern Nephes. The walls displayed tastefully curated paintings of different continental landmarks. Mireille recognized most, but a few were completely foreign.

She paused before a beautiful landscape rendered in soft pastels. An opalescent palace stood above a field of white flowers. Due to the impressionistic style, Mireille couldn't tell what type of flowers they were. Her wolf settled, a peaceful calm sweeping away her earlier foreboding.

"Keep up," Ronin whisper-shouted from down the hall, his face half shrouded in shadow.

They crept up another staircase and came upon a circular landing with a single door. "We're in the west turret," Ronin murmured. "This must be Otto's office. I saw him watching from the window when we arrived this afternoon." He tried the handle. It didn't budge. "Guess that would've been too easy."

Mireille surveyed the small landing, then glanced out the window to the estate entrance. Down between the mountains, the city of Kheimos flowed like a spill of liquid glitter.

She unlatched the window and shoved it open, poking her head outside. This high up, the wind howled violently, whipping through her copper hair.

She brushed the strands away, then spied an open window to her right. Given the height of the turret and the smoothness of the wall, she didn't question why. It was damn-near inaccessible.

For most individuals.

She pulled back inside, then bent down to remove her heels.

"What are you doing?" Ronin grabbed her arm, forcing her upright. "You're not seriously about to climb out of the fucking window, are you? Dressed like *that*?"

She twisted out his grip. "You worried about me putting on a show for the birds?"

Ronin poked his head outside. "No, I'm worried about you falling to True Death."

Mireille shrugged. "I'm not."

"There's barely anything to cling to."

"There are pockmarks in the stone." She elongated her fingernails. "Just large enough for me to sink my claws in."

"Let me do it," he demanded.

Mireille straightened, hands on her hips. "You won't even fit through the window. Not to mention, you're twice as heavy as me." She dragged a pointed gaze down his massive form. "Gravity is not your friend." She shucked off her heels, then shoved them toward Ronin. "Here. Hold these for me."

Ronin took them, his face a mask of panic. Why did he care so much if something happened to her? And why did just asking herself that question terrify her? She needed to shut it down.

"Mireille, I'm supposed to protect—"

"Oh, please. Don't pull that macho bullshit on me. I'm not some fragile little female who needs a big strong male to do her dirty work. I've been working for the IA, by myself, for *centuries.* If you can't handle a little danger, just go back down to the party. Maybe start another fight with Kosera if you need to feed your ego."

Hurt scurried across his face, swiftly replaced by indignant anger, and she knew her blow had landed. Thank the High Gods. Better that than to have him looking at her with such care and concern.

But he crowded in closer, his jaw clenched, cradling

her heels in one enormous hand. "I am not going to let you—"

"*Let* me?"

"—do this. I don't care if you think you're in charge—"

"*Think* I'm in charge?"

"—there's got to be another way to get into that room. If you'd just give me a minute to…"

He muttered a low curse, reaching for her as she climbed onto the ledge and swung out into the open air.

THIS WAS A TERRIBLE FUCKING IDEA.

Her wolf's bellow was drowned out by the roaring wind.

Mireille's ice-blue dress billowed around her legs and her hair whipped into her eyes. Her arms trembled and her calves burned as she fought to maintain her hold in the pockmarks, digging her claws in so forcefully she was worried they might crack.

That open window had looked far closer from inside the turret. And the window she'd climbed through looked equally far away.

No turning back now.

She wrenched her left claws from the wall, and the wind tugged at her arm with such force that she nearly lost her balance.

Be careful! her wolf yipped. *You need to—*

If you keep screaming at me, I'm going to lose my concentration.

Her wolf growled low, but shut her yap.

Mireille tossed her hair out of her face, her stomach roiling, then dug her claws into the next pockmark.

She picked her way slowly across the wall, cursing herself for her overconfidence. What had she been trying to prove? There were a thousand other ways she could think of, even at this very moment, to try to get into that room. She'd grasped at the first option she'd landed on, like an overeager rookie.

She blamed Ronin.

He was messing with her instincts, turning her usual careful planning upside down. And now she was hanging off the side of a building in the middle of the night with her panties visible to anyone who might decide to exit the main house.

She smothered her frustration. Now was not the time to indulge it. She needed to *focus*. Needed to find her next foothold.

The wind picked up again, a fierce, soul-freezing torrent that had her pressing so firmly against the wall that she almost tried to grip it with her teeth.

Her frozen arms quaked, her feet cramping, and despite being only several feet from the open window, she wasn't confident she had the strength to reach it.

The wind died, praise Anaemos, and Mireille took a deep breath.

I know I told you to shut up, but I'm going to need to use your strength for this last push.

Oh? her wolf crooned. *And* why *should I help you after you scolded me, huh?*

Because if you don't, we're both going to be pancakes.

The creature huffed, but Mireille's limbs strengthened and enough power flowed through her muscles that she was able to make a final push.

She strained for the ledge, the claws of her left hand digging into the stone. She was going to make it.

Her feet slipped.

She bit her lip to cage in a scream, didn't want to draw any attention, and said a silent prayer in her mind to whatever Gods were listening.

She put all of her strength into her left arm, clinging to the ledge with her claws.

"Fuck, fuck, *fuck*," she hissed, her toes scrabbling to find purchase against smooth stone as she struggled to pull her body up.

Gritting her teeth, she surged her right arm upward, just barely hooking her claws over the edge.

After an agonizing, muscle-trembling pull-up, she managed to swing a leg onto the ledge, then hoisted herself up.

She stood on the narrow ledge, pressing her forehead to the cool stone as a hysterical laugh tore up her throat.

You are a crazy bitch, her wolf chuffed. *I love it.*

Mireille smirked, then reached her arm toward the open window.

A surge of energy shot through her veins, blasting her backward.

Time slowed as her breath whooshed out of her lungs, the free-falling sensation silencing her wolf.

She was about to die. Or be severely injured, at the least. In this stupid dress. On this stupid assignment. For these stupid males.

Another hysterical laugh bubbled through her as the wind tore at her body. She closed her eyes, waiting for the ground to break her.

She slammed into something hard, yet...*warm.*

Ronin let out an airy grunt, then stumbled backward, cradling her in his arms as they both fell onto the gravel driveway.

She sucked in a gasping breath, the movement bringing her awareness to every place their bodies touched. His hard chest rose and fell beneath her, and she swore she could feel every ridge and dip of his abs against her back. Not to mention a very considerable something pressed against her ass.

They stayed like that for several minutes, Ronin's powerful arms banded across her chest and hips. She didn't even feel the bite of the teeth-chattering cold, not with Ronin's radiant heat seeping through the thin silk of her dress.

She was about to open her mouth when Ronin shifted beneath her, scooping her into his arms and marching her through the front door.

The foyer was empty as he carried her into the front parlor, then set her down in a maroon velvet armchair beside which she spied her shoes.

He gripped the armrests, bringing his face in line with hers, caging her in.

His narrowed eyes blazed, though neither of them uttered a word as she studied him. The hard line of his usually soft mouth. The sharp cut of his jaw. The patrician slope of his nose. All combined into a breathtaking vision of wild, savage beauty.

Of wild, *furious* beauty.

A bolt of pure, raw need shocked through her.

She wanted to devour the distance between them, slant her mouth over his, taste his anger.

But she didn't give in to the foolish impulse, likely

inspired by the adrenaline still coursing through her veins.

"What happened?" His voice was a faint, guttural sigh.

"The window was warded."

"I gathered that." He pressed his lips together. "I meant before. When your legs gave out." His face was so close that his breath ghosted over her mouth. Had he been watching her the whole time rather than trying to get into that room?

"Foot cramp," she whispered.

His eyes scanned hers, but he said nothing further as he lowered to his knees and crouched at her feet. And began to rub them.

She didn't say a word as he worked, swallowing a blissful moan as he ran a strong thumb up her aching sole. He curled his fingers between her toes, loosening the tension, and heat coiled in her lower belly. *Fuck*, there was something so erotic about his calluses scraping across that soft, rarely touched skin.

"You know," he murmured, concentrating on his masterful work at her feet, "if you had just given me a moment to think through our options before barreling out of that window…"

"Don't start," she grumbled.

Ronin squeezed her arch and the pressure was so delicious that Mireille released a pleasure-soaked whimper.

His golden-blue eyes darted to her mouth. "I'll take a thank you at any time."

"The fall wouldn't have killed me. I would have healed. Probably."

He snorted a laugh as he plucked up a shoe. He cupped her calf, his warm fingers a brand against her cool skin, then slipped it onto her right foot. "One of these days, Valette, you're going to admit how much you need me."

He tucked her left foot into the other shoe, and she pushed up out of the chair, towering over his kneeling form. "Immortality is an *awfully* long time to wait." He dipped his head, snickering, as she vented an irritated sigh. "We're going to have to figure out another way to get into that office."

"Maybe you should try climbing out of the window again." He stood, a raven eyebrow cocked beneath his messy white strands. "That ward that blew you off the turret was probably just a one-time activation."

"Ass," she muttered, trying not to stare as he sunk his sharp canines into his luscious bottom lip to cage in a laugh.

"You were right about the show though." He angled his head. "Caught a glimpse of your panties as you were careening toward me. Black lace. I'm into it."

She smacked his arm but couldn't help a soft snicker. "We should probably get back to the party before anyone starts to question where we went."

"Well, if you walk in looking like *that*, I know what they'll assume."

Mireille stepped over to a gilded mirror and nearly burst out laughing. Her hair stuck up at all angles, a tangled copper halo. She smoothed her fingers through it, trying to tame the nest. "There was a black pad outside the office door. I wonder if anyone besides Otto has access to it. Do you think—"

Voices echoed down the hallway.

"Let's go," Ronin said. "No more scheming today, you reckless female. Weren't you the one who commanded we just spend tonight mingling with the guests?”

She huffed as she let Ronin lead her out of the parlor and back toward the greenhouse.

“Come on, Matakos. Where's your sense of adventure?”

Then laughed in earnest at his low, rumbling growl.

CHAPTER NINETEEN

*R*onin and Mireille headed out to the gardens just before sunrise for the first performance —an aria from the opera *Ignesh Tremani*, which translated to *Wings of Fire* from the Aramaelish.

They'd spent the last few hours mingling with the other guests in the greenhouse, Ronin watching Mireille like a hawk after her brush with death. He'd tried to hold it together after he'd caught her, but High Gods, he'd been fucking terrified. And *furious* that she hadn't taken even a second to talk through the decision with him before shoving out of that window. If he hadn't thought to go outside and spot her, and if she'd hit the ground instead of him...

He tried to convince himself that the only reason he'd been so scared was because if Mireille had been injured, if they'd been caught, then this assignment would be a failure. No uncaged wolf.

But deep down, he knew that wasn't true.

He'd pushed those thoughts aside as he watched

Mireille chat with the other guests, yawning the entire time, her eyelids drooping.

Several times, Ronin had almost said *fuck it* and carried her back to their suite to force her to get some rest. But every time he tried, she refused. Said they needed to stay and observe, despite learning nothing useful.

Well, Ronin had learned something—Mireille worked herself way too hard. And was far too willing to risk her safety for a job. He was starting to realize that in addition to protecting her from Otto, he should also be protecting her from *herself*.

Outside in the gardens, an arrangement of chairs was set upon the flagstone patio. A flaming wooden arch carved into the shape of wings stood in front of them, surrounded by three ice sculptures—the ones Ronin had seen from their window yesterday.

In one sculpture, the High God Anaemos soared for the sky, wings outstretched.

In another, he brandished a lit spear, his arm cocked back moments before release.

In the final sculpture, he floated to the ground, wings aflame behind him.

It was a familiar story, one in which every young Fae had been indoctrinated since the Empire had come into power.

The myth claimed that though Anaemos's wings had ignited, they hadn't been destroyed. A gift from the grateful sun to the High God for blooming it into existence.

Ronin was pretty sure it was bullshit. Though he didn't quite believe Selene's tales about where the Fae had come from either, that they'd been created by Adelphinae along with the humans and all other life on Ethyrios eons ago.

As Ronin passed a sculpture, Mireille shivering beneath his arm, the air warmed. Otto must have erected some kind of shield around the performance space so the spectators wouldn't freeze.

Good thing for Mireille, who still wore nothing but that sleeveless blue dress that would certainly be imprinted on Ronin's brain for months. Years, maybe.

Excited, drowsy whispers rippled through the expectant guests as Ronin and Mireille settled into the back row.

Otto entered through the hedge maze wearing a vibrant suit covered in swirling flames with a regal Beastrunner female on his arm. The skirt of her elaborate gown fluttered in petals of lemon, apricot, and persimmon.

Gasps hissed through the guests as Otto positioned her before the flaming arch, and Mireille let out a joyous little squeak, gripping Ronin's thigh. He may have edged in closer.

"Do you know who that is?" she whispered, nearly vibrating.

"Should I?"

"That's Odelle Carmina, the most legendary mezzo-soprano to sing with the Imperial Opera. Though she hasn't been seen publicly in years. I wonder how Otto persuaded her to come out of retirement."

Ronin bit his cheek to suppress a laugh. Mireille got excited about so few things, but when she did, her silver eyes burned and her skin flushed.

He wouldn't mind seeing that flush more often.

A teasing smirk graced his lips, though secretly, he delighted in *her* delight. "Like I said before. Nerd."

Mireille scoffed. "I'm not a nerd just because I appreciate the *arts*, Matakos."

"No," Ronin cocked his head thoughtfully. "I guess that's not the only reason you're a nerd."

She elbowed him in the ribs, and he threw an arm around her shoulder. His wolf chuffed affectionately as she relaxed against him.

Otto patted Diva Carmina's hand, then addressed the crowd.

"Friends and fellow Fae," he began, sweeping his viper's eyes across the gathered partygoers, "welcome to the first of our stories. This morning's performance of the famous aria *Iae Tombilae, Iae Nost Thanatem Sompros* from the thrilling opera *Ignesh Tremani*, will be performed by a female who we're sure needs no introduction. Diva Odelle Carmina!"

Applause peppered the air, several Fae rising from their seats, and Ronin whispered into Mireille's ear, "What does that mean?"

Her lips grazed his cheek as she answered him, and his wolf bounded across his heart. "*That Which Falls is Not Always Fallen.* It's the finale, occurs just after Anaemos has fallen from the sky with his wings aflame. On stage, the aria is sung by a maiden spirit, a being who occupied Ethyrios during the Gods' Age. In the story, she heals his wings and he falls in love with her. The Erabis family claims their lineage traces back this coupling. They insist the color of their wings proves it—scorched black with the iridescence of solar fire."

Otto continued, "The remaining two performances will be revealed as our time together marches along." He preened, drinking in the attention as jubilant murmurs flitted through the crowd. "Now, sit back, relax and enjoy what is sure to be a stirring rendition of the aria by the most celebrated voice in the history of Ethyrios!" He bowed to Diva Carmina, then took his seat in the front row.

The diva returned a subtle nod, then fluffed out her skirt, settled her stance and placed her hands at her diaphragm.

She had the ethereal, graceful beauty that all Fae nearing the end of their centuries-long existence possessed. Fae aged much slower than humans, and it was only in their post-millennial years that they began to show signs of mortality: graying hair, wrinkled skin, a slow stiffness of movement.

Standing proud and tall, her chestnut eyes landed on Ronin, and an unexpected dread settled upon him. He had no idea where it had come from. The diva's gaze revealed no hint of emotion beyond contentment.

He shifted in his seat, nerves prickling, and she stared at him for so long that he wondered if she'd forgotten the words.

Then the rising sun broke across the horizon, casting bands of salmon across the snow-covered fields, and Diva Odelle Carmina opened her mouth.

MIREILLE HAD HEARD this aria performed live a number of times, mostly by traveling companies visiting the Grand Ethyrian.

But nothing prepared her for the sound that wavered through Diva Carmina's lips as the sun crested.

The first plaintive note, held for an impossibly long time, showcased the spirit maiden's horror upon seeing her beloved High God plummet to the ground, wings aflame.

There were only a handful of performers capable of the notoriously difficult introduction. And even fewer who could manage it with perfect pitch.

The diva not only achieved it, but also imbued the opening with heart-wrenching shades of shock and longing.

It took Mireille's breath away.

Her eyes stung and her throat burned as she tried to remember when she had last heard such beautiful music.

She swiped away embarrassing tears, then noticed Ronin, of all people, doing the same.

He shrugged through a watery smile, and some hard, ice-cold part of her melted.

So the beast did appreciate *some* culture.

She nestled closer, and he squeezed her shoulder in recognition of the soul-stirring performance.

Diva Carmina continued with the aria, a master technician who hit every note with otherworldly precision. But far more arresting than her technical skill was the diva's ability to infuse each phrase with so much genuine emotion, one might assume she was the spirit maiden herself reborn.

She held the crowd within her enchanting spell for the full ten minutes of the aria.

As she built toward the climax, a gauntlet of octave jumps and glissando scales, she barely took a breath until she reached the final line.

"Raetyndra meos, amaternum mei." A cracked whisper borne on a puff of wind.

"What does that mean?" Ronin whispered in Mireille's ear, as though he was desperate to learn the answer.

Mireille's voice broke, and she could've sworn she heard him return a stifled sob at her answer. "Return to me, my eternal love."

Diva Carmina held her anguished face for a moment longer, then her lips parted into a dazzling smile as the spectators surged to their feet, cheering and whistling.

Otto rose from his seat, clapping and shaking his head in awe.

"Bravo, *bravo!*" He clasped one of the diva's hands. "Ethyrios is not worthy of such a spectacular treasure."

Diva Carmina demurred, bobbing a curtsy to the eccentric old billionaire.

They smiled at each other, the nascent sunrise gilding them in a shimmering halo.

Otto slashed out with his other hand, the steel within catching the light.

The diva's eyes widened as Otto plunged the dagger into her heart.

And the crowd devolved into terror.

CHAPTER TWENTY

orror coiled in Ronin's gut as the diva crumpled onto the flagstones.

He shot to his feet, shoving Mireille behind him. The crowd fled their seats, knocking over chairs, trampling each other in their rush to escape the gardens.

"STOP!" Otto shouted, brandishing the bloodied dagger. His command stilled the crowd, who regarded him with terrified eyes and stifled whimpers. "Calm down, friends. Calm down. Allow us to explain."

Mireille clutched at Ronin's back, poking her head around his shoulder. He could hear her pulse pounding, could scent traces of her fear.

Otto handed the dagger to Julius Kosera, who wrapped it in a handkerchief. "There is no magic without sacrifice. No divine blessings without proof that we are willing to suffer, even give up our lives."

"Did Diva Carmina know she was *giving up her life?*" Ronin snarled.

Otto turned to him, his eyes glittering with sick

amusement. "No. She did not. But her death will not be in vain, this we promise you."

"Sick bastard," Mireille whispered against Ronin's shoulder.

Otto continued, "As gruesome as this act may have seemed, we assure you it was in service of a greater good. One that will benefit most, if not all, of you here."

The guests eyed each other warily.

"Long before the great war cleaved our world in two, there was a time when *all* sub-species, not just Windriders, were capable of wielding elemental magics. Water, lightning, even fire. We have researched for centuries, traveled the continent in search of a way to restore these powers. And lucky for you, we believe we have found a method to do just that."

Mireille squeezed Ronin's shoulder, her nails digging into his flesh.

"Each performance this week is intended to dishonor the false *High Gods*. A message sent to the true Creator, Adelphinae. And after the final one, she will bless us all with a transformation."

"How do you know it will work?" Nero Beruglia shouted.

"We don't," Otto shrugged. "But the potential reward is worth the risk, do you not agree?"

Mireille stepped out from behind Ronin. "Tell us how you plan to achieve this. You owe us that much."

Otto's fangs popped. "We owe you *nothing*. You have all come here willingly, availed yourselves of our food and drink and hospitality. Just witnessed the greatest performance of that aria that anyone in Ethyrios has ever seen. And those of you that leave this estate will return to your daily lives as some of the most powerful Fae on the continent. Are you not sick of being subjected to rule by the Windriders? Do you not agree that it is time we Beastrunners and Deathstalkers leveled the playing field?" Murmurs rippled across the crowd. "We do apologize for the shock. Take some time to think. Rest up and relax. Our next event will take place on Thursday at sunset. You'll receive further details that morning."

Ronin wondered how many guests would even still be here by Thursday.

The crowd filed out of the gardens, and the human staff herded them back into the house.

"Breakfast will be delivered to your rooms presently," Otto called out from underneath the smoldering arch. "Thank you for your attention and attendance!"

Ronin and Mireille followed the guests back into the house, then headed up to their room.

He ushered her in, and as soon as he shut the door, she whirled, her eyes darting wildly.

"We need to get the fuck out of here."

"Now hang on a minute." Ronin stepped forward as if to touch her, calm her.

She couldn't stomach the kindness, took a giant step backwards.

He paused, something like hurt mixed with exasperation flitting across his face.

He plopped into a leather armchair by the fireplace. "Let's talk this through before you make any more impulsive decisions."

"Impulsive decisions? Otto just *murdered* Odelle Carmina."

Ronin rested his elbows on his knees. "Is that really a shock to you? Do you think Larissa Bisere is just having a fucking tea party somewhere on this estate?"

"We need to contact Skanisse and get more reinforcements up here. This is bigger than you and I can handle on our own."

She sank into the chair opposite Ronin, his face full of grave intensity. "I will not let him harm you, Mireille."

High Gods, she actually *believed* him. And that was even more shocking to her than the murder she'd just witnessed.

A knock sounded at the door. "Master Matakos? Mistress Valette? We have your breakfast."

"Just leave it out there," Ronin barked. "We'll come get it when we're ready."

The voice chuckled, assuming far more intimate reasons for why Ronin and Mireille weren't answering the door. "Of course, sir. Just leave the tray outside when you've finished. I'll be back around to fetch it."

"Look," Mireille said, "I've dealt with plenty of killers before. This isn't my first dangerous assignment. But you know what's kept me safe and *alive* through all of them? My instincts."

"Oh, like your instinct to jump out of windows?"

She leveled an icy glare at him. "Something even more dangerous than we imagined is happening here. We need. To contact. *Skanisse.*"

"Fine." Ronin rose from his chair and strode to the nightstand to grab his commstone. He placed the violet stone beneath his ear, then closed his eyes and said, "Hugo Skanisse."

He waited several seconds, then said the name louder.

Mireille's anxiety rose as he continued to wait with no answer.

Ronin said the name one more time before ripping the stone away and chucking it back onto the nightstand. "It's not working. Try yours."

Mireille crossed to her side of the bed to grab her own commstone. Setting the cool stone in place, she closed her eyes and pictured High Councilor Skanisse in her mind, then said the male's name three times. The stone beneath her ear remained cool after each utterance, not warming in the tell-tale sign that the connection was about to be made.

"Mine's not working, either." She frowned.

Frustrated, Ronin carved a hand through his hair. "Otto must have deactivated them somehow."

"Then we need to get out of here," Mireille prodded.

Ronin shook his head. "I'm not leaving."

"What?" she reared back. "Why?"

He tilted his head, his expression inscrutable. "What did they offer you?"

An answer, Mireille thought. *The chance to know where I came from, to finally understand who I truly am.*

She'd have to find some other way to convince Skanisse and the Emperor to reveal the information. Or figure out how to track it down on her own. She'd gone this long without it, what was a few more centuries? And if she died here at the estate, it wouldn't fucking matter anyway.

But she wasn't about to share any of that with Ronin.

"Why? What did they offer *you*?"

His blue-yellow eyes blazed and she could've sworn the tattoos on his neck and forearms began to glow. "They're going to uncage my wolf."

"A big payout," she admitted with a hesitant nod.

"The biggest." He blew out a long breath. "And the only thing I've wanted for the last three centuries. And now that you know why I'm so *invested*, tell me what they offered you."

Silence stretched between them, thick with renewed tension. Until her sharp answer sliced through it. "No." She leapt from her chair and crossed to the closet, stripping off her dress and pulling on a pair of leggings, a long-sleeved shirt, and her wool jacket. "I'm leaving."

Ronin settled back in his chair, refusing to look at her. "Do whatever you want, Valette. Tuck your tail and run back to the IA. I thought you were supposed to be a skilled field agent."

"A *skilled* field agent knows when the game is unwinnable. When it's better to remove yourself rather than suffer the loss."

Ronin snorted, fist at his chin. "Never pegged you for a fucking quitter. I thought you were better than that."

His words stung. They should have been enough to chase away her *useless* sense of guilt at the thought of leaving him here alone.

She snatched her bag from the floor and stuffed her commstone into it. Her fingers brushed against cool glass.

She placed the clear vial on the table before him. "Veiling potion. The more you take, the longer it will last. The whole bottle is a twenty-four hour dose."

Ronin didn't look at her, continued to stare at the cold, empty fireplace, his expression stony.

She stood in front of him, hands on her hips, waiting for a thank you that didn't come.

So she slipped out of the room and shut the door behind her.

The hallways were empty, save a few dazed members of Otto's human staff, as Mireille dashed down to the first floor.

The parlors and sitting rooms were similarly unoccupied, the guests sleeping off both last night's party and this morning's shocking performance.

She was a bit surprised to find no one else attempting to leave. Had they all been seduced by Otto's mad promises?

She pushed through the glass double-doors, welcomed by a blast of frosty air. Rows of icicles hung from the cornice above, like dripping fangs in the morning sun.

She couldn't get Ronin's harsh words out of her mind.

Never pegged you for a fucking quitter.

She wasn't *quitting*. She was making a prudent decision based on newly revealed information. Ruthless fucking efficiency. If Ronin couldn't understand that, then best of luck to him.

Mireille slipped off the patio and into the gardens. The chairs had been removed, the empty flagstone square dusted with a thin covering of sugary snow. Wisps of smoke curled off the smoldering arch.

She aimed for the waist-high hedges beyond which she'd spied a path leading into the woods. She kept her footsteps slow, glancing up at the estate's windows. If anyone saw her, she needed to appear to be on a casual stroll.

Wending down the path, she tried to not let the eerie quiet spook her. She heard not a single call of any winter bird, nor the rustle of any other small woodland creature. Snow fell from spindly evergreens, swallowing every sound save her crunching footsteps.

She'd only been walking for a few minutes before she slammed into something hard.

The air wobbled, and she cursed softly, shaking off her smarting hand and knee. She flattened a palm against the source of the vibration. The barrier was solid, yet pliable, and as she tried to force her hand through, it molded around her fingers, stretching like taffy but not breaking.

Otto had erected a security ward around the entire estate. She scolded herself for not considering the possibility. Especially after she'd experienced the effects of his wards last night.

Following along the slight shimmer in the air, she paused every few feet to check for cracks or weaknesses. She found none.

And with each pause, her panic grew. Her wolf paced within her mind, releasing soft snarls and chuffs of frustration. Claws poked at Mireille's fingertips, her canines creasing her bottom lip.

She cracked her neck, breathing deeply and banishing her beast.

She placed her commstone beneath her ear. Maybe this close to the barrier, she could get a signal?

No luck. The stone remained cold and dead. She slipped it back into her bag.

There had to be a break in the barrier somewhere. Possibly at the front of the estate by the towering entrance gate?

She secured her bag, ready to make a run for it, when a deep voice boomed behind her.

"Where do you think you're going, little ballerina?"

FUCK HER.

Seriously. *Fuck.* Her.

It had taken less than twenty-four hours for Mireille to ditch Ronin. To decide she'd rather risk the wrath of Skanisse and the Emperor than see this assignment through with him.

Whatever they'd offered her must not be that enticing. And he realized just how little he knew about her when he couldn't think of what it could possibly be.

Had they offered her wealth? A position of power? Mireille didn't seem like the type of female who would care about either of those things. But maybe she'd been playing him all along.

She was so High-Gods-damned stubborn. And bossy. And independent to a fault. Ready to dash away without even having a proper conversation like a *good* partner would have done. He shouldn't have been surprised, given that stunt she'd pulled outside Otto's office last night.

He slouched in his chair, wishing the morning meal had come with a Delirium as he sipped his cold, bitter tea and tried to puzzle out his next move.

How would Otto react once he realized Mireille had left?

"Fuck," he muttered, dipping his head into his hands.

Go after her, his wolf piped up.

Why? She wants nothing to do with us.

Go after *her,* his wolf insisted. *Partners do not leave each other behind.*

That's exactly what she just did to us!

Are you five? Apologize. Grovel. Do whatever it takes. You cannot do this without her.

Thanks for the vote of confidence, asshole.

Ronin exhaled an irritated sigh. Deep down, he knew his wolf was right. If he had any chance of completing this bat-shit crazy assignment, any chance of getting the beast back, he needed to find the little she-wolf and convince her to return.

He pushed out of his chair, shrugged on his leather jacket, and went to hunt down his fucking irrational, infuriating, beautiful partner.

ADRENALINE COURSED through Mireille's veins in a tingling rush, a warm contrast to the breeze biting her cheeks and tossing her copper strands.

With the barrier at her back, there was no way for her to escape the massive Beastrunner standing before her, his arms at his sides and his fists clenched. Primed for a fight.

"I... I just... I needed some fresh air. I thought we were allowed to roam the estate while we're here."

"You're awfully far away from the main house." Kosera's voice sounded like boulders crashing together. "Why'd you come so far into the woods?" He stepped forward, her neck straining as she craned her head back. Wrath of fucking Vestan, he was the tallest Fae she'd ever met.

"I was..." Her mind spiraled, searching for a reason why she might be out here.

Every clever lie she'd ever spun eddied from her mind. She should have eaten breakfast. She was exhausted. And her mental state was in shambles after her near-death experience last night, the emotional roller-coaster of this morning's opera performance, and the terror of Otto's cryptic plans.

"Answer me, little ballerina," Kosera growled, crowding her further. "Or perhaps we should go see Master Otto together?"

"No," Mireille stammered. "Nuh-no. I came... I'm out here because I—"

"Needed an open space to practice." A familiar, sly voice bounded through the trees. "There you are, love. You weren't about to start without me, were you?"

Her knees nearly buckled at the sight of Ronin traipsing through the ankle-deep snow, his marbled eyes laser-focused on her.

Kosera whipped his head around, frowning. "Practice for what?"

"That nugget of information hasn't worked itself

through the guests yet? Mireille's been giving me dance lessons."

Ronin stepped casually up to Kosera, and even though the Greyhorn had at least half a foot on him, Ronin's presence loomed larger. He locked eyes with Kosera. *Try me, asshole*, his gaze said.

He'd gone mad. That was the only explanation Mireille could conjure. Kosera could shift, Ronin couldn't. If the Greyhorn decided to show them both exactly *why* he'd earned that nickname, she doubted Ronin could fight off a five-thousand pound bull.

Kosera surveyed the woods skeptically. "Doesn't seem like the most conducive space for a dance lesson, *champ*."

"On the contrary," Mireille piped up, stepping out from behind Kosera and placing herself between him and Ronin. "I've been going too easy on him. Wanted to give him the challenge of trying to keep his steps in the snow."

Kosera's brows pinched. "Bullshit. Show me."

Mireille swallowed, about to open her mouth to protest, but Ronin grabbed her wrist, running a thumb across the base of her palm. Lightning shot through her veins at his touch.

He shucked off his jacket, handed it to her, then pushed up the sleeves of his tight black shirt to expose his toned forearms. "Get ready to have your mind blown," he said, aiming a smirk at Mireille.

He stepped into a tiny clearing amidst a ring of trees, flurries tumbling around him, then closed his eyes and brought his palms together at his chest.

Kosera crossed his arms and cocked his head while Mireille said a silent prayer.

Ronin's eyes popped open, and he launched into the most ridiculous, unhinged dance routine she'd ever seen.

He swirled his arms, kicking his legs up and throwing flakes through the air. He leapt and crouched, slamming his massive hand into the snow.

At one point, he circled his arms above his head and fluttered his feet, moving sideways with his gaze glued to Kosera. Thankfully, he didn't turn to Mireille or she might have burst out laughing.

He spun and jumped and lunged, limbs flailing. Mireille had no idea what music he heard in his head. She struggled to find any discernible beat. But his movements were graceful and confident, despite the fact that he obviously had no idea what the fuck he was doing.

He skipped to the back of the clearing, took a deep breath, then raised onto his tiptoes—a feat in itself in his unlaced boots. Waving his arms in front of his chest, he ran forward, then leapt into the air, legs split, and landed in a crouch with his head bowed, breathing heavily.

Mireille jolted as a sharp clap echoed through the clearing. Kosera mashed his palms together as Ronin rose, wiping his hands on his pants.

"That was the worst dancing I've ever seen," Kosera said. "Don't quit your day job, Butcher."

Ronin's face fell, and the look of false dejection he aimed at Mireille had her choking down laughter. "I thought you said I was getting better."

Mireille turned to Kosera. "Now you see why he needs the practice. Leave us, please. I'm sure you could tell how nervous he gets in front of an audience."

Kosera threw his hands up and turned away, shaking his head and muttering obscenities as he stalked out of the clearing.

Mireille approached Ronin, waiting until Kosera was out of view and earshot, then doubled over in the most belly-clenching laughter she'd experienced in decades. Centuries, maybe.

Once her hilarity subsided, she glanced up at Ronin, who had the biggest, goofiest grin on his face. It was somehow even more devastating than his sly, charming ones.

"You are a fucking idiot."

He shrugged. "It worked, didn't it?"

"Was that the—"

"Dying cows from your dumb ballet? Yes." He rolled his sleeves down and she handed him his jacket.

She snickered. "Honestly, you weren't half bad. I might be able to find a part for you next season if you're interested."

They continued to stare at each other, something charged passing between them before Ronin looked away and dragged a hand through his hair to brush away the flakes.

"Don't fucking do that again," he snapped.

"Do *what?*" Her indignation instantly resurfaced.

"Run away from me. Make decisions without discussing them with me. We're *partners*, Mireille. We need to be able to trust each other or we're never going to get through this." She sighed, and he gripped her chin, tilting her face up and forcing her to look at him. "I mean it. If we disagree about something, we talk it out. *Work* it out. I'm seeing this through to the end."

Mireille scoffed. "Because you want to get your wolf back."

She tried to pull away, but he held firm. "Yes, that's certainly a very motivating reason." His eyes softened. "But it's not the only reason. Nor the most important. I'm supposed to *protect* you. But I can't do that if you don't talk to me. You're way fucking smarter than me. If anyone is going to figure all this out, it's you."

She wanted to throw his statement back at him. Protest that he was taking advantage of her. Letting her do all the work while he sat back and did nothing.

But even as the words rose to her tongue, they fizzled. He *had* made several breakthroughs down in Kheimos. Not to mention the quick thinking he'd just demonstrated with Kosera and his willingness to make an utter fool of himself to cover for her.

"Okay," she breathed out.

Ronin cocked his head, an incredulous look passing over his handsome face. "That's it? Okay? You're not going to fight me on this?"

"I… I suppose I can admit when I'm wrong," she bit out through clenched teeth.

He patted her cheek, then pinched her nose. "Based on how difficult it looked for you to admit that, I actually *believe* you." He bent down to examine her face. "You look exhausted. Come on, let's go back to our suite so you can get some rest before we find out what nonsense Otto has in store for us next."

"Wait." She grabbed his wrist. "You need to see this."

He let her lead him toward the barrier and she flattened his palm against the invisible wall.

Ronin sucked in a sharp breath. "What is this?"

"Some kind of ward. Probably what's deactivated the commstones. It's impenetrable. We're locked in."

Ronin vented a bitter laugh. "So *that's* why you agreed to stay. You still want to leave, but you can't."

He turned to walk away from her and she grabbed his hand again.

"No, Ronin, you're right. I'm not… I'm not good at

this. At having someone else to depend on." His brows rose. "I'm sorry I ran away without discussing it with you. I won't do that again."

She intertwined their fingers, and he dipped his gaze to the contact, his breath shuddering out.

"Thank you," she whispered. "For catching me last night. And for rescuing me today when I didn't deserve it."

He raised their intertwined hands to his chest.

"You *always* deserve it, Mireille." His face was intense. Sincere. "I'm not going to abandon you over a screw-up or two. That's what friends do—we take on the messy shit *together*."

A lump formed in Mireille's throat, and she dug the nails of her free hand into her palm to keep from crying.

Friends.

It was a concept she was wholly unfamiliar with. No one had ever promised *together* to her before either. She knew it was her own fault. Knew *she* was the one who'd never let anyone behind her defensive walls. And perhaps it was her utter exhaustion, but she could feel them crumbling.

Here in this snowy clearing, standing before a male that she had made far too many assumptions about, she vowed to try harder. To do better. To be a good partner— a good *friend*—to Ronin. At least until the end of the assignment.

"Friends." She shook his hand, then let out a tiny shriek when he scooped her into his arms. "What are you doing?"

"Friends don't let friends trudge through the snow when they're tired. And don't think for a second that I'm not going to force you to eat when we get back to our suite."

Mireille smiled against his shoulder, his leather jacket a cool comfort against her cheek. She allowed herself a rare moment to lay back and let someone else take the lead for a change.

She was surprised by how much she enjoyed it.

Mireille felt refreshed when she awoke from her nap.

Or at least she did for the split-second before glancing out the window to see the first bruised hints of dusk breaking through pines.

"How long did you let me sleep?" she grumbled.

"As long as you needed," Ronin murmured from the armchair, elbows on his knees, hands clasped beneath his chin. A chessboard, mid-game, perched on the table before him.

Anxious energy buzzed through Mireille's veins, and she shot to the bathroom.

She wanted to lash out at him. Ask him why the fuck he let her sleep so long. The stakes of this assignment were so much higher than she'd imagined. And now that she'd fully re-committed herself to it, there was so much they needed to learn. She should have spent the after-noon doing *anything* other than napping.

Chewing on her irritation, she scrubbed her face with

cold water then ran a brush through her tangled hair. Despite her annoyance, she had to admit she felt better. Clearer. As if the food he'd insisted she eat and the rest he'd encouraged her to take had lifted some invisible weight. The weight that had convinced her she couldn't do this? That she'd needed to run in the first place?

Such an odd thing, for someone else to recognize her body's needs. To know what she needed even as she pushed herself to the brink.

"You alive in there?" Ronin called out.

Mireille exited the bathroom, and as she sank into the chair across from him, he assessed her.

"Don't even think about it."

"What?" He moved a piece across the board, the picture of innocence.

"I got plenty of rest. While you were playing with yourself?" She gestured to the game.

He chuckled. "Gotta keep my skills sharp. My sister is ruthless. We have a decades long tournament going at the moment, and I am way behind."

A flutter stirred Mireille's chest. He continued to surprise her, this *Butcher* of Aethalia. So full of contrasts.

"Do you play?" he asked.

"No, I never learned. Where did you find the board?"

"Top shelf of the closet."

Mireille gnawed her bottom lip, her mind churning.

"Nope," Ronin said, popping the last syllable.

"Nope what? You don't even know what I'm going to say."

"I know *exactly* what you're going to say. But we can't go sneaking around the estate right now. While you were snoring away in dreamland, this arrived."

Ronin handed her a cream card as she fought to

suppress her embarrassment. Had she been snoring? She was amazed she'd let herself be that vulnerable in front of him, to sleep that deeply.

When she slept next to her marks, she'd lie on the edge of wakefulness the whole night. Even if she managed to drift off, not a single mark had survived long enough to mention her snoring.

As if he could read every twitch of her face, he added, "Don't worry. It was less snoring and more a delicate whistling noise. Like an off-key clarinet. Fucking adorable."

She blushed, glancing down at the card. Printed in swooping script, it read: *Master Matakos and Mistress Valette - your presence is requested this evening in Master Otto's private dining quarters. A servant will arrive to fetch you at seven o'clock. Please dress appropriately.*

"Please dress appropriately?" Mireille snorted. "What does *that* mean?"

"You've seen the shit he wears." Ronin moved another piece across the board. "I think the technical term for it is *absurdist whimsical chic*."

She couldn't help the rumbling laugh that poured out of her as she crossed to the closet. She flipped through the dresses she'd brought, most of which she'd worn on previous assignments. "What time is it?"

"Quarter past six," Ronin answered, not looking up from his game.

"Are you kidding? It'll take me half that time just to shower. Why didn't you wake me up earlier?" She flew back into the bathroom to get ready.

Forty minutes later, she emerged to find Ronin waiting at the door with his back to her, dressed in a sleek black shirt and pants. Which he'd topped with a pair of checkered suspenders, of all things.

He turned at her snicker, his breath catching as his eyes traveled the length of her shimmering gold gown. She'd left her hair down again. Not for him, she lied to herself.

He continued to stare, his heated gaze a physical weight upon her body, stealing her breath.

"Ready?" she wheezed out, frozen in place.

Rather than opening the door, he prowled toward her. "You forgot a piece of your armor." His voice was low and silky as he tugged her across the room.

He wrapped his tattooed hands around her waist and hoisted her up onto the vanity, grazing her knee with his fingertips and encouraging her to spread her legs. As he settled between them, she had to restrain herself from wrapping her thighs around his waist.

He plucked up her lipstick and wrapped his hand around the back of her neck.

"Part your lips for me, love."

There was no reason for him to call her that in the privacy of their suite. Part of her wanted to scold him, maybe even tease him, but his proximity chased away her ability to speak.

She did as he'd commanded—trying to ignore how much she *liked* taking commands from him—and his eyes fell upon her mouth as he smoothed the creamy color across her lips.

His gentle attention was so different from the brutality she knew he was capable of. Such a contrast to the feral, caged beast lurking beneath his skin. She was certain he could hear her rapid heartbeat.

He placed the tube beside her, then pulled back to

inspect his work, running a thumb beneath the swell of her lip to wipe away a smudge.

Their eyes connected and all the air sucked out of the room, a magnetic pulse flowing between them.

He leaned in closer. So close that all she'd have to do was inch upward, and their mouths would be touching.

She settled her hands on his hips, and a low growl scraped up his throat. His grip on her neck tightened.

He poked his tongue out to lick his lips and she swore she felt it on her own.

Her muscles tensed, half of her wanting to close the hairsbreadth of space between them, half of her screaming that it would complicate her assignment. Her *life*.

Do it, her wolf whispered.

"*Ronin*," she breathed out, pushing up, their mouths grazing—

The quick knock at the door broke the spell.

Ronin closed his eyes and pulled back, a soft breath shuddering through his chest.

"Master Matakos? Mistress Valette?" the servant called out. "Master Otto is ready for you."

Ronin helped Mireille off the vanity, chasing away his heated intensity with a familiar teasing smirk. His go-to tactic to hide his true feelings. Mireille recognized the play, one she often executed with icy indifference.

"Guess I shouldn't mess up my handiwork," he said as he opened the door.

She huffed a laugh, grateful for the eased tension, as she took his proffered arm.

And tried not to think about how much she *wanted* him to make a complete and utter mess of her.

"How do you know how to apply lipstick?" Mireille murmured to Ronin as the pair followed the servant down a hallway in the west wing.

"Twin sister, remember? My *only* sibling. We were each other's sole entertainment."

"And what's with the suspenders?"

"Gotta keep up with our fashionable host."

Her lips curled into a tiny grin, and he tried not to stare at the outfit *she* had changed into. The outfit that had caused whatever madness had just transpired between them.

The glittery gold dress was practically painted on her, clinging to every tantalizing curve. From his vantage point, the scooping neckline offered an incredible view of her stunning cleavage, and the high slit down the front bared a shapely leg with every other step.

High Gods, what he wouldn't do to kneel before her again, worship those legs. But maybe this time, he'd throw one over his shoulder, kiss and lick up that sculpted thigh, slow and teasing until she was begging him to put his mouth—

"We've arrived," the servant uttered, dissolving Ronin's fantasy as they stopped before a pair of double doors carved into the shape of a curving snake.

He needed to clear his head and *focus*. This dinner would be a test of wits. They'd need to learn all they could about Otto's plans without giving any hint of their true intentions. Ronin would need his sharpest headspace to accomplish that. He couldn't afford to have it tangled up with thoughts of the varied and numerous filthy things he wanted to do to his partner.

His *friend*.

When was the last time he'd been just *friends* with a female? He honestly couldn't remember.

The servant swung open the door into a cozy, candlelit room. Beyond the round black table in the center, Ronin spied the other side of that stained glass window, the one depicting the High God Stygios on his throne. The second pair of watchful, serpentine eyes that Ronin would have to contend with this evening.

Their host stood at the window, hands clasped behind his back, wearing another suit that Ronin would definitely describe as absurdist, whimsical chic. As Otto turned to welcome them, Ronin noticed that what he'd thought were dots within the maroon-and-indigo paisley pattern were actually tiny skulls.

Not creepy at all.

"You may go." Otto signaled to the servant, who bowed then shut the door with a quiet snick. Ronin swore he felt Mireille tense, and he placed a hand at her lower back. "Ronin. Mireille. Thank you for joining us for dinner this evening."

Did we have another choice? Ronin thought, before noticing how Otto had addressed them. "Dispensing with the formalities tonight, Master Otto?"

"Please," their host preened, spreading his palms. "Tonight, we are simply...Jurgev."

Ronin bit back a snicker. He didn't think there was *anything* simple about the Deathstalker male who plucked up Mireille's arm and led her to her seat. The one closer to himself, of course. Ronin was forced to take the third seat on the other side of the table.

As she sat, Otto pushing in her chair, she shot Ronin a conspiratorial look. *We're in this together*, it seemed to say, and he offered her a subtle nod, returning the sentiment.

Otto slid into his black chair, then poured Mirielle a glass of red wine from a sculptural decanter. "We'd offer you some, Ronin, but we believe you have different drink preferences."

Ronin didn't miss the judgment in the male's tone as another human servant bustled through a hidden door and placed a glistening bottle of Delirium before him.

He slid his gaze toward Mireille, barely able to see her above the swollen bouquet of blue roses—a well-placed barrier that Otto had likely placed there on purpose.

Mireille's silver eyes glistened in the flickering glow of the candles framing the bouquet. And despite the low light, the pleading within them was crystal clear.

Please don't. I need you.

He could do this. He was *going* to do this. For her.

He pushed aside the Delirium, his wolf howling, and sweat dampened his palms. The mere thought of denying the elixir made the back of his eyeballs ache.

He nearly jumped out of his seat as Mireille's foot climbed his shin. As if she could sense his struggle and wanted him to know that she'd support him.

He shot her a grateful look before snatching up his wine glass and shoving it toward Otto.

"Actually, Jurgev"—he loaded as much disdain as he dared into the male's name—"I'd prefer wine tonight."

Otto cocked a thin, black eyebrow. "Are you sure? We've got plenty of Delirium. We find that Fae like your-selves who drink it often don't typically like to be without one."

Ronin clenched his other fist, keeping his eyes glued

to Otto and not casting them toward the glowing, seductive bottle.

"I'm sure," he gritted out through a tight grin. "If you've chosen red for the meal, who am I to question your impeccable taste?"

He didn't miss Mireille dipping her head, hiding a smirk.

Otto tilted his head, suspicion narrowing his eyes. But he kept quiet as he reached around the bouquet to fill Ronin's glass. "Guest's choice, we suppose."

The servant returned, setting down small plates of salad.

Otto gestured to the Delirium. "You can take that away. It seems Master Matakos is breaking with tradition tonight."

Ronin had to physically restrain himself from snatching the bottle from the servant.

Don't let him! his wolf howled. *We need that!*

You're gonna have to deal without it tonight, buddy, Ronin answered. *She needs us present and focused.*

His wolf barked out a frustrated growl that turned into a whine. *I suppose we can manage for one night.*

How magnanimous of you, Ronin added sarcastically. But to his wolf's credit, he settled.

Ronin took a sip of the wine. Of course, it tasted incredible. Silky smooth, but with a lingering roundness after the swallow that tasted of currants and oak. Divine. But not what he truly wanted.

He picked up his fork, and across the table Mireille did the same.

"So," she began, poking at her greens, "Jurgev. We're delighted you've invited us to dine with you privately this evening. But I'd be lying if I said we weren't curious about why."

Ronin noticed her emphasis on the word *we*. Proving to Otto that he and Mireille were a unit. Something fluttered through his chest at her insistence. Something that made his aching desire for a Delirium slightly easier to bear.

"We'd be a little disappointed in you if you weren't," Otto said with an indulgent smile that he aimed solely at Mireille. Bastard scooted his chair closer to her, and Ronin's wolf burbled a warning growl.

Ronin stabbed a sliced cucumber as Otto continued, "Since you two were a late addition to the guest list, we wanted to get to know you better. We've already researched the histories of the other guests, but we're afraid we don't know much about either of yours. At least, not more than the rest of Kheimos already knows." He winked at Mireille.

She offered a tight smile that looked more like a grimace, then crunched down on a piece of lettuce.

"Why don't we start with you, dear?" Otto hadn't even picked up his fork, his salad untouched. Ronin wouldn't have been surprised to learn that the Deathstalker didn't eat normal food at all. Maybe dined on the organs of his victims.

Mireille shrugged, her sparkling gold dress shifting in the candlelight. A portion of her coppery hair slid down her shoulder, and Ronin caught himself staring just as intently as their host.

Fuck, she looked even more radiant than normal tonight. There was a softness to her face that he hadn't yet seen. Was it an act for Otto? Or could their truce this morning have had something to do with it? Ronin didn't dare hope.

"What would you like to know?" Mireille lifted her glass to her burgundy lips, the lips Ronin himself had painted, and a small seed of warmth bloomed in his chest.

Otto's forked tongue darted past his teeth. "Start at the beginning. Where were you raised?"

"In a small village in Cernodas," Mireille answered, and Ronin noted how vague her answer was. A small village of *two*.

"And your parents? Where were they from?"

Ronin hoped Otto didn't catch the flicker of pain that darkened Mireille's gaze, the tension that stole through her body. She smoothed both out with practiced nonchalance.

"My mother was a Beastrunner. She ran a small school and travel lodge in our village. My childhood was rather uneventful. I left home at eighteen and came up here to Kheimos to dance."

"And your father?" Otto asked.

Mireille's fork screeched across her plate. She set the utensil down, then moved her hands into her lap. Likely to hide the shaking Ronin was sure had overtaken them. "I…"

"Mireille's father was a choreographer," Ronin chimed in, and Mireille shot him a shocked look.

"Is that so?" Otto's viper eyes bored into Mireille, examining every nuance of her expression. To her credit, she'd stilled her shaking, offered Ronin a dreamy smile. Just a besotted female delighting in her lover's thoughtful attention to her history. High *Gods*, it looked so real.

"Yes, he's right." Mireille scooped up her fork. "It was my father who taught me to dance."

"Anyone we would have heard of?" Otto offered her an expectant smile.

"I doubt it. He worked for a small company in one of the larger towns not too far from our village."

"What else can you tell us about your father?"

The servant bustled in to clear their salads. When he reached Otto's, the Deathstalker snatched a cherry tomato from the plate. He bit into it, and the juicy insides spurted down his chin. It felt like a threat.

Mireille reached for her napkin, then cradled Otto's face and wiped away the smear. Ronin tried not to howl with jealousy as hunger brightened Otto's eyes.

"There's not much more to tell," she said. "He was a Beastrunner as well. A stallion bi-form."

Ronin was in awe of how smoothly Mireille spun her lies. Though, he wondered if perhaps she'd already had this story ready. An invention to fill the hole in her heart where the truth of her father should have been.

"What part of the continent was he from?" Otto asked. "Not many stallion bi-forms are native to Cernodas."

Ronin could almost hear Mireille mentally cataloging the home territories of the other guests. When she answered, she'd chosen a territory that hadn't yet been mentioned by any of them.

"He was from a town in northern Nephes."

Otto may have been slick, but he wasn't completely unreadable. Ronin could sense the male's disappointment and confusion at Mireille's answer.

"Are you quite sure? How many generations of his family lived there? We've traveled all over the continent, and have never come across anyone from Nephes with the surname Valette."

Mireille took a gulping sip of her wine, but was spared from answering as the waiter returned and set down their main courses.

It was some kind of savory pie, blood-red juices oozing from the tiny holes in the top. Ronin held his breath as he sliced into the flaky crust, slightly terrified of what he might find, then loosed it when he beheld the contents. Just chopped, cooked beets dotted with flecks of white cheese.

He took a tentative bite. The dish was unexpectedly delicious, the earthiness of the beets offset by the creamy tang of the cheese. The crust was perfectly crisp and buttery as well.

"This is divine, Jurgev," Mireille said. "Do you grow beets here in your greenhouse?"

"We do," Otto answered before taking a bite of his own meal. "At this stage in our life, we no longer have the stomach for meat. All the meals this week will be vegetarian. We do hope that's not a problem, Ronin. We have heard you have a particular taste for flesh."

Bastard. Needling Ronin with his wartime exploits. But Otto was going to have to try a lot harder than that to bait him. He shoveled in another mouthful of pie, smirking at Otto as he chewed.

"Valette is my mother's last name," Mireille cut in, severing the building hostility.

"What?" Otto asked.

"It worked better as a stage name, so I used that instead of my father's last name."

"And what *was* your father's name, if you don't mind our asking?"

"Amiel," Mireille answered swiftly.

"Like Irina Amiel? The prima ballerina?" Otto cocked his head, considering.

"Yes, but I don't believe they were related. Or if so, it was only distantly."

"What a pleasant surprise that would be for you." Otto sliced through his pie, and a rush of crimson juice spilled out. "Perhaps that's where you acquired your talent."

"Perhaps." She dipped her chin, eyelashes fluttering.

Otto crossed his fork and knife atop his plate, then patted his mouth with his napkin, never once tearing his eyes from Mireille.

Ronin was beginning to feel like he were crashing *their* date. But he didn't think it would be wise to force himself into the conversation. For now, he was content to sit back and observe. Why the hell had Otto invited him to this dinner anyway?

Otto trailed a finger down the long, silver scar on Mireille's forearm. "And how did you acquire this? Rare to see such an ugly scar on a Fae."

"Oh, it's nothing." Mireille shivered as Otto continued to caress her skin. "Just a childhood accident. Got a little careless with a friend's Typhon dagger."

Ronin reached for the decanter to pour himself another glass of wine. Neither Mireille nor Otto glanced at him as he did so. He'd noticed Mireille's scar, of course. It was hard to ignore. But he'd never asked her how she'd acquired it. He highly doubted what she'd just told Otto was the true story.

So quickly that Ronin barely saw him move, Otto snatched up Mireille's forearm, then sniffed her scar. He ran his forked tongue along the puckered skin, and Mireille let out a breathy little noise. Otto whipped his eyes toward Ronin, victory flashing through them. As if Otto were winning a game that Ronin didn't even realize they were playing.

"Hmmm," Otto said. "We smell no traces of dragon fire. That tends to linger within scars caused by Typhon steel."

"It was quite a long time ago that I acquired it."

Otto blinked, his lavender lips parting into a sly smile. "That's one explanation, surely." He rose from the table, then offered Mireille a hand and helped her out of her chair. Ronin gulped down the rest of his wine before rising as well. "Thank you both for indulging an old Fae's curiosity. Dessert is being served in the main dining room. Shall we join the other guests?"

As they turned away from the table, Layla Fetar stalked into the room. "Jurgev. A word." She didn't seem dressed for dessert, wearing her leathers with her throwing knives glinting at her waist.

Otto nodded to Layla, then trailed his fingers down Mireille's exposed back as he guided her out the door. Ronin followed, fighting the urge to slap Otto's hand off her. "We will join you downstairs shortly. Thank you for the enlightening conversation."

Mireille gave him a shy smile as Ronin dragged her from the room, the double doors shutting behind them.

Once they were alone in the hallway, Ronin leaned down to whisper, "Well, that was—"

Mireille raised a finger to her lips, then gestured toward the doors. She pressed her ear against one and Ronin did the same at the other.

Layla's husky voice was low, but still discernible. "She's refusing to come."

"Why." Otto's short, sharp bark wasn't even phrased as a question.

"She said she'll only make the journey if *you* escort her personally."

"We cannot leave our gues—"

A metallic hiss sounded, likely Layla unsheathing one of her knives. "I could persuade her, if you'd like."

"No," Otto sighed. "No, that won't help. She's a stubborn old bitch, but she is essential to the next performance. She knows it must occur when the Scales of Nyctima grace the sky and the pathway opens."

"Does she often use blackmail to attain your company?"

"More often than not." Otto's response held a hint of begrudging respect. "We will fetch her. You and Julius must keep an eye on the guests while we're gone. Keep them entertained and...pliable. With any luck, we'll return from Listhima by Thursday afternoon with not a moment to spare."

Footsteps approached the door and Ronin grabbed Mireille's hand, rushing her down the hallway and around a corner. He poked his head around in time to see Otto exit the room, followed by Layla.

"What was *that* all about?" Mireille whispered. "Open pathway to where? And who is *she*?"

"I don't know," he answered, rubbing his eyes with his thumb and forefinger. His head was pounding, the need for a Delirium throbbing through his veins.

"And did you hear the name of the village he mentioned? Listhima. That's the village where anastasium originated. Do you think that's where Otto is from?"

"Guess we'll have a few days to poke around and try to figure it out while our illustrious *host* is away."

She nodded, lost in thought. "That was pretty odd dinner conversation, too. He didn't ask you a single question."

"Of course he didn't. He's obsessed with you." He couldn't help the bite in his tone.

She waved a dismissive hand. "Oh, please. Don't tell me it bothered you. It's the whole point of why we're here. Just think of it like your chess games. Moves and counter-moves, right?"

"I guess." Ronin chewed his lower lip, and Mireille's eyes darted there briefly, her cheeks reddening. The sight emboldened him. "How's this for a counter-move then?" He stepped in closer, leaning down to whisper in her ear. "Have I told you how beautiful you look tonight?"

"You haven't." She gifted him an incandescent smile. He knew it was more real than any she'd offered their slimy host this evening. His chest squeezed, his jealousy dissolving.

"You look incredibly, breathtakingly beautiful tonight, Mireille."

She dipped her head and hooked a strand of copper hair behind her ear, peeking up at him through her lashes. "I might say the same about you, but your checkered suspenders are ruining the effect."

He bit back a laugh then plucked up her arm to lead her down to the main dining room.

"Don't even try to deny it," he said. "You fucking love them."

CHAPTER TWENTY-THREE

"That was some fight the other night, Butcher."

Ronin tried not to flinch as the Death-stalker female seated next to him wrapped a hand around his forearm. On his other side, he swore he felt Mireille tense, though she didn't break her conversation with Nero.

The Beastrunner had made a beeline for her as soon as the guests had retired to the parlors after dessert. Nero had been chewing her ear off for the entire hour they'd been here. Ronin hadn't bothered to listen in—none of Nero's inane chatter had any relevance to their case.

Ronin had no idea why Mireille was humoring him—maybe out of some newly-found font of patience? Or maybe *she* was gleaning something from the conversation that Ronin couldn't discern.

He probably should have gotten up earlier, done his part to mingle, but he was afraid of what he might do if he left Mireille's side. A gleaming row of Delirium bottles beckoned from the credenza. But he was determined to keep his promise to her tonight. To not indulge his addiction. To keep his mind clear.

Plus, he was waiting for the rest of the guests to retire. He'd noticed something about this room during their arrival tour and wanted to scope it out with Mireille.

"You were there?" he said to the Deathstalker as she ran her sharp, purple fingernails along his tattoos.

The female nodded, her sleek sable bob shining beneath the crystal chandelier. "For one heart-stopping moment, we were sure you were going to kill Callum Maloney. Pity you didn't."

Ronin snickered softly. "Not a fan?"

Her red lips parted into a predatory smile. "We have been hoping for his defeat ever since he took down the champion of Nephes."

"Are you from Nephes?" Ronin remembered that the male currently drooling all over his partner was from a town in Akti. As were most of the guests Ronin had spoken with over the past few days.

"No. But we did spend a rather long and enjoyable weekend with their former champion," the Deathstalker purred, raking her serpentine eyes over Ronin's torso. "We're originally from a town in what's currently the Desolation. It was destroyed during the war, so we left. Moved up here to Kheimos."

Something hot and achy tore through his chest at her casual mention of the war, bringing to the surface his own memories. Without the numbing effect of the Delirium, his wolf thrashed against his ribs.

As if she sensed his discomfort, Mireille wrapped her fingers around the hand he'd left on the settee between them. His wolf calmed, the guilt and regret dissipating. He felt a surge of gratitude for his friend before refocusing on the Deathstalker female.

"Quite a different climate up here," he said. "Do you miss the heat?"

Her forked tongue flicked out to graze his cheek. "We find there are plenty of other ways to generate heat in the Northern Territories." Her eyes flicked to Mireille. "If you and your lover are interested... Have you ever tried venom-play?" She licked one of her fangs.

He fought to suppress a laugh as his wolf shuddered within him. *Absolutely* not.

"A generous offer," he said out loud, "but I think we'll pass for tonight."

She leaned back, disappointment dulling her pale green eyes, and shrugged. "Don't knock it until you've tried it. Enjoy the rest of your evening, Butcher."

She slunk off the settee and exited the parlor. Probably in search of another willing victim.

A few of the other guests followed her out. If Ronin had to guess, it was approaching midnight. He wondered if Otto had left for Listhima yet. Ronin suspected he had —their host hadn't shown up downstairs after their private dinner.

"Nero!" A high-pitched voice rang out from the parlor entrance, where a thin, severe-looking Beastrunner female with curly brown hair was stalking toward the settee.

Nero shot to his feet, jostling Mireille into Ronin. He hooked an arm around her shoulder, his fingers lingering on her bare skin.

"Ce-cecelia!" Nero stuttered, darting his eyes between

his mate and Mireille. "I've been looking everywhere for you."

Cecelia placed a hand on her hip, reaching out the other for her wayward mate and throwing a sharp look at Mireille. "Looking real hard, it seems."

Nero took his mate's hand, muttering apologies. He threw one last, wistful glance toward Mireille as Cecelia dragged him from the parlor.

Ronin laughed as they exited. "Nero better be careful. If Otto catches him fawning over you…"

"I think his mate might be more of a danger to him than our host," Mireille smirked.

Ronin swiveled his gaze around the parlor. There was one last couple lingering in the corner, a Beastrunner female perched in the lap of a Deathstalker male, his hand roving over her thigh, heads bowed in quiet conversation.

"The guests you've been speaking with," he whispered, "which territories are they from?"

Mireille didn't even ask why he'd asked, seemed to catch the direction of his thoughts. "They're all from Akti. Why?"

"That Deathstalker female I was just speaking with… she's from the Desolation. Doesn't fit the pattern."

Mireille grunted. "She looked like she wanted to suck you dry. And not your blood."

Ronin smirked. "Jealous, Valette? I'm surprised you even noticed, since you were so tied up with Nero."

She waved him off. "Anyway, the Desolation borders Akti. It could still fit."

"Do you think the locations signify something?"

Mireille brushed her hair off her shoulder, wafting her sweet, musky scent over him. His wolf took a deep whiff, sighing contentedly. "I'm sure they do. I just don't know what yet. We could probably figure it out if we could get into Otto's office." She released a frustrated grumble.

"The servants have access to the room."

She perked up. "What? How do you know that?"

"Took a little surveillance tour earlier while you were napping." He winked. "I saw one of the servants press his palm to that pad outside the door. That short, older man with the silver hair who distributes the breakfast trays."

"That's *excellent* news," she grinned. "I think I know how we can get in there."

"Veiling potion?"

Mireille shook her head. "No, the veiling potion only affects one's outward appearance and scent. It couldn't recreate his essence. I have something else in mind." She tapped at her lip. He felt a tiny stab of disappointment that the color he'd put there earlier had worn off. "Though it will take a full day to produce. Did you bring those Lethaphyll cigarettes Mattias gave you?"

Ronin nodded, but didn't press further as the couple in the corner finally left the parlor. As their footsteps faded down the hall, he pulled Mireille from the settee.

"Now that we're alone, I want to show you something."

She glanced playfully at his lap, cocking a sleek eyebrow. High Gods, he couldn't get enough of mischievous Mireille.

"Not that, filthy little she-wolf." He pinched her nose, then padded to the side wall, running his hands along the trim. "I noticed a door here when we first arrived. A servant dragged that blond man through it. Thought it might be useful for us to see where it leads."

"Good thinking." Mireille stepped up beside him, her gold gown rustling across the carpet, and began searching as well.

He pressed the wall and a soft click sounded as a portion opened, revealing a white stone corridor lined with dim sconces.

Mireille poked her head through, then retracted it. "After you, big, scary boyfriend."

He chuckled and ducked through the small entrance, Mireille on his heels as the door snicked shut behind them.

His wolf perked up, sniffing at the air and whining.

What is it? Ronin asked.

That scent again. It's far more concentrated in here. Death and...ashes.

Ronin shivered, scenting the smoky tinge on the air. He heard Mireille sniff behind him as well.

"What *is* that?" she asked, covering her nose. "It smells like burnt hair."

He swallowed her small hand in his own, his wolf pacing and growling as they crept down the sloping corridor. Their footsteps were far too loud in the dreadful silence.

Ronin paused at the corner, then angled his head around and sucked in a breath.

The vast, empty chamber was built from the same white stone as the exterior of the estate. Evenly spaced columns climbed to the curved ceiling like the rib bones of some gargantuan creature. Rows of stone benches jutted up from the floor on either side of a long aisle leading to an altar.

Diva Carmina's bare body lay atop it, two strips of cloth draped over her breasts and pelvis and two puncture wounds in her neck. Behind her loomed the strangest fireplace Ronin had ever seen.

The stone was sculpted to look like the skull of a giant serpent, its sharp fangs framing a charred pit.

As they approached the altar, Mireille let out a choked noise. "What a terrible, wasteful end for such a supreme talent. She didn't deserve this."

As Ronin approached the snake head, he noted a barrel behind the altar. He removed the lid, and pale blue stones glistened back at him. "Is this…"

Mireille leaned around him, her soft breasts pressing against his back as she cupped his waist. He tried not to let it distract him.

"The anastasium." She rounded the basket, bending over to examine the facets of the apricot-sized gems.

Footsteps pounded down the hall outside the chamber.

"Fuck." Ronin snatched Mireille's hand and rushed down the aisle in search of a place to hide.

At the chamber's entrance were two dark alcoves, each containing a statue of Deathstalker males who bore a striking resemblance to Otto. His ancestors, perhaps.

Ronin shoved Mireille into the alcove on the left. He nestled in behind, tucking her against his chest and placing his palms against the back of the statue. Her hair tickled his chin and her ass pressed against his thighs, tantalizingly close to his cock. He fought an urge to pull her closer.

Better cover her mouth, his wolf added. Unhelpfully. *She might scream if she gets frightened.*

She's not that kind of female, Ronin hissed back.

Still, put your hand there anyway. We want to know what her lips feel like.

Ronin's height afforded him a clear view of the altar around the statue's head. Two human servants—a taller man with shoulder-length, coffee-colored hair and that same older man with the silver hair who Ronin had seen outside Otto's office earlier—approached the diva's body. The tall man cradled the diva's shoulders while the other grabbed her ankles, and they maneuvered her onto the floor within the snake's mouth. The tall man plucked an anastasium stone from the barrel and placed it over one of the diva's eyes, while the older man traced a finger along a triangle etched into the wall beside the fire place.

Thunderous grinding filled the chamber as the snake's throat opened, two stone slabs parting to reveal a wall of flame. Undulating swirls of red, orange, yellow and blue oozed across the floor to caress and blister the diva's body.

Ronin's gorge rose at the unmistakable scent of burning flesh and hair, and Mireille covered her mouth, emitting a small yelp. She flattened herself against Ronin, who wrapped an arm around her waist.

See? his wolf piped up. *Screamer.*

Ronin shook him off as he watched the fire devour the diva's body.

The tall man traced the triangle on the wall again, and the flames sucked back into themselves as the stone slabs rumbled closed.

There was no trace of the diva left in the fireplace. Just a pile of ash topped with an anastasium stone, which was now emanating an internal glow.

The silver-haired man hoisted a shovel from a rack next to the fireplace to fish it out.

The other approached with a small, felt-lined box,

and his partner placed the stone inside, then flicked the lid shut.

Ronin held his breath, felt Mireille do the same, both afraid to let out a single sound lest the two men discover their hiding place.

He only released it once their footsteps had faded, and he and Mireille crawled out from behind the statue.

"What *happened*?" she asked. "I couldn't see anything, only smell…"

Ronin explained the triangle symbol, the burning, the glowing anastasium stone. "Does any of it sound familiar to you?"

"No…" She trailed off, but Ronin could practically hear the gears in her head turning. "But if the stone was glowing after, do you think the fire is what activated it? Is fire the source of Stygios's power?"

Ronin scratched at his cheek. "Seems too obvious. Wouldn't someone have figured that out by now?"

She shrugged, then yawned against the back of her hand.

"We'll do some more exploring *tomorrow*," he said. Mireille shot him a sharp look, about to protest. "On clear, sleep-fueled heads."

The corner of her lip twitched, as if she were about to argue, but to Ronin's surprise, she merely nodded as she let him lead her out of the chamber.

As they reached the hidden door to the parlor, voices echoed from the other end of the stone corridor and Mireille shot him a panicked look.

He pulled her into the empty parlor as the voices grew closer. Too close. They wouldn't make it out of the room in time.

Ronin crowded Mireille against the wall and cupped

his hands beneath the base of her skull, threading his fingers through her hair and tilting her face up.

As he inched his lips dangerously close to hers, his whisper was steady despite the rapid acceleration of his heartbeat.

"Be a good girl and play along."

Then his lips met hers and the world melted away.

CHAPTER TWENTY-FOUR

Maybe it was because Mireille hadn't been properly kissed in decades.

Maybe it was because Ronin hadn't yet given up on her. Had taken all her vicious barbs and thrown them right back at her. As if he enjoyed the challenge. As if he enjoyed *her*.

Fuck, maybe it was just because he'd called her *good girl*.

It could have been for any of those reasons, or maybe none of those reasons, why she curled her hands around those *ridiculous* suspenders and pulled him closer, sealing their lips together.

He pushed his tongue into her mouth with an aching groan. Like he'd been anticipating this moment as much as she had, desperate for any excuse to perform their fake roles.

Her wolf loosed a victorious howl.

He cradled her cheek in one hand as he slid the other down her body. Heat flared in its wake, too brief passes along the side of her breast and the curve of her hip. His fingers crept up her shaking thigh, slipping through the slit in her dress and hauling her leg around his waist.

"Mireille," he murmured on her lips, eyes closed, as lost in this show as she was. He dove back in again, drinking her down in tiny sips, savoring her with slow strokes of his tongue. Flavors of frosted evergreen and sugared lemon filled her mouth. Fresh and sweet and sharp.

Why in Ethyrios had she waited so long to taste him?

A moan slid up her throat and he hardened against her as his fingers coasted beneath her panties, squeezing her ass. So dangerously close to exactly where she wanted them. She released his suspenders, gripping his shoulders as he thrust against her, pressing her into the wall.

He broke the kiss, pinning her in place with a raw, heavy-lidded stare, then fisted her hair and yanked her head back.

It fucking hurt.

She loved it.

He nipped down her throat, across the mounds of her breasts. Jolts of electric pleasure zapped through her each time his cool, wicked fangs met her heated skin.

Fuck. Yes. *More.*

She panted against his soft hair, his fingers at her ass drifting lower as he bit down harder on her neck. A callused pad grazed the bottom of her slit, but before he could push in fully, find out how real this was, how wet she was for him, the hidden door crashed open.

The two men from the crypt strode through and her wolf barked out a curse. *Impeccable fucking timing, assholes.*

Ronin removed his lips and teeth from Mireille's

flesh, resting his forehead against her collarbone. As if he needed a moment to compose himself.

She tried to remember how to breathe.

Reluctantly, Ronin slipped his fingers from her panties, then rested his palm on her hip.

A hand appeared on his shoulder.

Ronin grabbed it and spun, angling the tall man's arm behind his back and baring his teeth against the man's throat. The servant didn't cower, his instincts dampened by whatever spell Otto had woven over his staff.

"Take your party to the privacy of your room, please," the man intoned. "The parlors are closed for the night."

A low growl burbled up Ronin's throat, the tips of his fangs digging into the man's flesh, nearly hard enough to break skin.

Mireille placed a hand between Ronin's tense shoulder blades.

Thank the High Gods, her touch worked. Ronin looked as if he'd been seconds away from ripping out the man's throat.

Shaking his head and releasing the servant, Ronin said in a calm voice that belied his earlier aggression, "We were just about to."

The man's gaze flicked to Mireille.

"It's true," she piped up, watching the hairs on the back of Ronin's neck prickle at her voice.

The man swiveled his head, the movement as slow and deliberate as a puppet, as he said to the silver-haired servant beside him who was still holding that small box, "Is that what it looked like to you?"

Ronin laughed incredulously, pulling Mireille out from behind him. "Take a good, hard look at this *stunning* female and then tell me you would have been able to wait to get her upstairs before pouncing on her."

His praise set her entire lower body on fire again, and if she were less wise, she might have even thrown caution to the wind, dragged him back to their suite, and *let* him pounce on her.

Ronin pulled her out of the parlor, and she could feel the men's eyes boring into the back of her head.

She winked at them over her shoulder, then blew a kiss as she and Ronin turned down the marble-floored hallway.

Once they'd reached the guest wing, Ronin leaned against the wall and dipped his head.

"I…" He scrubbed his hands over his face. "It was the only thing I could think to do in the moment."

Mireille crossed her arms over her chest, rubbing the spots on her neck and breasts where he'd nipped her. Trying not to think about how much she wanted him to do it again.

"It was good, quick thinking," she offered.

He stared down at her, a question in his eyes that she didn't yet know how to answer, then shook his head as he opened the door to their suite.

Mireille was exhausted. It had been a very long, very strange few days. And that kiss had just short-circuited her brain.

Ronin blew out an extended breath as she swept past him into the room. He struggled to find his words, and Mireille was simultaneously relieved and terrified that he seemed to be just as affected by their kiss as she was. "Mireille, I…"

She turned back to him, kept her expression as

professional as possible, and whatever he saw there stilled his tongue.

There were no more words exchanged between them as they changed into their nightclothes, then climbed into bed together, each keeping to their own side.

And though she desperately needed it, sleep took its sweet time claiming her that night.

It was chased away by swirling speculations on what, exactly, Ronin had been about to say.

CHAPTER TWENTY-FIVE

Mireille returned to their suite the next morning, cheeks reddened and blood flowing.

She'd woken before Ronin, had spent several indulgent minutes watching him sleep. His rhythmic breaths stirring his snowy hair. The soft curve of his plush lips. His tattooed hand rising and falling where it lay across his bare chest.

She had immediately decided that a run through the frozen estate was the best option to keep her from doing something *very* stupid.

Like pulling down those blankets, kneeling between his legs, and waking him up with her mouth.

The short jog had only partly helped. She'd wanted to let her wolf out—she was feeling a bit feral after three days without shifting; High Gods, was this how poor Ronin felt all the time?—but didn't think it wise to run around the grounds in that form. None of the other Beastrunner guests had done so this week.

Every puff of frosty air that left her mouth tasted like his tongue. But fortunately, by the end, the exercise had done what exercise normally did for her—cleared her mind, allowed her to focus on their assignment rather than on how much she wanted to tangle herself up with her partner again. Surely just a side effect of the lack of shifting.

She'd made a second pit stop on her journey as well—a trip to the greenhouse.

She had the bounty she'd acquired tucked into her jacket pocket as she strode through the door to find Ronin dressed for the day. He was seated in an armchair, their breakfast tray spread out onto the low table before him.

The silver serving platter was filled to capacity with a basket of steaming biscuits, two fluffy omelets, and crispy potatoes, plus a bowl of berries, a carafe of coffee and a pot of tea.

The delectable scents only served to make Mireille keenly aware of her hunger. She stripped off her jacket and plopped into the seat across from him.

"Good morning." Her voice came out far more high-pitched and squeaky than she'd intended, so she cleared her throat and tried again. "Good morning."

Ronin smirked, as if he knew exactly why she was nervous. But he didn't tease her as he filled a mug with coffee, then added two spoonfuls of sugar and a splash of cream before handing it to her.

She couldn't help the small smile that tugged at her lips. "You remember how I take my coffee?"

"Well," he said, his own lips turning up, "since you wouldn't share your kinks with me, I had to remember something."

She took a tentative sip of the scalding drink, the sweet, creamy bitterness releasing some of the tension in her shoulders, then dug into the omelet and potatoes.

"Fuck," she said around a crispy mouthful. "This is really good. Why do the insane ones always serve the best food?"

Ronin polished off his own omelet in three bites, then shoveled the entire pile of potatoes in his mouth.

Mireille snickered.

"What?"

"You eat like a wolf," she said, amused.

"Old habits." He brushed his mouth with a cloth napkin. "Where'd you go this morning?"

"Took a little jog to clear my head."

His grin exposed a hint of fang and her neck prickled. As if her body remembered just how incredible they'd felt on her neck last night. "Why'd you need to clear your head?"

She ignored his question, hoping the flush from her run was hiding the new flush blooming on her cheeks. "Who dropped off the tray this morning? The silver-haired man? Same one we saw in the crypt last night?"

Ronin nodded, plucking up a strawberry and sinking his teeth into it. High Gods, why did that look so enticingly obscene? Her thighs clenched, and she turned away to rummage through her jacket.

She pulled out a pile of soft pink petals, then spread them onto a napkin.

Ronin's brows rose. "I saw those in the greenhouse the other night. While Nero was drooling over you. They were under glass. I assumed they were poisonous." His eyes scanned her face, as if he were worried she'd inadvertently hurt herself.

"Not poisonous." The tension in his shoulders melted away. "But they are extremely prone to dehydration. They dry out faster than almost any other flower. They're called Bleeding Hearts. The dried petals can be brewed into a tea that makes someone…let's just say, *very susceptible* to suggestion. And if I mix in some of those dried Lethaphyll leaves from the cigarettes Mattias gave you." She brought her fingers to her temple, popping them out to mimic a small explosion. "That servant won't remember a thing after."

Ronin's brows rose further, a broad smile forming. "You're a fucking genius."

She smiled back. "Told you I'd surprise you one day, Matakos."

He shook his head. "You being a genius doesn't surprise me at all. Gonna have to try harder than that. When can we use it?"

"It'll take about twenty-four hours for the petals to fully dry out. We can brew the tea tomorrow morning and give it to our servant when he comes back to pick up the tray. And then persuade him to let us into Otto's office." Mireille folded the napkin over the petals, then hid the parcel on the top shelf of the closet.

"So, what's the plan for today then?" Ronin drained his tea to the dregs. "Where are we going snooping?"

Mireille turned back, smirking at him. "We're not going snooping, we're going hunting. For Fallen Goddess relics.

"Time to tour Otto's galleries."

RONIN'S FOOTSTEPS echoed off the flagstone path that led to Otto's famous galleries, a wide, white building that bled into the surrounding snow.

Beside him, Mireille was a coil of barely contained energy. He couldn't decide where it was coming from—the run she'd taken this morning, her excitement at touring a private art collection that barely anyone on the continent had ever seen, or…

Their kiss last night.

He certainly hadn't been able to get it out of his mind. More than once in bed he'd had to talk himself out of rolling over, grasping her soft body to him, and burying his fingers inside her. Doing some more rehearsing of their roles.

He'd almost confessed it to her last night. How he was feeling. How the lines between what was fake and what was real were starting to blur.

For him, at least.

The look she'd given him after that mind-obliterating kiss, all cool calculation and professional distance, had dissuaded him from revealing what was creeping into his heart.

They still had a job to do. He didn't want to make things awkward.

He jogged up the shallow steps to the gallery entrance, then hauled open the heavy door and held it for Mireille. He certainly did *not* breathe in her sweet scent as she swept past him, her eyes widening as she took in the high-ceilinged room.

Rays of cold sunlight streamed in through the glass dome, illuminating the statues arranged throughout the hall. From this center gallery, four archways led off into what Ronin assumed were other galleries housing the paintings and more delicate artifacts that could be damaged by natural sunlight.

"Well," he said, clenching his fists and trying to stop himself from putting his hands on her, "where should we start?"

Mireille didn't acknowledge him as she approached the colossal statue greeting visitors just inside the entrance. It was, of course, another shrine to Stygios. This one depicted the High God embroiled in a battle with his famous pet, Nyctima.

The serpent was coiled around Stygios's muscular—and very naked—frame, the High God's wrathful face twisted toward the creature. He was holding something against his pursed lips.

Mireille bent down to read the plaque at the statue's base, and Ronin crept up to peer over her shoulder.

"*The Taming of Nyctima,*" he read out loud. "I don't recall that myth, do you?"

Mireille's copper hair glistened in the sunshine as she nodded. "That flute." She gestured to the instrument in Stygios's hand. "The story claims he used it to call her forth from the depths of the planet. To mesmerize her, turn her into his reaper."

Ronin shivered as Mireille moved further into the hall. A few other guests were milling about, quietly appreciating the statuary.

Ronin hustled to follow, but she didn't stop at any of the other pieces. "Where are you going?" he whisper-shouted.

She halted abruptly and he nearly slammed into her back, placing his hands on her shoulders to steady himself. The heat of her skin burned beneath his fingertips and he snatched them back. He hadn't been worried about touching her before, but now every touch felt... *loaded.*

If she felt similarly, it didn't show on her face as she turned to whisper, "Nothing in this hall is old enough. Everything's in the post-war style. If Otto's got any artifacts from Adelphinae in here, they'd be housed along with more ancient pieces."

Her gaze caught on a small sculpture at the far end of the hall and she sucked in a shuddering breath. She stalked toward it, dipping her hand into the pocket of her long black cardigan.

If Ronin hadn't known any better, he might have assumed Mireille herself had been the model for this particular sculpture. The lines of the ballerina's limbs were just as shapely and elegant as her own, though the face was different.

Far less striking.

Mireille pulled something from her pocket, nestling it in her hands, her silver eyes glistening. He glanced toward the plaque on the wall. "Irina—"

"Amiel," Mireille finished for him, her voice tight.

"Who was she?"

"A famous prima ballerina who danced with the Imperial Ballet in Delos." She turned to him, opening her palm. The tiny ballerina figurine held the same pose as the statue before him. "This must be a replica of..." Her voice broke, as she held up the figurine. The paint was rubbed off in several places, the face cracked with age. A well-worn, long-cherished treasure. "This is the only gift I ever received from my father. It was in a music box he left for me when I was a child."

She'd never spoken to Ronin about her father before. At least not directly.

"He's the reason I'm doing this," she whispered.

"What do you mean?"

Her eyes filled with tears and Ronin's heart broke for her. "I never… He left the gift, but I never actually met him. My mother wouldn't even tell me his name. I've been seeking information about him for centuries. The Empire claims to have learned his identity. Skanisse is going to reveal it to me when we complete the assignment. *If* we complete the assignment."

As if Ronin weren't already determined enough, he now had an entirely new motivation to finish this job. To remove the centuries worth of grief he now beheld in his friend's eyes.

"We *will*, Mireille. I promise you."

She swiped a tear from her cheek, then donned a far more determined, and familiar, expression. "Let's go. We've got a lot more rooms to explore."

He shook his head as he followed, muttering under his breath, though based on her sly grin, she'd heard him perfectly clearly.

"Taskmaster."

THE REST of the galleries were much dimmer than the main hall, with cones of light spearing from small holes in the ceiling to illuminate glass-cased treasures and gilt-framed paintings.

A quiet peace settled over Mireille as she absorbed the curated beauty: sun-dappled landscapes painted by human artists before the war; burnished bronze masks with severe, animalistic expressions worn by the warrior women of Syvalle; blown-glass pieces by the masters in

Nephes that were so thin and delicate it looked as if a shout might shatter them. All of it centuries old.

Mireille had always found it easier to experience emotions through art, be it a painting, a book, a piece of music. All necessarily solitary endeavors with no reciprocal expectations placed upon her. A one-way conversation, of sorts.

When she was forced to interact with sentient beings, that's when things became difficult. She knew, of course, how to fake the appropriate emotional responses to manipulate her audience.

But a true, authentic expression of her feelings? Sometimes she wasn't even sure what that *was*. Like that part of herself was buried beneath the severity her mother had drilled into her.

She suppressed the thought as she and Ronin sauntered into the final gallery. They'd found nothing in the others, no hints of the Fallen Goddess's tell-tale fire opals anywhere.

Mireille was growing more and more frustrated by the minute.

The only thing calming her was the steady, silent presence of her partner as he drifted along beside her.

Ronin seemed...*different* today. Throughout their assignment, she'd often caught him staring at her with that heated possessiveness she so frequently inspired in males. But now there was something almost wistful in his gaze. Something soft and precious—and terrifying.

And even though her own emotions were difficult for her to interpret, she had centuries of experience reading others.

He was starting to *feel* things for her. She honestly couldn't think why. She'd been nothing but horrible to him since they'd met. Maybe he was some kind of masochist.

Still, his care today had been a comfort. Had helped her maintain her focus.

Crazy that a caged wolf bi-form who could barely control his own impulses was keeping *her* in check.

She snickered to herself as she approached a long case containing an array of decorative vases. She stepped closer to examine the green illustrations on the first vase, then sucked in a sharp breath.

Ronin was instantly at her side. "What? What did you find?"

She grabbed his arm to pull him closer, definitely *not* testing his rock-hard biceps, and gestured toward the vase. "Look at these."

They side-stepped down the glass, examining illustrations that seemed eerily similar to what they'd witnessed in the crypt last night.

On the first vase, a group of Deathstalkers—marked by their serpent's eyes and elongated fangs—were gathered around a prone figure atop a wooden pallet.

On the second, a Deathstalker in a black robe—some kind of holy male, perhaps?—placed a round object onto the dead Fae's eye.

On the third, flames licked across both the pallet and the body.

And on the fourth and final vase, the holy male had raised the stone, now surrounded by a radiating halo, above his head and beneath a word written in swooping calligraphy.

"Psychis," Ronin uttered. "What does that mean?"

Mireille's stomach dropped to her feet. "Soul. Psychis means soul in Aramaelish."

"Are you telling me the diva's *soul* is what made that anastasium stone glow?"

"That's not all I'm telling you. *Death* is what activates the stones. That's the source of Stygios's power." Her face was ashen as she turned to him. "Death itself."

She rushed over to the plaque beside the case, Ronin right on her heels, and her fingers shook as they traced the provenance of the ancient vases.

Listhima.

CHAPTER TWENTY-SIX

In their suite the next morning, Mireille brewed a special batch of tea—Ronin sipping his own—as they awaited the silver-haired servant's return to gather their breakfast tray.

After their discovery in the gallery yesterday, the rest of the day had been rather uneventful. Dinner with the other guests had been a whirlwind of speculation about what, exactly, tonight's performance would entail. Guesses ranged from the mundane (another opera performance) to the fantastical (silk aerialists in the bioluminescent section of the greenhouse) to the violent (a fight to the death among the human servants). Mireille and Ronin had played their parts, offering up their own suggestions.

Given that Otto had said the opening performance was intended to dishonor Anaemos, Mireille suspected tonight's theme would involve another of the High Gods. Stygios, if she had to guess based on what she and Ronin had overheard Otto and Layla discussing. Something about the Scales of Nyctima and opening pathways. But she didn't offer up that little tidbit of information to the other guests.

Otto had not yet returned from his journey to fetch tonight's performer from Listhima. Mireille wondered if the female—Otto and Layla had been referring to a "she" —would suffer the same fate as Diva Carmina. She shuddered at the thought, wondered if she might be able to warn the performer beforehand.

She tried to banish that worry, focus on her task this morning—infiltrating Otto's office to see if they could find anything that might help them weave together these odd threads of his plans.

She and Ronin ran through what they'd learned while she waited for the dried Bleeding Heart petals and Letha-phyll leaves to steep.

"So," she began, "let's go over what we know." She held up a finger as she listed off the facts. "One: Otto has been luring Fae with elemental magic in their ancestry to his estate. And they're all from either the Akti territory or the Desolation. Which borders Akti. But we don't know what those locations signify."

Ronin nodded, drinking from his tea cup. He hadn't had a Delirium in three days. He was managing well enough without it, though he seemed more tense than usual, his fuse much shorter. Especially when he'd almost shredded that servant who'd interrupted their kiss. And she'd noticed him gazing longingly at the bottles during last night's dinner. She was incredibly proud of his restraint, had told him so at the table, but he'd waved her off like it was nothing.

"Two"—she held up a second finger—"he's using the anastasium stones to capture souls. But, we don't know what he's using the activated stones for. Nor where he's hiding them."

"Three," Ronin held up three tattooed fingers, "he's a fucking crazy psychopath who wears weird fucking suits, doesn't eat meat, and has a strange obsession with the High Gods and the Fallen Goddess, but is rich and influential enough to have lured a bunch of power hungry Fae who haven't run away from him even though he murdered someone right in front of them. Oh, and they don't seem to have noticed that he's warded us all in here. Or, if they have, they don't care. And he's got a household full of spellbound human servants and even though he invited you here to get into your pants, he left to fetch some other mysterious *she* after you answered his questions about your heritage with lies."

Mireille lifted the lid of the tea pot, sniffing at the contents within to see if they had been steeping long enough. Nearly there. "That was way more than three things."

Ronin barked a sharp laugh. "Am I wrong?"

"No, but none of it answers any of our questions. And what about the illegal relics of the Fallen Goddess that he's supposedly been gathering? We didn't find any here in the main house, nor in the galleries. He must be hiding them somewhere else."

Ronin slumped down in his chair, thunking his teacup onto the table. "How do you deal with this?"

She cocked her head. "With what?"

"Gathering all this information, keeping it straight, figuring out which parts are pertinent and which are dead-ends. It's fucking confusing." He raked his fingers up the shaved sides of his head.

She leaned back in her chair, caressing the buttery

leather armrests. Picturing her fingers in place of Ronin's on those soft sides of his head. "It always comes together in the end. Like a puzzle full of missing pieces. We find more, we fit them into place, and the picture suddenly becomes crystal clear."

"Frustrating to be in the middle of it."

"Welcome to the life of an IA agent," she snickered. "And don't lose hope. Imagine what we might find in Otto's office this morning. Maybe even the one piece that makes sense of all this."

"Doubtful," he grumbled.

A knock rang out across the hall, followed by murmured voices—the servant making his rounds to collect the breakfast trays.

Mireille checked the teapot once more, the liquid now a deep fuschia and wafting that unmistakable licorice scent. She poured out a steaming cup, grinning. "Showtime."

Ronin sauntered over to the door to await the servant's knock.

It came mere seconds later, and when Mireille called out for the man to enter, he swung open the door and Ronin was upon him.

The old, silver-haired man didn't struggle or scream as Mireille stalked over, leveling what she hoped was a non-threatening look. "We're not going to hurt you. I need you to drink this for me."

The man pressed his lips together, but Ronin cupped his chin and squeezed his cheeks, forcing his mouth open.

An image flashed through Mireille's mind: Ronin performing the same hold on Dimi. Something hot and prickly snaked through Mireille's lower belly, a heady mixture of lust and jealousy. She shook it away before Ronin could sense anything, but the knowing gleam in his golden-blue eyes told her she hadn't quite succeeded.

She tipped the cup to the man's mouth, pouring half the liquid down his throat. Ronin's massive hand covered the man's entire lower face as he pinched his nose. The man had no choice but to swallow.

The tea took effect instantly, the man's pupils blowing so wide his hazel irises nearly disappeared.

Ronin released him, and the man swayed on his feet, his eyes glued to Mireille. His new master, according to the extract of Bleeding Heart flower coursing through his system.

"I need you to do something for me," she whispered.

"Anything," the man groaned.

So Mireille led him out of the suite, through the quiet halls, and over to the west wing.

THE CURVED walls of Otto's office were lined with shelves crammed with books, small sculptures, masks, and carvings. The space was neat and tidy, not a single element out of place.

Outside the door, the servant stood sentry, instructed to whistle if anyone approached.

"So," Ronin began, rounding the large black desk in the center of the room and poking through the drawers, "what exactly are we looking for?"

Mireille shrugged, stepping over to one of the bookshelves. "Anything of interest."

"Helpful," he grumbled as Mireille examined the titles.

Two entire shelves were taken up by a collection of

encyclopedias, the recorded history of Ethyrios dating back several centuries before the war. There were also travelogues, collections of the mythologies of the High and Lesser Gods, plus an entire shelf full of folk stories and fiction.

Based on the state of the spines, many cracked and worn, she had no trouble believing Otto had read every one.

She pulled one of the mythology collections from the shelf, stories of the High Gods. Entire paragraphs had been highlighted, sections crossed out in violent, ink-black strokes. Scratched notes and odd symbols deco-rated the margins—the scrawlings of a mad, obsessed mind.

She returned the book, her gaze snagging on a thick folio on the bottom shelf. It contained an assortment of maps, including an ancient one that showed the conti-nent several centuries before the war. Before the Empire had come into power, and before the land had been divided into its current territories.

Mireille hauled the folio over to the desk and spread it open. Ronin came up behind her, placing a palm on the surface and curving over her back.

She dragged a finger across the symbols littering areas that were now portions of present day Akti and the Desolation.

"What do those symbols mean?" Ronin's breath kissed the back of her neck and she fought to suppress a shiver.

She pointed to an upright triangle. "This one must mean fire. It's the same symbol that was etched onto the wall beside the fireplace in the crypt."

Ronin nodded, his chin grazing her shoulder. "And the others?"

"Safe assumption that this one"—she pointed to an upside-down triangle—"means water. And this one—"

"Lightning," Ronin finished as she gestured to the tiny bolt. "They're concentrated in the areas where the guests are from."

"Not all the guests. Neither you nor I are from there."

Sympathy softened Ronin's eyes. "You don't know that for sure though, do you? Your father could be from one of those towns."

"I suppose it's possible," Mireille muttered, that familiar, empty ache hollowing out her stomach as she closed the folio and returned it to the shelves. She continued to peruse them as Ronin resumed rifling through Otto's desk.

"Come look at this," Ronin called a few moments later. He'd opened a thick leather ledger.

Mireille stepped up beside him. "What is that?"

Ronin flipped through the yellowed pages, hundreds of them, with handwritten names scrawled beneath branching lines.

"Looks like family trees," Ronin murmured.

"Did Otto compile all of these *himself*?"

"It's all in the same hand-writing. It must have taken him years to record all this." Ronin flipped the ledger over, scrolling through the pages then stabbing his finger on one at the back. "Here."

Mireille leaned in, reading the bottom of the page.

Larissa Bisere.

Above her name, her lineage was scrolled out in lines of black ink, dating back at least five generations. At the top, what would have been Larissa's great-great-grandfather's name had a star next to it.

Mireille traced a finger over it. "What does the star mean?"

Ronin scrubbed a hand over his jaw. "Perhaps they were the last of their family members to possess elemental magic?"

"If that were the case, why is he labeling them with stars instead of the elemental symbols?"

He shrugged, flipping through several other pages. There were stars on many of the other trees, always more than three or four generations up.

"Are the names of any of the current guests in here?" she asked. "See if you can find Nero's."

Ronin expelled a tiny huff at the Beastrunner's name as he searched the back of the ledger. "Here." Similar to Larissa's, Nero's chart went up several generations, but there were no stars. Though there was a question mark next to one. They studied several more entries, finding them similar to Nero's, with question marks instead of stars.

Frustrated, Mireille returned to the shelves. Perhaps there was some kind of legend or index that would reveal the meaning of those stars and question marks.

"Mireille." Ronin's voice was thick with dread. "Come back and look at this."

His pale face froze the blood in her veins and her limbs grew heavy. Crossing to the desk felt like walking through syrup.

She glimpsed the final entry in Otto's ledger, and her mouth went dry, her throat closing.

Her own family tree.

Though only one side of the page was filled, four generations tracing up from her mother's name.

The space where her father's name should have been was empty, save for a question mark.

"What does that mean?" She could barely get the words out.

"Have you…" Ronin hesitated, as if he didn't want to dredge up her pain. "Have you ever felt stirrings of elemental magic? Like what we saw Mattias demonstrate?"

"Never," she choked out as Ronin gripped her shoulder, the gesture calming her, slowing the rapid pounding in her chest.

As she examined the names on her mother's side, she realized she'd never heard a single one. Vivienne had never shared any of them. It rankled that *Otto*, of all people, had more information about her own family than she did. And when had he collected this information? It must have been before she'd even arrived at the estate. Before she'd told him all those lies at dinner. The names on the tree were Valois, not Valette. Dread trailed icy fingers down her spine.

"Valois," Ronin whispered. "Is that your real last name?"

She nodded. "My mother's. I changed it before I came to Kheimos. But kept the first three letters the same, just in case he…"

She pushed the fear down, tucked it alongside that long-buried grief that had been prodded far too often by this assignment.

Had her father wielded elemental magic? She supposed that could be the reason her mother had fled from him and her pack, not wanting her and her daughter to be hunted down by the Empire because of it.

Her father's words from that night floated into her mind.

...needs to understand who she is...

She closed her eyes and took a deep breath, searching through herself for any hint of hidden magic. Nothing called back.

"Are you alright?" Ronin asked.

She smoothed over her expression, burying her pain and confusion and readjusting her armor. "Yes. Just put it away and let's keep looking."

They searched through every drawer, every box, every hidden corner of Otto's office but found no signs of any relics of the Fallen Goddess, nor even the box with the glowing anastasium stone containing the diva's soul.

Ronin flopped into a chair. "This is pointless. I don't think we're going to find anything else. We should leave before someone finds us in here."

"You sure you don't want to spend a few more hours reading through an encyclopedia on the history of Ethyrios?"

"That sounds more like *your* idea of a good time."

She smirked at him. "I'd ask what yours is, but I think I can guess."

A low whistle trilled from outside the door and Ronin shot her a panicked look.

But there was no one except the servant in the hallway when Mireille whipped open the door.

"He has returned," the man said, his pupils still blown wide and his eyes glazed. "I can sense him."

Mireille glanced down the staircase. "Come with us."

The trio hustled back to the guest wing, and as soon as Mireille shut the door to their suite, Ronin asked, "Why did we bring him back here?"

Mireille guided the servant into an armchair, then perched on the table before him. "Seeing if we can get any additional information before we set him loose." The servant merely sat there, waiting expectantly, his eyes glued to Mireille. "Where is Otto hiding the Fallen Goddess relics? And what are they?"

"I don't know."

Mireille vented a frustrated grunt while Ronin merely crossed his arms, leaning against the mantel and observing the interrogation. "Did Otto know who I was before he invited me here?"

"Who are you?" The servant cocked his head. Mireille didn't answer.

"Worth a try," Ronin murmured. "Ask him about the stones. He was in the crypt two nights ago."

"The anastasium stone that you took from the diva's ashes. Why was it glowing?"

"Her soul was captured within it."

Mireille nodded, encouraging him. One theory confirmed, at least. "And what is he doing with the glowing stones?"

"I don't know." The servant shook his head, frowning. As if it pained him to not have the answers Mireille sought. Then he perked up slightly. "But I do know where he's keeping them."

"Where?"

"Where the souls will be contained. Where death feeds life and life feeds death."

"What the fuck does that mean?" Ronin muttered.

Mireille grasped the man's shoulders. "Can you be a little more specific?"

"I..." The man's eyes rolled back in his head, exposing whites, and his body began to shudder.

Ronin leaned over the back of the chair. "What's happening to him?"

"The Bleeding Heart is wearing off." She swept the old man out of the chair and pushed him toward the door. "Go back to your quarters. Tell no one what happened."

The man's features slackened, confusion and obedience warring on his face as he slipped out of the room.

Ronin shut the door behind him. "You are fucking *ruthless*, Valette. Remind me never to cross you."

Mireille slumped into a chair and Ronin sank into the one across from her. "Where the souls will be contained. Where death feeds life and life feeds death… what do you think that means?"

Ronin leaned forward, forearms resting on his knees. "Sounds like the crypt. But we saw him taking the stone out of there…"

Mireille's mind swirled with possibilities, eddying around the edges of something she couldn't firmly grasp. Their discovery in Otto's office, half her family history laid bare, hogged her attention.

They sat in silence, both in quiet contemplation of the servant's words, when something swished underneath the door.

Mireille rose to pick up the card, then turned to Ronin, reading it: "The second performance will take place this evening at sunset in the Main Ballroom. Cocktails and hors d'oeuvres will be served until precisely two minutes before midnight, at which time a revered visitor will guide us in a seance in dishonor of Stygios the Reaper, High God of Death and Destruction." Mireille snorted. "That doesn't sound ominous or anything."

Ronin slumped further into his chair. "This is officially the weirdest fucking job I've ever worked. Company's not too bad though." He slid his eyes to her, gauging her reaction. Bracing himself for a barbed retort.

This male had already saved her life twice. Both times *after* she'd stubbornly refused to accept his help. He'd cajoled her into eating and sleeping, made sure she took care of herself even as her mind roared at her to ignore her bodily needs and keep working. Kindnesses no one had ever bestowed upon her.

Kindnesses she'd never *let* anyone bestow upon her.

So she clawed back her instincts to push him away again, to retreat into her safe solitude, and answered him.

"Not too bad at all, Matakos."

CHAPTER TWENTY-SEVEN

The cocktail hour before the seance was a more animated affair than the previous two nights' gatherings. As if the whispers of Otto's return, performer in tow, had stirred the guests into an excited frenzy.

Ronin thought they were a bunch of short-sighted, power-hungry idiots.

He and Mireille had decided to mingle separately tonight, to probe the histories of the guests, see if they could figure out what those question marks on their family trees had signified.

They were also keeping their ears open for mentions of locations around the estate that could be *where death feeds life and life feeds death.*

Ronin hadn't learned anything useful during the three hours of inane conversation he'd already subjected himself to, so he was taking a well-earned break.

The main ballroom spanned the entire length of the west wing. More a cave than a ballroom, the room was entirely black and lit only by flames dancing in marble braziers. Outside the few large windows, the first iridescent hints of the Scales of Nyctima swirled over the Blackspurs.

But the room's most unnerving feature was its thick glass floor, so clear it gave the impression of walking on air. Many of the guests were keeping their eyes aimed upward, and he'd seen more than a few near stumbles, many hands grasping elbows.

Ronin thought it perhaps just another of Otto's tactics to keep his guests off-kilter.

Mireille didn't seem to have any trouble navigating, even in the ridiculously high heels she was wearing.

Not that Ronin was watching her like a creep from across the room or anything.

And even if he was, it was only in a professional and strictly platonic capacity as her protector, partner and recently-crowned friend.

No, he certainly *wasn't* tucked between two blazing braziers, sipping at a tumbler of iced vodka and monitoring her every move. She flitted between groups of smartly-dressed Fae, most of whom had worn black for the High God of Death. Ronin wondered whether they'd selected their outfits before they knew the entire room was black. It was like looking into a sea of floating heads.

Mireille was wearing another skin-fucking-tight dress, on theme in black, with a high neckline. Her right arm was concealed beneath the sole long sleeve. He suspected it had been a purposeful choice, to hide her scar from their host, discourage any further *inspection*. The hem barely covered her ass, and her legs looked miles long, especially in those crimson heels.

He tracked multiple males—and several females— eying her legs with a hunger that surely mirrored his own. And every time he caught someone looking, his wolf growled a warning.

One he didn't bother shushing. He just let the possessiveness sear through his veins. Hoping that maybe if he didn't fight the feeling, it would go away.

It wasn't fucking working.

Why are you standing here doing nothing? his wolf ground out. *They should all have their eyes gouged out for staring at her like that.*

Ronin snorted. *You've got a lot to learn about modern ideals, my friend. You can't just blind everyone who looks at your female.*

So you are admitting she is our female? Finally.

That's not what I—

Another female broke through his laser-focused line of sight to Mireille, slinking toward him in a dress with even less fabric. He thought he also caught the glint of a knife through the left slit in her dress. Then realized it was definitely a knife when he caught another glint through the right slit.

"Butcher," Layla Fetar purred as she approached, lifting her amber drink in a toast. "I don't believe we've yet had the pleasure."

Ronin reluctantly tore his gaze from Mireille, who'd just let out a bubbling little laugh at some inanity being spewed by Nero Beruglia. It looked like she was about to place her hand on Nero's shoulder, and Ronin silently thanked the High Gods for Layla's distraction.

"Mistress Fetar." He lifted his glass to return her salute. "Are you sure about that? Heard a rumor you were at my fight last weekend."

Her black-painted lips curved into a coy smile. "Take a walk around the room with me?"

She extended her hand and he offered her an elbow.

"So, you and Mireille Valette. How long has that been a thing?" Layla dug her sharp fingernails into his forearm.

He was surprised at his wolf's silence. Layla was undeniably beautiful. And smelled delicious. Exactly the type of female that would usually have his wolf salivating, but there wasn't a hint of movement or even a peep from the creature.

Ronin didn't dare think too long about why.

"A few months." Ronin cut his gaze to the circular dais in the center of the room. Two human servants had entered carrying a hefty chair, a throne really, that looked suspiciously like it was stitched together with bones. Whether they were Fae or human, Ronin couldn't tell from his vantage point. Though truthfully, there was no easy way to tell—human and Fae bones looked exactly the same. Some kind of point to be made there, surely, about the similarities between the two species once all the skin, muscle, blood and magic was stripped away.

"Quite an odd pairing, the two of you," Layla muttered.

"Really? Why do you think so?"

Layla laughed, a harsh sound that held not a bit of genuine mirth. As cutting as the blades strapped to her thighs. "From what I've heard about you, she seems a bit *vanilla* for your tastes."

"And what, precisely, would you know about my *tastes*, Mistress Fetar?"

"Layla, please. And certainly you must know how much the females of Kheimos enjoy their gossip." She stopped him and tugged on his elbow, encouraging him to lean down. Her lips skimmed his earlobe. "Rumor has it you're the best fuck in town. Though I've also heard you don't often provide that service more than once."

Layla gestured with her glass toward Mireille, who was still laughing with Nero. Lucky bastard.

"I'm wondering how *that* one finally tamed the notorious Butcher of Aethalia." Layla wrapped her black lips around the edge of her glass and took a short sip.

Ronin couldn't get a precise read on Layla. Was she jealous? Surely not. Otto had probably put her up to this, an attempt to seduce him away from Mireille so that the Deathstalker himself could close in.

"The heart wants what it wants." Ronin shrugged. "I can no more explain that than I can explain why someone as skilled and ambitious as I've heard you are would want to work for a rich old billionaire up here on the edge of nowhere. You were a Shadow Maiden for Empress Mila, were you not?"

Layla's kohl-lined eyes rounded, though only briefly. But enough for Ronin to tell he'd caught her off-guard.

She smoothed over her expression and emitted an amused little laugh. "You've been looking into my history? I'm flattered. And impressed. Let's just say the post no longer suited me, and leave it at that." Layla grasped his elbow and resumed their walk around the room. "What do you know of Mireille's personal history?"

Ronin was careful with his answer. He didn't know much, other than the few crumbs she'd offered him these past weeks. "A bit. Like I said, we've only been together for a few months."

And though he knew he shouldn't be asking Layla this question—if he wanted to know about Mireille's history, he should ask her himself, give her the chance to answer in a way that wasn't filtered through the mouths of their enemies—he couldn't help himself.

"What do *you* know of her history?"

Layla paused their stroll and stood in front of him, holding her glass against her chest. "She keeping secrets from you, Butcher? Doesn't sound like a love match to me."

"Who said she's keeping secrets from me? I'm just trying to discern how skillful your information mining is."

Layla gave him a razor-sharp smile. "She is not what she appears to be."

Ronin's stomach dropped.

What the fuck did *that* mean?

He took a sip of his vodka, an effort to calm his pulse so that Layla wouldn't be able to read how much she'd thrown him.

"Well, to me she appears to be the most beautiful wolf bi-form in the room. One who seems poised to charm the pants off of your master." He pointed over Layla's shoulder, who turned in time to see Otto—looking like a walking skeleton tonight in a black suit decorated with anatomically-correct bones—approach Mireille and pull her away from Nero.

A stab of fear pinched Ronin's gut. Based on those family trees they'd found in Otto's office, their host had to know Mireille had been lying at dinner the other night. Would the Deathstalker call her out on it?

Layla turned back to Ronin. "A wolf bi-form, you say?" Her dark eyes twinkled with merriment. And menace. "Are you so sure about that?"

What in Ethyrios was Layla talking about? Ronin

knew, without a shadow of a doubt, that Mireille was a wolf. Her scent alone was enough to verify the fact.

But then he remembered that other note in her scent. The one he couldn't identify. The one that smelled like a flower poised for decay.

"What else would she be?" Ronin countered, hiding his racing heart behind a nonchalant smirk.

"Perhaps you should look a bit deeper before you tie yourself to her."

Ronin couldn't discern Layla's angle. If there *was* some massive secret in Mireille's heritage, why was it so important? And how was it different from the other guests? Perhaps Layla didn't know herself, and was trying to fish an answer for Otto.

"Enjoy the seance, Ronin." Layla sashayed away from him, joining a group that included Julius Kosera, several other Fae, and even a few humans who were being fed from. The tangy scent of mortal fear wafted through the room as they wept, paralyzed by their Fae predators.

Layla herself approached a stunning dark-haired woman who bowed her head in deference. Ronin turned away just as Layla whipped one of her knives out of her thigh-sheath and held it against the young woman's throat as she fed.

Ronin took another bracing gulp of his drink, then laid it away on a side table. Though his need for a Delirium was damn-near unbearable, he refused to get that high through a live—and most certainly non-consensual—feeding. There were still a few boundaries he was unwilling to cross.

He surveyed the space for Mireille, his gaze catching on her unmistakable fiery red hair. She was standing atop the dais, Otto looming over her and gesturing toward the throne of bones. Mireille looked enraptured by whatever he was saying, and Ronin couldn't tell if it was fake or not.

Knowing Mireille and her unquenchable thirst for knowledge, her interest was likely genuine.

Go rescue her, his wolf piped up, finally stirring back to life after that odd conversation with Layla.

Doesn't look like she particularly wants or needs to be rescued, Ronin answered, turning away to seek another drink and a guest to interrogate.

Before he got the chance, a bell jingled, and the entire room turned their attention to Otto.

Mireille had stepped down onto the glass floor, glancing up at Otto just as expectantly as the other guests.

What secrets in her heritage had Layla been referring to? Surely it had something to do with that family tree they'd seen in Otto's office yesterday. Had something to do with Mireille's father.

He was about to rush to her side, warn her of what Layla had said, when Otto spoke up and the entire room went silent.

"Cherished guests," he intoned.

"It is time to begin our seance."

MIREILLE WATCHED Otto from the side of the dais, her mind aflutter. He hadn't uttered a word about her lies, those fabricated stories she'd spun about her parents. Her heart had been in her throat during their entire chat, waiting for him to drop some hint that she'd exposed herself. Instead, he'd regaled her with the incredible history of the piece at the center of the dais.

The Deathstalker had claimed the throne was stitched together with the bones of every Otto male going all the way back to Magnus Otto, the progenitor of the line. Otto had pointed out each bone, naming every male family member, and while Mireille had been fascinated, she also couldn't help asking herself why they'd only included the males. Who wouldn't have even existed without the females who'd birthed them. Then thought to herself, maybe it wasn't such a terrible fate that the females hadn't been forced to have their bones turned into a chair to house their male progeny's ass for thousands of years.

"Now, the vast majority of you may *think* you know what to expect tonight," Otto addressed the crowd, "but we can assure you that this particular seance will be unlike any you have ever experienced."

The crowd burbled, exchanging excited whispers, and Mireille used the pause to scan the room for Ronin.

It wasn't difficult to find him; other than Kosera, who was guarding the room's sole entrance, Ronin was the tallest male in the room, his white hair standing out against the black walls.

He turned to her as soon as her eyes landed on him. As if he could sense her attention. She offered a smile, which he returned, flicking his eyes toward Otto then back to her again. Asking if she got any important intel.

She offered a slight shrug, trying to convey *yes and no*. In truth, other than regaling Mireille with the history of the throne, Otto hadn't given her much.

The Deathstalker himself spoke up again. "And we

have invited another very special guest to guide us in our transcendental quest."

Otto signaled to Kosera, who opened the ballroom door to reveal an ancient Deathstalker female. Her coal-black pupils were lined in white, her ashen dreadlocks a grizzled nest around her head and shoulders. She was dressed in a sweeping, high-collared jacket woven with green-black feathers. Mireille had a ghastly suspicion they'd been pulled from a Windrider's wings.

The crowd parted as the old female shuffled toward the dais, hunched over a knobby cane topped with a carved snake's head, its fangs cradling a milky rock the size of a duck egg.

A fire opal.

The relic of the Fallen Goddess they'd been seeking?

With every strike of her cane, the female took a single step forward, and the long trail of her coat slid across the floor.

Clack, hiss.

Clack, hiss.

Clack, hiss.

The room was grave silent, the guests not daring to even breathe.

As the female reached the dais, Otto bent down to grasp her elbow and haul her up. He tucked her cane under his arm as he escorted her to the throne.

She wheezed as she sat, then closed her eyes and leaned her head back, her dreadlocks snagging in the rough bones.

Otto said nothing, merely stood beside her, surveying the guests with calm amusement.

The female sat so still that Mireille began to wonder

if the short walk to the dais had too thoroughly exhausted her and she'd met True Death.

In a flash, the female's drooping lids popped open and her milk-edged eyes bolted straight to Mireille, who had to fight the urge to flinch.

The old female muttered something to Otto in Aramaelish. Mireille was close enough to catch a few words.

Souls.

Anxious.

She dug her nails into her palms, the pain forcing her to stay present and not give in to her rising anxiety.

The Deathstalker female touched a wrinkled hand to Otto's forearm, signaling him to proceed.

"Ladies and gentlemales, we have the extreme honor this evening of introducing you to a female who has been conversing with the souls of our dearly departed for longer than anyone in this room has been alive. Souls who are not, as you have been led to believe, living their eternal lives in the realm of Stygios, but are in a very different place altogether." Otto paused, and the crowd strained forward. "They are in the Halfway."

A Beastrunner near the dais piped up. "What's the Halfway?"

"A sort of...repository. An area between worlds guarded by the Creator herself." Otto's eyes sparkled with gleeful menace. "You will see."

The ancient Deathstalker female's lips spread into a toothless grin, and she released a sound like a puff of dust escaping a dessicated corpse.

Otto touched her arm. "Our grandmother will lead you there tonight." Delighted gasps bubbled through the crowd, along with a smattering of respectful applause as

Otto bent down to press a reverent kiss to the old female's cheek. "The most powerful chronomancer our world has ever known. Nostrata Otto, everyone!"

The applause grew louder, and Nostrata allowed it to continue for several moments before raising a wobbly hand.

"Ethyrians," she croaked, her voice struggling up her ancient throat, "we come before you tonight as a conduit. When the Scales of Nyctima grace the sky, a path will open and we will travel to the Halfway in search of souls who have connections with each and every one of you in this room. You may encounter many different faces in the Halfway. Some are mere visions, spectral reflections conjured by the souls who reside there. But the souls themselves, those who have already passed, will emit a rainbow glow. Seek them. If you are lucky, they may bring you a message."

A chill ran down Mireille's spine, and she sought out Ronin, who had gone similarly pale.

Between the two of them, there were likely many, *many* departed souls in the Halfway who would have not-so-kind messages for them.

Nostrata began instructing the crowd. "Lie back on the floor and close your eyes."

Mireille had been trying all evening *not* to glance at the floor. It was extremely unnerving to feel like one was walking on air. Especially since the drop underneath was many thousands of feet down, the rocky, pine-laden cliffs of the Blackspurs cascading to the valley floor.

She steeled herself, and looked down. The sight was very different now that night had fallen. Only blackness shown beneath her feet. As if she were floating in the middle of nowhere.

But she did as the ancient female had instructed, stretching out across the glass and closing her eyes.

A cool mist flowed into the room, kissing her ankles then wending its way up her body. It was thick and creamy, but light as air. Like being coated with dry foam.

She recognized what it was as soon as the smoky, licorice scent hit her nostrils.

Lethaphyll.

She tried not to panic as the hallucinogenic drug seeped into her lungs. The effects were instantaneous, her body melting into the glass floor.

The sounds in the room faded, leaving only her own heartbeat pounding a slow, mesmerizing rhythm. As if she'd returned to the womb.

She nearly burst into euphoric giggles at the thought. No one had memories of being in the womb.

Or did they? Perhaps every single memory she'd ever had was still within her, buried in the cobwebbed depths of her subconscious.

Nostrata's raspy voice floated over, softened by the hazy smoke. Mireille cracked an eye open to watch the ancient female.

"Adelphinae, our Creator. We come before you, humble servants, to request passage for but a few hours into the Halfway."

Nostrata cracked her cane upon the floor—the violent boom shaking Mireille's bones—and the opal on top glowed even more fiercely. As if the light from the Scales of Nyctima outside the window were flowing through it.

Mireille's wolf was calm, sitting back on her hind legs with head cocked, tail waving, and ears perked. Listening.

Nostrata's voice rose again, softly, carried upon the mist itself into Mireille's mind. "What messages do the wayward souls have for us this evening, Creator?"

The last syllable dissolved into a fading echo, then transformed into a susurration of hushed voices. They were faint at first, then grew louder, and louder, and louder still. So loud that Mireille was certain her vibrating brain was about to leak out her ears.

At the point where Mireille couldn't take it anymore, ready to run screaming from the ballroom, the voices abruptly faded as a single one crystallized in her mind.

A feminine voice with a hard edge that Mireille hadn't heard in nearly three hundred years.

A voice she'd never expected to hear again. At least not until she herself was but a mere shadow of a soul.

"Mireille," the voice whispered.

"My girl."

CHAPTER TWENTY-EIGHT

Mireille was seated at the dining table in the cabin in the Oread Woods, her soft, chubby fingers resting on the surface.

By the hearth, Vivienne was bent over a copper pot, a faint, prismatic glow surrounding her. Their cabin was so remote that it had never been outfitted with any magical energy or appliances. It had never bothered Mireille in childhood—she'd never known anything different.

"Mother?" Mireille's hands rushed to her throat. Her voice was high and youthful. Innocent. Centuries away from her current cynical tone.

Vivienne didn't answer, just kept stirring that pot.

Outside the window, time was not obeying its normal cadence. In the span of a minute, the sun rose and set twice, and the leaves of the trees vibrated, as if stirred by a violent breeze. A raven with green-black feathers landed on a trembling branch, and a fox scurried through the trunks, a blur of red and brown, its eyes incandescent streaks in the false night.

"Mother," Mireille asked again, and as Vivienne turned, Mireille braced herself. The last time Mireille had seen her, Vivienne's throat had been a gruesome mess of torn flesh and serrated muscle.

Mireille vented a relieved sigh as Vivienne faced her, neck smooth and unmarred. She looked exactly as Mireille remembered her.

Vivienne's coal-black hair was coiled into a low bun, a severe part bisecting her skull. She wore a simple black shirt tucked into a pair of wool trousers.

Her cold, silver eyes swept across her daughter as she joined her at the table. Mireille could count on one hand the number of times her mother had looked upon her with anything resembling true affection.

Whatever was on the hearth continued to bubble and pop in the pot. It had a rich, mouthwatering scent—some kind of meat cooking in broth with a peppery punch of rosemary.

But there was something beneath it. Something game-y. Something that made Mireille's mouth water at the same time as her stomach roiled with instinctual disgust.

"I had to do it." Vivienne's brows knit together in feigned regret. "It was the only way to protect you." Vivienne grasped Mireille's hand. Her mother's fingers were ice-cold, another sign that this was not a true memory. They had always been so hot and dry, as if her wolf had evaporated any lingering moisture from her skin. "I didn't want him to know you existed, but he tracked us down. He was always the most skilled of hunters."

Mireille's gaze caught on something in the window. A

cloaked figure, its face half-hidden in shadow, emanating that same multicolored shimmer as Vivienne. Above its broad shoulders rose the pommel of a sword carved into the shape of a grinning skull.

The pale moon crested the figure's head, a ghostly halo, and in a flashing blur, it moved to the door and began pounding.

"Do not worry," Vivienne said, emotionless despite the frenzied thuds. "He cannot get you in here. He will never find you again."

A thump shook the door, but the hinges held. A male voice roared from the other side. "Let me see her!"

"What is in the pot, mother?" Mireille whined, a tear slipping down her cheek.

Vivienne slapped her across the face. "What have I told you about crying? Do not *ever* show that weakness. You and I are strong, lone wolves." Vivienne stood from her chair and knelt before Mireille, digging claws into her shoulders. Mireille cried harder. "You *must* stop, Mireille."

Vivienne grabbed a cloth napkin and scraped the wetness away, the harsh starched fabric scratching Mireille's cheeks.

The pounding at the door continued. "Let me in, Vivienne! It's been centuries. She needs to *know*."

Vivienne crossed to the pot and scooped up a serving of stew so deep red it was almost black. She set the steaming bowl before Mireille—the game-y scent was even more powerful, overtaking the rosemary—then placed a pewter spoon beside the dish and tucked the napkin into Mireille's collar. "Eat."

Mireille hesitated, and Vivienne pressed the spoon into her palm.

"Now, Mireille." Vivienne's silver eyes blazed with fury and the kaleidescope of faint color surrounding her pulsed brighter. "Eat!"

Mireille dipped her spoon into the stew and pulled out chunks of reddish-brown meat dripping with dark crimson juices.

Mireille swallowed her rising disgust and took a tentative bite.

It didn't at all taste how it smelled. It wasn't revolting.

It was *delicious*.

It tasted like a warm hug. Like tears of joy. Like a blissful day spent with bare toes in the grass and a cloudless, blue sky overheard.

As she chewed, the taste changed.

Bitter fear coated her tongue. The horror of a loved one's lifeless eyes. The yawning dread of a world coated in ash, burning bodies strewn across a smoldering wasteland.

She chewed once more, and the flavor changed again.

The spicy, hot rage of frustration, with ankles and wrists bound. An inferno of anger. The most familiar taste.

She swallowed, and a blinding spear of pain tore through her. A red stain bloomed on the napkin covering her chest.

Vivienne grabbed her by the chin, then forced Mireille's spoon back into the stew. "Finish it."

The cloaked figure had ceased his banging. Was peering through the window, his gloved hands pressed against the glass. She still couldn't see his face beyond the shadows of his hood. But she could feel his eyes upon her. Could feel his love and anguish radiating toward her.

Vivienne forced the spoon into Mireille's mouth, closing a palm over her lips and forcing her to swallow.

She didn't even taste the chunky lumps as they burned down her throat. Another gush of liquid poured from her chest.

She choked against her mother's hand, and Vivienne pushed the bowl away, the liquid spilling across the table and onto the floor.

Vivienne swept Mireille into a crushing embrace. "You did it. Mother always protects you."

Mireille tried to conjure up any feeling at all for these words, but there was a hollowness in her chest. As if something was missing.

Something vital.

Mireille's face went slack against her mother's shoulder.

Vivienne stroked her hair, cooing soothing words. "You'll be safe now. You never need to worry about him or anyone else discovering your secrets. Ruthless efficiency, my pup."

Vivienne settled Mireille onto her feet and removed the cloth napkin to reveal a large, gaping wound in Mireille's chest.

Right where her heart should have been.

CHAPTER TWENTY-NINE

oming out of the vision was a far more violent experience than falling into it.

Mireille's eyes popped open as her body convulsed, her skull smashing against the solid glass and rattling her bones.

She turned her head and vomited. To her utter horror, it was the same color and consistency as the stew from her vision: a viscous spill of maroon liquid with chunks of brownish-gray scattered throughout.

Head swimming, she pressed panicked hands to her chest. To her overwhelming relief, it was intact. No gaping wound.

She sat upright and surveyed the ballroom. The mist had evaporated, though several guests lay prone on the floor, blinking away the effects of the lethaphyll. The ammonic tang of urine mingled with the sour scent of vomit. She was one of the last to awaken.

Holy High fucking Gods, what *was* that?

She knew it wasn't a memory. Yes, her mother had

often been cold and unfeeling, and had expected the same from her daughter, but she'd never force-fed her. And certainly not whatever…*meal* had been in that pot.

She suspected the cloaked figure must have been her father. And if his soul had been in the Halfway, bathed in that iridescent glow, then he had passed.

A wave of grief, cold and disorienting and so all-consuming it felt like her heart had been ripped out of her chest all over again, washed over her.

She swallowed it down as she noticed both Otto and Nostrata staring down at her from atop the dais, the latter's face awash in rainbow light from the fire opal atop her cane. Nostrata whispered something into her grandson's ear, never tearing her eyes from Mireille.

Mireille ignored them, searching the room for Ronin.

He was nowhere to be found.

Disappointment pinched her gut. Had he gone back to their room? Had his visit to the Halfway been as unsettling as hers?

And, most importantly, how had he become, in the span of a few weeks, the person she wanted to run to for comfort? She needed his insouciant smirks, his gentle teasing, to chase away her churning horror and freshly-tilled sorrow.

Otto broke the silence from atop the dais.

"Welcome back, dear guests. We trust your conversations with the souls were revealing. Nostrata has already told us they were, as she checked in on each of you during your visits." Mireille recalled that raven with the green-black feathers, the same that decorated Nostrata's coat, that had been lurking in the trees outside the cabin. "She and I will spend the rest of the night interpreting your visions and will fetch you tomorrow morning for a private consultation. Stay here as long as you need to gather your wits."

Several Fae groaned as they pulled themselves to shaky feet. Mireille attempted the same, then crashed back down to her knees, sparking electric pain throughout her body.

Otto flew from the dais to help her up, and she fought an urge to swat him away. There was still far too much that she and Ronin didn't know; she couldn't risk insulting him.

Otto murmured, "We're very much looking forward to *your* reading tomorrow."

She glanced toward the ballroom door, where the other guests were dazedly filing out.

"Did you…" She coughed, clearing her throat, as rough and scratchy as if she'd awoken from the grave. "Did you see where Master Matakos went?"

Otto's lips pulled into a cruel smile. "Some Fae are far too cowardly to face the souls' messages. We are afraid your *lover* was one of them. Not ten minutes into the session, he awoke and fled the room."

Mireille blanched. "I'd better go check on him."

Otto squeezed her arm tighter. "You need do no such thing. He's perfectly fine back in your suite. Layla saw to the task herself." He gestured to the beautiful Beastrunner, who aimed a black-lipped smirk at Mireille.

"How long was the session?" Mireille asked, trying not to focus on Layla's lingering stare.

"You have all been in your trance state for three hours." Mireille bit back a gasp. That vision had only lasted several minutes. Though, she recalled the odd way time moved in the Halfway. "Layla attended to Master

Matakos for nearly the entire time. He must have required quite a bit of calming."

The vision of what Mireille had seen in those showers, Ronin thrusting into Dimi, flooded her mind.

At that time, she'd been aroused and intrigued. Now, the thought of Ronin fucking someone else made her want to scream, slit a throat or two.

Had things changed between them so dramatically since then? There had been the conversation about their partnership—their *friendship*, even. Then the kiss, of course, which neither of them had yet addressed. Certainly not enough to cause such a violent reaction.

Otto whispered into her ear, "He's a complete and utter fool if he could possibly have eyes for anyone else, Mireille. You are the most exceptional creature we've encountered in our five centuries of life." The tip of his forked tongue brushed her neck and she choked down a revolted shudder.

She was sure Otto had somehow orchestrated Ronin's removal. She needed to check on him. *Now.*

But first, she needed to slip her slithery host.

"You are too kind, Master Otto." She dipped her chin, peeking up at him through her lashes as he pressed closer.

"Jurgev," he exhaled.

"Jurgev." She licked her lips. "I look forward to our private meeting tomorrow. Though I'm quite worn out at the moment. Probably best if I rest up?" She slid a hand up his arm and he let out a quivering breath.

"Of course," he conceded with an expectant smile. "Sweet dreams, Mireille."

His serpent's eyes crawled over her flesh during her entire long walk out of the ballroom.

CHAPTER THIRTY

ireille returned to the guest wing, then pressed her hand to the panel outside their door. "Ronin?" she called out as it swung open.

The main room was quiet. And cold. He hadn't lit the fireplace.

The armchairs were empty, as was the bed. Which was still made and seemed unruffled. Relief rushed through her.

"Ronin."

A rumbling grunt came from the bathroom as she opened the door, her hand flying to her mouth.

Ronin slumped in the bathtub, fully clothed, his long legs stretched out beneath the water and his white dress shirt plastered to his impressive torso. His tattooed muscles peeked through the transparent fabric.

His suit jacket was strewn across the floor and four empty bottles of Delirium perched on the lip of the tub.

A fifth, half-empty itself, was clasped in his massive

fist, stopped halfway to his lips. His blue-yellow irises were tiny rings around his blown-out pupils.

The corner of his mouth kicked up as Mireille approached.

"My little she-friend," he slurred, wet strands of white hair clinging to his black eyebrows. "I mean, my girl-wolf." He shook his head and cackled, tipping over the bottle and spilling glowing Delirium into the bathwater.

"What are you… Ronin, what happened?" She knelt beside the tub, the floor cold and damp against her knees. Not cold. *Freezing*.

How long had he been sitting in here like this? She plucked the bottle from his fingers and he didn't protest. Just stared at her face, blinking, water beading in his dark eyelashes.

"Amatu save me, you're the most exquisite thing I've ever seen," he breathed out, and her face flamed. "Are you real?" He brushed wet fingers against her cheek, jolting in disbelief. "You *are* real. My fucking lucky night."

His eyes were glazed and hooded, and as he attempted to lift himself out of the tub, his arms gave out and he crashed down, sending a wave over the lip and soaking Mireille's black dress.

"Sorry," he giggled.

Tears prickled the backs of Mireille's eyes. It was gut-wrenching to see him struggle like this. He'd been doing so well, avoiding Delirium for the past few days. He must have seen something truly awful during the seance to have gone overboard like this.

She rounded the tub, then bent down to snake her arms underneath his armpits. "Okay, Matakos. Come on. Get up."

"Why?" he shivered, trying to wriggle out of her

grasp. "I like it in here. It's… well, it *was* warm." His teeth began chattering, as if he'd just noticed how cold the water had become.

"Up." Mireille hauled him to his feet. She didn't know how in Ethyrios she managed it—Ronin was six-and-a-half feet of solid muscle and fucking *heavy*—but she was able to help him out of the tub without either of them slipping.

He stood, swaying slightly and pulling at his shirt. "Why's my shirt look funny? I can see my nipples." He howled with laughter, tipping backwards, and Mireille rushed over to steady him.

"Okay, let's get you out of these wet clothes" —his eyebrows shot up and his lips curved into a grin— "and into some dry ones." He pouted, but didn't protest as she slung his arm over her shoulder and marched him into the bedroom.

She planted him at the end of the bed, then guided his hands to the footboard. "Hold on to this."

"Mmmm." His hum was a deep, surprisingly seductive sound given the state he was in. "I like where this is heading."

"I'm going to undress you," she stated.

"Now I *love* where this is heading," he slurred, reaching back for her. The motion set him off-balance and he smacked his hand back to the footboard to steady himself. "Though maybe we should wait until another night. I'm not sure I'm capable of giving you my best performance right now."

She stepped behind him, wrapping her arms around his torso to undo the buttons, then lifted each hand as she stripped the sleeves down and peeled off his shirt. His muscled back was no less tempting than his front.

She scolded herself. Her poor friend was clearly struggling, and here she was ogling him.

She trailed her hands down to his waistband and he thrust his hips forward.

"*Fuck*, yeah."

"Ronin," she snapped, and he seemed to return to himself for a moment.

"Sorry," he mumbled. "I'm not—"

"It's fine. Just hold still while I take your pants off."

He groaned. "This is fucking humiliating."

She unhooked the button and pulled down the zipper, trying not to make contact with the very impressive bulge underneath. Pushing his pants down his legs, she lifted his ankles one by one and shucked them off.

Free of his clothes, he rounded the footboard and toppled onto the mattress.

"Oh no," she said. "You need to sober up first."

Though regular liquor didn't give Fae hangovers, Delirium was another story. If he was going to be of any use at all tomorrow, to be alert and on guard for Otto's continued madness, she needed to make sure he had a clear head before falling asleep.

He grumbled and whined, but sat upright as she strode to the closet. She found a black t-shirt and cotton pants, then handed him both.

As he dressed himself, she *may* have allowed her gaze to linger just a few seconds longer than necessary on his decadently sculpted torso, the powerful sweep of his thighs, the faint smattering of snow-white hair that trailed into his underwear. Though she did finally avert her eyes when he stripped off *that* particular article of wet clothing.

Once he was decent, she helped him into an armchair

and lit the fireplace. She changed into her silk pajamas, then flopped down into the chair across from him.

"What will help?" she asked.

He leaned his head back, staring at her from underneath slitted lids. "What will help with what?"

"What can I do to sober you up? I've never… I don't drink Delirium, so I don't know how to counteract it. I'm guessing just water or coffee won't do it?"

He shook his head, his wet hair squeaking on the leather.

"Blood," he murmured.

"What?"

He leveled a wobbly gaze at her. "Your clean blood. It will speed my healing, help my body counteract the Delirium."

It wasn't the craziest suggestion. Fae blood *did* have healing properties.

"Okay," she breathed out. "How?"

He didn't answer, his head lolling on his shoulder and his ragged breathing slowing.

"Ronin."

No reaction.

Fuck, he was worse off than she thought.

She bolted out of her chair and jerked his shoulders. *"Ronin."*

His chest stilled, and panic frosted her veins.

"RONIN!" She cocked her arm back and punched him in the jaw.

He surged to life, wrapping his arms around her waist, and hauled her into his lap.

And she tried not to scream as Ronin fisted her hair, exposed her neck, and sank his sharpened canines into her flesh.

A HEADY, succulent liquid flowed into Ronin's mouth, singeing down his throat and through his veins.

It tasted like a snow-dampened bonfire, smoldering embers on the back of his tongue.

It tasted like a forest floor covered in pine needles and icy moonlight.

It tasted like a *wolf.*

Mirielle's wolf. That familiar combination of musk and overripe flowers.

His own wolf howled, dissolving the Delirium stupor.

There was a soft body cradled in his lap. Feminine hips pressing against his cock. Muscular legs straddling his waist. Silky hair tangled in his fingers.

He slowly became aware of his lips on Mireille's neck, his teeth piercing her flesh as he sucked down mouthful after mouthful of the most intoxicating blood he'd ever tasted.

Snippets of their conversation pelted him. Something about him needing to sober up.

Frenzied Dienses, what the fuck was he doing?

And why couldn't he stop?

Pliant in his lap, Mireille whimpered as his throat worked, drinking her down.

Was she enjoying this?

Her delicate hands rested on his shoulders, steadying him. Or perhaps steadying herself.

As the fog of the Delirium lifted, he removed his mouth from her addictive flesh. He shortened his canines, panting as he pressed his forehead against her chest.

Fuck, she tasted good.

She stroked the back of his neck as he returned to himself, and when he lifted his head to look at her, there was fear in her eyes.

But not for herself.

For him.

As if he were fucking *worth* something.

"Are you okay?" she asked. "Did you take enough?"

He licked the smear of blood off her neck, and the two puncture wounds began threading back together. "I… I think I'm good."

She made no move to remove herself from his lap.

He cupped her face, gratitude squeezing his chest. "So fucking brave." Another shiver of pleasure ran through her at his praise.

His wolf was frantic, the infusion of Mireille's blood stirring the creature into a frenzy of indecipherable yips and barks and howls.

Which was probably a blessing. Ronin didn't want to hear any of the beast's vulgar ideas, especially since his and Mireille's limbs were still tangled together. Their faces were so close that he could feel her warm breath on his lips.

Her silver eyes searched his, scanning between them. Answering those questions he'd been too cowardly to ask her after their kiss.

His jaw ached, and he hissed as he brushed the tender spot. "Did you… Did you punch me in the face?"

She rolled her eyes, chasing away whatever had just passed between them. "Trust me, you deserved it. And I was trying to wake you up. I thought you were… I was so…" She shook her head, chasing away a confession.

She pushed out of his lap, and his wolf let out a frustrated whine. She adjusted the waistband of her silk pants—to Ronin's utter delight, the same she'd been wearing that night at the theater when they'd teased Otto —and pulled her collar up. It fell back down, exposing her shoulder.

And even though his lips had just left her skin, he wanted to put them back there. Immediately.

She settled into the chair across from him and tucked her legs up, the fire's golden glow dancing in her coppery hair. "What happened to you tonight?" Concern twisted her features.

Had anyone, other than Selene, ever looked at him with such concern?

A deep ache gripped his heart, so intense he felt like he was dying.

"Otto said you woke up about ten minutes into the seance and fled the room. Said that Layla had to accompany you back here." There was an edge in her voice when she said the other female's name that he thought it wise not to comment on.

Ronin spread his legs, sinking deeper into the cushions with a long exhale. All the Delirium in the world wouldn't dull the terror he'd felt as soon as he'd crossed into the Halfway.

And had seen who was waiting for him.

Once he'd awoken, gasping and sweating on the glass floor, he'd fled the ballroom. Layla had chased him back to the suite, then called down to the servants for a case of Delirium. She'd drank one with him, then left him to his own uncontrollable devices. She hadn't hit on him—not any more than she had at the party beforehand—and now, with a clearer head, he wondered if this had been her plan all along. To disorient and distract him. To put him out of commission or weaken him somehow. Get him to abandon his task of protecting Mireille and leave her vulnerable to Otto's machinations.

Luckily, Mireille seemed unharmed. Other than the two faded pink marks that he himself had placed on her neck.

"The seance…" he started, unsure of how to convey what he'd seen. No, not unsure. *Ashamed*. A writhing, oily, poisonous shame.

Compassion softened her gaze, as if she could sense his churning emotions. "Who visited you, Ronin?"

He crumpled forward, his forearms crashing to his knees. He scanned the room for another bottle of Delirium. High fucking Gods, he wanted another one so badly. Even the embarrassment of feeding from his partner couldn't quell the craving.

This *hurt*.

It hurt so fucking bad, all the guilt, and his heart was going to pound through his chest, and he couldn't breathe, and—

Gentle fingers brushed across his scalp, and when he looked up, Mireille stood before him, his eyes level with the sliver of creamy skin between her waistband and her shirt.

"Let it out." Her voice was so soothing he could hardly bear it. A garbled sob clawed up his throat as she knelt at his feet, clasping gentle fingers around his hand. Grounding him. "Tell me. Unburden yourself. That's what friends are for, right?"

She looked exhausted. Letha only knew what kind of message the souls had offered *her*. But despite all the shit she was carrying herself, she still wanted to help carry his.

Something cracked open in his chest. Something vast and boundless and eternal.

So, Ronin opened his mouth.

And revealed his tortured soul to his friend.

"There were human soldiers," Ronin whispered, his voice breaking. "Thousands of them."

Mireille rested her cheek on his thigh, still grasping his hand. Just those two small points of contact. Any more than that, and she didn't know what she might let him do.

Seeing him so vulnerable, so undone by his guilt, had shattered her last lingering perceptions of him.

She'd thought he was arrogant, narcissistic, lazy. Coasting through life thanks to his reputation.

But that hadn't been true at all. Underneath those layers was a male haunted by the things he'd done.

Haunted by a pain so ingrained that he had to numb it with the very substance that had been the catalyst of his downfall.

Mireille didn't often feel pity for *anyone*, believing that people deserved to suffer the consequences of their actions. Their *choices*.

But seeing Ronin struggle with his own had her tapping a well of compassion she hadn't even realized she possessed.

Ronin sighed, his leg shifting beneath her cheek. "As soon as I crossed over, they swarmed me. And they weren't..." He choked down a sob. "They weren't even angry. That was the worst part. I could have dealt with that. They..." He swallowed. "They showed me the lives I had stolen from them. The wives and husbands and chil-dren they'd left behind. Grand-children they'd never even met. Not after I... after I'd killed them." Glistening tears bathed his cheeks. "There were so many. A sea of human faces all blurred together, some glowing and some just visions. I could barely distinguish them. I did that. I caused all that devastation, and I can't..."

She wanted to tell him it wasn't his fault. That he was just following orders. That those human soldiers had taken to those battlefields knowing the potential outcomes. But she didn't think he wanted or needed to hear that right now.

"I'm a coward," he howled. "I should've stayed. Should've listened to their grievances. But I just ran away again. Like I've done for the past three centuries."

"You're not a monster, Ronin," she whispered.

"Yes, I fucking am. Someone with true strength wouldn't have used it on opponents who were so much weaker. I deserve this cage."

"Prove them wrong," she said.

"Wh-what?"

"Prove them wrong. Once we finish this assignment—and we *will*—when they uncage you, don't let the Empire use you like that ever again. Forge a different path."

"What kind of path?"

She shrugged. "I can't answer that for you. But what I do know is you have a choice right now. You can continue to beat yourself up, wallow in your regret, or you can change things. Be *better*. Do better."

He exhaled slowly, brushing a finger along the bite marks on her neck. "Did I hurt you?"

She angled into his touch, letting him stroke her skin. "No. I, uh... kind of enjoyed it. In case you couldn't tell."

Ronin chuckled and the sound was a balm. "Mmm-mm," he purred, igniting sparks throughout her body. "Kinky. I knew it."

She didn't know what came over her. Perhaps it was his openness tonight. Perhaps it was this crazy, emotional roller coaster of an assignment. Perhaps it was just Ronin himself—so powerful, yet so vulnerable in his unmasking.

And so incredibly beautiful that looking at him was as glorious and painful as the harsh glare of the sun after days spent in darkness.

She forced herself to hold his molten gaze. "If we get out of this alive, maybe we could…go on a real date?"

He chuckled again, ran his thumb across her bottom lip. "That better be a promise."

She shrugged. "We make pretty good partners."

"The Butcher and the ballerina. Look out, Kheimos."

"I'll get you box seats next season, since I know how much you love watching the ballet," she snorted.

Affection softened his eyes. A look that Mireille had rarely received from anyone. "I love watching *you*, Mireille."

Radiant warmth stole through her as she stood, then offered her hand. Ronin took it, his calluses scraping her soft skin, and pulled himself to standing, so close that a breath would've pressed their chests together. "You okay now?"

He nodded, blowing out a long exhale. "I think so. Though I'm not sure I'm going to be able to sleep."

Mireille stepped back, giving him space. "Me neither."

Ronin cocked his head, scrutinizing her. "What did *you* see? In the Halfway?"

Her limbs stiffened, her gorge rising at the phantom

taste of that stew on her tongue. The taste of her own fucking heart. "I don't want to talk about it."

Ronin regarded her carefully, the decision not to push settling into his features.

She nodded her chin to the half-finished game of chess on the table. "You up for a game?"

Ronin smirked. "I thought you didn't know how to play?"

"I don't," she said, picking up a piece that looked like a tiny turret. "What's this one called?"

"Guess," Ronin grinned.

"Castle?"

"Guess again."

"Fortress," she tried.

"Nope."

"Stronghold."

"Try again."

"Turret. Tower. Citadel. Outpost," she peppered him, earning shakes of his head every time. "What the fuck is it called then?"

Ronin's soft mouth formed a delighted smile and she wanted to leap into his arms and kiss it off of him. "Rook."

"*Rook*? That makes no fucking sense."

He threw his head back and laughed. So different from his earlier gloom. "I didn't name the pieces."

"Why's it called a rook?"

His dark brows furrowed. "I honestly have no clue."

"Teach me. Payment for your fake dance lessons."

His grin grew wider as he gathered up the board and strode to the bed where he sat cross-legged, beckoning her to join him.

Outside, snow continued to fall, large, fluffy flakes

dotting the darkness and imparting a coziness to the room despite the lurking dangers.

She climbed onto the mattress and flung her hair over her shoulder as Ronin arranged the pieces with long, elegant fingers.

"Go easy on me, Matakos."

The smile he aimed at her was a thing of dazzling, heart-wrenching beauty.

"Never, Valette."

CHAPTER THIRTY-ONE

Something hard and sharp dug into Ronin's ass cheek.

He groaned awake, lifting his hips and pulling out a black chess piece—the bishop. He tossed it to the foot of the bed where the board and remaining pieces lay in a haphazard pile.

He took a moment to study Mireille's peaceful, sleep-softened face on the pillow beside him. So different from the hard-ass exterior she put on while awake.

He was growing to appreciate both sides of her.

Maybe too much.

He barely remembered what had happened last night, but his head was blissfully clear thanks to the blood she'd given him.

And likely also thanks to her listening.

He brushed a strand of red hair behind her ear, then tugged the blankets up to cover her shoulder, running his thumb over a freckle. The two puncture wounds from his bite last night had faded.

He got out of bed, then cleaned up the chessboard.

"Another round?" Mireille murmured into her pillow.

Ronin chuckled. She'd been a very quick learner, absorbing the rules and strategy more quickly than any novice he'd ever played. Not that he was surprised, with that cunning, steel-trap mind of hers.

He hadn't gone easy on her. He'd won the first three games, then had been genuinely thrilled when she'd won the fourth. She'd accused him of letting her win, and he couldn't tell which had turned him on more: her fiery anger that he'd gone easy on her or her sheer joy when he'd insisted she really *had* beaten him.

Her eyelids drooping, she'd demanded they play again. But by then, dawn's mauve light was crowning the Blackspurs and he'd convinced her they should get some sleep. She'd told him about her impending meeting with Otto this morning, and he wanted her to meet it fresh and alert.

He was surprised he'd been able to sleep at all. He'd struggled these past few nights, without the aid of the Delirium. And after their little liaison in the chair last night, he'd yet again been completely sober.

But as he'd fallen into bed with Mireille, close but not touching, her soft breaths and sighs had lulled him into his own restorative slumber.

It was…nice. Sharing a bed with a female without trying to fuck her.

Not that those thoughts had been too far from his mind as he'd drifted off.

She pushed up from the mattress, the bright morning sunshine haloing her silky hair and glinting in her silver eyes.

His heart somersaulted in his chest.

Ours, his wolf whined.

Not yet, Ronin answered. *But...maybe someday.*

You should offer to clean her. A proper tongue bath to help her wake up. Start with the fur between her legs.

Honestly, I thank the High Gods every day that I'm the only one who can hear you.

His wolf chuffed, then panted as Mireille raised her arms above her head and exposed the taut planes of her stomach.

Ronin turned away, not needing that particular distraction, and headed for the bathroom.

"You chickenshit, Butcher? Afraid you'll lose again to someone who just learned how to play your silly horse and castle game?"

Ronin crossed his arms and leaned a shoulder against the door frame as Mireille's gaze blazed a trail across his bare torso.

"Pretty cocky for a female who only won because she dipped her neckline down to distract me with her gorgeous breasts while I was trying to concentrate on my move."

Mireille cupped those gorgeous breasts, and Ronin's wolf howled. "I will never understand why males are so distracted by these, but I thank Faurana the Mother for them every day. Makes at least one of my jobs so much easier."

Ronin hooked a thumb over his shoulder. "Mind if I shower first?"

Mireille waved a permissive hand. "All yours. Try not to drown in the tub again, please. I need my partner."

Ronin laughed, loving that she could be playful about last night. He should have been so fucking ashamed of the state she'd found him in. And under other circumstances, he might have been.

But the beautiful, fierce little female now performing her morning stretches had chased all that away.

He gazed at her from the bathroom doorway, reluctant to turn away, when a knock broke the silence.

All the contentment drained from Mireille's face, their little bubble of false peace burst.

She darted fearful eyes toward him as she opened the door, and he sauntered over, placing a comforting hand on her shoulder.

That silver-haired servant stood in the hallway, breakfast tray in hand. There was no hint of recognition or wariness in the man's eyes, as if yesterday's episode wasn't even a distant memory.

"Master Otto requests your presence in his study, Mistress Valette." The servant passed the tray to Ronin.

"Immediately."

THE SERVANT RAPPED on the door to Otto's study, and Mireille straightened her shoulders and donned her mask. The aloof one she'd abandoned so many times this week.

With Ronin Matakos, of all people.

"Enter." Otto's voice slithered into the dim hallway before the servant pushed the door open, encouraging Mireille to step inside.

Seated behind his desk, that leather ledger open before him, sunlight sparkled around Otto's edges, shadows casting him in silhouette.

Beside him, Nostrata Otto dozed in an indigo chair,

her snake-head cane leaning against the armrest. The ancient female appeared far less regal this morning, dressed in a plain white nightgown and shawl. She startled awake when the door snicked shut, loosing a series of hacking coughs.

The harsh morning sun was not kind to the old Deathstalker, her fragility more apparent than it had been in the dark ballroom last night. She seemed entirely drained. How many more trips to the Halfway could she manage?

Otto stood, his silky, poppy-patterned dressing gown billowing around him, and Mireille settled into a chair. An expectant smile curved his lips. "Good morning. May we offer you something to eat or drink? We apologize for asking you to skip breakfast, but after Nostrata and I discussed your vision, we thought it imperative we speak with you as soon as possible."

Mireille glanced around the room, not seeing a breakfast tray anywhere, wondering where Otto would conjure his offer from. Then realized he likely expected her to refuse it.

Was he so sure of all her answers this morning? It unsettled her. All this information he was withholding.

She decided to throw him off.

"Thank you, Jurgev." She purred his name, a lover's caress. "I'd love some coffee."

Otto frowned, then barked for another servant to have a carafe brought up before turning back to Mireille. "Far be it for us to deny the wishes of our most honored guest."

Mireille was so sick of his slimy confidence, his certainty that the Fae he'd lured here were mere puppets dancing on his tangled strings.

She'd never been able to stomach bullies, even as she recognized that she herself often was one. Perhaps that was why Otto bothered her so much. She saw too much of herself within his careful lies and constant scheming.

They waited in silence until the servant bustled in with a carafe of coffee, three mugs, and a basket of honey-soaked pastries.

Mireille took her time indulging in the spread, relishing Otto's obvious impatience. She stirred sugar and cream into her coffee, then sipped it slowly between bites of the flaky, sweet pastry. When she was finished, she licked the sticky glaze from her fingertips, and Otto's forked tongue darted erratically as her mouth held him in rapt attention.

She pushed her cup and plate aside, then folded her hands atop the desk. "Why am I here?"

Otto cocked his head, as if trying to decipher what she meant by *here*. Here in this office? Here at the estate? Perhaps even here on Ethyrios. "Therein lies the question. Do you remember what we said to you all during the arrival party?"

"You said many things during that speech. That we're all living in delusion. That our hearts and minds would be forever changed by our experiences with you."

"We did say that, didn't we?" Otto flicked through the ledger, and adrenaline scorched through her veins as she saw what page he'd landed on. The one with her own family tree. And in place of the question mark, Otto had scrawled a star. The ink gleamed, still wet. "Have your heart and mind been changed yet, Mireille?"

Her thoughts instantly turned to Ronin. To the feel of his teeth on her neck, his hand fisting her hair, his powerful body beneath her. To his tears and vulnerable confessions. To his laughter and teasing over a trivial game of strategy.

And to waking up this morning to his citrus and pine scent after the most restful sleep she'd had in centuries.

How much could Otto read on her face? Her impervious mask was cracking, her efforts to hide her true feelings disintegrating.

Mireille wrangled herself under control. "That would be quite a feat for you to pull off after only four days, wouldn't it?"

Otto leaned over the desk, propping his chin on interlaced fingers. There was dirt caked into the beds of his normally pristine fingernails. "It has happened in less time than that before, we assure you."

Mireille's mind strayed to Mattias Bisere, to his sister Larissa and the strange dream he'd had after she'd disappeared. Mireille wanted to probe, see what she could get Otto to reveal, but couldn't quite conjure an angle to get there without exposing her own deceptions.

"We also mentioned stories, if you'll recall," Otto crooned. "So many stories, told by so many different groups of people. What stories have you been telling *yourself*?" She sat up straighter, her eyes involuntarily darting to the ledger page dimpled by Otto's elbows. "Have you figured out the meaning of your message from the souls last night? Figured out who that cloaked figure was, pounding on the door of your cabin, *desperate* to reach you?"

Cold fear sluiced through Mireille's limbs, sweat slicking her palms as she raised her chin. "It was my father. Obviously."

Otto's serpentine eyes sparkled with smug amusement. "Odd for a *choreographer* to be carrying a sword, don't you think?"

Mireille would never forget that grinning skull pommel. She'd never seen its like, despite all the missions she'd executed for the IA.

Otto stalked to an overstocked shelf and fished out a tiny book.

Mireille's fingers trembled as he handed it to her and she beheld the title, scrolled in golden print across the tattered fabric cover. One of the few titles written in the common tongue rather than Aramaelish.

A Comprehensive History of Ethyrian Weaponry.

The air in the room thinned, and a pounding rush overtook her mind as her lungs tightened.

"Turn to page one-hundred-and-ninety-four, if you'd be so kind." Otto returned to his seat.

Mireille did as he asked, arriving at a page with an illustration of her father's sword with all the parts identified—fuller, edge, cross-guard, point, grip.

And pommel.

Mireille's vision swam as she attempted to read the words.

The skull pommel represents mortality, a common symbol used across various human weapons.

This had to be some kind of trick. This book couldn't be real, just another of Otto's lies.

Her breakfast threatened to crawl up her throat as Mireille gripped the edge of the desk, certain she was about to pass out.

"You lied to us the other night, Mireille," Otto said, basking in her confusion. "Your father was not a choreographer. He wasn't even Fae.

"Your father was *human.*"

CHAPTER THIRTY-TWO

Mireille's entire childhood flashed before her eyes.

Her mother's insistence that she control her emotions. Her irrational fear of Mireille shifting. Her determination to keep Mireille away from anyone who might be able to sense what her daughter was.

"Did you know?" Otto asked.

"No." A choked whisper.

Her wolf snarled at Otto's gleefully smug grin.

Mireille pushed down the rage, the grief. Calmed her wolf. Smoothed everything over with that glacial detachment she'd always found it so easy to conjure. "This is why you invited me."

"We've met so many interesting individuals in our travels throughout the continent. Including a rather forthcoming wolf pack in a small village in Akti a few decades ago. One wolf in particular told us the most incredible story about a female named Vivienne Valois who'd fallen in love with a human, then fled her pack in fear when she realized she was with child. They tracked her down eventually, of course. But the fierce female—and her even fiercer daughter—fought them, chased them away. Though not before both females sustained some rather nasty injuries. Including a gash to the younger she-wolf's front right leg." Otto gestured to her scar. "Valois sounds an *awful* lot like Valette."

Mireille could barely breathe. Who else knew about this? The Empire had claimed they'd discovered her father's identity. If so, and if they knew she was half-human, why hadn't she been arrested? Unless they'd suspected Otto's plans all along, had thrown her in his path on purpose. Used her, yet again, for their own gains.

"When we saw you at the ballet last week, saw that scar on your forearm, we knew. And your lies at dinner the other night, not to mention your revelatory vision in the Halfway, only confirmed our suspicions." Otto steepled his fingers atop the desk, leering. "We have been searching for you for quite some time, Mireille Valois."

She raised her chin, refusing to show Otto how much he'd thrown her. "Why?"

"We've sought Fae with human heritage for centuries. Sometimes we are wrong, but more often than not... We were correct about nearly every guest this weekend. Their visions confirmed it when they were visited by their human ancestors. Though most of their mortal blood is removed by several generations. They possess seeds of elemental power, but their magic will not be as strong as yours. We have different plans for them."

"What *plans*?"

"So many questions," Otto chuckled and Mireille fought the urge to call upon her wolf and kill Otto right here, right now. Stop all this madness.

But her wolf was just as shell-shocked as she was, reeling from the world-altering information Otto had just shared. Why had her mother never told her? And did Otto know more about her father? His name, perhaps?

"We told you that the theme of this week was stories." Otto cocked his head. "It seems that you have been told some very *inventive* stories for your entire life. How does that make you feel?"

She nearly snarled at him, but didn't answer.

He continued, undeterred. "Though that pales in comparison to the greatest storytellers our world has ever known. Can you guess who they are?"

Again, she kept her silence.

"The Erabis family." Otto spat the name, and beside him, Nostrata hissed. Mireille almost fell out of her seat. She'd forgotten the ancient female was present. "Centuries ago, they began weaving their tales. Tales that called for the separation of the species. Tales that questioned Adelphinae's teachings. Tales that raised up their own false High Gods in place of the true Creator and split Ethyrios into its current hierarchies, with Beastrunners and Deathstalkers beneath Windriders, humans discarded in the colonies."

"For what purpose?" Mireille asked, more to keep him talking than anything else.

"Power. Influence. Wealth. What other purposes are there? They must have foreseen the consequences of discouraging interspecies breeding, must have known that to do so would weaken the other elemental magics beyond their own wind. Give them a reason to hold their dominion over the rest of us."

Mireille's mind swirled, trying to keep up. "That

makes no sense. How have they kept their wind magic as the other elemental powers have faded?"

Otto dipped his head. "Adelphinae has not yet provided us with a clear answer to that question, though we have asked repeatedly."

"What about the sources of the High Gods' magic throughout the continent? The ones that power the god-touched stones? How can those exist if the High Gods aren't real?"

"*All* magic on Ethyrios is a gift from the Creator, despite what you've been told," Otto snarled.

"You worship the Fallen Goddess?" Mireille swept her gaze around the room, over Nostrata's cane. "Your house seems more like a shrine to Stygios."

"Well, one must maintain appearances throughout these days of Imperial conquest, no?" Otto smirked. "As we bide our time and prepare to make our stand."

"Make a stand?" she scoffed. "How is restoring elemental powers to a group of less than forty Fae going to help you defeat the *Empire*?"

"Who said anything about restoring their power?" Otto popped his fangs and leaned back in his chair, intertwining his fingers across his stomach. Again, Mireille reeled. Why was he confessing all this to her? "We intend to take it for ourselves. And restore yours, if you'll join us."

Mireille massaged her temples, trying to chase away the headache forming behind her eyeballs. "Join you how?"

"Tomorrow, you will have the opportunity to gain more power than most Fae on Ethyrios could only dream of possessing. Afterward, we're going to raise a weapon that has been slumbering for centuries. One left in this world by Adelphinae herself."

"What *weapon*?"

Otto regarded her from beneath lowered brows. "You will see. With these gifts from the Creator, there will be no limit to what we could accomplish together. We could raise armies, abolish the Empire, remake the world as *we* see fit. Wouldn't you like to know what that feels like?"

Mireille sat back in her chair. What Otto was offering —even if she believed for one second that he'd revealed the full truth of his plans—was not any kind of future she would have imagined for herself. Nor was it one she wanted. She wasn't a *leader*. She could barely stand inter-acting with people. Not to mention, she suspected that her and Otto's visions for what the world should be were dramatically different.

Still, she thought it best to play along right now. She inclined her head. "A very *tempting* offer. What will you require of me?"

"Our final performance will take place tomorrow at noon. This one will be a story to honor Faurana the Mother, High Goddess of Land and Life. Well, not to *honor*. Surely you can see that the past two performances have been more of an upending of the High Gods' worship. Sacrificing the diva. Journeying to the Halfway. All intended to reveal the Empire's lies and prove our faith to the Creator."

Was everything that Mireille had thought she'd known of the world a lie? Or was the liar seated before her?

Magic *existed*. That much she was sure of. Whether it had been gifted by the High Gods or the Fallen Goddess, she had no idea. Perhaps it was gifted by neither, just a quirk of nature bloomed into existence by Ethyrios itself. Still, she couldn't deny the reason in what Otto was saying. If the High Gods *weren't* real, who was benefiting the most from those myths? The Empire.

Her head swam, and for a moment she wondered if Otto was telling her all this to confuse her. Throw her off balance and get her to blindly agree to his request. "What kind of performance?"

Otto's eyes shined with manic glee as he placed his palms on the desk, Mireille's gaze darting again to those half-moons of dirt crusted in his nail beds. "We are surprised you have not guessed it already. It is another reason we were so eager to have you join us this weekend.

"You will be performing the final solo from *The Curse of Faurana.*"

She's been gone too long, Ronin's wolf whined.

I'm sure she's fine, he consoled the creature. *In case you hadn't noticed, she can handle herself.*

Ronin was also attempting to console *himself.* Had spent the entire time Mireille had been with Otto pacing the room, wondering if he should go check on her.

He knew she wouldn't want that. Whatever play she was making, he wanted her to be able to execute it without his interference. He trusted her. She was the cleverest person he knew. Far cleverer than he was.

But none of those thoughts made him feel any better that it was coming up on an hour since she'd left.

Just when he was about to throw caution to the wind, tear through the estate, and go rescue her, the door swung open and Mireille stepped in. His shoulders relaxed at the sight of her, intact and unharmed, but worry stirred through him at her troubled eyes and fraught expression.

"What happened?" He rushed to her, gripping her

upper arm. Needing to reassure himself of her physical presence.

Her lower lip quivered as a small breath escaped. She pulled out of his grip and plopped down into an armchair, avoiding his gaze. "Otto told me something about myself this morning. A secret my mother kept from me my entire life."

Ronin fell to his knees before her, clasping her hands. Mimicking her supplication before him last night. "Whatever it is—"

"My father was human," she blurted, and Ronin clenched the armrests to keep from toppling over.

She brushed a hand through her hair, and her scent washed over him. The notes in it crystallized with stunning clarity. That underlying sweetness, that floral note on the edge of decay.

Mortality.

The answer had been, quite literally, right under his nose and on the tip of his tongue this entire time.

Ronin sat back on his heels, placing his palms on her thighs, trying to offer whatever comfort he could. Based on her age, he knew her father must have passed. His chest squeezed painfully for her. To find out the truth about her father at the same time as any hope of ever meeting the man was snatched away... Fuck, that was rough.

Not to mention terrifying. Ronin remembered what had become of anyone accused of being a half-breed during the war; they were hunted by the Empire, exposed by newly paranoid friends and neighbors, then thrown into Tartarus. He wondered how many of those prisoners had been taken based on rumor and speculation alone. Outwardly, there was no way to tell a full-blooded Fae from a half-breed. Well, other than that extremely faint dissonance he'd recognized in Mireille's scent. Did the Empire know of it?

"They were from Akti," Mireille choked out. "Both my mother and my father. I should have…should have realized earlier the significance of that territory, its proximity to the Desolation. It's where the majority of the human settlements were before the war. Where the most interspecies breeding would have occurred."

"So the other guests…"

"All have humans somewhere in their bloodlines. It's what those stars signified in their family trees."

"Mattias and Larissa…"

Mireille nodded.

"But Mattias *could* wield fire magic. Even if it was an extremely low level. If mixed human and Fae blood is what supplies it and you're half human, why can't you?"

"I don't know," she whispered. "I've never… Maybe the awareness of it affects one's ability to wield it? I had no idea that I possessed it, so why would I have ever tried to access it?"

"If awareness is the key, then why can't Nero access water magic?" Ronin countered. "He suspected his ancestors possessed it, so surely he would've been able to conjure *something*."

Mireille growled in frustration. "I don't *know*."

He squeezed her thighs tighter, his eyes softening. "I'm so sorry, Mireille. So sorry that you had to learn about your father this way."

He sensed the shift immediately. That cool facade returned, her entire countenance hardening. Her shoulders stiffened as she pulled herself upright.

"I'm fine. Otto shared more important things with me that you need to hear."

"Mireille…" He reached for her cheek, but she swatted him away.

"I said I'm *fine*, Ronin. This isn't over. And if we don't figure out *exactly* what the fuck Otto is up to, there are going to be far worse consequences for everyone here than some inconsequential secret of my parentage."

Ronin wanted to argue with her. Wanted to shout that her feelings about this *were* important. That she deserved some time to process them. Deserved to give herself some of that compassion she'd shown him last night.

But he knew that work was her favorite distraction. So he didn't push.

Not yet.

"Tell me," he said, crossing to the other chair and listening as Mireille explained everything that Otto had told her this morning. About his search for Fae with human heritage. About the purpose of these bizarre performances, an attempt to appease the Creator.

About his desire to raise some weapon to take down the Empire, for fuck's sake. The old billionaire really was off his fucking rocker.

"Otto will be distracted for the next several hours as he meets with the other guests." Mireille pushed herself up out of her chair. "We should take the opportunity to see what else we can learn about this weapon he's hoping to unleash. He offered me an unintentional clue this morning about where we should look."

Ronin rose, stepping past her to open the door. "Your lead, Valette. Where are we headed?"

He was heartened by the small smile she offered him.

"To the place where death feeds life and life feeds death.

"The greenhouse."

MIREILLE LED Ronin through the halls of the guest wing, then down the staircase to the first floor.

In the parlors, small groups of guests chattered in excited speculation about their readings with Otto and Nostrata this morning.

Mireille held her tongue, though she wanted to scream at them. Wanted to warn them about what Otto had told her.

But causing chaos right now was not the most prudent move. They needed more information, needed to get a better grasp on Otto's plans in order make their own to defeat him and save the guests.

Plus, even if she was able to convince them all to abandon this crazy pursuit, no one could go anywhere until Otto lifted that ward surrounding the estate.

Just as she and Ronin reached the double-doors to the patio, a hand gripped her upper arm.

"I was right!" Nero Beruglia gushed in Mireille's ear as he pulled her aside. Ronin paused by the doors. "I just had my reading with Otto and Nostrata. I *knew* there was water power in my bloodline. My great-great-great-grandfather visited me in the Halfway. He was human, if you can believe it."

Mireille plastered on a friendly smile. "I can believe it."

"Otto says he's found a way to restore the power to me." Awe rippled across Nero's feline features. "Something about a final performance tomorrow? I cannot wait to see what he's got planned for us."

Guilt twisted Mireille's gut. She wanted to warn Nero to be on his guard, but something about the blatant hunger in the male's eyes stilled her tongue. Mireille wasn't confident he'd even believe her.

"How did Cecelia take the news?"

Nero's face fell. "Her reading was not as…successful. No mixed bloodlines in her heritage. But she is excited for me. Wait until our children hear about this. I wonder if Otto will allow them to come here for a treatment as well."

Mireille jolted. She'd never even considered what Otto might do to the guests *without* human blood.

"Just…be wary tomorrow. You've heard everything Otto said. About blessings not coming without sacrifice? Think long and hard tonight about what sacrifices you are willing to make."

He waved her off. "Nonsense. I would make *any* sacrifice to reclaim the power that's been taken from my family."

Mireille's gaze drifted to the parlor, full of Fae showcasing the same ravenous excitement as Nero. All firmly within Otto's thrall. She returned pleading eyes to Nero, but he was lost to his dreams.

"Mireille," Ronin called out, shooting her a questioning glance.

"Take care, Nero." She loaded as much warning as she dared into the sign-off.

The male nodded, then bounded back to join the jubilant conversation in the parlor.

"What was that all about?" Ronin asked as they stepped out onto the patio.

"Otto's got them all wrapped around his slithery fingers. They'll do whatever he says in exchange for these *gifts* he's promised them."

Ronin remained silent as they hurried down the steps and into the greenhouse, the humid warmth within a balm against the freeze.

They clomped down the iron staircase, their footfalls echoing into silence broken only by the faint buzzing of insects and the eerie whisper of rustling leaves.

Inside the stone circle, those bushes of pale blue roses beckoned. Mireille could've been mistaken, but it almost seemed as though the blooms had grown larger since she'd last seen them.

"So," Ronin whispered, "what, exactly, are we looking for?"

"There was dirt caked around Otto's fingernails during our meeting this morning." Mireille swept her gaze down several of the leafy pathways. "Let's split up and look around. See if there are any areas where the soil looks recently disturbed."

Ronin nodded, taking one of the pathways to the left as Mireille stalked down one to the right.

Despite her anxiety, despite her world-rocking conversation with Otto this morning, she couldn't help but feel a sense of awe at the specimens around her, had to stop herself from abandoning this task and going on a foraging adventure through the impressive collection.

She passed a tufted row of dienswort, small red blooms against a sea of deep green, and her fingers itched to pluck up the flowers. Dienswort was difficult to come by, and expensive. She stepped away from the bounty with a mournful sigh, then rounded a corner and skidded to a halt.

Towering nearly all the way to the domed ceiling was a tree that Mireille had read about, but had never seen in real life. And if the legends were true, *no one* had seen one in centuries. A thick, stark white trunk speared up into a canopy of foliage in a vivid spectrum, every color in the rainbow and all the hues in between. Gauzy green moss draped from the branches, and Mireille couldn't help but gawk.

Resurrection trees once covered the plains in the Desolation. Legend stated that their leaves had a myriad of magical uses. Including the ability pull a Fae back from the brink of True Death. But they'd all been decimated during the war, destroyed by the humans in retaliation against the Fae and their magic. She wondered how Otto had managed to get his hands on one, much less kept it alive. They were very temperamental, especially outside their native climate.

She was so awestuck, she almost didn't notice the dirt dusted across the pathway.

"Ronin!" she called out. He must have been close, because he was beside her in an instant. "Look." She pointed to the trail.

He cocked an eyebrow and they both stepped over the low fence to examine the tree.

Ronin ran his fingers through the leaves as Mireille crouched, circling the trunk. At the base, right at the edge of the soil, was a small knot. Smoother and shinier than a knot should be. As if fingers had often rubbed across it. She pressed against it, and the ground beneath them lowered, a slow descent accompanied by a waterfall of soil.

The platform hit the ground with an echoing boom, and as soon as they stepped off, it rose again, closing above and leaving them in a darkened, white stone hallway.

Mireille grabbed Ronin's hand and he intertwined their fingers.

To their left, faint blue light crept across the walls. To the right was nothing but solid stone. Ronin swiveled his head, sniffing the air. "I think the crypt is on the other side of this wall."

They turned a corner, and Mireille gasped.

The white walls gave way to packed dirt, an underground cave containing a honeycomb of crevices carved into gargantuan, gnarled white roots. Each crevice, about a hundred in total, held a piece of glowing anastasium. The stones pulsed, brightening and dimming. As if they were breathing.

Ronin bent down before a crevice to examine a stone. "Are these—"

"They're souls," said a low female voice behind them.

Mireille whirled to find Layla Fetar standing in the entrance to the chamber.

Before Layla even had a chance to continue, Ronin rushed the tiny female, wrapping his hand around her throat and slamming her against the dirt wall.

"What the *fuck* do you want?" he snarled.

Layla clawed at his hands, face purpling, choking down sips of air.

"Ronin," Mireille muttered a warning.

"Not what you think," Layla wheezed.

"Try me." Ronin leaned in closer and extended his fangs. His claws as well, the thickest slicing into Layla's flesh and drawing a line of blood.

Layla's foot shot out, connecting with Ronin's groin in a well-aimed, forceful blow.

He doubled over, retching, and Layla dropped to the floor, landing gracefully on her feet. She whipped out a throwing knife and pointed the tip at Ronin's eye.

Mireille bounded between them. "What *do* you want? Other than to damage goods I had plans for later?"

Layla breathed heavily as she tried to recover from Ronin's attack. "Drop the act. I know you two aren't really an item."

Mireille assisted Ronin to the floor as he cradled his injured groin. "Not an act," he rasped.

"I know why you're really here," Layla said. "And I need your help."

Ronin tensed, though both he and Mireille kept their expressions neutral. "Bullshit. You tried to have me killed at the fight last weekend."

"I didn't," Layla hissed. "Who do you think paid Maloney to curb the killing blow? Otto was furious when his plan to eliminate his competition for Mireille didn't pan out, though he never suspected why. I've been protecting you the whole time. He wanted to send Kosera after you when you woke up during the seance last night too, rough you up a bit. But I convinced him to let me do it instead. Promised to incapacitate you with Delirium. I knew you'd recover." Layla bent forward, bracing her forearms on her knees, chest heaving.

"Why didn't you tell us before?" Mireille asked.

"I thought I could take Otto down on my own, that I wouldn't need to endanger anyone else. Or involve two spies sent by Imperial Affairs." Layla cocked an eyebrow. "But I'm out of time. High Gods Matakos, that's some grip you have." She broke into a coughing fit.

Mireille approached, palms raised, then faster than Layla could stop her, had the female disarmed. She flipped a throwing knife in one hand as she winked at Ronin over her shoulder. He shot her a heated look.

She leveled the knives at Layla. "Explain. If I like what you have to say, *maybe* I'll let you have these back. Though I can't guarantee it. These are so light and well-balanced. Might just keep them for myself."

Layla massaged her throat, the redness already fading thanks to her Fae healing. "If you help me, I just might let you."

Mireille ambled over to Ronin, placing herself before him, the tip of the blades still aimed at Layla.

"I don't work for Otto," Layla said, trying to convey her sincerity with unwavering eye contact. "Or rather, he *thinks* I work for him, but I've been doing quite the opposite for decades."

Both Ronin and Mireille remained silent.

Layla smirked. "Saving your questions until the end? I like you two." Her features hardened. "I work for an organization called the Teles Chrysos. I'm going to assume you've never heard of us."

Mireille hadn't heard of them, though she did recognize the word Teles. The name of that symbol long associated with the Fallen Goddess, a circle slashed through with a vertical line.

"We are working to keep Adelphinae's faith alive. Her *true* faith. Not whatever bastardized version Otto believes he's supporting." Layla ran a hand down her white braid, the black one blending in with her tight leather uniform. "Otto has been hunting down information about the Fallen Goddess for centuries. At first, we thought to recruit him, but he's stymied all our efforts at contact. Pursing his own agenda. Our leadership decided it would be wise to put someone on the inside. To make a move against him, if necessary."

"Let me guess," Mireille chimed in. "Now's the time to make the move."

Layla nodded. "Everything he's working toward culminates tomorrow."

Mireille aimed a careful glance at Ronin. Could they trust Layla? Ronin gave her a subtle nod.

"The Empire has assigned us the same task," he said. "We've been sent to decipher his plans and thwart them. Take him down."

"One of the rare occasions where our goals align with the Empire. The Erabis family are worse than you can imagine. They will be the destruction of this world if their power remains unchecked." Mireille remembered Layla's history. That she'd been a Shadow Maiden to Empress Mila herself. Must have had a front row seat to the Erabis family's evils. "But they aren't the most immediate threat. If Otto is able to raise his weapon…"

"What *is* the weapon?" Mireille asked.

A look of pure horror twisted Layla's delicate features. "He intends to resurrect Nyctima."

"*What?*" Ronin spat at the same time Mireille whispered, "How is that even possible?"

"Nyctima is a *myth*," Ronin said.

Layla shook her head. "The most powerful myths are woven with threads of truth. Nyctima was once very much real. An emissary, of sorts, for Adelphinae on Ethyrios. They say it was Leonin Erabis's grandfather, Phaeban Erabis, who destroyed her over a millennium ago, back when their family first turned from the Creator's faith. He used her bones to build parts of this estate."

Mireille shuddered. Cathedral of Bones. *Literally.*

"How was he able to destroy her?" Ronin asked.

"He summoned her with a flute made of fire opal. A powerful object that Adelphinae had gifted to the Delphine, the head of her priestesses here in Ethyrios. Phaeban sacked one of her temples and stole it. Stygios's myth, *the Taming of Nyctima*, is a bastardization of Phaeban's story, twisted to make it seem as if the High God himself turned Nyctima into his own *pet.*"

"The statue in the galleries," Mireille turned to Ronin. "Stygios was playing a flute."

Ronin didn't respond, was still carefully regarding Layla. "How do you know this? And why does no one else on the continent speak of it?"

"Only a few very brave, and very old, Fae have dared keep the true word of the Creator alive against the Empire's wishes. Many are members of our organization."

"The real fire opal flute," Mireille asked. "Don't tell me that—"

Layla nodded. "Otto has acquired it."

"*How?*" Ronin asked, incredulously. "And why would the Empire be so careless as to let an object like *that* slip through their fingers?"

"It was lost during the chaos of Leonin's war with the humans. I have no idea how Otto finally managed to track it down after all these years."

"And you're sure he has it?" Mireille asked.

"He speaks as if he does. It's central to his plans. Though I've searched this entire estate and have yet to see any sign of it."

"Still," Ronin said, "if Nyctima was destroyed, why

would the flute summon her? How does Otto intend to *resurrect* her?"

Layla pointed toward the alcoves. "By using those."

Mireille turned to survey the glowing stones.

"Those are the souls of the Fae that Otto has been luring to his estate with promises of restoring their elemental magic," Layla said sadly. "Souls of mixed species heritage. Offerings to the Creator and the very fuel that's rebuilding her fallen emissary. He's been feeding them to Nyctima's spirit. Strengthening her. The tree above keeps them intact, a symbiotic relationship of sorts. The souls give life to the tree and in return, the tree restores them after Nyctima's feedings."

"Where death feeds life and life feeds death," Ronin whispered.

Layla continued, "Her spirit comes to feed every one-hundred-and-five days."

"The Scales of Nyctima," Mireille breathed. "Those lights that appear in the sky. They actually *are* Nyctima?"

"Sort of," Layla confirmed. "They are a cast-off of her spiritual energy, the only part of her that still remains. When they appear, a path between this world and the Halfway opens, allows Otto and Nostrata to perform those seances."

Mireille gestured toward the stones. "So, is that what he intends for the other guests tomorrow? To burn them and capture their souls to feed to Nyctima once he summons her?"

Layla shook her head again, her mouth drawing downward. "No. This is the final feeding. A *live* feeding. It's why he's gathered so many guests. He only invited one at a time before he acquired the flute. This will be a group offering to both Nyctima and Adelphinae that

Otto hopes will persuade the Goddess to bless him with fire magic."

"He has no human heritage, though," Ronin chimed in. "How could he hope to acquire it?"

"He may not have human heritage, but he does have mixed blood running through his system." Layla shuddered. "He drinks from the guests. After he kills them and before he burns them. He's consumed plenty these past decades."

"Why doesn't he just drink from humans?" Mireille asked.

"He's convinced it has to be mixed blood." Layla shuddered.

A crushing sadness weighed on Mireille's shoulders. All this senseless death. She remembered the one that had kicked off this fucking bizarre week. "The diva—"

"He fed from her, yes. Then fed her soul to Nyctima to open the Halfway last night, to confirm his suspicions about the heritage of this group of guests."

Ronin crossed his arms over his chest, skepticism overtaking his handsome features. "Why is the Teles Chrysos trying to thwart him? Wouldn't you all *want* Otto to resurrect a weapon that can take down the Empire?"

Layla scoffed. "And give *Otto* all that power? Whoever wields that flute will *control* Nyctima. Can use her as a tool for either good or evil. Which do you think Jurgev Otto will choose? Besides, it is not yet time for us to take on the Empire. The prophecy has not yet been fulfilled."

Mireille waited for Layla to elaborate, but her candor had come to an end.

"Why are you trusting *us* with all this?" Ronin asked. "We work for your enemies."

Layla leaned back against the wall. "I can't take him and Nostrata *and* Kosera down alone. I need your help. We work together to defeat him, then go our separate ways. And you promise not to reveal anything about our organization to your bosses."

Mireille glanced to Ronin again, reading the same thing on his face that she had felt after her conversation with Otto this morning.

Fuck the Empire.

Not only had they punished Ronin for following *their* orders, she had a sneaking suspicion that they'd been hiding things from her as well. That they, and Skanisse, knew far more about Otto's plans than they'd revealed. Had known *exactly* what Mireille was and had put her squarely in Otto's crosshairs.

Layla continued. "Whatever Otto's got planned for tomorrow—"

"He wants me to perform the final solo from *The Curse of Faurana*," Mireille cut in. "As a dishonor to the High Goddess to appease Adelphinae. I don't think he means to kill me at the end of it, like he did the diva."

"You don't *think?*" Ronin growled.

"He wants me to join him."

Ronin's face paled. "What the *fuck?* You didn't say yes, did you?"

"Of course I did. Let him think what he wants." Mireille approached the roots, surveyed the stones. Close up, she could see a faint, rainbow shimmer running through them, small, nearly microscopic particles.

Was that really all a soul was comprised of?

"Do you remember a Beastrunner female named Larissa Bisere?" Mireille asked.

Layla cocked her head. "Coyote bi-form?" Mireille

nodded. "Yes. She was one of Otto's most eager guests. She asked so many questions, about herself and her heritage. I liked her; she was spunky. I almost tried to save her, but she was so desperate for Otto's offerings that I'm not sure she would have believed me even if I'd tried to talk her out of it."

"Was Otto able to restore her fire?" Mireille asked.

"He's never even tried," Layla whispered. "He kills them before they even get the chance."

"Which one of these stones belongs to her?"

"Why?"

"Because her brother deserves a chance to say good-bye," Mireille answered. Ronin squeezed her shoulder.

Layla pointed to the center crevice.

"How do you know which stones belong to which slain guests?" Ronin asked.

"Because I bore witness to each of their deaths." Layla squared her shoulders, pain and regret passing over her beautiful features. "It was the least I could do."

"What does he do with their ashes?" Ronin whispered.

"He uses them to fertilize his rosebushes." Layla sneered. "Bone meal is full of nutrients. The traces of anastasium are what gives those roses their pale blue color." She plucked up Larissa's stone and handed it to Mireille.

"Why give this to me now?" Mireille slipped the cool stone into her pocket. "Won't Otto realize it's missing tomorrow?"

"We'll just have to make sure he's too distracted to notice." Layla's grin was savage. Deadly.

"Follow me."

CHAPTER THIRTY-FOUR

*L*ayla led them out of the chamber and into the white stone hallway.

Ronin had no idea what to make of everything the female had shared, so he focused on a single goal.

Survive tomorrow. And ensure that Mireille did as well.

Layla took a forked path that led into another chamber filled with tables and racks of weapons—swords, maces, hammers, and an entire wall of axes in different shapes and sizes.

A devilish glint shone in Layla's espresso eyes. "Take your pick."

Mireille and Ronin shared a mischievous grin, then bounded into the room.

This was more like it. Slicing and stabbing, not snooping and spying. His comfort zone.

His wolf panted, craving the violence promised by this bounty of honed steel.

Mireille bent over a table, running her fingers down

the length of a long broadsword with a skull-shaped pommel. "This is a human sword." There was something thoughtful, yet pained, in her examination. "I saw my father carrying one like it in the Halfway. Is it Typhon steel?"

"No. But it's sharp and heavy enough to kill a Fae if you know where to strike. My advice? Go for the head." Layla loosed a wicked cackle.

Mireille raised the sword in a two-handed grip, her fists tightening on the hilt. Ronin swallowed.

Was there anything sexier than a beautiful female wielding an instrument of death?

She angled the sword, then brought it down in a swift, diagonal arc.

He prayed to whatever Gods existed that he'd get to witness Mireille use that cut on Otto. A sight he suspected would live on in his dreams for centuries.

"I want this one," Mireille said, her face a mask of delicious savagery.

"Excellent choice," Layla answered over her shoulder, her fingers dancing across a shelf of daggers. "Butcher?"

Ronin approached the axes, plucking up the selection he'd made as soon as he'd seen the weapon.

The two sharp curves of the double-headed axe held no carvings or markings. Just a simple, effective tool of destruction. A replica of the axe wielded by Vestan the Warrior, the very same that appeared on the Northern Territories' sigil.

And what was Ronin if not a warrior? Perhaps even the greatest warrior Ethyrios had ever seen. At one time, at least.

He called upon that strength again, that *purpose* he'd

felt on those battlefields, twisted though it had been for the Empire's goals.

Now he would use his strength for his own purpose. To protect the daring she-wolf beside him. To protect the world from devious power-players like Otto.

To take a step toward the role he still had to play, the one that voice in the chronomancer's shop—perhaps the Fallen Goddess herself—had alluded to.

He slung the axe over his shoulder and sauntered over to Layla, who nodded approvingly.

"Do you know what that one's called?" she asked.

"The axe of Vestan?" Ronin guessed with a chuckle.

Layla shook her head. "Vestan is an ancient human god. No more real than the High Gods themselves, but as Otto has always said, there is power in stories. In the *collective belief* in stories. Adelphinae knows this better than anyone. It's why she has been so angered that her own story has been erased from our history. Those ancient humans believed that Vestan used that axe to shape the skeleton of this world, carving the mountains, rivers, lakes, and sea beds. So it was only natural they gave his weapon an appropriate name."

Layla elongated her fangs, bloodlust rising, and the words she uttered stirred Ronin's soul.

"They named it *Bonecleaver.*"

CHAPTER THIRTY-FIVE

Snowflakes drifted past the window, falling stars against the pitch-black night.

In the bed beside Mireille, Ronin's breathing whispered a peaceful melody. *He* certainly hadn't had any trouble falling asleep tonight.

Mireille, however, had been awake for hours, going over plans in her mind that seemed both too hastily thrown together and yet the only possible solution to acquire the flute and defeat Otto.

The plan was brutal in its simplicity.

Layla would hide the weapons Mireille and Ronin had chosen behind the statue of Otto's ancestor in that alcove in the crypt. And as soon as Mireille began her dance, Ronin would grab them to make their final stand. She would have to give the most mesmerizing performance of her life to keep the Deathstalker billionaire and the guests enthralled.

The whole plan seemed patently ridiculous and

hinged on so many things going right. But they were out of options.

And out of time.

Even with all those thoughts swirling, the one really keeping her awake was the bomb Otto had dropped into her own personal history.

Mireille was *half-human*.

On the one hand, it explained so much about her life. She'd always felt different from other Fae. Always felt like an outsider. In the past, she'd attributed it to her solitary upbringing.

But her sense of otherness had never gone away, not even when she'd finally joined society in Kheimos. Her fellow dancers had always been a mystery, puzzles Mireille couldn't solve. Even Juliet, who'd seemed inclined to reveal her full picture. Mireille had thought she'd figured it out once, with Josef, but that disaster had only strengthened her long-held belief: she was different. And better alone.

She sighed, grabbing the small ballerina figurine from the nightstand.

The mattress shifted, followed by Ronin's deep rasp. "Can't sleep?"

She turned, tucking the figurine under her cheek as she shook her head.

"Are you worried about tomorrow?" he asked, tucking his own hands under his cheek. His tattoos shimmered across his biceps, and Mireille tried to ignore her sudden, intense desire for him to wrap her up in those impressive arms, hold her close, and tell her everything was going to be alright.

Just a stupid fantasy, really.

Mireille had pushed people away her entire life,

drifting from performance to performance, never exposing her true self. She had made this bed and was now, quite literally, laying in it.

"No. I never worry about my assignments. I know I'll be able to handle whatever gets thrown at me tomorrow. Even after all the shit I just learned, I trust myself."

"And your partner?" He tossed her a sleepy smile, and she had to physically restrain herself from leaping for him, threading her fingers through his tousled white hair, and kissing his fucking face off.

"I guess I trust him, too." She smiled back. "After all."

He tucked a strand of hair behind her ear, his palm lingering on her cheek, and a shiver coursed through her. "Wow, after only two weeks? You might want to sharpen those survival skills, Valette."

She snickered, pressing her cheek into his hand. High Gods, had it only been two weeks? She felt like she'd known him far longer.

"How are you feeling about the other news you received today? About your father?"

They hadn't had a chance to discuss it after their meeting with Layla. Otto had insisted everyone attend a raucous dinner party to celebrate the results of their readings.

Most of the guests had been just as jubilant as Nero, who'd spent the hours-long dinner regaling his seatmates with his plans for his newfound *power*. Mireille had dropped as many hints as she dared that tomorrow may not go how he expected. By the end of the meal, a shred of doubt had started creeping into his eyes.

They'd discussed it with Layla, the possibility of warning the guests. Maybe even recruiting them to take Otto down at dinner. But they couldn't risk the loss of the flute, couldn't risk it slipping out of their grasp and into potentially even more dangerous hands.

Mireille pulled out the figurine, twirling the little ballerina on the bed between her and Ronin. "When I was younger, I had all these theories about who my father might be. A rich merchant, a skilled tradesman, a bladesmith perhaps? Maybe even some important advisor to the Emperor. But do you want to know what my favorite theory was?"

Sympathy shone in Ronin's blue-yellow eyes. "Tell me." A soft request. "Please."

"You guessed it at dinner with Otto the other night. That he was a choreographer. The great mastermind behind the scenes at the Imperial Ballet in Delos. Providing the steps for every dancer who graced that legendary stage. Even Irina Amiel. What other reason would he have had to gift me the music box that contained this?"

Mireille held the figurine in a band of moonlight. Hairline cracks spider-webbed across the ballerina's tiny, painted face.

"Ever since then, I thought if I could just be perfect, if I could manage all the steps, if I could follow life's chore-ography...that maybe he would—" Her voice cracked and Ronin wrapped a large hand around her forearm, a comforting, though respectfully distanced, pressure. "That he would come back for me."

She saw her own pain reflected in Ronin's gaze.

The pain of doing everything right, but still being discarded.

The pain of locking down one's true self.

The pain of being alone in the world.

She sucked in a shuddering breath, her eyes stinging

as she asked the question that had dogged her for centuries.

"Why didn't he want me, Ronin?"

RONIN'S CHEST ached at Mireille's anguished question.

He didn't hesitate, wrapped her in his arms and let her cry against his chest as her icy exterior melted away.

And though some callous part of him had taunted her days ago that there was nothing beneath it, deep down he *knew* that this is what her tears would reveal.

A shattered soul left to fend for itself. A vulnerability so deeply rooted that to expose it to *anyone* would require tearing out too many vital parts.

The very same things that were underneath *his* exterior. He and Mireille were more alike than he'd ever thought possible.

He stroked a hand through her hair, waiting for her sobs to ebb.

Once they did, he sat up against the headboard and pulled her into his lap. "Do you know what I like most about you, Mireille?"

She tipped her chin up to look at him, and her tear-soaked eyes were so unguarded he could barely fucking stand it.

"Your imperfections. Like this one right here." He kissed the small freckle on her shoulder. "And this one." He lifted her forearm, running his thumb along the silver scar. She released a shuddering breath, nestling in closer.

"And especially this one." He tapped a finger against her temple. "Your mind works differently than anyone

I've ever met. I don't think it ever stops." She huffed a small laugh.

"But the best imperfection?" He flattened his palm against her chest. "It's this. Your broken heart."

He lowered the strap of her silk camisole, pressing a gentle kiss upon the frantic organ. Then breathed his final confession against her soft, warm skin.

"Let me help you piece it back together."

His words were kindling. She turned in his lap, her thighs bracketing his hips, and grasped his cheeks. Glistening fire blazed in her silver eyes as he wrapped his arms around her lower back.

And then her mouth was on him, and any worries he had about tomorrow or the day after or the day after faded away into blissful oblivion.

CHAPTER THIRTY-SIX

No one had ever looked at Mireille the way Ronin was looking at her. Had ever said such things to her. Had ever seen her so clearly, despite her efforts at obfuscation with every word, every gesture, every fight these past weeks.

She had no words to offer him. He'd just uttered all the most meaningful ones. So she kissed him again instead, pushing her tongue into his mouth. Her entire body lit up at his responding groan.

He massaged her ass as she ground her hips against the growing hardness beneath his loose sleep pants.

Sweet Amatu, she'd never been so happy that a male slept without a shirt on. She pulled away to marvel at his sculpted, powerful beauty, dragging a finger across the glacial swirls on his chest.

"Will these disappear when they uncage you?" she asked, her lips swollen, her mind loose and hazy from his drugging kisses.

He shook his head. "They're permanent. Only the magic within the ink itself will be removed."

She curled her fingers around the back of his neck. "I kinda like them."

He bent down to slant his mouth over hers again. "Good. I'm hoping you'll be seeing them often."

His kiss wasn't nearly as gentle as hers. Hand fisting her hair, he surged upwards, tilting her head back and taking what he wanted, his body curving over her.

He yanked her hair harder, and she moaned at the delicious pain.

"Take control, Ronin," she begged. "I'm so sick of clinging to it."

She felt his smirk against her mouth. "I fucking knew it."

She rolled her eyes and he smacked her cheek, hard enough to startle but not hurt.

"First rule," he said, all the playful smarminess fleeing his face. "Do not roll your eyes at your master."

A tentative giggle escaped her as his eyes narrowed. "Sorry... Sorry. It's just so..."

He cupped her skull, his thumbs tilting her chin up and forcing her to look at him.

"Are you sure you want to do this?" She nodded at the tenderness lurking beneath his dominance. "Then before we start, we should probably discuss some boundaries."

"Okay," she tittered nervously. "Like what?"

"Tonight will be all about your pleasure. Don't forget that. Even if it seems like I'm in control, remember that you have control too. I will only go as far as you allow me to go." A dull, heated ache throbbed in her low belly. "I think you *want* to submit to me. To take your body to the razor-thin edge between pain and pleasure. Am I right?"

Fuck, yes, that's what she wanted. She nodded enthusiastically.

"I need to hear you say the words."

"Yes. Yes, it's what I want."

"Anything off-limits?"

"No ass play."

He chuckled, dragging a gentle thumb across her bottom lip. "Got it. Anything else? Slapping? Spanking? Biting?"

Heat crawled up her neck and cheeks. "I am *very* much on board with all of that."

He raised her hand to his mouth and nipped the base of her thumb, his canines dimpling her flesh. "Safe word?"

"Spiders."

He threw his head back in a hooting laugh. "Good choice." The smirk gracing his soft mouth set her stomach fluttering. High *Gods* she wanted that mouth back on her immediately.

"What about you?" she asked.

"Me?"

"Is there anything you don't want me to do to you?"

"Nothing," he answered, his gaze so bright and open and honest that her chest squeezed. "Fight me, kick me, punch me. Give me your worst. I'll happily take it."

Her breasts pebbled and his eyes dipped straight there. "Hmmm." His low grunt crept up her thighs, a rumbling caress. Too much fucking talking. She wanted him *now*. "So that's what does it for you. You want to fight me off, don't you?"

Her breathing grew rapid. She'd been wondering

what it would feel like to be Ronin's prey. And the fact that she was about to find out? Fucking *bliss.*

Bait him, her wolf piped up.

What?

Hit him, the creature purred. *Trust me.*

Mireille's lips curved into a wicked grin, and she slapped Ronin across the face.

His shock was genuine before it turned into something else. Something molten.

"Oh, little she-wolf," he purred, grabbing her wrist as she attempted another strike. "You have no idea what you just started." He shoved her out of his lap, all traces of teasing gone. "Go stand over there."

Her palm stung and her heart slammed against her ribs, her knees wobbling as she padded to the center of the room.

Her wolf chuffed. *Told you.*

Keep it down in there.

Killjoy.

Mireille turned back to face Ronin, who was sprawled against the headboard, long legs spread.

A king of beasts awaiting his sacrifice.

With one hand behind his head, he dipped the other below his waistband, stroking himself. Pinning her in place with his heavy-lidded stare, a faint smirk twisted his soft, cruel mouth. "Here's how this is going to go. From now on, you are under my command. If you're good, if you please me, I will reward you. If you defy me, you'll be punished. Do you understand?"

She nodded, the tumultuous beat in her chest matching the pulsing, liquid heat slicking her panties.

"Say the fucking word, Mireille," he growled.

"Yes," she breathed. She could barely stand upright. Wanted him to touch her so badly it physically *hurt*.

"Good." The headboard creaked as he settled back against it. "Take off your clothes. Show me what's mine tonight."

Clasping the hem, she lifted her shirt over her head. Ronin's attention seared across her exposed chest. She slid her silk pants off and tossed them aside, then stood upright, drawing her shoulders back and pushing her breasts forward.

She trailed her hands down her stomach, Ronin's gaze a fiery brand upon her overly sensitive skin, then reached for her panties.

"Leave those on. For now."

Unsure of what to do next, she left her hands at her sides, fingers trembling. Ronin seemed content to let her stand there, soaking up every inch of her as his hand moved below his waistband.

After what felt like an eternity, he shifted, throwing his legs over the side of the mattress and spreading them wide, palms braced behind him.

"Come over here."

She took a tentative step forward.

"No. On your hands and knees." His marbled eyes gleamed—a predator stalking through midnight woods. "*Crawl* to me."

His command pelted her, a physical blow that stole her breath and deepened the ache between her thighs. She crouched down, eyes glued to the soft carpet.

"Eyes on me." His lips curved upwards, exposing his sharp fangs. "I want to remember this. The impervious Mireille Valette, crawling across the floor, her body shaking with anticipation for my touch."

She held his gaze for the entire length of her journey, her back arched and her drenched panties chafing.

Electric energy flowed between them. As if everything they'd experienced together these past weeks—the bickering, the fighting, that explosive kiss, the blood drinking—had led them to the precipice of this moment.

Once she reached him, she sat back on her heels, knees spread with her hands on her thighs and her head bowed. Awaiting his next order.

At the heavy weight of his perusal, she dared a glance upward. The longing and lust she found on his handsome face nearly stopped her heart.

His hand shot out to grip her chin, and he turned her face side to side. "*Very* good." His praise trailed gentle fingers across her clit, and she sucked in a sharp breath as he ran a callused thumb along her lower lip. "Now show me what this pretty little mouth can do."

He released her face and leaned back on his palms, his stiff cock tenting his pants between them. A challenge. One she was determined to surmount.

She rose onto her knees, reaching for his waistband, but he slapped her hands away. "No. Mouth only."

She cocked an incredulous eyebrow, and he circled her wrists in a single hand, hauling her face toward his. "Really? Defiance already?"

His breath on her lips tasted like frosted pine needles, the cool, crisp scent heightening her arousal.

"Nuh-no," she shuddered out, and he squeezed her wrists, just this side of painfully tight. She knew he could break them with little effort.

"No, what?" he grunted.

"No, Ronin." She tried to look contrite. Normally,

pulling such an expression would have infuriated her, but she *wanted* to be good. Wanted to please him.

"Better." He released her wrists. "I want you to use my name tonight. Often."

Mireille clasped her hands behind her back, then leaned down over his waist, her copper hair spilling across his bare abdomen. She could've sworn she heard a soft moan. The sound enflamed her; he wanted her, *needed* her, just as badly as she needed him.

She grabbed his waistband with her teeth, and he lifted his hips as she tugged his pants down.

As his cock sprang free, her eyes widened, and her mouth began to water. It was just as glorious and brutal as the rest of him, the taut skin of his swollen head glistening with a bead of moisture above a thick, veined shaft.

She inched in closer, angling her head, then kissed up his length. His cock twitched against her lips, and he uttered a soft curse. Then groaned in earnest as she closed her lips around him.

The taste of his cock, salted and musky with that velvet-plush skin, made her ravenous. She licked, kissed, and sucked every incredible inch. Relaxing the back of her throat, she took him down so deep that the tip of her nose brushed the downy hairs dusting his lower abdomen.

He thrust his hips up to meet her strokes, and she sucked in her cheeks each time she reached the tip. She swirled her tongue around his head, drunk on the titillating symphony of his breathy grunts and rumbling curses.

Without the use of her hands, she couldn't help swallowing strands of hair as she sucked him.

He gathered her hair up, then held it in a single fist at the crown of her head as she bobbed in his lap. His voice was low and guttural as he praised her. "*Fuck*, you're good at this."

She relaxed her jaw further, holding herself still and letting him thrust up into her as hard and fast as he wanted. The head of his cock slammed into the back of her throat, and she gagged, her eyes watering.

She loved it. Wanted more.

He lifted her by the hair, pulling her mouth off his wet, hard cock, and kissed her fiercely.

Raw, burning need tingled across every inch of her body, and all she wanted him to do was touch her. Use her.

Punish her.

As his tongue stroked over her teeth, she cupped his balls, already firm and raised, and yanked down with all the force she could muster.

He tore his mouth away with a shocked gasp, then dug his fingers into her scalp and jerked her upright. She struggled to stay on her feet.

He licked up her stomach, his tongue shooting a quivering jolt of ecstasy straight to her clit, and whispered against her flesh, "What'd you that for, little she-wolf?" He elongated his canines and bit the underside of her breast. She moaned, the sound laced with pure pleasure. "I'm beginning to think you *want* to be punished."

He tugged her across his lap, then pressed a hand against the back of her neck, pushing her into the mattress. She turned her face to the side, watching him out of the corner of her eye.

Though his words were harsh, reverence filled his savage features as he traced his fingers down her spine, over her panties, and across the back of her thigh, dipping between her legs. So close, yet so far from where she wanted him.

She arched her back, begging for more of his touch, and he pushed her neck into the mattress harder.

"Stay. Still," he snarled, and her body flooded with heat again as she obeyed his command. She didn't know which turned her on more, his praise or his scolding.

He yanked up on the waistband of her panties, exposing the swells of her ass, and the tightened fabric against her throbbing clit dragged a low moan out of her.

He pushed his thumb past her teeth. "Quiet. You'll take your punishment in silence."

She bit down on the rough pad while he smoothed his hand over her left ass cheek, a teasing, gentle caress.

Though there was nothing gentle in the open-palmed, explosive smack he unleashed upon her willing flesh.

The blow shattered through her, the stinging pain like lightning in her veins, and she clenched down onto his thumb to stop herself from releasing a primal groan.

He rubbed her ass cheek, soothing briefly, before bringing his hand down again. This time, his palm lingered, his fingers digging into her flesh.

Each smack grew harder, the sting buzzing her skin, increasing her sensitivity.

Teeth clenched around his thumb, she darted her gaze toward him as he spanked her. He was feral, crazed with lust, a sight so erotic that she felt she might come just from witnessing it.

High Gods, she wanted this. Wanted him to be as rough with her as he dared. Wanted him to turn her backside into a flushed, pulsating mess. Wanted to feel his imprint there every time she tried to sit down for days.

"Are you going to defy me again, or are you going to obey?" He spanked her so hard that she lurched up the mattress. She released a garbled, incoherent sound and he smacked her again. "*Answer* me."

"Obey," she breathed out around his thumb, pressing her thighs together in an attempt to curb the desperate ache.

"Good," he whispered, shooting a claw from his fingertip and tracing it down her spine. She shivered as he sliced through her panties, then tossed the ruined silk to the floor.

He retracted the claw and removed his thumb from her mouth, using both his hands to spread her ass apart.

She tensed, worried about where he was going to put his fingers, but he didn't go anywhere near the space between her cheeks.

Just like he promised he wouldn't.

The thought of it, that he was respecting her wishes even as he delivered such delectable pain, made fresh tears squeeze from her eyes.

Tears that instantly dried the second he stroked a finger up her slit, her lips dripping for him. His dark, silken chuckle coasted over her skin. "You're so fucking wet. My twisted little ballerina."

She spread her thighs apart, pushing her hips back in an effort to impale herself, so desperate to have his long, elegant fingers inside her.

He pressed his forearm against her lower back and curled his hand around her hip, then used the other to tease between her legs in light, feathery strokes. "No squirming, or you won't get your reward. Can you stay still for me?"

He huffed a laugh as she went motionless.

"Yes, Ronin."

"Good fucking girl." He plunged his thumb inside her, and her body erupted. She chomped down on her tongue to keep from moving as waves of shimmering bliss rocked her limbs.

He pushed his thumb in and out in a tantalizingly slow rhythm, stroking his index finger along her clit in tandem. Drawing out her pleasure.

Keeping still under the ministrations of his wicked fingers was nearly impossible. Moans and whimpers bubbled up her throat and she pressed her mouth against the sheets, desperately afraid that if he heard them, he'd stop this seductive torture.

Her entire body quivered, her thighs shaking, her hard nipples coasting over the soft blankets. Trying to control her muscles as he fucked her with his fingers only provoked her impending release. She suspected he knew; that this was the reason he'd demanded she not move.

"Fucking *look* at you, Mireille." His quiet voice was near worshipful as he held her down, his fingers soaked with her arousal. "This perfect, pink ass." He squeezed a cheek with his left hand as his right continued to move inside her. "These powerful thighs." He trailed a hand down her legs. "This fucking *hair*," he groaned, fisting a handful of it again as he increased his pumping rhythm, circling his index finger around her clit.

She was nearly sobbing into the sheets, struggling to still her hips when all she wanted to do was roll back against his hand, his praise skyrocketing her to heights of sheer ecstasy.

Then, just when she was on the verge of pitching over the edge, her body a tight coil of pleasure begging to spring loose, the fucker *stopped.*

He removed his hands from her hair and between her legs, calmly placing them outside his hips, and gifted her a gorgeous, infuriating smile.

She bolted upright, her chest heaving, and straddled him. "What the fuck, Ronin?" She shoved his torso, but he didn't even flinch. Just continued to smirk as she beat him with her tiny fists.

He stopped her movement with a large hand on her hip, then grabbed her wrists with the other. "Oh, you thought the spanking was your punishment?" He had the fucking audacity to *laugh.* "The spanking was for *me.*" He brought his face inches from hers, breathing against her lips. "And you only get to come if you behave."

She snarled, then bit his bottom lip.

His eyes went molten as he tore away, then dragged a finger across his beautiful mouth, brows narrowed.

Her heart pounded in her chest. She was fucking furious with him. But still wanted him so badly. She'd agreed to this. Agreed to play along. He'd said this was about her pleasure, but how could that be true if he were denying her?

He licked the blood from his finger, his gaze sliding back to her, and all the air fled her lungs. "You *really* shouldn't have done that."

It was all the warning he offered before flipping her face down onto the mattress and bracketing her hips with his knees, folding her arms behind her. She tried to break free, his rock-hard cock bouncing against her back as she kicked and struggled beneath him.

He reached for the sheet, elongating his claws, then cut out a long strip of fabric and tied her wrists together. She bucked her hips, trying to throw him off, but he held firm. Once he had her arms secured, he flipped her over again, her bound arms pinned beneath her.

She kicked a leg out, aiming for his stomach, but he caught her ankle. "No, no. Unless you want me to tie these up, too?"

Amatu spare her, his wild, cunning grin made her impossibly wetter.

His strong hands clenched her thighs as he spread her open. Moonlight glinting off an exposed fang was the last thing she saw before he lowered his hungry mouth to her sex and she threw her head back in a shuddering scream.

Ronin's tongue was even better than his fingers. He laved her clit, kissed her lips, devoured her in long licks and gentle strokes.

It should have been painful since she'd been so close to orgasm before, but he knew exactly when and where to apply pressure, ratcheting her body to heights of pleasure she'd never thought possible.

"That's my angry little she-wolf." He pushed two fingers inside of her as he nipped her clit, the pain a jolt of pure ecstasy. She wanted her hands free, wanted to cup her breasts and pinch her nipples, needing more sensation.

Ronin dipped his head down, spearing his tongue inside her as he trailed a hand up her stomach. He squeezed her breast, then pulled her nipple, stretching it to a point of intense pain. Just as she was about to scream, he let go and a wave of body-shaking euphoria pounded through her body.

She couldn't believe it, but she was at the brink again. Riding that plateau, her muscles tightening and loosening. She arched her back and pushed her heels into the mattress, undulating her hips against Ronin's face as he fucked her with his tongue.

Just as she was about to come, he stopped.

Again.

She burst into frustrated tears and rolled onto her side, her arms still bound behind her.

Ronin slid up her body, bringing all of his weight on top of her. She hated him. Hated his control and how badly she wanted him. Hated all these stupid *feelings* he'd drawn from her these past weeks. She wanted to fucking come and she fucking HATED him.

But not enough to say her safe word.

Because this was exactly what she needed. A way to channel her rage and anguish, twist it into something else and burn it from her soul. Turn it into blazing passion.

And Ronin was the perfect partner for the task.

He brought his mouth to her cheek, his breath hot on her face. "This is what you wanted, Mireille, wasn't it? For me to show you *just* how little control you actually have? Fucking admit it."

"*Never*," she snarled against the sheets.

He turned her face and shoved his tongue into her mouth. She bit down nearly hard enough to sever the tip and a hot rush of iron-rich liquid flowed down her throat. Laughter bubbled out of her as he spat his blood onto her cheek.

"Fucking *bitch*," he growled, then flipped her onto her

stomach. He hauled her hips up and forced her chest against the mattress, wrapping a hand around her bound wrists.

And with no warning at all, Ronin thrust forward and buried his enormous cock inside her.

MIREILLE'S SCREAM as Ronin finally plunged himself into her hot, wet warmth was a sound of pure, undiluted pleasure.

Despite her tears.

Despite her rage.

Despite her violence.

He paused, allowing her to adjust to the sheer size of him.

He knew this was what she needed. A safe space to work through her feelings, all the hurt and anger. He wanted to prove he could take everything she threw at him. That he wouldn't abandon her. That she didn't need to be perfect to be worthy of pleasure.

She *wanted* to defy him. Wanted to be punished. And he was happy to oblige. But he needed to ensure she accepted the praise as well.

He understood Mireille better than any female he'd ever been with.

And she understood him too. His need to dominate, his need to strike back, his need to *fight*, even while they fucked.

His wolf was in ecstasy, growling and barking and howling, running through his mind in a panting frenzy, ears perked and attuned to Mireille's every sound.

She whimpered into the sheets, wiggling her hips,

urging him to move while muttering *please* over and over again.

The word was blazing fuel for his desire.

He pulled out slowly, her inner walls gripping him. As if she didn't want to let go. Then he pushed in even more slowly.

"Ronin," she groaned, and the sound shot straight for his cock.

He fucked her in languid strokes, and she melted beneath him, her thighs quivering as she released mewling coos and rapturous moans.

Her cunt pulsed around him, and High Gods, he could fuck her forever and never tire of it.

He watched his cock plunge past the two perfect spheres of her ass, still awash in that pink flush, her hair a coppery spill of molten metal across the moonlit sheets.

She tightened around him and he knew she was close again. He could've edged her at least three more times, but he was honestly worried she might kill him if he attempted it.

He huffed a laugh at the thought as he hauled her upright, her wrists bound behind her, and sat on his heels as he settled her back against his chest, her head on his shoulder.

He massaged her full breasts, kissed the soft mound of skin between her neck and her shoulder, licked the salty tears from her cheeks. All while continuing to thrust up into her magnificently tight heat.

Trailing a hand down her taut stomach, he began circling her clit with gentle pressure. He cuffed a hand around her throat, holding her against him.

He'd listed her imperfections, but in his mind, she *was* perfect. For him. Her strong, soft body, her flushed skin, her arousing defiance. Everything about her designed specifically to drive him wild.

And for the first time in Ronin's three-plus centuries of life, he understood the desire to promise himself to a single someone for the rest of his immortality.

He could so easily fall in love with Mireille.

He just wasn't sure she'd let him.

And he didn't want to ruin this electric connection with an awkward burst of *sentimentality*. Neither of them was the type.

So he tried to show her, with his gentle hands and roving mouth, how much he cared for her. How devoted he was to her pleasure, regardless of how she preferred to come by it.

She continued to move on him, moaning against his neck as he drove into her, massaging her clit.

Her inner walls tightened, pulsing around his cock, and her breathy pants accelerated.

"Ronin, *please*," she breathed, then issued her own command that he was helpless to deny.

"Let me come."

MIREILLE WAS PUTTY against Ronin's chest.

Every nerve-ending scintillated as she rode his thick cock, his callused hands caressing her body.

He was a solid presence behind her, and she leaned all her weight onto him, confident that he'd support her.

"You ready for this, little she-wolf?"

She was incapable of any movement more taxing than a subtle nod.

The ache between her legs was unbearable. Her spent

muscles quivered, exhausted from being pushed to the brink, denied, and then pushed to the brink again.

But as he stroked between her thighs, moving inside her at that slow, steady pace, everything coiled again, tightening her toward what she knew would be total and complete annihilation.

Her breathing grew erratic as she matched his thrusts.

He circled her clit with his thumb, pressing harder, and turned her face to his.

And as she stared into his beautiful, golden blue eyes, glowing with lust and affection, something rebuilt inside of her.

Those broken pieces of her heart fused back together, and a single tear stole down her cheek as he whispered against her mouth, "Let go, love."

He captured her lips in a bruising kiss as her body exploded with scintillating heat, her limbs trembling and her mind shattered.

She shuddered against him as he squeezed her closer, his chest crushed against her back, drinking down her moans.

For one heart-stopping moment, she could've sworn her soul left her body. Floated into the Halfway before crashing back into her. Was she still the same person she'd been an hour ago?

As her senses returned, she realized he hadn't yet climaxed, was still moving inside her.

"What are you waiting for?"

"Didn't want to distract you." He smirked, then kissed her nose. "You fucking earned that."

She'd never felt so used up, so *desired* in her entire life. Sated in the best way. She leaned her head back against his shoulder, sucking gently on his earlobe. His powerful body trembled, and she clenched around him, urging him toward his own *very* well earned release.

He kissed across her jaw and down her neck, then clamped his teeth on her shoulder. He increased the pace of his thrusts, tightening his arms around her breasts and waist. His fangs dimpled her skin, holding her in place but not sinking in.

His hot breath tickled as he pounded into her, crushing her against his chest and roaring his climax against her flesh. She immediately came again, aftershocks of ecstasy sparkling through her spent limbs.

Ronin fell forward, curving over her back and slamming his right palm into the mattress as he held her against him with his left. They panted in tandem as he pulled out, then turned her over and settled her against the bed.

"Are you okay?" he asked, adoration a fierce glow in his golden blue eyes.

She cupped his cheek. "Never felt better in my entire fucking life."

He chuckled, then lowered his mouth to hers, pressing a gentle, reverent kiss to her lips before he pushed off the bed and bounded for the bathroom.

He returned with a towel, cleaned between her legs, then tossed it to the floor and climbed back into bed. Circling an arm around her waist, he hauled her against his warm, sweaty body and threw a leg across her thigh.

His nose roved through her hair as he released a contented sigh. "*Fuck* me, Mireille, that was…"

"I know." She placed her hand atop his on her waist, entwining their fingers.

"Has it ever been like that for you before? With anyone?" His voice was a cracked whisper.

"Never. You?"

He shook his head against her hair.

It was all either of them dared say before Mireille closed her eyes, and, enveloped within Ronin's powerful embrace, promptly fell asleep.

CHAPTER THIRTY-SEVEN

The next morning began mostly the same in the Cathedral of Bones, with a knock at the door—that human servant with the breakfast tray.

The part that was spectacularly different was where Mireille found herself when the knock woke her.

Warm and safe and protected within Ronin's arms.

Dawn's buttery light caressed the pines outside as she cracked her eyes open, greeting the morning with a smile.

She *never* did that.

Twisting around, she found Ronin awake as well, wearing a sleepy grin.

Mireille was pleasantly surprised by the lack of awkwardness between them, given everything that had transpired the night before.

"Good morning," he purred.

She demurred, his gaze flicking to her mouth as she bit her bottom lip. "Good morning to you, too."

An insistent hardness pressed against her stomach, and a devilish glint shone in his eyes. "Shower?"

She nodded, and he rose from the bed, scooped her up and carried her into the bathroom. Where he proceeded to massage her sore muscles, wash her hair, and clean her body. Then fucked her hard and fast against the shower wall, her ass smashed against the cool tiles. He let her come as soon as she wanted this time.

They were eating breakfast in front of the crackling fire, chatting about nothing particularly important, content to ignore the difficult day ahead when another knock interrupted them.

Ronin, dressed in the same outfit he'd worn during their dinner with Otto—the black shirt and trousers with the checkered suspenders, that, okay, fine, she'd admit she loved—went to open the door.

Mistress Klovia stood outside, a garment bag draped over her arm. "Master Otto sent this for you, Mistress Valette. Your costume for the performance today."

Mireille, still wrapped up in a fluffy bathrobe, gestured toward the bed. "You can leave it there."

Mistress Klovia spread the bag upon the bed, then exited the suite.

A pang of guilt gripped Mireille's stomach. "Should we have warned her? About what's going to happen?"

Ronin contemplated her question, sipping his tea. Such an amusing, contradictory sight, his tattooed fingers wrapped around the dainty cup. Who would have thought that a male who looked like *that* drank tea? And played chess. And cried at the opera.

And fucked like a God.

Though to be fair, that might be the only assumption

she'd made about him that this whirlwind week *hadn't* obliterated.

She tried to banish those thoughts from her mind. They'd do her no good today. She needed to be on top of her game. In more ways than one.

"Too risky," Ronin said, his own face hardening. "Whatever influence Otto has over the humans here might compel her to tell him everything you said."

Mireille chewed her lip again, determined to ensure Otto's human staff wouldn't suffer today. She crossed to the bed and unzipped the garment bag.

Inside was a perfect replica of her costume from the Grand Ethyrian—the stiff tutu, the bejeweled bodice, the crimson pointe shoes. Had Otto or one of his minions returned to the theater to take it from her dressing room? Icy dread prickled down her spine.

Ronin stepped up behind her and turned her to face him.

He speared a hand into her hair, massaging the base of her skull as he stared down at her, worry tightening his handsome features. "You don't have to do this, Mireille. You can stay up here, locked safe away, and I can finish this on my own."

She grasped his muscled forearm, smirking. "What about your little speech about not abandoning your partner, huh?"

"That was before..." he sucked in a breath, "...before I knew the thought of you being harmed would make me feel this crazy. Like I want to go find Otto right now and tear his fucking throat out before you even take a single dance step."

She shook her head. "We need that flute. If he's killed

before revealing it, it could be lost forever. Or taken by someone *worse* than Otto."

"Like the fucking Empire?" Ronin grumbled.

Indecision wracked through her. She *certainly* didn't want to hand the artifact over to Skanisse, not now that she knew what it was capable of. But if they didn't…

"Well, we need *something* to give to the IA or your wolf will remain caged."

"I don't fucking care about that anymore," he growled, then tilted his head back and clenched his teeth, the muscles in his neck straining as his body went taut. Likely his wolf protesting violently. "I'd stay caged for the rest of my life if it meant keeping you safe."

She leaned into his touch, his words bathing her heart in radiating warmth.

"We keep each other safe, remember? I'm doing this for you, too." She rose onto her tiptoes and planted a sweet kiss on his lips. "Seems a little out of order after last night, but I am *very* much looking forward to our date once this is over."

His hand tightened against her scalp. "As long as you bring a better list of questions this time."

She laughed and kissed him again.

Then swept up the garment bag, strode into the bathroom, and changed into her armor.

THE CRYPT LOOKED EVEN MORE sinister than Ronin remembered, lit torches flickering shadows across the fanged fireplace, roughly-hewn benches, and columns that arced like ribs—probably *actual* ribs, based on what Layla had shared—across the high ceiling.

The statues of Otto's ancestors, half-hidden within the alcoves flanking the entrance, greeted the guests like serpentine gatekeepers.

Ronin slid his gaze to the statue on the right. Behind which, he hoped, were Bonecleaver and Mireille's sword. Assuming Layla had done her part this morning.

Unlike his prior visit, there was no stripped and cleaned body laying atop the altar. Instead, it held a small pyramid of glowing anastasium stones.

Ronin shivered as he took a seat at the bench farthest from the altar. And closest to the alcove.

Layla sauntered up the aisle in her skin-tight leather uniform, her throwing knives a glittering corset around her waist and her white and black braids bouncing against her back. She threw him a quick glance as she passed, which he returned with a wink.

The plan was still on.

Yes, it was *very* much on. Even more so after last night. His chest ached. He didn't want Mireille anywhere near Otto. Regardless of whether the Deathstalker had claimed he wasn't going to harm her. Ronin didn't trust a thing the slimy bastard said.

Layla had come to fetch Mireille soon after she'd changed into her costume this morning, to bring her to Otto as he made his final preparations.

That had been nearly an hour ago. Ronin had spent the time pacing around the suite, going through the plan over and over in his head.

As soon as Mireille took the stage, Layla would grab Nostrata at knifepoint, threaten the ancient Deathstalker's life if Otto refused to reveal the flute. And as soon as he saw Layla move, Ronin would grab Bonecleaver and Mireille's sword to take on Kosera.

But there were too many unknowns, too many factors that could go so poorly. What if they were rushed by the guests? What if Otto had some other trick up his sleeve?

Ronin tried to calm himself as hushed silence fell upon the room. Otto's slow, measured footsteps echoed up the aisle, followed by the *clack* and *hiss* of Nostrata's cane and feathered robe.

Ronin startled at the billionaire's suit—simple, stark white. Not a hint of pattern or color to be found. A giant fucking red flag.

Otto surveyed the guests, offering subtle nods and bows as he approached the altar, now flanked by Layla and Kosera. He took a brief moment to run his fingers along the stones before turning to address the crowd.

Ronin swore he felt a chill breeze sweep through the room, quivering the torches.

Otto folded his hands at his waist, his black fingernails a stark contrast with his pale skin. "And so, friends, we have reached the pinnacle of our time together. At the very moment when the sun is at the pinnacle of the sky. The time of day when change comes upon the world. When the light slips away to begin its solemn march toward darkness."

Nostrata huffed a cough behind him, leaning heavily on her snake-head cane with its fire opal. She appeared far weaker than she had the night of the seance. As if her life-force had been drained by the multitude of readings she'd performed over the past twenty-four hours.

"An appropriate time," Otto continued. "One carefully chosen to mirror your own impending transformations."

The guests tittered in hushed excitement, and Ronin

wondered how he was the only one in the room to recognize the cold menace in Otto's smile.

"But"—Otto raised a single finger—"before we seek our gifts from the Creator, we must first upend the story of our third and final false deity. Faurana the Mother, High Goddess of Land and Life." Otto dipped his head, emitting a disdainful chuckle. "Land and life. The very things Adelphinae herself has provided to our world. Faurana's stories are the most egregious, are they not?"

Otto took a long, pregnant pause, letting his words settle upon the crowd.

"The High Gods do not exist. And in denying our Creator, the Erabis family and their so-called Empire have stolen something from each and every one of you."

Ronin flicked his gaze toward Layla, her expression carefully smug as she bobbed her head in agreement.

"After today's performance, we will use a powerful artifact to call upon a weapon that Adelphinae herself has left in this world for us. A weapon that will bless you with the elemental power that has faded from your bloodlines. Should she deem you worthy, of course."

"What happens if we're *not* worthy?" Nero Beruglia piped up. Ronin was heartened by the biting edge in the male's tone. Nervous, fearful whispers rippled across the guests, along with several audible remarks of hesitation.

"An impossibility, dear friends," Otto preened. "The point of these performances has been to open your eyes, crumble any faith you may have had in the High Gods, allow the doubt to creep in. As long as Adelphinae can sense that you are open to accepting her into your heart, you will be fine. There is nothing to fear." The crowd fell silent, but Ronin noticed many of them glancing toward the crypt's exit. "But first! Please sit back and enjoy this final performance. A dance, performed by the prima ballerina of the Kheimos Company herself—*Mireille Valette!*"

Ronin held his breath as Mireille glided into the room, her pointe shoes thudding against the stone. Her tutu rustled with every step, and the torchlight gleamed off the jewels scattered across her bodice. Her copper hair was piled atop her head in a tight bun, exposing the elegant lines of her neck and back.

Though her gait was fierce, Ronin couldn't help thinking how small and fragile she looked in that costume. He fought the urge to dash out of his seat, scoop her up, and carry her far, far away from the monster holding court ahead of her.

Arriving at the altar, she turned to face the crowd, arms loose at her sides. Poised and ready to launch into her solo.

Otto's viper eyes devoured her body with blatant covetousness, and Ronin's wolf snarled.

Get her out of here, the beast whined.

Not yet, Ronin answered him. *We need to stick to the plan.*

You are a fool if you think that male has shared his full truth with anyone. *End. This. Now.*

Up at the altar, Otto positioned himself behind Mireille, his knobby fingers curling over her shoulders.

"Magnificent," Otto whispered, though it carried through the silent crypt, prickling the hairs on Ronin's neck. "We have learned something very interesting about Mistress Valette this weekend. Most of you have human heritage in your bloodlines that dates back many, many generations. But hers…"

An involuntary snarl ripped up Ronin's throat as Otto

wrapped an arm around Mireille's waist and hauled her back against him. "Mireille is half-human."

Shocked gasps exploded into the room, along with whispered speculations.

"...is she doing here?"

"Thought they were all sent to Tartarus..."

"...does that mean for her power..."

Otto pulled Mireille closer.

Her body was relaxed and her breathing appeared normal. Unafraid.

Ronin's heart glowed with fierce pride, even as fear chilled his blood, icing his veins and agitating his wolf.

"Perhaps," Otto said, his voice low and menacing, "we do not need her to perform today at all."

Ronin tensed into preternatural stillness, flicking his eyes toward Layla, whose face was carefully neutral despite the fingers twitching at her sides, closing in on her knives.

Otto popped his fangs, and Ronin barely had time to burst out of his seat before the Deathstalker yanked Mireille's head to the side.

And sank his teeth into her throat.

CHAPTER THIRTY-EIGHT

The chaos occurred in the blink of an eye.

Otto tore his fangs from Mireille's flesh, a confused expression flitting across his face, and she crumpled to the floor, her body thrashing as the Death-stalker's venom coursed through her.

Layla unsheathed a knife and rushed for Nostrata, stealing Otto's attention.

Several members of the crowd shot to their feet as Ronin darted for the statue to grab the weapons, slinging Bonecleaver over his shoulder. He rushed for the altar, head and heart racing. His wolf clawed frantically at his insides.

"Enough!" Layla roared, her knife pressed against Nostrata's throat as the ancient female choked out sinister laughs.

Ronin stopped before Kosera, brandishing both axe and sword. "You heard the female," he growled as Kosera lifted his palms with a knowing smirk.

Keeping his weapons aimed at Kosera, Ronin glanced

sidelong at Mireille. Deathstalker venom paralyzed other Fae, and was instantly fatal for humans. He had no idea what effect it would have on a half-breed. He wanted to rush to her, but didn't dare take his attention from the Greyhorn.

Internally, he begged Mireille to hold on just a few moments longer.

"Give us the flute, Otto," Layla snarled. "Or I swear by the Creator, I'll send Nostrata to True Death."

Otto wiped Mireille's blood from his mouth, then stepped over her prone body. She was no longer twitching, and Ronin was heartened to see her chest slowly rising and falling. A normal rhythm. How was that possible?

"Now, now," Otto said, taking a step toward Layla who pressed her knife harder against Nostrata's neck. A bead of green blood rose on her pale, papery skin, and she hissed in pain. "Do you mean this?" He reached into his tailored jacket pocket and pulled out the instrument. It was so much smaller than Ronin expected, little larger than Otto's index finger, and milky white with rainbow streaks running through it. "Layla. We are so disappointed in you."

He stalked closer and Layla backed up a few steps, dragging Nostrata with her into the mouth of the fireplace.

"Think about what you are doing right now," Otto snarled, his lips stained red.

Distracted by the spectacle, Ronin barely had time to twist himself away as Kosera lunged for him. Ronin smashed the flat of the axe onto the back of Kosera's leg, the force of the blow nearly shattering the Beastrunner's calf. Kosera fell to the floor, reaching for his awkwardly twisted leg and glaring up at Ronin, beads of sweat gathering on his bald head as he gritted his teeth against the pain.

Ronin bracketed the axe and sword around Kosera's neck. "Stand *down* or I'll cut your fucking head off."

"He's right, Julius," Otto said. "Just wait. This will all be over soon." Layla's frenzied eyes bounced between Otto's face and the flute clenched in his hand. "Nostrata has been ready to meet the Creator for centuries. Isn't that right, Grandmother?"

Nostrata managed a subtle nod above the glinting steel at her throat, croaking. "We're ready."

Layla didn't have a chance to move before Otto flashed to the wall in a supernatural blur, then traced his finger along the carved triangle and raised the flute to his lips.

Time slowed as the high-pitched, wavery note pierced the silence and the stone slabs rumbled apart.

But this time, there was no fire behind them. Only an endless black abyss.

Mesmerized, Ronin stared into the dark pit as something began to take form. A shadowy mass prowling forward.

An enormous, iridescent eye, slashed through by a slitted pupil, peered out through the slabs and a thunderous rumble shook the chamber. As if something monstrously powerful were slamming its body against the stone.

Guests screamed, bolting off the benches and scrambling for the exit while a few remained frozen in place by fear and curiosity.

Layla trembled, dropping her knife and releasing Nostrata.

Otto approached the eye, awestruck, and whispered a reverent breath. "Nyctima."

Beneath Ronin, Kosera was similarly captivated, staring at the giant eye as he clutched his broken leg. Which was healing quickly.

Ronin used Kosera's distraction to rush for Mireille, dropping the weapons at his side with a clang as he pulled her head into his lap.

"Mireille," Ronin croaked, smacking her cheeks and shaking her lightly. "Mireille, wake up!"

She's not going to answer you if she's paralyzed by the venom, fool, his wolf snarled. *Get her out of here!*

Ronin ignored him, his frantic fingers coasting over her throat, searching for a pulse. Her body was warm, her breathing normal. She didn't seem paralyzed, only unconscious.

A deafening crack tore through the chamber as chunks of stone plummeted from the ceiling in plumes of dust.

Ronin scooped Mireille into his arms, glancing over his shoulder.

What he saw hollowed out his stomach.

The triangular head of a giant serpent forced through the crumbling opening. Two rainbow eyes shimmered against its black scales as its forked tongue darted out to sniff Otto, who fell to his knees in supplication and released the flute.

It clattered across the floor, and Layla ran for it, darting a glance back at Nostrata who'd taken up a similar position of awe next to her grandson.

Layla bent down to grab the flute and Ronin's abandoned axe and sword. She high-tailed it toward him, and they fled up the aisle, pausing briefly at the exit as Otto's voice echoed through the chamber.

"Nyctima, please accept the gifts we have gathered here. Living souls, with the blood of both species running through their veins, trapped within these grounds for you to hunt down and devour. In exchange, we would ask that your mistress, Adelphinae, blesses us with fire magic. And that she may allow us to call upon you again when it is time to make war upon our enemies."

The snake rose up, towering over Otto and Nostrata, who both bowed their heads.

Layla pulled at Ronin's arm, but he was frozen in place, mesmerized by Nyctima regarding Otto with divine sentience. As if considering the male's request.

Movement by the altar caught Ronin's eye. Kosera, his leg fully healed, pushed upright, his gaze swiveling between the snake and the trio at the crypt's exit. Leaving his boss to fend for himself, he stalked up the aisle.

And behind him, Nyctima cocked her head, unhinged her jaw, and spewed a jet of fire that consumed both Otto and Nostrata in a smoky, blazing swirl.

RONIN AND LAYLA bolted down the stone hallway, Kosera's pounding footfalls echoing behind them.

"Take her and go!" Ronin shouted, shoving Mireille toward Layla. "I'll deal with the Greyhorn."

Layla placed Bonecleaver and the sword on the ground, then took Mireille from him with a pleading look. "Ronin—"

"There's no fucking time!" he roared, snatching up the

axe and laying the sword atop Mireille's body in Layla's arms. "Go! I'll meet you out front. See if you can wake her up. And figure out how to get that fucking ward down."

Layla glanced over her shoulder, eyes widening.

A colossal bull rhinoceros huffed less than twenty feet away, head bowed with its wickedly sharp horn jutting forward as its hoof scratched the stone floor. Readying for a charge.

Ronin shoved Layla behind him. "Fucking *go!*" He didn't understand why she was so hesitant to leave him.

With a final, shuddering breath over Ronin's shoulder, Layla obeyed, scurrying up the hallway and out the hidden door into the parlor.

The sound of slithering scales echoed from the crypt. As if Nyctima were on the move, in search of her next victim. Ronin snickered softly at the thought that Otto had been the final sacrifice after all.

He flipped Bonecleaver in his hands, then turned his attention to Kosera. "Your boss is dead. We don't need to do this. We should get out of here before that snake makes a meal of us all."

The rhinoceros snorted, then said in a deep, craggy voice, "I've been waiting to take you down for *years*, Butcher. Not missing my chance now."

Kosera barreled down the hallway, massive hooves thundering, and it was all Ronin could do to pivot out of the charge and flatten himself against the wall. Kosera blasted past him, skidding to a stop and turning back around.

Really wish you could come out right now, buddy, he begged his wolf.

Who took one look at the massive bull readying for another charge and said, *No, thanks.*

You DO realize that if I die, you die too?

You got this, his wolf said flatly. *I believe in you.*

Kosera exploded down the narrow corridor again, but this time when Ronin tried to swivel away, Kosera swerved, smashing Ronin against the stone. His wrist smacked the wall and he dropped the axe, then pounded his fists against Kosera's thick, rough skin. It was like trying to punch through a boulder.

Kosera dug his hooves against the floor, crushing Ronin with his heavy body. Ronin attempted to suck in a breath and something within him snapped. Jolts of electric pain seized his lungs as at least two ribs broke beneath Kosera's incredible force.

The rhinoceros released him, and Ronin dropped to the floor, chest heaving. He swiped a wrist across his nose and blood smeared the back of his hand.

He groaned, trying to push to his hands and knees, but couldn't manage it. He turned his head to the side, the stone floor cool against his cheek, and saw Kosera making a third charge.

He barely rolled away in time to avoid getting his head squished. His left arm wasn't so lucky. Kosera trampled it, the bone splintering with an audible crack.

Ronin roared, terrible, blinding pain lancing through him. He curled over his injured arm, dragging it across the floor as he crawled toward his fallen axe.

This was *not* how he was going to go out. Fucking trampled to death by a rhinoceros holding a grudge. And not without making sure that Mireille was safe.

The thought of her strengthened him. They would make it out of this.

Together.

Curling shaking fingers around Bonecleaver's wooden handle, he used every ounce of strength left in his legs to push himself to standing, back braced against the wall. His ribs and arm screamed in protest.

"Give *up*, Butcher," Kosera grumbled from the other end of the hallway. "Or I'll crush you into bloody pulp and bone ash."

Ronin held out the axe with his right arm, his left limp at his side, blooding staining his teeth. He barked out a maniacal laugh. "Come and get me, Greyhorn."

Kosera charged once more.

Ronin feinted left, as if trying to plaster himself against the wall. But when Kosera angled left, Ronin pivoted right.

And slammed Bonecleaver into the beast's neck.

Kosera's deafening squeal nearly burst Ronin's eardrums.

The blade of the axe dug in deep before Ronin wrenched it free, then bent over his knees and sucked down gulps of air to fight off the debilitating nausea.

Kosera shifted into his humanoid form, pressing a hand against the gushing wound at his throat. "That was a mistake." He rushed for Ronin, his nose elongating into a horn.

Ronin sliced out with the axe, barely missing Kosera's stomach as the male jumped backward. Ronin could feel his own broken arm and ribs mending, the bones stitching back together in a process even more excruciating than the breaks themselves. Delirious with pain, he had trouble focusing on Kosera's moves.

The Greyhorn slammed Ronin into the wall again,

hands wringing his throat as he pointed his horn toward Ronin's left eye.

"Such pretty eyes," Kosera snarled, pushing in closer.

"Flattered," Ronin choked out, "but I'm seeing someone."

Kosera hissed out a gravelly laugh. "I think I'll pop one out and take it as a trophy. What do you think?"

The tip of the horn dug in, and explosive sparks flared behind Ronin's eyelid. Enough to call forth a wave of panicked adrenaline. He lifted Bonecleaver and slammed the butt-end of the handle into Kosera's ear.

Roaring, Kosera backed away and Ronin fell to the floor, rubbing at his blissfully still-intact eye. He gripped the axe with both hands, his left arm throbbing through the repairing bones and muscles.

He arced the weapon down into the meat between Kosera's neck and shoulder with a crunching squelch.

Kosera dropped to his knees, choking, burbling noises accompanying the red bubbles spewing from his open mouth.

"Fucking bastard," Ronin screamed as he pulled the axe out. Blinding rage propelled him through the effort as he brought it down again.

And again.

And *again*.

His head rolled halfway down the hallway, Ronin's wolf piped up. *I think you can stop.*

Ronin brought the axe blade to the floor, then rested his forehead atop his clasped hands on the handle, chest heaving.

Following the long red smear, Ronin's gaze landed on the Greyhorn's severed head, rocking slightly where it had stopped. His fat, purple tongue lolled out of his twisted mouth, his beady black eyes blown wide in death.

A faint hiss crept around the corner, and horror coiled in Ronin's gut as a long forked tongue slithered across the stone, curled around Kosera's head, then dragged it back toward the crypt.

Ronin didn't wait a second longer to see if Nyctima intended to devour the rest of the Greyhorn's body.

He plucked up Bonecleaver, then fled the gore-streaked hallway.

He needed to get back to his partner.

CHAPTER THIRTY-NINE

Ronin burst through the arched doors to the estate, a welcome blast of air cooling his frenzied bloodlust.

Outside, the guests were scattered along the iron fence, most congregating by the towering entrance gate and trying to break through the air between the bars. To no avail. That warded barrier remained intact.

A panicked sweep around the circular driveway revealed Layla crouched over Mireille, prone in the gravel next to the empty fountain with that coiled, striking serpent statue.

Heart in his throat, Ronin hobbled over to the two females, his ribs and arm still aching, and roared at Layla. "Why hasn't she woken up yet?"

Layla raised her head, revealing two coppery red braids. On the ground before her, Mireille's bun was a swirl of black and white.

"What the—" Awe stopped his words as Layla's

features sharpened, her espresso eyes turning silver and her lips filling out into a very familiar pout.

At his feet, Mireille transformed into Layla, and her eyes snapped open as she sucked in a shuddering breath before popping upright.

Mireille stood, beaming at him. Though her smile dissolved as her eyes roved over his bloodied face, his awkwardly cradled left arm. "What happened? Are you okay?"

"I will be." He shook his head, tossing Bonecleaver to the ground and cupping her cheek with his right hand. "What's going on? What did you two do?"

Mireille aimed a smug smirk at Layla. "Took some extra precautions. We each took a small dose of veiling potion before the performance. Layla thought Otto might try to drink from me. Luckily, honey-badger bi-forms are immune to Deathstalker venom. His bite only knocked her out for a bit while the neurotoxins in her blood did their work." Mireille laughed, the merry sound music to his ears.

"What were you going to do if you had to go through with the dance solo?" Ronin asked Layla.

She shrugged. "We wouldn't have let it get that far. Mireille would've captured Nostrata before I took a single step."

He brushed a thumb across Mireille's cheekbone. "You should have told me."

She tipped up a shoulder, all cool nonchalance. "We needed your reaction to be genuine. Otherwise, Otto might have known we'd switched places."

He grabbed her by the back of the neck and pulled her in for a hungry kiss.

Layla rolled her eyes. "You two can quit pretending now."

Mireille gazed up at him, her icy silver eyes softer than he'd ever seen them, a strand of copper hair blowing across her face. She placed a hand on his chest, and his heart squeezed. "We were never pretending," she whispered, smiling, and sweet Amatu, it was the most beautiful fucking thing he'd ever seen.

Ronin leaned down for another kiss.

He never reached her lips.

The estate entrance exploded, a burst of tinkling glass and crushed stone that revealed Nyctima.

And Otto riding on the back of her head.

HORRIFIED SCREAMS and echoing clangs erupted through the courtyard as the guests began pounding on the iron fence.

Mireille grabbed her sword, Ronin lifted Bonecleaver, and Layla unhooked two throwing knives from the corset around Mireille's waist.

Nyctima lowered her head and Otto leapt down, his feet crunching through the gravel as he headed for the trio at the fountain.

The last line of defense between these monsters and the innocent Fae behind them.

Otto paused, blinking slowly. His skin had paled further, and his bright yellow viper's eyes had darkened to deep pits so black they seemed to swallow the gray afternoon light.

"He's mine," Mireille growled. "You two take Nyctima."

She stalked forward as Ronin and Layla pivoted for the snake, who was being lured toward the gate by the wailing, cowering guests.

Mireille tightened her grip on the sword as she stopped mere feet from Otto. "You look a bit different, Jurgev."

He cocked his head, the motion more serpentine than Fae, then hissed, shooting a jet of fire toward her that she pivoted away from.

"Lost your ability to speak when you got eaten by your little pet, huh?" Mireille taunted, inching closer. He smelled like singed hair and charred flesh, the skin on his palms melting onto the gravel in smoking chunks. "You wanted me to dance for you" —she leveled the sword at his face— "so let's fucking dance."

She lunged for him, slicing her sword toward his stomach, but he slithered away. His movements were hitching and jerky, like he barely had control of his muscles. A corpse risen from death.

He shambled toward the fence, aiming for the guests, and Mireille dashed after him.

She passed Ronin and Layla, both dodging Nyctima's giant fangs as they futilely attempted to pierce her hide with knives and axe. Every blow glanced off the shimmering black scales.

Mireille re-focused on Otto, arcing her sword down and catching his calf. It cut through his blackened trousers, digging into his flesh, but he didn't halt. He was beyond pain, beyond thought.

She crashed into his back, tackling him to the ground, and pressed her sword under his jaw. He didn't struggle, merely lay beneath her, smirking like he had some great secret.

Not a drop of blood emerged when she dragged the steel across his throat, even though the skin parted easily, releasing a cloudy gray puff. He laughed, a smoggy hiss containing no sound at all.

As if he'd been transformed into a being of pure fire. One her sword would be useless against.

He bucked up, throwing her off, then sent a blazing stream for her head. She raised a forearm to block it, and the fire scorched across the leather. She rolled away, dropping her sword and dousing the flames.

Time to come out and play, she called to her wolf.

Her limbs popped and lengthened, her muscles strengthening, fangs and claws elongating as she shifted into her copper-furred wolf.

She sprang for Otto, but he threw up a wall of fire, undisturbed as the flames poured off him, consuming his hair, clothes, and limbs.

She whined, backing away and crashing against the fence as Otto strode toward her, each careful step agonizingly slow. As if he had all the time in the world. As if her end was inevitable.

"Please," Mireille blubbered as Otto towered over her, his flames singeing her fur.

She swiped a paw at him, then yelped when he grabbed it, burning her skin and crushing her bones with unnatural strength.

She howled for Ronin and Layla, but couldn't see anything beyond Otto's dancing flames.

A shadow crawled over them, and Mireille tried to howl again.

No sound came out as Nyctima's massive jaws closed around her and Otto.

RONIN COULD DO nothing but watch in abject terror as Mireille and whatever *thing* Jurgev Otto had become were swallowed whole by Nyctima.

For a moment, time froze. The screaming of the guests, the metallic whine of Layla's knives scraping the impenetrable scales, the cold tang of snow, and the acrid bitterness of the guests' fear all faded away.

Ronin dropped to his knees, adrenaline fleeing his body, and Bonecleaver crashed to the ground.

The sound broke Layla's trance, and she paused her useless slicing to rush to him.

"Ronin." She shook his shoulders. *"Ronin!"*

He glanced up, jaw slack, limbs numbing as the fight seeped out of his muscles.

"Don't you fucking give up!" she screamed in his face.

As if lured by her scream, Nyctima twisted toward them.

Manic delight flashed through her rainbow eyes.

Manic delight and *challenge*.

It lit something within him. Not something. His *wolf*.

The creature howled to the sky, the most feral, furious sound Ronin had ever heard.

A howl borne from centuries of restrained misery.

A howl of world-ending fury.

A howl to cleave the cosmos.

Ronin staggered to his feet. His chest heaved, his muscles bulged, and his wolf's howl echoed up his own throat. His tattoos glowed, throwing off pulses of ice-blue light.

Layla backed up a step, muttering, "Bless the Creator."

The sound of Ronin's cage breaking was the sound of a fissuring glacier. Deep. Thunderous. *Bone-shaking.*

A shockwave burst across the courtyard, knocking Layla off her feet and sending her skidding into the fountain. The guests slammed against the fence in a series of thudding clanks.

Nyctima reared, her sheer size absorbing the blast.

And then, for the first time in nearly three-hundred years, Ronin Matakos shifted into his magnificent white wolf.

His massive paws slammed onto the gravel as he bared fangs nearly half the size of Layla herself. Panting breaths clouded the air as Ronin shook his enormous body, then crouched onto his haunches.

"My fucking turn," he rumbled.

He sprang off his heels and launched himself for Nyctima.

Ronin had nearly forgotten what this felt like. To be himself but not himself. Intoxicating power coursed through his veins. He chomped down on the snake, just behind its head, the scales no longer impenetrable thanks to his colossal fangs.

She twisted and thrashed, her body a solid column of pure muscle. As large as Ronin's wolf was, Nyctima was at least three times larger.

Something wrapped around Ronin's left paw and squeezed. Unbearably hard. Her tail.

With a swift jerk, Nyctima whipped Ronin across the courtyard. He skidded through gravel and snow, slamming into the fence and scattering the dazed, terrified guests.

"Get them out of here," he yelled to Layla in a low,

burbling growl as he lurched back to his feet, shaking stones from his gleaming white fur.

Layla slid a hesitant glance toward the manor, then herded the guests up the steps and through the destroyed doors as Ronin turned his attention back to Nyctima.

The two puncture wounds near her head oozed an iridescent substance that Ronin couldn't say for sure *wasn't* blood.

He readied for another assault, hackles raised, muzzle dripping saliva.

Nyctima pushed upright, half her body towering over Ronin, her forked tongue darting out to sniff the air. She swayed as if trying to throw off his aim.

Ronin rocketed forward, his paws pounding the gravel, then broke left as the serpent struck forward in a shining black blur.

Ronin leapt onto her back and sunk his claws in, and she flipped over, wrapping her body around him. Smooth, cool scales slid against his fur as he dug his claws in deeper, trying to rip through skin and muscle to get to the vital bits.

Nyctima barely noticed.

And before Ronin knew it, the snake had coiled around him entirely, her muscular body crushing his too-recently healed ribs.

Dimly, he heard Layla shouting for him as his bones crunched and his lungs compressed. He couldn't breathe, could only manage whimpering whines as Nyctima crushed the life from him.

If this was how he was meant to go, so be it.

At least he'd reunited with his wolf, one final time.

At least he and Mireille had made peace. Had become true partners. Friends. Maybe even something more than that, for one blissful night. Perhaps he'd find her again one day in the Halfway.

As the darkness crept in and his consciousness faded, his last thoughts were of her.

His little she-wolf.

CHAPTER FORTY

*M*ireille.

Mireille.

Wake up, my pup.

Cool grass tickled Mireille's cheek, and a child's buoyant laughter floated through her mind.

Along with a voice that, centuries later, she still recognized. Still *ached* for.

A glowing hand cupped her armpit and pulled her to her feet.

Warm sunshine bathed the cozy house, and white petals danced across the feet of a tall, broad-shouldered man with a braided beard and a young girl on the brink of human adolescence. Neither held that iridescent shimmer; they were visions, not souls. And they were sparring with wooden daggers.

An errant breeze pulled chocolate strands from the girl's messy plait as a grin lit up her freckled face.

"Keep that dagger up," the man ordered.

"I *know*," the girl said in a tiny, determined voice, her smile twisting into something fierce as she rushed him.

Neither of them noticed Mireille standing there.

Mireille wasn't even sure she *was* standing there. She couldn't sense the ground beneath her feet. Her body felt weightless.

Another presence drifted beside her, and she turned to find a pair of blue-gray eyes within a kind, lined face. The man was handsome in a stately sort of way, with short, dark hair that curled beneath his ears and a close-trimmed beard that hugged his jaw.

"D-Daddy?" she croaked out.

A tear dripped down the man's cheek, and he pulled her into a crushing hug. Despite her lack of form, she felt his strong arms wrap around her.

"How… how is this possible?" she asked.

"We're in the Halfway. But we don't have much time before Adelphinae realizes you're here. If she does, you won't be able to return to your world. So, you need to listen to me carefully." He squeezed her shoulder. "You need to *fight*, Mireille. You have to wake up."

Her knees weakened, and she collapsed against his chest. "I'm just… I'm so tired. Can't I stay here with you?"

"No, my pup." His eyes crinkled as he stroked her cheek. "I had many regrets in my life. But the biggest was that I didn't fight your mother harder for the chance to know you. By the Creator, I wanted to. But she convinced me it would be too dangerous. You mustn't be too hard on her. She was trying to protect you, the only way she knew how."

"Why?" Mireille sobbed.

"Because Ethyrios, as it is currently being run, is not a kind place for beings born of two species. Look what the Empire has done to you already." His expression hardened to something stony, something furious. "Used you up. Run you ragged. Turned you into a pawn in their twisted games." Mireille stared at him with wet, pleading eyes. "There is no such thing as linear time in the Halfway. The souls here can see the past, which has already been set, but we can also see all possible versions of the future. And I've only seen one in which you finally escape the Empire's clutches." He turned toward the man and the young girl, still sparring together beside them.

"Who is she?"

"Your destiny," her father breathed reverently. "And Ethyrios's only chance for salvation. You've got to find her. *Help* her. She's going to need you."

"How? How will I find her?"

"You'll know." Her father placed his hand over her heart. "In here. The path will not be easy. Nor quick. This girl is centuries away from existence. There's a chance she may not come into being at all. But there's only one way to guarantee it."

Mireille cocked her head, questioning.

"Hope," he said softly. "It's the most powerful force in this world. It's what kept me going all those years while your mother hid you away. Hope that you'd survive. Hope that you'd have at least some part of me within you. Hope that you'd be safe, even if I couldn't provide that protection myself." His hands were rough as he gripped her cheeks, a soldier's hands, and the skull-shaped pommel of his sword glinted over his shoulder. "I needn't have worried. I've been watching you, Mireille. I've seen what you've become. A fierce, powerful female who takes no shit from anyone." He chuckled softly.

"You're going to need to use that strength for what's to come."

Hearing the word strength sapped any that was remaining from Mireille's weary body, and she collapsed into her father's arms, sobbing against his cloak.

"I'm so proud of you," he whispered into her ear.

Mireille scoffed. "I'm a mess, Daddy. I've been a mess for a long time. I don't know how to change. How to be perfect."

He tipped her chin up. "You don't need to be perfect, Mireille. You are worthy of love and joy and peace just the way you are."

Something tugged at Mireille's chest. As if some force were trying to pull her out of this vision. Her father jolted. He felt it, too.

"You need to go, my pup. You need to wake up," he said. "Use your elemental magic."

"I don't want to leave you," she sobbed against his neck, clinging to him. "And *what* magic? I don't know what it is. I can't access it."

"You can," he insisted. "You *must*. All you need do is say the words. *Believe* them."

"What words?"

The tugging grew more insistent, and rainbow light shimmered around her father's increasingly transparent silhouette as he whispered the words into her ear, then pushed out of her arms.

"Don't leave!" she shouted.

"I love you, Mireille. I've always loved you."

"Wait!" She dropped to her knees, clinging to the grass as the force in her chest tried to pull her away. "What's your name?"

Her father dissolved into glimmering mist, his broad

smile, so full of love and affection and pride, the last thing to fade.

Tears flowed anew as Mireille watched the little girl and her father.

"Remember your mantra," the man said.

The girl lifted her dagger, the portrait of youthful determination. "Blade up, fear down."

Mireille said the words her father had spoken to her, then let the tugging sweep her away as his voice rang out in her mind.

"Gareth," he said.

"My name is Gareth Fortin."

CHAPTER FORTY-ONE

*R*onin wavered in and out of consciousness, unaware of anything except the scaled, muscular body wrapped around him.

I'm sorry, buddy, he said to his wolf.

I am not, his wolf answered. *I am thankful I got to feel the wind through my fur one last time. To fight for you and our female.*

She is our female, isn't she?

Only took her being eaten by a giant snake for you to finally admit it. I'd say I'm proud of you, but I think I'd rather scold you for all that wasted time.

We will find her again, Ronin whispered. *In this world, or the next.*

He unhooked his fangs from Nyctima's scales, his paws and legs going limp, and released a mournful howl.

He closed his eyes, resigned to his fate, when the vise-tight hold slackened ever so slightly. Cool scales grew warm against his fur as Nyctima unraveled herself.

Rising to unsteady paws, Ronin readied for another attack.

He didn't get the chance.

The snake thrashed violently, thumping the ground and throwing stones and puffs of snow, her stomach pulsating.

Ronin shifted back into his humanoid form, sprawled out on the gravel and clutched his aching, re-broken ribs, struggling to breathe.

A clawed paw, covered in fire, burst through the black scales, ripping through flesh and splattering goopy, iridescent liquid. Another flaming paw joined the first.

Nyctima tried, in vain, to sink her fangs into the thing gouging through her insides.

The serpent exploded into two halves, the stench of cooked meat filling the air as her tail slid into the fountain and her head crashed against the fence with a thunderous clang.

Then Ronin lost his breath entirely as he saw what had burst from the creature.

A wolf, covered head to toe in crackling fire, stood tall and proud, fangs bared. She tipped her head to the sky, releasing a victorious howl, and her flames glowed brighter.

She padded over to Ronin, flames flickering as she wove around smoldering chunks of flesh and chipped scales, then banked the fire away from her face.

Heat kissed his knuckles as he reached for her, his ribs screaming in protest. She nuzzled his hand, her nose wet and surprisingly cool.

"Mireille?"

He'd never seen anything like her.

Inside of him, his wolf bowed down and rolled onto his back. Submissive. He'd never done that for *anyone*.

The she-wolf's silver eyes glittered with fierce pride. A look which Ronin returned before the beast transformed, and Mireille, in humanoid form, crashed onto the ground next to him, panting. Curling tendrils of smoke rose from her naked skin.

Ronin gathered her into his arms, his own pain be damned.

Layla and a handful of the guests gathered on the stones of the ruined manor entrance, gaping.

Ronin stripped off his shirt, offering it to Mireille.

"That's never..." she croaked "...happened before."

"What, love?" Ronin asked, stroking her cheek.

"Clothes disappearing?" Her eyes were closed as she rested her head against his shoulder. Her skin was scorching, the falling snowflakes melting upon contact.

Ronin chuckled. "Most Beastrunners aren't on fire. I think you burned them off."

She laughed.

It was the most glorious sound in the world.

"What the fuck happened inside the snake?"

Something soft and sad crept through Mireille's eyes. "I went to the Halfway, saw my father there. He showed me a vision of someone I'm supposed to meet in the future. I think... I think whoever she is, she gave me the courage to believe the words."

"What words?"

"I am one with my power. And I am enough."

Ronin's brows rose. "The words from—"

"Mattias's dream. The ones Larissa said to him."

Ronin blinked slowly. "They activated his fire magic."

Mireille nodded, then looked at him, truly looked at

him, for the first time since she'd burst out of the snake. "Your tattoos aren't glowing anymore."

Ronin shook his head. "My wolf came out."

"How?" she asked breathlessly.

"I… I'm not sure. I think seeing you die—well, at least I *thought* you were dead, never been happier to be wrong about something in my entire life—it made him so furious that he was able to break through his bonds."

Layla approached, her feet crunching through the gravel. She crouched beside them, her black and white hair in disarray and her eyes filled with awe.

"You two are a sight to behold. Did you know you had fire magic? And that it would turn you into a flaming wolf?" she asked Mireille.

"If I had, I might have tried to access it sooner," Mireille said with a soft chuckle.

Ronin surveyed the carnage, the chunks of burning flesh, the exploded entrance of the manor. Otto's human staff were milling around, dazed yet aware. Reawakened from whatever spells Otto had been using to control them.

"What are we going to do about them?" Ronin asked.

"The Teles Chrysos will make sure they're cared for," Layla answered. "Many will likely wish to return to the colonies, return to the families they were taken from. We'll take care of the guests, too. Hoping a few of them might even want to join us after everything they've learned here. And we'll strip the estate of anything we don't want the Empire to get their hands on."

Mireille tensed in Ronin's lap. "There's a leather ledger, hidden in the desk in Otto's office. It's full of family trees, Fae with human heritage. The Empire could use that information to hunt them down. Make sure you destroy it."

Layla nodded, then pulled the opal flute out of her torn, bejeweled bodice. "What about this?"

"What about it?" Ronin asked.

Layla's lips thinned. "Nyctima was not the only emissary that Adelphinae left in this world. There are others. Larger, more powerful monsters, if the legends are to be believed. The Teles Chrysos may need this flute to summon them in the battles to come. Will you be returning it to the Empire?"

"No," Mireille said softly, cupping Ronin's cheek. "We're done with the Empire. We won't be returning to Kheimos. At least, not for long."

Ronin laid his hand over hers, whispering, "What do you mean?"

"Your wolf is *free*, Ronin. There's no need to go back." Her expression turned fierce. "We don't have to let them use us ever again."

"What about the information they promised you? About your father?"

"He told me his name. Gareth Fortin." Her eyes dampened. "He was…kind. *Brave*. And he" —her voice broke— "he loved me. Exactly as I am. That's all I need to know."

Ronin leaned down to kiss away her tears.

"If you won't be returning to Kheimos…" Layla cleared her throat. "Perhaps you'd consider joining us? The Teles Chrysos could certainly use two members like you."

Mireille didn't look to Layla, her gaze glued firmly to Ronin's own. "We're looking forward to some well-earned time off."

Layla stepped away to give them privacy, then headed

for the fence, where she pushed an arm through the bars. The ward had vanished now that Otto had finally met True Death.

Ronin huffed a laugh, then kissed Mireille's palm. "Should we celebrate first?"

"How?"

"A run through the woods?"

Mireille's excited smile stirred something in his chest.

"Just give me my shirt back before you shift," he said with a grin. "It's one of my favorites and I don't want you to burn it."

Mireille pulled at the black fabric as she stepped away from him. "What, this shirt? I think it's only fair, Matakos…" She burst into her wolf form, his shirt disintegrating, and bounded toward the edge of the forest.

"Guess I deserved that," Ronin laughed, then stood, his ribs barking, but fuck if he was going to let a little pain stop him.

Mireille turned back, her flames hissing in the swirling snow.

A majestic wolf of pure fire.

Ronin's heart had never felt so full.

As he began his own shift, he growled out, "I'll give you a head-start, little she-wolf.

"Run fast before I catch you."

CHAPTER FORTY-TWO

Chirping birdsong filled Mireille's ears as footsteps crunched through the pine needles behind her. Hazy mid-afternoon sunlight banded through the trees, illuminating the cabin's rotted door and broken windows.

"It looks smaller than I expected." Ronin's hand skated across her lower back.

Mireille blew out a long breath. "It was just me and my mother. We didn't need much."

Her fingers tensed around the file folder, a farewell gift from Sonya.

Her father's history.

After they'd left the Otto estate last week, they'd returned to Kheimos for a few days to tie up loose ends before making their final escape.

Ronin had stayed mostly hidden within his apartment, far too recognizable a presence to risk walking through the streets and word getting back to Skanisse that he'd returned to the city.

Mireille had used the last of her veiling potion to perform two tasks.

First, she'd visited Mattias Bisere, who'd been heartbroken, though not shocked, to learn his sister had met True Death at the estate. Though the blow was softened when Mireille had gifted Mattias the anastasium stone containing Larissa's soul.

Then, she'd visited Sonya at her home, not willing to risk a trip back to IA headquarters, even under the guise of the potion. She'd confessed everything that had happened, begged Sonya not to breath a word of it to Skanisse, then given the Windrider her father's name. Asked if Sonya would go to the archives, perform one last favor for her.

Mireille had waited at Sonya's for several nerve-wracking hours, half expecting the High Councilor himself to arrive with a cadre of agents to arrest her. She'd nearly collapsed with relief when Sonya finally returned and handed her the folder. Sonya had pulled her into a fierce hug, assured Mireille her secrets were safe, then told her to take care of herself.

That had been a week ago, and Mireille hadn't yet found the courage to read it. Wanted to do it here in the cabin where she'd first heard her father's voice. It felt like closure, of a kind.

Instead, the past week had been filled with exactly what she and Ronin had promised each other among the ruins of the Cathedral of Bones—rest and relaxation.

They'd journeyed out of Kheimos, traveling mostly in their wolf forms through the dense forests and snow-capped mountains, careful to keep out of sight.

Their blissful week had been full of barely anything

other than long conversations, longer runs, hunting for game and sleeping beneath the stars.

Well, to be fair, there wasn't much sleeping.

It was a wild, feral existence that Mireille was sure she could get quite used to. And Ronin hadn't had a drop of Delirium the entire time. She was incredibly proud of him.

Mireille thought often of the young girl she'd seen in the Halfway with her father. He'd said she was centuries away from existence and that, when the time was right, Mireille would know how to find her.

In the meantime, Mireille figured her life was her own to live until she was called upon to fulfill that role. Whatever it may be.

And right now, she wanted nothing more than to live a quiet life in the woods with the wonderful male standing beside her.

"Well," Ronin said, "shall we?"

Sweet Amatu, he is delicious, Mireille's wolf purred.

She pulled back her shoulders, gathering her courage. "Yes" was all she said before Ronin led her up the rickety steps and through the cabin door, which hung precariously on rusted hinges.

Her breath caught, and an ache pierced her chest at the sight of the small table before the crumbling hearth. Remembering the *meal* she'd been served in that vision during the seance.

She shook the thoughts away, then pulled out a chair covered in layers of dust and settled down gingerly. Ronin didn't bother with the other chair—no way would it hold his weight. Instead, he leaned Mireille's sword— the replica of her father's—against the wall, then came up behind her, a pillar of warmth and strength at her back.

"You don't have to do this," he offered, his voice low and soft as he rubbed her shoulders. "Maybe it's better to not know what happened to him. You said he seemed content in the Halfway. Perhaps it would be easier to remember him that way."

Mireille dashed away a tear. "No," she whispered. Then more firmly, "No. He deserves it. For me to honor his life after all those years of not knowing him."

Ronin brushed her hair aside, then kissed her neck. "Do you want me to stay? Or would you prefer to read it alone?"

Mireille thought for a moment. She was grateful that Ronin was here to support her. But perhaps this moment *was* something she should experience on her own. Something sacred between her and Gareth.

She clasped Ronin's hand, brushing her lips across his tattooed knuckles.

Inom Than. Become Death.

She thought he should change it to *Nikoch Than.* Defy Death.

She chuckled to herself. Too many letters.

"Wait for me outside."

Ronin nodded, then exited the cabin, ducking and angling his broad shoulders through the narrow door. He attempted to shut it, despite the useless hinges. Her chest tightened at the gesture. A radiant, achy longing she'd never felt before.

Love, perhaps? Whatever this *thing* was between them, it was all-consuming. Overwhelming in the best way.

What was it, if not love? Or at least the fragile seedlings of it.

With that thought bolstering her courage, she took a deep breath and opened the folder.

MIREILLE DIDN'T KNOW how long she sat there, staring at the chipped blue paint on the wall.

It couldn't be true.

She pleaded with whatever Gods actually existed for it not to be true.

Her knees buckled as she attempted to rise from the chair, instead crashing to the dusty floor. She rolled into a fetal position, clutching her stomach.

And her chest. Which had been cleaved in half.

A torrent of tears erupted, and she clapped a hand over her mouth to muffle them. Didn't want him to hear. Didn't want him to know.

Saliva and snot mingled on her palm as pain and anger and grief washed over her in relentless, violent waves. As if every emotion she'd kept caged for the past three centuries had finally broken free.

She'd thought she'd already freed them over these weeks with Ronin. Then realized she'd only freed the pleasant ones. The light ones.

The dark emotions were so much more powerful.

So much more *tempting*.

Her eyes darted to her sword, glinting with menace in the window's soft light.

Avenge him, it taunted.

This had all been a mistake. A distracting, foolish mistake.

Familiar anger consumed her, chasing away all those

other useless feelings. They'd never lasted longer than the pain anyway.

How could she have been so naive to think this time would be different?

She rose from the floor, swiping her nose with the back of her wrist, and stalked to the sword.

Then wrapped her hand around the hilt.

RONIN'S first sign that something was wrong was how long it was taking Mireille to read the contents of that folder.

He'd been standing outside the small cabin for a little over an hour, leaned back against a sticky pine tree, the resinous scent of sap stinging his nostrils.

Since his uncaging, his senses, even in his humanoid form, had heightened. Well, it was either the uncaging or his reduced Delirium consumption. It wasn't that he didn't need the elixir anymore. That craving, that *addiction*, would never go away. It was a part of him, just as much as his wolf and his now non-magical tattoos.

But for the first time in his life, Ronin had a reason to *want* to curb it. To want to be present for every moment he spent with Mireille.

The past week had been utter fucking *bliss*.

Deep down, he knew her feelings weren't as strong as his. Not yet. The minute he'd seen her burst through that snake in her flaming wolf form, he'd wanted to get on his knees and proclaim his undying love.

But she was still skittish, still adjusting to a non-solitary existence, and he didn't want to scare her away. So he'd be patient. Would wait to confess how he felt until a time when she'd be ready to hear it.

He'd wait forever, if necessary.

But right now, he was worried about her for a very *different* reason. Surely it wouldn't have taken someone as smart as Mireille this long to read that file.

Is she okay in there? he asked his wolf.

Another side-effect of his uncaging—their wolves could sense each other. They couldn't communicate in words, not like how Ronin and his own wolf conversed in his mind, but they had a general awareness of each other's presence. Could sense feelings, locations even. And according to his wolf's *very* colorful commentary every time he and Mireille had fucked this past week—a delightfully frequent occurrence—their wolves could feel it, too. The beast had been insatiable ever since.

His wolf let out a small whimper and Ronin tensed. *She is...angry.*

About what?

I cannot—

The door to the cabin banged open, then crashed off its hinges onto the porch.

Mireille stood in the doorway, her silver eyes ablaze with fury, the file folder in one hand and her sword in the other, her chest heaving.

"Mireille, what—" Ronin started, then stopped as she raised the sword and stalked down the steps, the wood groaning beneath her furious footfalls.

She paused at the bottom, her wet cheeks glistening in the approaching twilight. She tossed the file folder at his feet, and sheaves of paper spilled onto the dry pine needles.

"Read it," she snarled.

Ronin's chest hollowed out. He raised his palms, his wolf growling and scratching at his chest. Acknowledging a new enemy. "Why don't we just—"

"Fucking *read* it, Butcher." A hoarse cry edged in anger and tears.

Ronin's heart tripled its beat; she hadn't called him Butcher like that since the day they'd met at IA headquarters.

Mireille gripped the sword, flames licking her fingertips, but didn't move as Ronin bent down to gather the folder and papers.

He shot her a pleading glance that she met with that all-too-familiar imperviousness. Though something was different about it. It used to be icy, cold.

Now, it was the burning fire of a world-ending rage.

He opened the folder, his muscles twitching from the effort to contain his wolf, who slammed against his chest, desperate to come out and fight.

He shuffled through the papers, his thumb catching on a document that was thicker than the rest.

A death certificate.

His heart stopped beating entirely as he read the scrolling calligraphy, written in both Aramaelish and the common tongue.

Cause of death: Mauled on the battlefield at Aethalia. Casualty of the white wolf.

The folder fell to the ground in a cascading swish, and he raised his eyes to Mireille's.

In them, he found nothing but the deepest hatred. No fear, though. Pride swelled his chest even as it shattered to pieces.

"You. Fucking. *KILLED HIM!*" she roared, the sword

in her hands shaking violently as her fire swelled, crawling up the blade in a crackling blaze.

Ronin backed up a step, pleading. "I didn't know," he choked out. "I didn't know, Mireille." His wolf howled, raking claws against his bones, and he could barely hold back the shift. If he let his beast out now, he honestly didn't know what the creature would do to her.

"You slaughtered him before I even had a chance to —" Her voice broke, and Ronin couldn't help echoing her tears.

"Please. I didn't..." An image speared through his panic-fogged mind—a young girl with copper hair, holding the hand of a distinguished-looking soldier with blue-gray eyes. Like a tiny beacon in that sea of human sameness he'd encountered during his vision in the Halfway.

How in Ethyrios hadn't he known it was her?

"You're a fucking *monster*," she whispered. The pain and regret lacing her words broke him.

He crashed to his knees, paralyzed by guilt. "What can I do? How can I fix this?"

"You can't." She towered over him. "Bring out the beast so that I can have my vengeance."

She angled the flaming steel so close to his face that sweat pebbled across his forehead, and he squinted his eyes against the excruciating heat.

It was the last straw for his wolf. The creature took over Ronin's body, the shift so swift and violent that he vomited, bile bursting across his tongue as he bared his fangs.

Don't hurt her, Ronin begged, but he was no longer in control. All he could do was watch helplessly through his wolf's eyes as he crouched back onto his hind legs and lunged for Mireille.

She pivoted away with that dancer's grace, and Ronin crashed through the porch, the stairs crumbling to shards beneath him.

Mireille regained her footing and brandished her sword as a crazed smile tore across her face.

Ronin tried to memorize the sight. Even in her anger, in her hatred, she was glorious.

It was the last thought in Ronin's mind as his wolf stood, shook off the wooden shards, and rushed for her.

Then a blinding, fiery pain tore through Ronin's left eye.

And his world evaporated in a swirl of crimson.

CHAPTER FORTY-THREE

Something—or *someone*—had infiltrated her woods.

She could smell him on the wind, beneath the other scents. Rotting leaves. Lingering smoke. The pile of scat she'd used to track her kill. The blood coating her muzzle and spilling from the gash in the deer's belly.

It had been five days since the incident. She didn't dare call it anything other than that. Couldn't.

Every time she thought about him, about what he'd done, about what *she'd* done, something so violent and ugly and agonizing tore through her that she vowed she'd just stay in her wolf form for eternity.

Could a Fae die from a broken heart? Or would the wound keep healing and re-breaking? An endless, immortal cycle of grief. She'd carried grief all her life, but this time it was worse.

It was so much fucking worse.

She hadn't shifted into her humanoid form since it had happened. Had burned down the cabin—along with any dreams she'd had of what she and Ronin could have been there—and begun prowling through the Oread Woods, hunting and sleeping and running and forgetting. Or trying to forget.

She licked her chops, sniffing at the air. She knew the scent on the air, a congested, concrete-and-metal stink that reminded her of a city she used to live in. What was its name again? And had she lost the name so quickly in her quest to become more animal than Fae?

Her hackles raised and she growled a warning as the intruder's scent grew closer, the dry needles cracking beneath approaching footfalls.

A flash of blue appeared between the pines, about a hundred yards away.

For a split second, she thought to turn and run, but her base instincts wouldn't allow her to abandon her kill.

She stepped over the deer carcass, hiding it behind her mass of muscle and copper fur. No flames, today. She'd practiced with her power as well, during these long, blurry days. Learned to control her fire, to bank it when needed or to use it for warmth. She let the embers smolder within her, waiting. If needed, she'd call upon them to roast this interloper.

She bowed her head and bared her fangs as a Windrider with blond hair and sky-blue feathers stepped into the clearing. Instinctively, she knew he was a threat, though she couldn't scent any Typhon steel on him.

She realized why when Hugo Skanisse raised a stun pistol at her.

"Hello, Mireille Valette," he said in that high-pitched voice that grated across her bones. A familiar irritation. "Or should I say Mireille *Valois*."

She snarled at him, incapable of forming words in her

devolved state. She summoned her power and fire crackled along her limbs and torso. Skanisse waved a hand, sending tendrils of wind toward her. One by one, the flames snuffed out.

A seed of fear bloomed in her belly and she twisted around, poised to run.

"Ah ah ah," Skanisse crooned, cocking the pistol. "I wouldn't do that if I were you. There's a legion of Imperial soldiers surrounding us, waiting to strike on my command. You can either come with me willingly, accept your fate, or I can order them to put you down."

She thought he was bluffing until a new wave of scents reached her nose. At least a hundred Fae, mostly Windriders, as well as the metallic, fiery tang of Typhon steel. Along with the rustling murmurs of shifting feet, the whine of swords arcing through the air.

"You might have even gotten away, had we not discovered those documents Sonya stole last week."

She growled, sitting back on her haunches, blood and saliva dripping from her fangs. The tiny, non-bestial part of her, barely a drop within an ocean of wild rage, was wracked by guilt for endangering Sonya, who'd stuck her neck out for her so many times.

"Your ignorance of your own history was the only reason you weren't locked up years ago. Though it did prove rather useful to take down Otto. You always were the most successful of my agents."

Her eyes darted madly, seeking any escape, even as that tiny part of her wanted to ask Skanisse what had happened to Ronin. She knew she hadn't killed him with her final strike. Had watched as he'd fled, blood gushing from his blistered eye socket.

Clanking echoed through the pines as the soldiers

surrounded the clearing, their Typhon broadswords glinting in the sun.

"Time to embrace your cage, Mireille." Hugo raised the pistol higher.

She leapt for him, refusing to go down without a fight.

He pulled the trigger.

The last sound she heard as the energy blast consumed her, paralyzing her limbs and crashing her to the ground, was her own whimpering whine.

So, she closed her eyes, and let the darkness swallow her.

It had always been her fate, after all.

CHAPTER FORTY-FOUR

*V*oices outside the door woke Ronin from his piss-poor slumber.

Other than that first week he'd arrived back at his family cottage in Denevrae—blind in one eye and nearly bleeding out—he hadn't been able to get more than a few, restless hours.

Selene had healed him as best she could, begging him to tell her what had happened.

He refused to say a word. Wasn't ready to share any of his final, painful moments with Mireille with anyone, even the sister whom he loved, and who loved him so dearly that she'd tried everything to save his eye.

She couldn't, in the end.

Honestly, it was lucky Mireille hadn't killed him. Any deeper of a slice and that flaming blade might have pierced his brain, delivering True Death in one brutal, hate-filled stroke.

A part of him, a part that was growing smaller and

smaller with each passing day, hoped that maybe she'd held back on purpose.

He groaned as he lifted himself up onto his elbows, pain pounding through his skull. He reached up to touch his bandages, found them sticky and wet with pus.

His wolf hadn't said a word since they'd returned. Ronin counted it a blessing. Though he was still furious with the creature for forcing the shift, he was grateful he'd gotten them to safety. And thanks to Selene's skills as a healer, he'd likely have centuries to repair his relationship with the beast.

He couldn't say the same for Mireille. Whenever he thought about her, a stabbing pain lanced through his chest and the tears that rose to his injured, vacant eye socket stung nearly as badly as his battered heart.

She'd called him a monster. After *she* was the one who'd assured him he wasn't. She was the only person who'd ever said it that he believed, including Selene. And to have it rescinded…

He shook the thought away as the voices outside his bedroom—his fucking *childhood* bedroom—grew louder.

He sat upright, the blanket falling from his bare chest as Selene opened the door. Ronin startled at who accompanied her.

"Layla?" he said, his voice raw and scratchy.

The honey-badger bi-form was dressed quite differently than the last time he'd seen her, in an elegant cream top and tailored black pants, her typical leather uniform discarded. Save for that corseted belt of Typhon throwing knives. Seemed some things never changed, regardless of who she was working for.

She leaned down to inspect his wound, her smooth black and white waves tickling his chest.

"Damn, Butcher, she got you good," she said, her eyes tinged with sorrow. "What happened?"

Ronin rubbed at his bandages. "It doesn't fucking matter. What are you *doing* here?"

Layla aimed a look at Selene, a look that held far too much familiarity for Ronin's liking. Selene dipped her golden-blue eyes to her wringing hands.

"Do you two know each other?" he asked.

"Not…not exactly," Selene answered in a meek voice. "Though I do know the organization that Layla works for. Quite well, in fact."

Ronin jolted as if struck, remembering the *guests* Selene had been entertaining the last time they'd talked. Before he'd gotten sucked into… He wasn't going to think about the assignment. About Otto or Kosera or Nyctima or…*her* ever again. Tainted fucking memories.

High Gods, he wanted a Delirium. Selene had finally caved and purchased a case a few days ago. After Ronin had roared at her, said some very nasty things in his grief and anger, *begging* for a bottle to quiet his mind. Quiet his soul.

He didn't ask for one now though. Thought it best to see through this conversation as alert and focused as possible. He'd drown himself afterward. "How long?"

"Wh-what?" Selene asked.

"How long have you been a member of the Teles Chrysos, Selene?"

Her answer was barely a whisper, and she didn't look at him as she provided it. "For the past twelve years."

Ronin, shockingly, found a new reserve of anger. "Do you know how fucking *dangerous* that is? If anyone had ever found out—"

Color rose on his twin's cheeks as she finally met his

gaze. "I have never *once* judged you for your choices, Ronin. Do not presume to now judge mine."

"Bullshit," he laughed. "Where's my Delirium, huh, sis?"

She pushed her shoulders back. "That's different."

"*How?*" he roared, something within him stirring to life. Wrath of Vestan, it felt good to get the anger out. Even though he knew his sister was not who he wanted to take it out on.

Layla stood at the edge of his bed, arms crossed, not joining in the sibling rivalry.

"Because it's killing you!" Selene snarled, more ferocious than he'd ever seen her. "Because it's been keeping you from *living* these past years. You're a slave to it, and you don't even recognize it."

"And becoming a member of an organization that's planning to rebel against the Empire isn't going to kill *you*? I fail to see how this is different."

Layla piped up. "Hate to interrupt this lovely family moment, but you have a decision to make." She shot her gaze to Ronin.

"What decision?" Ronin leapt out of bed, the swiftness of the movement making his head swim. Staggering, he caught himself on the edge of the nightstand. Selene stepped over to help, her concern overriding any lingering irritation from their shouting match.

"I've come with an offer from the Teles Chrysos leadership. They want you to return to Delos, to the Empire now that your wolf is uncaged, and rejoin the Imperial Defense Council. And feed us any useful information you come across."

Ronin laughed bitterly. "You want me to play spy again? Why would I agree to that? And why the hell would the Empire take me back when I defied their orders and fled after what happened at the estate?"

Layla leveled a sympathetic stare at him. "Because she covered for you."

"What the fuck are you talking about?"

"She was captured," Layla said, and Ronin's heart fell to his feet. "Skanisse tracked her down, brought her back to Kheimos. Made a pretty big spectacle of it, too. She took the fall for everything. Said she orchestrated Otto's takedown in order to claim power for herself." Layla cleared her throat. "Said you were just a pawn and that she'd broken your cage to turn you back into a weapon to use against the Empire."

A vein jumped in Ronin's clenched jaw. "What happened to her?"

Fury tightened Layla's delicate features. "They sent her to Tartarus."

A big part of him was glad to fucking hear it, while another part... No one ever got out of the dangerous prison. Not alive, anyway.

"She sacrificed her freedom to save you, Ronin," Layla whispered.

He searched his chest for an ounce of sympathy to offer Mireille. And maybe it was even there. But if it was, it was buried beneath volcanic layers of rage and pain.

The centerpiece of his broken fucking heart.

She could *rot* for all he cared.

He knew he'd spend the rest of his life wishing he actually believed that.

"Still," he ground out, "why would I rejoin the fucking *Empire* for you and your zealots?"

"Because it's the right thing to do," Selene piped up. "Because this world cannot continue on in this way. Even if we could stomach the hierarchies, these separations between species and sub-species, it is not Adelphinae's will. And she will destroy us if we don't find a way to fix it."

Ronin remembered that meeting he'd had with the chronomancer, what felt like years ago. What that voice had said about him still having a role to play. He'd thought she'd been talking about the assignment with Otto. But perhaps his path was quite a bit longer than that.

Selene sat down next to him, placing a hand on his thigh. "Ro, *please*. I've never asked you for anything in my life, but I know... We need to do this. Together. Or else this world is not going to survive. Please."

Selene—twin sister and master manipulator.

He bowed his head in his hands. What *else* was he going to do with the rest of his immortality? He was finding it hard to give a shit about anything at the moment. But the thought of remaining here in Denevrae, in this claustrophobic cottage with Selene, doing... what exactly? Chopping wood? Gardening? Playing chess?

Harboring rebels?

When Skanisse had first approached him, he thought he'd have a chance to regain some of his lost glory. Maybe what Selene and the Teles Chrysos were offering would allow him to do that after all.

He shuffled over to his closet, then pulled on a shirt. "So what's the plan then? I just waltz back into Delos and what? Fall to my knees before Leonin Erabis? Beg forgiveness for my *sins*?"

"Something like that." Layla winked, then sashayed out of the room. When she returned, she was holding a familiar object in her hand.

Nostrata's cane.

"You'll arrive bearing a gift," Layla smirked, holding it out to him. "A genuine relic of the Fallen Goddess."

He took the cane, examining the carved snake head on top, the fire opal held between its fangs glistening in the early morning light. "Why would you surrender this to them?"

"It wasn't an easy decision," Layla admitted. "The Teles Chrysos leadership had many long, heated debates about it. In the end, it was decided that the information we could gain by having someone on the inside was worth the sacrifice. The Empire won't be able to do much with the cane—it can only be wielded by a chrono-mancer and even then, all it can do is allow them to visit the Halfway. Besides, offering it up will distract them from searching for the flute, which is far more powerful. And integral to our long-term plans."

Ronin blew out a long breath. "Alright." He turned to his sister. "But I'm only doing this for you, Leenie."

Selene winked. "Checkmate, big bro." She brought her hand to his face, running her thumb across his cheek-bone just under his bandages. "Come on, let's get you ready for your Imperial visit.

"I've made you a new accessory."

EPILOGUE

"And *that's* how I got the scar."

Ronin rubbed at his eye patch. A throbbing ache had gathered behind it as he'd recounted his sad, sorry tale.

A much sharper ache needled through his chest. The ache he'd tried—and failed—to soothe for two-hundred-and-six years. Not that he was keeping count.

Seated on the rough, black boulders next to him, Reena and Cassandra gaped, the former looking like she'd just swallowed her tongue and the latter…

He was still adjusting to seeing her with those incredible, iridescent white wings, her human features sharpened into something new and painfully beautiful. Something *Fae*.

And she was clearly still adjusting to the wings. They cascaded through the slats in her gray prison shirt, drooping down her back and resting upon the charcoal dirt.

No Windrider he knew *ever* let their wings drag upon the ground. She'd need to work on building up those muscles, would need to learn how to carry them properly. Not to mention figure out a way to hide the fucking things before the Emperor journeyed to the prison to deliver their sentences. Before Eamon Erabis found out what his brother Tristan had done. *Again.* Turned a human woman.

Creator save them *all.*

The trio gathered in a yard outside of Tartarus's intake tower, the place where new inmates were dumped before they received their sentences. Several other groups of shell-shocked, freshly-minted prisoners were scattered throughout the barren, dusty expanse, eying their new neighbors warily.

There were no guards at Tartarus. There was no need. The extensive wards surrounding the complex prevented escape and the inmates were left to fend for themselves— a violent, lawless existence that often resulted in bloody civil wars that served to cull the population.

A worry for another day.

"So," Reena said hesitantly, her golden tiger eyes glinting in the murky sunlight seeping through the warded dome above them, "she's here then? Your former—"

"She's *nothing* to me," Ronin snapped. "But yes. She's here."

He knew it to be true because as soon as he'd arrived, as soon as he'd woken up in his cell, his wolf had released such an anguished, mournful howl that Ronin's eardrums had nearly burst.

Oh yes, she was here. He could sense her. But he

didn't dare ask his wolf what state she was in, how she was feeling. He didn't want to fucking know.

The only thing he cared about was saving Selene, who was here as well. Captured by the Empire during a raid on the Teles Chrysos ten years ago.

He didn't even feel guilty that he hadn't told Cass that she and Mireille were destined to cross paths. That Mireille's father—one of Cass's human ancestors, for fuck's sake—had said Cass would need her help.

Maybe he'd tell her one of these days. But for now, he kept the information to himself. She had enough shit she was dealing with at the moment: being ripped away from Tristan, being shipped off to this High-Gods-forsaken prison.

Being Turned into an entirely new *species*.

But despite everything she'd endured, despite the raw, ever-present anger that lingered in her blue-gray eyes, she'd listened to Ronin's tale with compassion.

She reached out to squeeze his hand. "I'm sorry that happened to you, Ronin."

He shrugged and her grip tightened, nearly crushing his bones. *Fuck* she'd gotten so much stronger. Was she aware of it yet?

Her gaze narrowed, determination hardening her features. "But you need to get over it."

He startled, an amused smirk curving his lips. She was more like her half-human ancestor than she even knew. "And why's that?"

"Because if Mireille is here, has been here for *centuries*, then surely she's learned a few things about the prison. We need to find her so she can help us."

Ronin scoffed. "Help us do what?"

"We're breaking out of here." Cassandra gritted her teeth, her muscles tensing as she spread her glorious white wings wide. Rainbow light shimmered through her feathers, glowing with divine fire.

"And then we're going to end the Empire."

ACKNOWLEDGMENTS

Never in my wildest dreams did I imagine I'd write three books. All while staring down middle age, no less. Sometimes, I get paralyzed by the fear that I've started this journey too late, that my dreams are too far out of reach, and that I'll never catch up to them.

Here are just a few of the people who have helped me conquer that fear.

Forever first, to my husband Mark. I'm not getting any better at balancing all of this, and I'm eternally grateful for your patience, sacrifice, and support. I love you. Across time and in all worlds.

To Susan, my story guru. No matter how much I love my manuscript when I deliver it to you, I love it a thousand times more after incorporating all of your thoughtful, insightful, and sometimes diabolical feedback. You're a master and I'm so lucky to have you in my corner.

To Noah, my prose connoisseur. Thank you for helping me polish my words and tighten up my sentences. And I swear I'll figure out those commas someday.

To Rena, every cover gets better and better and better. I don't know how you weave your special brand of magic, especially when I offer so few details, but I am thrilled that you practice your sorcery with me. Let's do it again, yeah?

To my ARC readers, particularly those of you who have been with me since the beginning, thank you for your enthusiasm and encouragement. And please never stop sliding into my DMs to yell at me.

To all the incredible artists I've had the privilege to work with: Sally, Austen Marie, Kaja, Charlotte, and Jessica. You all do such amazing work and I'm honored that you've brought my characters to life in each of your unique styles. Nothing compares to the value of real, HUMAN artists.

To my friends and family, thank you for never making me feel like I was insane to embark on this path.

And to you, dear reader. Thank you, thank you, thank you for taking a chance on me and my stories. I, quite literally, could not do this without you. Well, I guess technically I could. But it wouldn't be nearly as enjoyable. You make it all worth it. And I hope you'll come back for the next leg of this crazy journey!

ABOUT THE AUTHOR

Kris K. Haines is a fantasy romance author and lover of stabby, swoony stories. A Jeopardy!® silver medalist and self-proclaimed adrenaline junkie, Kris can be found barreling down mountains in the winter and hugging the turns on her motorcycle in the summer. That is, when she doesn't have her nose stuck in a book. She lives outside of Philadelphia with her supportive husband and two sassy pugs.

www.ingramcontent.com/pod-product-compliance
Lightning Source LLC
Chambersburg PA
CBHW061857310726
48972CB00004B/1068